Dial B for Bondage

Kathy Kulig
Delilah Devlin
Samantha Cayto
Francesca Hawley

BEGGING FOR IT

Delilah Devlin

She needs punishment…before she deserves pleasure.

Tragedy scarred TJ Lipton. Now the only way she can find pleasure is when it's delivered with a heavy-handed dose of S&M. But finding a lover who can give her what she needs proves an elusive quest—until she finds the sex club Unfettered and a Dom named Cross McNally.

Cross understands all too well what drives TJ. He takes command of her body to give her everything she needs—restraint, the stinging kiss of a flogger, the thrill of a three-way—a sexual adventure that pulls her beyond her painful past and has her begging for more of his tender brand of domination.

CONTROLLING INTEREST

Francesca Hawley

Mozelle "Mouse" Vincent inherits money, a club and her boss' son as a business partner when society leader Regine Stuart dies. Torin Stuart knows what his late mother's wishes were for his exclusive BDSM club, Erotically Bound, but he's pissed that he's forced to trust Mouse—especially when her inherently submissive nature arouses the sexual Dominant in him.

After baring all in a heated, intense scene, Mouse realizes they still have to work together, but now Tor challenges any business suggestion she makes. When she wants to offer education classes, Tor dares her to organize the class and participate—as a submissive.

To his chagrin, Mouse agrees, but he can't stand the thought of any other Dom touching her. Suddenly there's far more at stake than the controlling interest in their club…because love is the ultimate prize in their power exchange.

MISTRESS MINE

Samantha Cayto

FBI agent and ex-military man Trey Boudreau likes to be in control and issue orders. But the bedroom is not a battlefield. His secret desire is to submit his body to a strong, older woman. He discovers a card that promises him the right one to bring him to his knees.

Juliette Coyne is a Domme determined to overcome a past experience that left her questioning her ability in the lifestyle. She is challenged by Trey, a strong, younger man in need of a good lesson or two. Old habits die hard, however, and the past continues to haunt them. Trey and Juliette grapple with each other and themselves for control, trust and a future together.

EMERALD DUNGEON

Kathy Kulig

Dana's summer job as a musician in an Irish castle takes an adventurous turn after she witnesses a BDSM scene in the dungeon, and her submissive side awakens. Jack is a sexy Dominant who recognizes the sub smoldering beneath her demure exterior. His skillful commands take Dana beyond her darkest erotic fantasies.

Whips, restraints and increasing levels of pain heighten her passion, but complete surrender and ecstasy are out of her reach. Secrets and strange events around the castle only add to the couple's troubles. Will a summer affair be enough to find what they both need? The appearance of a mysterious business card may help guide them. If Dana can accept Jack with complete trust and surrender, then ultimate pleasure and true love are possible.

An Ellora's Cave Publication

www.ellorascave.com

Dial B for Bondage

ISBN 9781419965081

Edited by Mary Moran and Helen Woodall.
Designer and Photographer: Syneca.
Models: Cole and Shannon.

Trade paperback publication 2011

DIAL B FOR BONDAGE

ഗ

The Magic

ℵ

The magic begins with the appearance of the business card. Sleek black print on a pristine white background—unassuming in its appearance. Those brave enough to call the number will begin a journey that will explore their greatest desires.

Once the call is made, the Operator goes to work. Somehow he knows just what every caller needs, always able to find the answer the caller seeks.

Callers may be directed to Unfettered, a new club in town, one nobody has heard of. It provides a safe haven for all who enter. Members are free to explore their every desire…even those they weren't aware of. Little do they know Unfettered will disappear once those yearnings have eased.

Submissives who don't know how to handle their Dominants. Masters looking for the perfect sub. People who need just a little push to admit vanilla isn't their favorite flavor. The card finds them all.

And once you dial 1-800-DOM-help, anything can happen.

BEGGING FOR IT

Delilah Devlin

Trademarks Acknowledgement

Chapter One

ᘓ

She awoke, gasping, inhaling smoke, and then began to choke. Which forced her to close her mouth and breath through her nose – a mistake because the smell of burned rubber, gasoline and something mustier and more frightening turned her stomach. She feared she'd vomit, but her seat belt gouged her waist as she hung upside down in the harness.

Something was in her eyes. She blinked but couldn't clear the viscous fluid. Panic swelled, and then she heard a sound beside her, an odd rhythmic gurgling, and she remembered.

The driver.

Blind, she reached for him, but her fingers sank into warm, sticky blood. She began to scream…

"TJ— Yo! Wake up!"

Tansy Jo Lipton jerked, banging her head against her monitor. Sitting back, she rubbed her head and glared at her partner Marnie Croft.

"You were asleep and moaning." Marnie's dark curls shivered around her face as she shook her head. "Did you call that VA shrink? Honey, you can't keep this up much longer. You need to talk to someone."

TJ frowned. She didn't like discussing her problems with anyone. Her demons were ones she preferred to wrestle on her own. In her own way. "We talk."

"But do you tell him anything he needs to hear? Does he know you're still havin' the dream?"

Giving a shrug, TJ's glance slid away. Then she lied through her teeth to her best friend. "I don't get it so much anymore."

Marnie snorted and turned away, closing TJ's office door without saying another word.

Not that TJ blamed her friend for her anger and frustration. Marnie had held the business together when TJ was called up. She'd hoped to have her burden lightened when TJ returned from Iraq.

The problem was TJ had never really come back. Not fully. She'd left part of herself behind in the bloody hell and had returned a wizened shell of her former self.

The dream was a nightmare. One she couldn't outrun. She'd slept so little the night before, she'd planned on only taking a catnap at her desk. However, if the puddle of drool on her desktop was any indication, she'd been out for a while. And the dream had found her again, leaving her cold.

She still shook with the horror of it.

TJ checked her watch. It was nearly time to call it quits for the day anyway. She turned off her computer, shuffled unfinished proposals into a neat stack and figured that was all she was going to accomplish. Nothing mattered anyway.

Who cared whether they raked in another fifty-grand contract for renovating office space in downtown San Antonio? Was anyone going to die if they failed?

She closed her office door and slinked down the corridor, whipping quickly past Marnie's door. Letting Marnie down did make her itch with guilt, but not enough to spark a fire for her to do her job.

She headed toward the underground parking lot, but music blared from the door of The Shamrock, just across the street. Would Brent be there again? Would he be up for a little sex? She was bored with him. He didn't really hit her buttons, but he was a good-looking guy with a willing dick. What more could she ask for when she needed a quick fix?

Standing at the curb, she waited for the traffic to pass. A car slowed, a darkly tinted window rolled down. A man peered up from his steering wheel.

"Not even in your dreams," she called out, and darted into the street behind his vehicle, strangely gratified by the sound of squealing brakes.

The bar was packed with happy-hour customers. She combed her hair with her fingers and made a beeline for the tables in the back.

Brent was parked in a booth and gave her a crooked smile as she approached. "Wondered if you'd show."

She slung her purse onto the seat opposite him then scooted in beside him, her hand going straight between his legs to cup his sex.

He jerked but eased his thighs open for her to give him a deeper caress. "I take it you're back for more," he murmured, and turned to nuzzle her ear.

She leaned away from the kiss he pressed against her skin. She wasn't here to cuddle. "Let's slip out back."

"Now, why do I suddenly feel cheap?" he muttered.

"Because you know I only want your body."

He grunted but let her tug his hand behind her as she slid from the seat and walked to the corridor at the back of the bar. She passed the restrooms, the bar owner's office, and pushed open the rear exit.

There, in the middle of the alley, she reached under her skirt and pulled off her panties.

"It's not even dark yet. Anyone could see," he said, his voice tightening with annoyance. "And it stinks out here."

TJ leaned into him, grabbing his hand and tucking it between her legs. No way could he miss the fact she was wet. Maybe he'd think she was hot for him. "Then go inside," she said, raising her chin. "I'll find someone else."

His gaze narrowed. "Anyone ever tell you you're a bitch?"

She smirked. "You. Last night. Tell me you weren't waiting with a hard-on just thinking about what we did. I'll call you a liar to your face."

He shook his head, his eyebrows drawing into a frown. "Girl, you've got issues."

"Not anything I don't already know. But right now all I want is you inside me—and give it to me rough."

She reached for his zipper, but he shoved her hands away and made quick work of his belt, his fly, and then shoved his pants off his hips, just far enough to free his cock, which sprang eagerly from the opening of his pants. He pulled a condom from his pocket and rolled it down his shaft. Then he reached for her. "Let's make it quick," he whispered urgently.

Fine by her. She put her back against the wall and let him lift her by the ass until she wrapped her legs around his waist.

When he started to push inside, she bent toward his ear. "Slap me."

Already looking sex-dazed, he shook his head. "What?"

"Slap my ass. Pinch me."

"All right," he growled then juggled her a bit to free a hand and tap her butt.

"Not hard enough."

He slapped her again.

She lifted her upper lip and snarled, "Harder, baby. I need it to sting."

"Fuck." His cock was poised at her opening, barely inside, but he cupped her butt and gave her a harder swat then followed with a biting pinch.

She kissed his cheek. "Now, bang me," she whispered. "Right here against the wall. Leave the imprint in my skin." She wrestled out of her blouse, letting the sleeves drop to her elbows. Not for him to admire her white, lace bra but because she wanted the bricks scraping her back.

He growled again and ground into her, thrusting inside and beginning to crash her against the wall. "You're fucking crazy, you know that?" he said beside her ear. "Fucking out of your mind. We're both gonna get arrested."

"Just do it," she said, giving his cheek a sharp tap. "Do it!"

He banged her pussy, jouncing her on his cock, driving her against the wall until the dirt and grit scraped her skin raw. This was how she liked it. What she needed. These days, she couldn't get off unless it hurt.

Only then did she deserve it.

Except he was already coming, giving a muffled shout into her ear, his movements growing erratic. When he halted, he pinned her to the wall and leaned back. "We're done," he said, his voice ragged. "Baby, I can't give you what you need."

No, he couldn't. He couldn't grind away the pain. Couldn't keep her mind so filled with sex that she didn't for even one second forget the jumbled images in her head.

And he was right. The alley stank. Not like the smell of loosened bowels and blood, but bad enough that it was all she could think about. "Let me down."

He raised her, disengaging, then set her on her heels.

She closed her blouse, tugged down her skirt and kicked away the panties lying beside her feet. As she walked away, she wondered if she was losing her mind. He certainly thought she had.

And she didn't blame him. Brent was basically a decent guy. It wasn't his fault she had so much baggage she couldn't let him fuck her the way he preferred. Last night, he'd pleaded with her to let him take her home.

Inside the bar, she headed back to the booth but found it occupied by a man—a big, burly guy with a thick neck and arms so big they could bench press a Cadillac. Her interest sparked immediately, but Brent was striding up behind her. "That's my purse on the seat next to you."

The man raised an eyebrow and gave them both a curious look, his gaze sliding over her disheveled appearance and likely coming to all the right conclusions.

TJ stared right back. There was something familiar about him. Something in the hard glint in his brown eyes. Or maybe it was just the short buzz cut that left his dark hair standing up in bristles on the top of his head. Like a Marine. That must have been it.

Without a word, he lifted her purse and handed it to her. She glanced behind her to say her farewell, but Brent was already striding out of the bar. Getting away from her as fast as he could, and she couldn't blame him.

She was the freaky chick. The one a guy thought he wanted until she had him banging her cunt in a dirty alley.

God, she needed a bath.

She turned away, but her heel caught in the carpet and she fell forward. The guy in the booth shot out a hand to grasp her upper arm, saving her from landing on her face.

She'd have bruises. A big black-and-blue bruise for every thick, hard finger that squeezed her arm. "Thanks," she said, and she meant it.

Cross McNally watched the woman walk away, her back straight, but her chin tilted at an angle that betrayed her inner turmoil. He'd seen her cross the street and thought he'd recognized her, but she'd given him a sneer when he'd slowed down.

He'd parked in front of the bar and followed her inside. When he'd seen her drag the dude in the Brooks Brothers suit out the back, he'd hurried out the front and around the side to watch.

It was shadowed where they stood, but he hadn't needed to see clearly to know what they were doing or what it was doing to her. Her groans had been edged with desperation.

The hard, crunching thrusts had to have rubbed her back and ass raw.

A familiar ache settled in his chest. The last time he'd felt it, he'd held her against his chest while she'd beaten him with bloody fists.

Cross left the bar and walked back to his car. He opened the door and slid behind the wheel but paused for a long moment before kicking the ignition. It must have been fate that had him on this exact street at just the right moment to find her.

And it looked as if he'd have to rescue her all over again. He just hoped this time she wouldn't hate him.

* * * * *

TJ unlocked her apartment and walked inside, slamming the door with a backward kick of her foot and passing the beeping telephone. No doubt a message from Marnie asking her when she'd finish the proposal for next week's bid deadline.

She walked straight to her bedroom and began to strip. Her shirt stuck to her back and she winced. She gave it a quick tug, pulling it away from her sticky skin. When she held the shirt in front of her, she saw an ugly red stain. She'd bled.

Shame burned the back of her throat. She balled up the shirt, strode into the bathroom and pushed it into the bottom of the trash can. When she slipped off her skirt, she didn't bother checking for blood but pitched it as well.

Her reflection in the mirror made her stomach hurt. Her face was white, her blue eyes haunted. Her makeup was smudged beneath the lower rim. When she turned, red, pimpled abrasions covered her back and the top of her hips, along with two deeper scrapes that were coated in blood.

What's wrong with me?

Only she already knew. The VA counselor, who didn't know the whole story of what was going on with her, had told her—PTSD mixed with a shitload of survivor's guilt.

All because she'd lived and PFC Sammy Figueroa hadn't.

TJ showered, dressed in a tee and sweatpants, and then headed into the kitchen to fix a bite to eat. Her phone chirped inside her purse, and she wrinkled her nose.

Soon, she promised herself, she'd get her life back in order. Just not tonight. Still, the sound was annoying. She opened the flap of her handbag and reached inside for her phone, hitting the button to silence it. When she drew out her hand, a card tumbled out.

It landed on the floor face up. It was a plain white business card with bold lettering. *Call 1-800-DOM-help.*

Her head canted as she read the words and numbers again. It wasn't something she'd tucked inside her purse. She'd have remembered. The way the telephone number reverberated inside her, the images it conjured—she wouldn't have forgotten it. The pictures flashed through her mind—ridiculous ones of men and women dressed in leather and PVC, dragging each other around by leather-studded collars and leashes. Of women stretched in chains with floggers stinging their backs and buttocks.

The sting of her own scrapes flared, which nonsensically caused her clit to throb.

She bent to pick up the card, intending to drop it into the trash, but her fingers curled around it instead. A deep ache settled in her belly. Tears burned the backs of her eyes.

What the hell anyway? She'd been battling urges that crippled her with horror ever since her return. She couldn't sleep. Couldn't work. Couldn't have a normal conversation with friends.

Maybe some man tricked-out in leather could give her the kind of pain she sensed she needed to find at least a temporary release from all of her problems.

She uncurled her fingers from around the edges of the card and reached for the phone.

Chapter Two

ꕤ

TJ stood on a sidewalk outside a building in the warehouse district. Tall streetlamps gleamed up and down a row of hollow, abandoned structures, leaving dark pools of shadow.

She tugged up the collar of her jacket to shield herself against a sudden chill. The building in front of her, a tall, square box with garishly painted doors and a neon sign that flickered and buzzed was named Unfettered.

And it was a club. One the operator she'd spoken to last night described as an "alternative".

"To what?" she'd asked.

"To everything you've tried before." His voice had been silky and deep, soothing her nerves as she'd clutched the handset so tightly the slip of her fingers squeaked.

It had felt as though he knew her pain. But perhaps he'd had hundreds of calls from people every bit as twisted and broken as she was.

The door opened. A woman stood at the top of the steps. She was tall with black hair that reached to her waist. She didn't beckon but simply held the door, her expression unrevealing as TJ fought the urge to turn and run.

This wasn't her. It couldn't be her.

"Chickenin' out before you even have a look inside?"

She jerked and swung her head toward the voice, only to find the burly man from the bar standing several feet away, his narrowed gaze watching her. Her shoulders fell. "You put the card in my purse."

"What card?" But then he smiled and waved an arm toward the entrance of the club. "After you?"

He was dressed in jeans that molded thickly muscled thighs and a black long-sleeved tee that could have been painted onto his torso, and which revealed the heavy musculature that cloaked his frame.

Her mouth dried. He'd be strong. Stronger than her.

"Tell me you're not tempted."

Lord, had he read her mind? No, he was talking about the club. "Why'd you do it?" she asked, knowing she was stalling the inevitable. And he knew it too.

His shrug was nonchalant, but his gaze fell away. His lips curved into a slight, tight smile. "I saw you in the alley. Looked like your boyfriend couldn't get you off. Looked like a nice guy." What he left unsaid was that he was not.

Still, she didn't like being played, moved around like a marionette. "I'm out of here."

She flicked a glance at the woman at the top of the stairs who still hadn't moved then turned on her heel and walked away.

However, footsteps shadowed hers. She glanced back. Big and burly was several steps behind but had halted when she had. "Stop following me. I'll call the police."

His smile widened, and his hand reached into his back pocket. He pulled out small, black wallet and gave it a flick. A gold badge shown in the lamplight.

"That's supposed to make me feel better? Anyone can buy one of those."

"I'm a cop. East substation. You can call if you like. But you already know I'm tellin' the truth."

She raised her chin. "Then you know better than to stalk me."

"Not stalkin', baby," he said in a lazy, Texas drawl. "I'm here to help."

TJ looked away and swallowed down a bitter lump. "Sure you are," she shot back, but her voice was thick. The endearment, even thrown around casually, made her wish for something she couldn't have—arms to hold her, a man who loved her.

He blew out a deep breath. "Look, I left the card in your purse, but it was your choice whether you called that number or not. And you're here. Why not see if this is what you've been lookin' for?"

She kept her back to him, afraid he'd read her expression and know that her hesitation was because she was afraid to walk away. She'd called the number out of desperation. "What is it you want out of this? You into freaks?"

"You're not a freak. But I know a little something about what you're goin' through."

She snorted. "Oh yeah? Think you know me so well?"

"I saw you with that guy. Or rather heard you. You wanted to be punished."

Her lip lifted in a snarl, and she swung toward him. "That your thing? You like watching? Or do you like slapping girls?"

"Not so much. But I am good at readin' what a partner needs. I'll give it to you. You won't have to beg me for it. You comin'?"

TJ swallowed, this time because her mouth had gone dry. He was good. Knew just what to say to get her to melt. Her nipples were erect. Her clit swelled.

His expression was still hard, uncompromising. But this time she took comfort from his strength. When he lifted his hand, she found herself raising hers and sliding her palm against his.

Cross slowly closed his fingers around her hand and pulled her. She came a step closer, and he pivoted so they stood side by side. He encircled her waist with his arm, lightly bracing the small of her back. He half feared she'd jerk away, but she eased into the embrace, seeming to relax a little. Letting him take charge. She was already learning to lean on him.

And it was sweet, even if her lips were twisted in a snarl.

TJ was skittish—and she had reason to be. If she had any clue what was going through his head right now… His body was taut, groin aching—had been since he'd first glimpsed her striding toward the club.

Fuck, she was beautiful tonight. Her tawny-brown hair was loose around her shoulders, and she wore a skimpy top, a black, silky sleeve that hugged her breasts. She'd come braless—he knew because her nipples poked against the fabric. Long, pencil-thin black jeans skimmed her legs. Her red-painted toenails were framed by silver sandals. He'd never been into toes, but swore he'd get off sucking on them.

They walked back to the club, and he raised his face to meet Dru's stoic gaze. The manager of the club gave him a subtle nod, and her lips formed a soft smile before she glanced at the woman he guided firmly up the steps. "TJ, right?"

TJ cleared her throat. "Right. How'd you know?"

"You're the only newbie scheduled to arrive. I've been keeping an eye out for you. The neighborhood can be a little intimidating. Come inside. I'd offer to show you around, but Cross, here, has been around a time or two. You're in good hands."

Cross raised an eyebrow. He didn't know how she managed it, but Dru knew everything that went on inside the club and probably knew all too well that he'd greased the wheels to get TJ here. When he'd first hit town, he'd needed a place he could go where he could feel as if he was in charge of his own destiny. A business card tucked into the corner of a bathroom stall door with the club's 1-800 number hadn't seemed like the answer. However, Unfettered had fit the bill to a "T".

Last night, he'd told the Operator that he thought TJ might find the club just as "therapeutic".

Cross passed Dru, who gave him a surreptitious wink, then guided TJ through the dark foyer and into the main room of the club. Music played, a throbbing techno beat, but not so loud he couldn't hear the rumble of conversations all around him.

TJ's head turned, glancing left then right, and her steps slowed. He pressed the small of her back, urging her forward. She didn't resist. She was clearly curious about everything happening around them.

There were small, lit stages positioned around the room, raised daises really, where several scenes were playing with onlookers admiring the techniques of those providing the demonstrations.

Her attention snagged on a woman whose chained arms were stretched toward the ceiling and who stood on tiptoe. She was a busty blonde, and each swat of a paddle against her generous buttocks shook her heavy breasts.

He was sure it was the woman's expression that fascinated TJ. A look of pure bliss accompanied the blonde's loud, staccato moans.

He bent toward TJ's ear. "Would you like a drink?" he asked, pointing toward the bar that stretched across the back of the room. "Sorry, no alcohol served here. If you've never been to a place like this, it's frowned on because alcohol messes with a person's judgment." At the questioning arch of her brow, he added, "A Dom needs to stay aware, know when he's pushed a sub to his or her limits. A sub needs to be clearheaded for the same reason."

Her eyebrows lowered. "Look, I don't care about learning about this lifestyle. It's not my thing."

"And yet you're interested in what's happening there," he said, pointing toward the blonde whose Dom was releasing leather cuffs to free her.

"But it's stupid, all that ritual. All that 'yes Sir, no Mistress' crap. The gestures, poses..." She waved toward a man who knelt in front of woman, his hands behind him, his head bent as the woman stroked his shoulders with a quirt. "I'd never do that."

Cross bit back a smile. He'd bet money she'd eat those words before the night was over. "It serves a purpose, sweetheart. It's a discipline. We need rules. Etiquette. To keep things safe."

She swung toward him, her expression belligerent. "Can we skip that part? I'm not... I don't think I could stand that."

"Because you're just eager to have sex, right?" He ignored the instantaneous thrust of her lower lip—and the answering surge in his groin. "You might not be into this thing, but you still need to know the rules. They're for your well-being."

She snorted. "You're gonna talk to me about safe words now?"

Cross didn't let her little outburst faze him. Too much rode on getting her alone tonight. The last thing he'd let happen was her escalating an argument to the point she walked. "Are you always so quick to jump ahead? You want to talk about safe words now? All right. Choose one."

Her fists curled at her sides. "I don't want one."

"Then a signal," he said agreeably. "So you have control."

"I don't want control. I don't want some pussy stoplight when things get tough."

Cross held still. "You want me to decide?" he asked softly.

Her chin jutted, pulling the skin taut over her cheeks, accentuating the haunted shadows in her eyes. "I don't want you to stop."

His jaw sawed shut. "All right, sweetheart. I'll give you what you need."

TJ shivered at the promise in his voice. Perhaps tonight she wouldn't be left disappointed.

A hand slid along his arm, and his head swiveled toward the manager who gave him a polite smile while her gaze reflected her doubt. She'd heard them arguing.

"Would you like her prepared?" the dark-haired woman asked.

"I'll do it," Cross said, biting out the words.

The woman's chest rose as she took a breath. Her gaze went from him to TJ, who kept her expression neutral. "Then I'll leave you two alone." To TJ, she tilted her head. "He really is very good. I vetted him myself. Trust in him to guide you."

Once they were alone, TJ glanced around the room. "Will anyone be watching us?"

"We'll have a private room. No onlookers."

"But will anyone see?"

"You should know that all the rooms are monitored."

She snorted. "For my safety. Right."

Cross edged closer. She almost took a step back but straightened her spine. When he put his arm around her and pressed against the small of her back to get her walking, she gave a little shiver, and her pussy grew moist.

If he could manage that kind of reaction with just a gentle nudge, what might that hand do when it landed sharply on her bare skin? They walked, in no apparent hurry, down a long corridor with doors on either side.

Pausing in front of one room, he slipped a card from his pocket. It looked like a hotel room passkey, and he swiped it through the reader. A soft snick sounded, and he pulled down the latch. He waited while she passed inside.

The room was lovely. The colors soothing. The walls were a soft sage, the carpet navy. The furnishings were mostly padded affairs with navy leather upholstery and dark, burnished wooden frames. Candles burned atop a long cabinet with lots of closed drawers.

She stood still in the center of the room, waiting for him to move closer.

However, he remained by the closed door, standing with his hands hanging loosely at his sides.

"Well?" she asked, hating the grating sound of her own voice. God, she was a bitch.

The corners of his mouth twitched. "I'm waiting for you."

Was he laughing at her? "What? You want me to strip here?"

"That would be a start, but not the one I want. I want you to tell me what you think you need."

"What's anyone *need* who comes in here? The subs. They want someone else to make the decisions."

"That's not true. Subs know the possibilities. They can be surprised, pushed beyond what they thought they could bear, but at least they have a structure to rely on. You don't know those possibilities. Tell me what you want."

TJ turned to the side so she didn't have to meet his steady gaze. She felt uncomfortable beneath his stare. Even despite, or perhaps because of, his implacable façade, he made it so tempting for her to confide. She crossed her arms over her chest, hugging herself. "I need pain. For you to make me hurt or I can't get off." There, she'd said it. Now he'd know she really was a freak.

"You're sure about that?"

She nodded jerkily, still not meeting his eyes.

Cross walked toward her, his tread light despite his size. His hand lifted slowly. A finger tucked under her chin to raise her face, forcing her to look at him. "We don't always get what we want, TJ. But I'll give you what you need. Now strip. Put your clothes on the table beside the door. Folded neatly."

She almost balked but sensed that while he was relaxing some of the rules for her, he wouldn't budge on much more. In any case, she was more than ready for things to move along.

Her body was a bundle of pent-up energy. She'd had nothing to think about all day beyond what would happen this night. For the first time in months, she'd felt hope that she'd find release. That she'd enter the zone where her mind could let go of her memories. Just a few moments' ease might save her sanity.

So, she stripped in silence, removing her sandals then her jeans, leaving only her silver bikini panties to cover her below. Then she wriggled out her blouse, easing it down her hips to the floor, not glancing up because she wasn't sure she'd have the nerve to continue. He intimidated her. Which excited her beyond all common sense.

When she stood in only her panties, she took a deep, steadying breath and turned slowly to face him.

His gaze scanned her body quickly then rose to meet her eyes again. "You're lovely."

Perhaps he'd said it to reassure her. She couldn't really tell, but she'd never had any complaints. Her body was still toned, although she hadn't worked out since she'd left the Army. And she'd lost a little weight. "What now?" she asked, surprised to hear the husky note in her voice.

"After you remove your pretty panties, you'll undress me.

Undressing him wasn't something she minded in the least. But the panties?

She'd been casual about dropping hers in the dirty alley with Brent, but she wanted just a little "armor" against Cross' intense scrutiny. Her fingers fumbled as she pushed the satin fabric down her hips and let it fall.

His gaze dropped to her pussy and lingered there a moment. His nostrils flared. When he looked into her face again, she felt moisture pool between her legs at the way his features hardened to granite.

One dark eyebrow arched.

With surprising grace, she walked toward him, circling behind him, then reached for the bottom hem of his tee. She stripped it up his torso, and he raised his arms for her to pull it off. When she stood back, she stared at his back, at the naked breadth of his shoulders, the deep indent of his spine and his narrow waist.

She cleared her throat. "I suppose you want me to fold your clothes too?"

"Of course," he said, without glancing back.

And yet there was amusement in his voice, and she hid a smile as she folded his shirt and placed it on the table next to her clothing. Which made it easier somehow when she walked around him to kneel and untie his boots.

His large hands braced against her shoulders, shifting his weight to her—something so simple and natural, but that reassured her because he was heavy. It reminded her of his strength.

She stripped off his socks and rolled them together into a tight ball, tucked them into his boots and placed them beside the growing piles.

When she reached for his waistband, his chest rose. She thumbed open the button and drew down his zipper, her mouth growing dry because the long ridge of his cock was thickening against his leg, lifting the fabric.

She tugged down his jeans and his cock sprang free, bobbing once, gliding like hot satin against her cheek. The impulse to slide her cheek along his length a second time was overwhelming, so she followed the urge and rubbed her skin against him, closing her eyes to inhale his musk and fill her nostrils with his scent.

Hands petted her hair gently—fingers combed through the strands. "Whenever you're ready, I want you up on that padded table, sweetheart."

Her eyes snapped open, blinking, and she quickly pulled his pants the rest of the way off. She folded them, tossing them carelessly on the stack, and went to the padded table he indicated. She jumped up and began to lie on her back.

"Other side," he said. "Rest your head on your arms and relax."

The relax part was impossible, but she lay down, closing her eyes and listening to his sounds as he moved around the room, opening cupboards. When he came back, he stood beside her. Warm liquid poured onto her back, heated oil, she surmised when he began to massage it into her skin.

He started at her shoulders. "These abrasions…I'll try to be gentle. Did those happen last night?"

"Yes."

"There's grit worked into the scrapes. They look inflamed. You won't do that again."

Not his call, but she didn't see a point in arguing. She'd decided the same thing herself.

His large hands rubbed the oil into her skin then he kneaded her shoulder, the tops of her arms. He didn't linger long enough for her to complain about the fact she wasn't there for a massage. He glided lightly over the scrapes. When he palmed her buttocks, she stiffened and lifted her head.

"I'm going to touch you everywhere. Get used to it." And with that, he traced the line bisecting her buttocks, glancing over her anus but coming back to swirl atop the sensitive opening.

TJ pressed her face into the padding, gritting her teeth to suppress a moan of pleasure. But then he moved on, spreading oil down the backs of her thighs and the pads of her feet.

"Roll over."

Lord, she wasn't ready for this. A fucking would be less intimate, but every smooth glide of his hand had given her a pleasure she hadn't known in a long, long time. So, she rolled, coming to rest on her back, her hands crossed over her belly.

He plucked them from her stomach and stretched them along her sides. Then while she watched this time, he tipped a bottle of oil and streamed it over her breasts and belly, into the top of her folds where it ran the length of her slit and pooled beneath her. He poured oil down the tops of her legs.

When he rubbed her this time, she couldn't escape his cutting gaze. "Why the guy in the alley, TJ?"

She jutted her chin. "Why not?"

"He wasn't doing it for you. He's not your type."

"And you are?"

He raised an eyebrow.

She grunted. "Okay. He was easy. Followed directions, to a point," she said with a one-sided smile.

"Like I said—not your type. The fact you had to order him to spank you made that crystal clear."

She hated that he'd seen that. She'd been weak and acted like a crazy whore. "You always spy on people?"

"I was watching out for you."

"You didn't know me. Why would you do that?"

His mouth tightened. "You remind me of someone."

TJ shook her head, wondering what his problem was that he'd be drawn to a woman like her. "Was she as big a bitch?"

Chapter Three

ꟸ

His teeth flashed, and TJ felt an instant wave of heat that didn't have thing to do with the fact his hands were rubbing oil onto her nipples, thumbs and forefingers pausing to pluck and twist the tips. That smile softened his expression and made him handsome.

Downward he roamed, slicking over her belly then onto her thighs, her knees, calves. *Lord, her toes.*

Each was parted, kneaded. And then his glance sliced to her pussy. "Part your legs for me, sweetheart."

She was embarrassed by how fast she complied, but he didn't smirk. He simply glided a fingertip along her nude folds, up and down then in between, tracing the edges of her thin, inner lips.

Her pussy clenched then opened, making a moist, sucking sound that snared his attention and made her blush. "I like a nude pussy," he murmured. "Keep it like this."

He said it as though they'd see each other again. Frankly, she hoped he'd last longer than Brent.

Fingers parted her and pulled up her folds to bare her clit. Air hissed between her teeth at the first, oily swirl atop the hard, rounded knot.

"Same sweet pink as your lips."

She rolled her eyes. "We are *not* discussing my pussy."

His eyebrows waggled. "Even if how much I like it will mean I spend some extra time there?" Fingers thrust inside her, two—thick, hard digits that twisted and thrust.

Of their own volition, her knees rose and parted.

"Yeah," he breathed. "I like it too, but we're not there yet." He withdrew and wiped his fingers on a towel. "Get on up."

His hand extended, and she gripped it without hesitation, letting him bring her up to sit on the edge of the table with her thighs parted around his hips. His cock angled toward his belly, and she wondered what he'd do if she shimmied her butt closer until it snuggled against her sex.

His gaze dropped to where their bodies almost met. His firm mouth curved. "You need a little softening," he said, his tone even.

"Softening?" she whispered, leaning back on her hands, all but inviting him to come over her, here and now.

"You'll like it. It's right up your alley." When his head came up, the hardness of his stare told her the use of the word "alley" had been deliberate.

She straightened and pulled her legs to the side, closing them. "You sound pissed, and you've no right to be. What I do with my body is my bus—"

"You're right. But you're also impatient as hell for me to *make* your body my business."

"You're an ass."

"And you're a bitch."

"So we're even?"

He snorted and shook his head. "We're back to rules. One I have to insist on now."

"Which is?"

"Call me Sir when you address me."

She turned away. "And if I don't?"

"Don't think disobedience will earn you the punishment you want. If you refuse, I walk. And it's not a tease. I won't stop at the door to give you a second chance."

TJ gave him a fierce frown. "Why's it so fucking important to you?"

"It's a sign of respect. Yours for me."

"You haven't done a thing to earn it."

"I'm here," he said, planting his hands on his naked hips. "I've seen the shit you dish, the stupid risks you take. But I'm still here."

"If I'm such a loser, why bother?"

"You really have to ask? When you saw me at the bar, there was a moment, wasn't there? You sized me up, and if your 'dick with benefits' hadn't walked up, I'd bet you'd have slid onto the seat with me. You knew in an instant that I could give you what you want."

He had to say that while they were both naked. While her nipples were hard and her pussy soaked. He'd oiled her up and gotten her stoked so she'd be weak. So willing to follow where he led that she'd beg for it. Damn, she was tempted to whine.

"What's it gonna be? Do you want me to stay?"

She swallowed down her pride but kept her face averted so he wouldn't see that she was secretly pleased he was placing limits on her. Like invisible bonds. "Please, Sir," she whispered. "I want you to stay."

Fingers slid into her hair, and he pulled to tilt back her head. Then he leaned toward her, closing the distance between them but never touching her with his chest or cock.

One breath, a slight arch of her back and she'd be able to scrape her nipples over his lightly furred chest. But his gaze warned her not to.

His mouth covered hers, suctioning slightly, then drew away.

She blinked open her eyes to find he'd never closed his. He studied her expression then his eased a fraction. "TJ, go to the bench behind me and bend over it. And no more questions."

"Yes Sir," she said, her voice husky.

He lent her his hand as she edged off the table and hopped to the floor. Her legs felt like rubber, and she wobbled a bit, but she strode around him toward the bench. A spanking bench, she guessed. She'd read about them but had never actually seen one. She climbed onto the platform, knelt on a padded step and leaned over it. It was surprisingly comfortable, even if the position left her completely vulnerable with her ass and pussy exposed. And she was comfortable—until he used straps to secure her wrists.

Cross smoothed his hand on her slick skin, from her shoulders to her buttocks. Then both hands closed around one thigh, slid up and down, and lifted it to widen her stance. He repeated the actions with the other. His palm cupped her sex, warming it. A finger slid inside her. "You'll let me do whatever I want?"

"Yes Sir," she gritted out, trying not to clench around the invading digit.

"But you want it rough." Another finger slid inside and both pushed deep.

"Yes," she hissed. Without thinking, she tilted her hips to stick her ass up higher, inviting him deeper. A thicker single digit—his thumb?—pushed against her asshole.

Her head sank as she breathed deeply, trying to relax the tight, little ring. Gradually, he eased inside then fucked all three fingers in and out, slowly.

Arousal slid from inside her to coat the long fingers thrusting in her pussy.

Pursing her lips, she breathed slowly, deeply. She knew he had no intention of getting her off this way, but she was content to let him set the pace.

His fingers withdrew. He padded silently away, toward a dark oak cabinet with slide-out trays of sexual implements. She watched from the corner of her eye as he ran his fingers over the flanges of a flogger, but he passed over it in favor of a paddle—a long, wooden paddle with holes drilled in its surface. Then he opened a drawer and pulled out a blindfold.

His gaze darted toward her, catching her watching. He whipped out the blindfold, making it snap, and she smiled then trained her gaze straight-ahead. A blindfold didn't worry her.

His steps approached again and halted behind her. His body leaned over hers, the heat from his skin warming her back although he never touched her. The blindfold came under her face, and she closed her eyes obediently as he tied it.

"Can you see anything?"

"No Sir," she said, smirking.

"Good."

The door to the room whooshed open, and she jerked up her head. When Cross didn't say anything to whomever had entered, she tightened. She wanted to ask who'd come in and whether it was part of his plan, but he'd ordered her not to question him.

Did he expect her to balk? Footsteps treaded lightly on the carpet, stopping in front of her. A hand cupped her chin. Not Cross'. It didn't feel quite large enough. A thumb stroked her bottom lip, but she kept her mouth firmly closed.

The hand withdrew. The sound of latex snapping came from right in front of her, level with her face. She began to shake her head.

A smack landed on the back of one thigh. Delivered by a hand—this time, certainly Cross'—and hard enough to sting. She jerked, tightening her lips.

Another slap landed on the other thigh then one against her right buttock and the left. She breathed noisily through her nostrils, knowing now what Cross hoped to achieve. *Bastard!* she wanted to say. But then he'd know he'd surprised her. She wouldn't give him the satisfaction of knowing she'd wanted him. *Him alone.*

A latex-covered cock stroked her cheek, but she turned away from it.

Cool gel squirted between her buttocks. Something with a rounded point slid between her cheeks. When it circled her hole, she groaned deep in her throat. As it pushed inside, she opened her mouth around a gasp, and a thumb entered her mouth, dragging down her jaw. The cock pushed between her teeth, but she couldn't object because the thing Cross pushed inside her ass was widening, stretching her. Her jaw opened wider for her to breathe around the cock pushing its way deeper inside her mouth.

TJ's entire body tightened. Her breasts hardened—her nipples grew painfully engorged. The plug Cross pushed relentlessly inside at last narrowed, and his palm snuggled against the base to push it the last little bit, but the toy wasn't going anywhere. The bulbous shape kept it trapped by the tightening of her sphincter.

He'd accomplished what he set out to do. Force her to accept another man's cock—a stranger's. The man in front of her stroked forward and back into her mouth, and she sucked him, obedient at last.

The hard surface of the paddle rubbed over her ass, and she tried to back off the cock to tell him no, that it was going to be too much.

"Don't fight. And for fuck's sake keep your lips around your teeth. If you hurt him, we're done."

He had her. Whatever he commanded, she'd obey. The hard paddle was a promise—her reward for good behavior.

And even before it left her skin, she closed her eyes. Her heart slowed. She locked her jaws wide open, prepared.

The first firm smack jolted her body. She groaned and the cock resumed shafting her mouth, in and out. She sucked hard, drawing on it.

A series of sharp slaps struck her buttocks and thighs, never the same spot, and as her skin warmed, her entire body quivered. Her mind let go, drifting in a luxurious haze.

A smack landed against the center of her ass, tapping the plug, and her pussy and ass clenched. Moisture trickled from her, running to the top of her folds and then her belly. With each slap after, she glided on wet heat. The fact of it registered, but she was far away, lost in a dream state where every part of her body blushed with heat. Every nerve ending sparked. She felt alive but removed.

The cock withdrew. Latex stretched. Then flicks of hot, thick sperm struck her face, her lips. The paddle skimmed her skin again, up her thighs, over her bottom. Then it fell away.

Footsteps padded away. The door opened and closed.

She was alone with Cross again. Her pussy was aching, so engorged it throbbed. She slumped against the bench.

The plug slid smoothly out. Velcro scratched, and her hands were freed. The blindfold loosened then drew away. "Open your eyes."

She blinked. Cross knelt in front of her, his intense, brown gaze locking with hers. He held a wipe and used it to clean her face.

"Any questions left?"

Just one. "Will you fuck me?"

His lips twisted in a grim smile. "That's the first one that came to mind?"

She nodded, tears burning her eyes.

Cross' expression softened. Then he straightened and lifted her from the bench, sweeping a hand beneath her knees when they threatened to buckle. He carried her to the table and sat her on the edge.

Her breath hissed as her inflamed skin met the cool leather. Already she could feel the welts rising.

"Lie back."

"Y-yes Sir."

When she lay back, she stretched her arms to either side. The euphoria hadn't fully receded from her mind. She felt mellow—her heart beat at a slow, steady thrum.

Until he bent toward her sex, and his fingers scraped the hood stretched over her aching clit. The first flutter of his tongue there had her arching her back. Her hands covered her breasts, comforting herself, kneading her nipples as he plied her with wicked, targeted laps and flicks until she exploded.

She hovered in ecstasy, blood pulsing through her pussy, rushing to her clit. His tongue soothed the knot until the last of her convulsions faded, and then he kissed her there and rose, leaning over her, his cock trapped against her folds but not entering her.

His hands cupped the back of her head, cradling it gently. "I'll see you again tomorrow."

She blinked. "But..."

He gave a grimace that eased into a crooked smile. "It's not about me getting mine, TJ. This was all about you. You'll learn to trust me on that—but you're right, trust has to be earned."

TJ lifted a nerveless hand and cupped the side of his cheek. "I don't understand. I'm willing, even eager for you to fuck me."

"Sweetheart, *fucking* isn't what I'm after."

"Then what?" she asked, her voice aching like a raw wound.

He shook his head. "No more questions. I'll help you dress." First, however, he leaned down and gave her the deep kiss she hadn't known she needed.

Chapter Four

ꟿ

TJ placed the draft proposal in a folder and turned off her computer. For the first time since she'd come back to San Antonio, she hadn't just shown up, she'd done a full day's work.

Not that she had any illusions she was "cured" or even on a road to recovery, but she'd slept dreamlessly the night before, floating on a cloud after her session with Cross.

Cross. She wondered what his last name was and just what kind of cop he was. She could imagine him in black SWAT gear, ready to storm an armed robber, but she'd much rather seeing him push paper at a desk. She'd seen enough rugged, honorable men in uniform spilling their blood.

And she did consider him honorable. The fact he'd withheld his pleasure the night before had gone a long way toward proving that. She'd been completely seduced, putty in his hands, and yet he'd held back. His cock had been red and engorged from the moment she'd slid down his jeans, so she knew it wasn't because he didn't find her attractive.

Something she still couldn't get her head around. He'd seen her with Brent. Knew she'd be into a quick fuck. She couldn't figure out what it was he wanted from her, unless his pleasure was a deeper sort of mindfuck.

Why should she care so long as she got what she needed from him?

TJ picked up her purse and headed down the hallway toward Marnie's office. Her friend was busy reviewing blueprints spread on a table.

TJ cleared her throat. "I finished the quote."

Marnie didn't turn, but her back stiffened. "Great. Leave it on my desk, will you? I still have some work to finish up."

It was on the tip of TJ's tongue to offer to help, but something in Marnie's posture warned her not to try. She had fences to mend there, but she knew she had to prove she was really in this thing, that she wanted to be a full partner again. So, she dropped the proposal into the inbox, satisfied that Marnie would have no complaints over the quality or the figures. If they won the bid, well, maybe then they'd talk.

Truth was TJ wasn't sure she wanted to stay in the business. The spark that had fueled her ambition was gone.

She exited the building, waving to the building's receptionist, and stepped out into sunshine. Turning her face upward, she let the warmth infuse her. She'd woken up refreshed, but she'd stayed feeling that way all day not because she'd slept well but because she looked forward to tonight.

Music blared from The Shamrock across the street and she turned toward it.

"TJ."

Her steps slowed, and she glanced behind her. Then her heart kicked into high gear.

Cross unfolded himself from where he'd been sitting against the hood of his dark sedan. He turned toward The Shamrock then gave her a pointed stare.

"I wasn't going there." *Not that it's any of your business*, she said to herself. But even to herself, she admitted that wasn't exactly the truth. He'd made her his business.

"Didn't think you would," he drawled. "There's nothin' for you there."

"Really? You think I wasn't even tempted?"

"You tryin' to piss me off?" he asked, a grin kicking up one side of his mouth.

"What would it get me?" she asked, both hands clutching her purse in front of her.

"Not what you're hopin'."

She bit her lip and felt a wave of shyness sweep over her. Strange, given he'd seen her completely naked, from every angle possible—some completely unflattering. "What are you doing here?" she asked breathlessly.

"I want you to come with me."

She gave a soft murmur, pleased he'd been just as eager to see her. "I realized today, I don't even know your full name. You don't know mine."

"TJ Lipton. Tansy Jo."

Her mouth gaped then snapped closed. "You went through my purse?"

He gave a sharp, unapologetic nod. "Checked your ID before you and boyfriend came back to the table."

"He's not my boyfriend," she blurted. "And you had no right to go through my bag."

"No, I didn't. And I apologize, but I wanted your address."

"Some girls might find that a little creepy."

His dark eyes narrowed. "Do you? You have to tell me the truth."

Flustered, because she felt equal parts outrage and flattered, she evaded answering. "This part of the rules?"

"My rule. Do you find me creepy?"

Lord, she found him intimidating, arrogant and so damn sexy her panties were already soaked through. But not creepy. "No Sir," she said quietly then gave a quick glance around because this conversation and her reactions were quickly becoming intimate.

Cross stepped close, his hands sliding over hers still gripping her purse. "Do you have any idea how I feel when you call me that?" he said, his voice a deep, growling rumble.

She swallowed. "Turned-on?"

He nodded.

"Then it's mutual."

"Name's Cross McNally."

He bent, but she didn't wait for him to plant one on her lips. She came up on her toes and leaned into him, the purse trapped between them as he devoured her mouth.

His lips were firm as he dragged them over hers, forcing her to follow his lead, just as he had last night. When his tongue stabbed at the seam of her mouth, she relented, opening to allow him inside.

Their tongues slid sensuously together. Her breaths deepened as she gave herself up to the pleasure of his kiss.

When he pulled away, his hands gripped the tops of her hips to steady her. "Will you come with me? No questions?"

She nodded and let him take her hand and lead her to the passenger side of his car.

Once she was inside, she sat at an angle to watch him as he drove, not caring to know where they went. "How long were you waiting for me?"

"Not long."

"If we'd missed each other, would I have seen you at Unfettered?"

"I wasn't going to miss you."

She narrowed her blue eyes, and when he glanced her way, he smiled at her expression. "I took one of your business cards when I went through your purse. I'd have come to your office if you hadn't walked out soon."

She laughed. "Am I really worth that kind of bother?"

His glance cut her way briefly. "TJ, I wouldn't be here if I didn't think so."

Pleasure warmed her, and she relaxed, glancing around at last and realizing that they were heading out of the city. "You live far?"

"No questions, remember? But I have some instructions for you to keep you from getting bored."

Instructions. Her nipples tightened, and he hadn't even said what he wanted her to do.

"I like your skirt, but I want it and your panties off. And you can't remove your seat belt."

"You don't want to make this easy, do you?"

White teeth flashed against tanned skin. "Wouldn't be as much fun."

She toed off her pumps and pulled her seat belt to give her a little extra wiggle room then lifted her butt to pull her panties down. She dangled them on the end of her finger. "Where do you want these?"

"Glove box."

"Do you collect them?

"No, but they're wet, right? I'd like to keep something with your scent."

She wrinkled her nose. "That's a little gross."

"Maybe to you. The skirt?"

She unbuttoned it then cursed under her breath as she worked it over her hips. "The glove box too?"

"Toss it on the backseat."

Without looking, she tossed backward. Now she was nude from the waist down.

The bleep of a siren sounded behind them. Her gaze darted to Cross. He rolled down his window and slowed, turning down a gravel road then reaching out an arm to wave the cop around them.

Odd behavior in her mind, but she wasn't really thinking because panic was starting to build. "Will you reach for my skirt? I don't want to flash anyone."

"You'll stay just like you are," he said then gave her a pointed stare. "And put your hands beside you. Don't even try to cover up."

Heat flooded her cheeks. Not the sexy kind. She burned with embarrassment while a cop pulled in front of them then got out of his car, halting to place his cream-colored cowboy hat on his head before striding toward them.

She began to cross her legs, but Cross placed a hand on her knee to hold her there. He leaned his head out the window. "Hey there, Tanner."

Why was she surprised they knew each other? "Tanner" approached the passenger side of the vehicle, and she squeezed her eyes shut. She heard the crunch of his footsteps then there was a silent pause.

No doubt he'd peeked into the vehicle and seen her.

Her window glided down. Footsteps crunched closer. She peeked up into the deputy's face that revealed nothing of what he was thinking. Tall and well-built, he was good-looking with close-cropped brown hair, blue eyes and a dimple in his chin.

"Sir," the deputy said, directing his words to Cross but keeping his eyes on her naked pussy. "Do you know you were speedin'?"

"Saw you a half mile back and stepped on it," Cross said, amusement in his tone.

Tanner's mouth twitched and his narrowed gaze shot to Cross. "There a reason your girl's half-naked?"

"I like her that way."

Tanner nodded, still fighting a smile. "Reason enough, I s'pose. Anything I can help you with?"

"Deputy, TJ here might be carryin'."

"I see." Tanner's expression turned stern when his glance cut to her face. "I understand now why you waved me past," he murmured. "My camera's runnin'." He tipped back his hat and gave TJ another slow look. Heat banked in his gaze, and he stepped away. "Ma'am, I need you to step out of the vehicle."

Her gaze shot to Cross.

"Do as the man says. *Everything* he says."

She read the hard glint in his eyes and realized the dominating man from the night before was back. Damn, she'd leave a puddle on the seat, and he'd know in a heartbeat just how turned-on she was.

Tanner lifted the door handle and stood back, his expression set in hard lines.

TJ glanced toward the main highway, but they'd pulled pretty far down the dirt road. No one would see. Still, she felt awkward stepping out half-naked onto hot gravel in her bare feet.

Her skirt landed on the ground beside her. Cross gave her a wink.

She stepped on the gabardine skirt, grateful for the buffer, but her shirtwaist blouse only covered her to the top of her mound.

"Face the car, ma'am."

She took a deep breath and turned to place her hands against the car.

"Spread 'em."

"What? No foreplay?" she muttered, but braced apart her legs. Air flowed between, reminding her just how vulnerable she was.

A soft chuckle sounded behind her but stopped the moment the trooper's hands smoothed over her shoulders, slid along her sides, over her hips and down each leg. When he came up, his hands trailed the inside of her thighs, coming to a halt at her pussy, which he cupped then probed with a finger.

"Think you're wrong, Cross," he drawled. "Nothin' hidden up here."

"Then do me a favor and put this inside her."

She couldn't see what Cross handed to the officer but felt something cool and round slide between her lips. Fingers followed it inside, pushing it deeper.

A hum started immediately, and she moaned, swaying for just a second as the vibrator started up. Tanner's fingers slid out.

"Were you thorough, Tanner?" Cross called out.

"Guess it's better to be on the safe side," Tanner said, a hint of laughter in his voice. "Bend over a little, sweetheart," he whispered next to her ear.

TJ blew through pursed lips then lowered her torso, gripping the bottom of the window for balance.

Tanner's hands cupped her buttocks, giving them a squeeze, then he tucked a finger between them.

"What is it with my ass?" she said over her shoulder, embarrassed because she was so aroused by the intimate touch.

"Be surprised the things a criminal can hide up there."

His finger penetrated, and TJ couldn't help it, she bent lower, her eyelids drooping. Her glance found Cross watching her through the window.

As Tanner swirled his finger inside her, the vibrations increased. "She's tight and clampin' down hard."

"Don't come for him, TJ. Not yet." Cross opened his door and came around the car.

Tanner cupped her belly and walked her back a step from the vehicle, just far enough that Cross was able to kneel in front of her. Then with Tanner holding her, fingering her asshole, Cross leaned toward her and tongued her pussy.

She was so taut with excitement that the first flick of his tongue caused TJ to give a yelp because it was so engorged.

The hand pressed against her belly tightened. "She's sweet, Cross. Perfect. Fuck, I'd love to have this ass."

Cross rolled his tongue over her nub then eased back a fraction of an inch. "If she's good, I might let you do more than take her mouth next time."

TJ barely registered that this was likely the guy who'd striped her face with cum the night before.

Cross latched on to her clit and sucked it hard.

She came up on her toes and reached out to brace herself on his shoulders. Tension wound inside her, curling in her womb—so tight it was nearly painful.

Fingers thrust inside her and snagged the vibrator. Then something long replaced it, coming up inside her.

She curved to see Tanner push the end of his nightstick up her pussy.

"Ride it, baby," he said. Fingers thrust into her ass, and his stick fucked her pussy at the same time.

She was there, right there. Her whole body began to shake, knees ready to give any second now.

Cross released her clit. "Come all over his stick, baby. Do it now." Then he toggled her clit with his fingers, working it fast.

The stick pushed up then came down, pumping easily inside her slick walls.

TJ rode the edge for a long moment then shook her head. "Can't. *Please*, Cross."

Cross sighed but reached up and slapped a breast hard enough to make it sting then pinched the tip.

She shot out of the stratosphere, convulsions working up and down her channel, her ass clamping hard around Tanner's fingers.

Cross let go of her nipple then gave her clit a long glide of tongue before sitting back on his haunches.

TJ held his shoulders while Tanner removed his fingers and pulled his stick free. He pinched her chin and pressed a kiss against her swollen lips. "Nice meetin' you at last." Then he tipped his hat at Cross and left.

She didn't watch as his squad car pulled away. She stood on the edge of a road in the middle of nowhere, half-naked for anyone to see. When Cross opened his arms, she straddled his hips, sighing when his arms closed around her in a fierce hug.

"That was the nastiest thing I've ever done," she said, although she wasn't complaining. Far from it.

Laughter gusted against her neck. "You're welcome."

Chapter Five

ꕥ

"What was that all about?"

Cross didn't scold her for asking. It had taken her several minutes to settle in the seat beside him after he'd helped her back into her skirt. She'd brushed at dirt, fiddled with her seat belt. Anything but look his way.

From the corner of his eye, he could see how red her cheeks were. She might have banged a stranger in an alleyway, but having him watch while another guy touched her intimately had rattled her.

He hadn't planned it. Sure, he knew Tanner's schedule and what strip of highway he'd be patrolling, but it had been fate, again, that enabled him to engineer that little scene. Something that would surprise and unsettle her, however pleasurable.

"Maybe I wanted to see how well you'd follow my lead." No maybes about that.

"You want some little wind-up doll?"

He snorted. "Sweetheart, you're not that easy."

She sighed and glanced out the passenger-side window. "I haven't always been like this. Manic, you know."

He pretended a casual interest even while his heartbeat sped. Would she really let him get that close? This soon? "Tell me about it."

She shook her head. "It's not something I discuss." She gave him a sultry smile. "And there are other things I'd rather think about."

He let it go. Soon enough, he hoped she'd open to him. Share something of the pain she was going through. "What things would you rather think about?"

"What you look like when you come would be good for starters."

Cross smiled. She was grousing because he still hadn't taken his own pleasure. "Anything you want to do about that?"

Her head turned. "Fucking's nice."

"Fucking's easy."

"You could let me return the favor…"

He arched a brow. "Wanna give me a blowjob?"

Her thighs pressed tightly together. "Yes Sir."

She said it so breathlessly that his entire body reacted, hardening to stone. "Good thing we're here," he murmured as he pulled into the drive.

TJ didn't wait for him to come around the car to open her door. She flipped the handle and stepped out. She held back a second as she patted a hand on her backside. A frown drew her tawny brows together.

"Wet?"

Her nose wrinkled. "I'll have to sponge it off before I send it to the cleaners."

He chuckled and preceded her along the walkway to the porch that stretched across the front of his white-limestone, ranch-style house. When he flung open the door, she stepped past him but halted at the entryway to glance around.

"It's a work in progress," he said, wondering what she thought. It shouldn't matter so much, but he knew she was in the business of renovation, and he hoped she wouldn't pick apart his efforts. "This room's a mess," he said, striding in to pull a piece of plastic from a countertop. "I was paintin' the ceiling last weekend."

"Nice moldings," she said, looking up.

Cross nodded proudly. He'd spent hours at a place in Dallas looking for just the right molding to frame the tall ceiling covered in punched, tin tiles.

"The colors are fabulous."

"Not too bright?" he said, eyeing the sunset-gold walls.

She gave him a smile. "I wish all my clients would be as fearless. No furniture yet?"

"I pulled it out of the living room when I had the floors tiled. It's in storage."

Her gaze narrowed. "Any furniture in the bedroom?"

He gave a waggle of his eyebrows. "Don't you worry. The bedroom's finished."

TJ didn't wait for an invitation. She trailed down the hallway, her hips swaying in a sassy wag.

Cross grunted but followed on her heels. "Last door."

When she opened it, she halted, standing in the doorway.

Casey waited while her gaze swept the room. "Yeah, looks like a brothel, huh?"

TJ shook her head. "It's gorgeous. Decadent. You did this?"

He nodded. Fiercely glad she liked it. He hoped she'd like it well enough to come here often. "I worked on it a little at a time. It's been therapy since…" But that was for another time. "Had some help choosing the paint. Wanted it red, but not like a blister."

"It's lovely." Her gaze landed on his bed. It was a tall, dark-walnut poster bed, and he'd hung gauzy gold and ivory curtains around it.

"Not a brothel—it looks like a harem," she murmured.

"The curtains serve a purpose."

Her eyebrows rose. "Oh?"

He pulled the curtains aside to reveal ropes hidden behind them. "For suspension."

"Of what?" she asked, but her voice was so airy, he thought she'd already guessed.

"Have to leave a few surprises, sweetheart."

She blushed and glanced around again then looked up at the ceiling. There he'd painted the tin tiles a rusty bronze, but that wasn't what snagged her gaze. She'd found the hooks in the ceiling and the ornate chains that dangled with padded cuffs at the ends.

He walked up behind her and laid his hands on her shoulders. "They're screwed into studs.

"What?"

"The chains can take weight without pulling the ceiling down."

She laughed and shook her head. "Never put screw and stud in the same sentence." Her hand reached to finger the leather cuffs.

He bent toward her ear. "Want to try it?"

A delicate shiver vibrated down her back. "Maybe later. Satisfy my curiosity first."

He squeezed her shoulders. "Are we back to what I look like when I come?" he asked, close enough his breath feathered the hair beside her ear.

She gave a shaky breath then turned her head to meet his gaze. "You've seen me come apart," she whispered. "I feel a little overexposed right now."

Cross released her and stepped away. "I'm all yours."

She turned to face him, her expression reflecting skepticism. "Really?"

It might kill him, letting her take the lead, but if he hoped to deepen their bond, she needed to trust him and herself. "I'll let you be in charge—whatever you desire."

Her chin came up, the glint in her eyes sparking with the challenge. "I want you naked."

His mouth twitched. "That was quick. Think about that long?"

One brow lifted in a wicked arch. "Since the last time I saw all of you. It's been hard to get you out of my mind. I like a strong man." She lifted her chin again. "Quit stalling. Naked. Now."

"Want to help me get that way?"

TJ shook her head. "Uh-uh. It's my turn to watch."

Cross narrowed his eyes but sat on the edge of the bed to remove his shoes.

"Leave a mess," she said, a dimple digging into one cheek as she crossed her arms over her chest.

He chunked the first shoe in the corner then the second and his socks. He drew his shirt over his shoulders and stood.

She was standing close and backed up, her gaze blinking as she eyed his chest and shoulders. Then her gaze reached his face. Her head tilted back. "You're a big guy."

"That scare you?" he growled.

"No. Makes a girl feel safe."

When he reached for his belt, she didn't move away. He unbuckled it and slid it from the loops of his jeans. Before he'd finished chunking it with the rest of his clothes, she'd thumbed open his buttons. He pushed down his pants but let them hang around his thighs.

Just as he'd hoped, she took over, bending to help him out of his pants, serving him again, even though this was supposed to be her turn to be in charge.

Lord, her face was right beside his cock but tilted down. When she tossed aside his pants, she turned and gave his dick a long, thorough inspection. Her expression would keep his fantasy fucks vivid for months.

Her lips parted, nostrils flaring as she took in his scent. Her tongue stroked her bottom lip, nearly killing his composure. Restless beneath her scrutiny, he gripped his shaft and ran his hand up and down his length.

Apparently, that wasn't a big enough hint.

TJ watched him stroke himself and creamed right then and there. His cock was impressive. Heavy, ruggedly veined like the rest of him. Even his balls didn't look vulnerable, not topped with all that masculinity. With his hand running up the flagpole, fingers balled around it, she wanted him so badly her belly hurt.

"Spread your legs a bit," she whispered.

Cross widened his stance while his head bent to watch her.

She felt a moment's trepidation. He'd been so good with her. So masterful. She hoped she didn't disappoint, but she was also selfishly involved here, wanting to learn his flavors, his textures, how his shaft felt stroking inside her mouth.

However, his ball sac drew her first. She leaned toward it, opened her mouth and stroked him with her tongue.

The skin there felt like velvet and was hairless. She wondered about that, but appreciated the fact just the same. She broadened her tongue and lapped around and around then drew one ball into her mouth while his fingers climbed his shaft again.

He tasted salty, and his masculine musk inflamed her. She grew greedier, sucking both stones between her lips. Then she went wild, tonguing them inside her mouth. They grew harder, drew closer to his groin, but she pulled gently, bobbing in shallow motions that fed the need for her to rock against him.

His breaths shortened, and he gave a low groan. Fingers combed through her hair then cupped the back of her head to pull her up. Trying to take the lead.

She released him and sat back, wiping a hand across her mouth as she looked up.

His eyes were narrowed slits. Skin stretched taut around his square jaw.

TJ backed away and stood, quickly stripping off her clothes until she was nude as well and panting with excitement.

"What do you want, baby?" he asked with another slow up and down glide.

Lord, who the hell was in charge here? Not her. His strokes made her jealous of his hand. She wanted all that thick hardness crammed up inside her.

"We need a condom," she said, quietly, urgency straining her voice.

"The bedside stand," he said, aiming his chin toward it, giving up even a pretense that she was still in control.

Eagerly, she went to the stand and opened the top drawer. She found the box of unopened Trojans and fought with the plastic and the lid then drew out a packet. Her hands shook, so she held it out to him.

His lips crimped into a small smile, but he bit the foil and drew out the latex circle, rolling it skillfully down his massive shaft. When it was in place, he glanced her way and quirked an eyebrow.

"The bed," she bit out. "I need you on the bed."

He sat on the edge then slid his thickly muscled legs over the side. Was there anything about him—his toes, maybe?—that didn't make her melt? She'd never felt so feminine, so weak beside a man before. "Scoot," she said then climbed onto the mattress to kneel beside him.

She bent over his cock, slid her nose along his cloaked shaft, nuzzled the crisp, curling hairs at the base of his cock then trailed the length with her tongue to learn by feel every little ridge and vein.

When she came to the cap, she sucked it between her lips and teethed it, careful not to pierce the latex. "I wanted to do this without the condom," she murmured, "but I knew I wouldn't last. I want you inside me. I want you to come for me. I need to fuck you hard, Cross."

"Will you come?"

"You know how to make me come, so hold off until you're close."

He nodded, his gaze dipping to watch her pussy as she spread her thighs over him and funneled his cock inside.

He was broad at the tip but arrowed. He stretched her opening, filled her better than the cold, hard stick his friend had stroked inside her. "Have you and Tanner been friends a long time?"

"Long enough."

She swirled her hips to wet the tip of his cock. "He the guy you had fuck my mouth last night?"

"Yeah, does it bother you, putting a face to the dick?"

A shallow pulse forced him inside an inch. "Yes, I didn't want him last night. I wanted your cock."

"I was a little busy giving you what you really needed."

He said it in a gruff, masculine tone that clued her to the fact he was just as tightly wound as she was. She pressed down, taking the cap inside another two inches. Her thighs flexed, and she fought the urge to shove downward. She wanted to savor the stretch—this fuck had been a long time coming. And because she was a little annoyed that he'd made her wait, she asked, "Do you like fucking?"

His smile was a quick, tight flash. "One of my favorite things to do."

Her nipples were hard, aching, but she resisted the urge to cup them. She wanted his hands there but wasn't able to command him. Her voice would lack strength. She feared he'd laugh if she tried because she shook with need. "Why didn't you take me? You knew I wanted you to do it."

"I told you, baby. It was about you. What you needed. And I wanted to build your trust."

She came up but missed the solid heat of him filling her and pushed quickly down again, taking him deeper. Sweet Lord, she was wet. He slid inside with a succulent sound. "You don't need my trust. Not for this," she said breathlessly. "You can have me. Have me any way you want, so long as you do one little thing for me. You know what that is."

"Have you any time? More than just today?"

She shook her head but dug her fingers into his chest as she gave him another shallow stroke. "Don't go getting possessive. I don't need promises. You don't want mine."

"You don't want to see me again?"

Her mouth gaped as she slid down a little farther, almost dizzy with relief, feeling as though every inch she consumed deepened their emotional connection. She shook her head, waging an internal battle for control. "I don't want to make plans. Don't want promises," she lied. "But I wouldn't mind you knocking at my door some night."

His jaw flexed. "For a quick fuck but not a date."

"This isn't good for you?" She was wetter now, and the glides were faster, getting deeper, her breaths shortened and her face flushed with heat. His strong hands took some of the burden from her straining thighs.

"This isn't enough for me, TJ," he said, slamming her down his cock now. "I want the whole woman."

She slowed, shuddering hard. "That's the problem," she said, smiling with tears in her eyes. "I'm not whole."

His palms slid up to cup her breasts, gently kneading them. "Tell me, sweetheart. Tell me why."

She blinked away the moisture. "Just be quiet. Please."

His lips closed, forming a thin line.

Closing her eyes to his disapproval, she continued to rock, but even though her body melted all around him, even though arousal curled inside her, she knew her limits. Her thighs gave way and she sank against him. "Cross?"

"Open your eyes when you speak to me."

She gave him a glare but knew the corners of her mouth were pulling downward and that her bottom lip was trembling.

"What do you need?"

Her shoulders fell. Her head bent. "For you to take over. For you to punish me."

"Do things my way?"

She nodded.

"Will those legs hold you up if I tell you that you have to stand?"

She nodded again then gave a little, gasping hiccup. She hated being so needful, so out of control. He'd think she was a complete basket case, but maybe that was already too late.

His hands cupped her ass and he lifted her. His cock slid from inside her and bobbed against his belly. "Go stand under the hooks."

Her nipples spiked. Fluid dripped from inside her, and he knew because a fingertip followed the trail. He brought her moisture to her mouth and painted her lips with her own arousal.

TJ moaned and leaned down to kiss him.

His hand fisted in her hair to anchor her close and his lips roamed over hers, rubbing hard, before he pulled her hair to raise her head. "Go now," he rasped.

Even though she trembled with need, she pushed off him and slid from the bed. The bed groaned behind her. His footsteps shadowed hers.

When she stood beneath the hooks, she raised her arms obediently and let him close the padded cuffs around her wrists. With she was secured, he walked to the wall and pulled down a handle where the ends of the chains were wrapped around a small wheel. He began to turn it, tightening the sturdy linked chain above her but was still able to stand on her heels.

"Higher," she grated out.

"You want to be stretched? Like the girl at the club?"

She nodded, and he winched her higher until she swayed on her toes.

"If this gets to be too much, if your arms go numb, you'll tell me."

She nodded, but it was a lie. Numbness would be a blessing. Pain would be rapturous. Already she felt a dull ache swell in her shoulders along with the lump burning the back of her throat.

Cross went to the dresser and pulled open a drawer. Poised on her toes, she peered down to see an array of implements. He picked up a flogger but discarded it. Then another. He drew a finger across the suede leather ends then glanced up at her. "I'm in charge now."

She nodded, even though he hadn't worded it as a question. Licking her bottom lip, she whispered, "Yes Sir."

Chapter Six

ℵ

Cross cursed under his breath. He knew what he had to do. What she really needed. And it wasn't about getting her off. Hanging her up would just be about softening her, getting her emotions all roiled up before he took her to the bed for the hard part.

Tansy Jo Lipton had lived a nightmare and had swept him right along into that dark place. And she didn't even know it. Every time they came together, he ruthlessly held himself back, knowing he couldn't give her everything she wanted or they'd be done.

He had to string her along. Seduce her. Make her lean on him when all she wanted to do was withdraw and keep her pain tightly leashed inside. But damn, she was gonna kill him first. The feel of her cunt sliding down his shaft had been pure hell to resist.

Steeling himself, he sought that place he had to go, the one where he could go to work on her body, feather and lash her with the strands of a flogger when all he wanted to do was drive deep inside her body until the anguish and lust inside himself was freed.

He forced his expression into a mask, kept the heat from his gaze and walked back to her.

Her glance left the flogger then roamed his face. Her tongue made a nervous foray over her bottom lip.

He stood close, letting the heat from his skin warms hers but without touching. She swayed toward him but couldn't quite reach.

"Still no safe word?" he murmured.

Her nostrils flared. Her lips closed, tightening. She gave a short, sharp shake of her head.

"Stubborn, that's what you are. Not good sub material at all. Not really. You think you want a man to take control but only because you want to fight. You want to be punished. Do you know why?"

She shook her head, but a shadow crossed her face.

"Liar," he whispered. Then he stepped away and ran the soft flanges down one side of her body and up again, pausing to trace around and around one breast. He tipped back the flogger then gave it a little flick, hitting the nipple.

Her body jerked. Her teeth sank into that wet, lower lip. He wanted his teeth there, biting, sucking then watching it stretch around his cock again.

He gave her breast a second flick then trailed the flogger down her belly, stopping to snap here and there, making her belly quiver and jump and leaving red splotches in his wake.

When he traced the contour of her mound and slid the soft, leather strands between her legs, she tried to open her thighs but couldn't because she was braced on her toes. He wet the strands in her arousal then walked behind her, ignoring the soft, sobbing quality of her breaths.

Done teasing, he flicked her buttocks and the backs of her thighs then stood to the side to stripe her with longer, harder slaps. He painted her pink then red, and still she hung on her chains, her chin level with the floor.

Cross tossed down the flogger and went back to the drawer. This time, he selected a braided leather quirt. He snapped the end against the air, liking the sharp sound it made, then glanced her way.

Her dewy gaze sharpened.

When he approached, he slid a hand between her legs and cupped her pussy. Her lips were hot, swollen, throbbing to her heartbeat. Moisture coated her sex and inner thighs. He swirled a fingertip around her hard, little clit. "You don't want a safe word, but I'll give you one anyway. *Fallujah.*"

TJ inhaled sharply and anger firmed her mouth. "Strange choice."

"Then you'll remember it, right?"

She shook her head, eyes glaring. "I won't use it."

"Suit yourself." He walked behind her, slightly to her left, then stood still for several moments, waiting while she fought her pride. Only when she glanced as far back as she could to see what he was doing did he raise the quirt. The snap he gave her ass raised a welt. A red, painful-looking one that for the first time since he'd entered the life, he regretted.

He felt remorse because before her head snapped around to stare at the wall in front of her, he'd seen the sheen of tears fill her eyes. With this woman, he couldn't close off his feelings, couldn't do what was needed. Not without feeling the cut himself.

Damn her stubbornness. Why couldn't they have a conversation like two mature people and talk about their past? But he knew. The moment she learned who he was, she'd shut off like a spigot and walk away.

Anger seared him. He breathed through his nostrils, seeking control of himself. Only then did he give her a second then a third stinging lash.

Her body rocked in the chains. Her back bowed and her expression, even in profile, blurred in subspace bliss.

She was serenely beautiful. But removed, he sensed. The next lash was sharper and forced a gasp. Her eyes blinked at tears, and at last, her toes crumpled. Only the cuffs held her suspended. Her breaths came in short, jagged bursts, but still she didn't relent—wouldn't give him the word—the name of the place that bound them.

Instead, he surrendered. He walked to the wall and unwound the chain. As she sagged, he stepped forward to catch her against his chest.

Tears wet his skin, and he cursed under his breath. "Why didn't you just say it?"

"I want to come. With you. But I don't deserve the pleasure."

He closed his eyes and held her close. "Not true. Not true at all," he whispered.

A sob racked her body. He scooped her into his arms and strode for the bed. There, he crawled onto the mattress, still clutching her against his chest until he was in the center of the bed and she was stretched beneath him.

Weight supported on his elbows, he cupped her cheeks and licked away her tears.

She gave a mewling sound and turned her face to capture his mouth.

He kissed her, thrusting his tongue inside and groaning because she tasted like her salty tears. Ending the kiss, he nuzzled behind her ear. "Open for me," he whispered.

TJ dragged in a deep breath and slowly parted her legs, bending her knees to make room as he centered himself. Her eyes were closed, her wet lashes forming spikes against her cheek.

"Look at me."

She blinked slowly, her gaze focusing on his face.

When her chin trembled, pain lodged next to his heart. "Guide me inside you."

Her fingertips scraped down his chest, his belly, and his cock jerked as she drew near. The fingers of one hand wrapped around his shaft. The others slid between her legs to part her folds, and then she pulled gently, bringing the tip to her entrance.

Cross straightened his arms then scooped his hips, flexing to impale her. He slid swiftly inside, not stopping until her walls surrounded him in wet heat. "Say my name."

"Cross," she gasped.

He pulled out then stroked forward with more force. "Say it again."

"Cross," she repeated, her voice breaking.

He resettled his knees, readying himself to power into her, but held still to make sure he had her full attention.

TJ raised her legs, framing his hips with her thighs, then tentatively clasped her ankles to surround him, waiting now for him to begin.

Suspended above her, Cross forced his breaths to even out. "Baby, what do you want?"

"For you to fuck me."

"Now tell me what you need."

She shook her head, pretending confusion, but as he hovered, unrelenting, her face crumpled. "I need all of you. All the way inside me."

"Good enough for now," he muttered, and drove into her, over and over, not breaking rhythm as he built frictional heat between his shaft and her tightly clasping cunt.

She was hot, wet, and beginning to roll her hips to meet his strokes. Her breaths sighed around him. Her moans broke shyly at first then deepened, becoming a staccato chant as he quickened his motions.

When she began the spiral, her head tossed on the coverlet, and he watched, gauging the depth of her pleasure by the way her teeth raked her lower lip and her eyes squeezed tightly. Things he'd noted when he'd eaten her out, because he'd never let her lie to him, never let her think she could fake a response.

Her pleasure was his to give. Soon, she'd surrender everything—her stubborn pride, her nightmares. He'd be the rock she clung to through the storm.

Cross braced his weight on one arm and curved a hand beneath her bottom, pulling her closer as he shortened and sharpened his thrusts. "Now, baby. Fly for me now."

Her hands slid around his back, her fingernails digging into his spine, and then she arched, thrusting her pussy upward to slam into his groin, grinding against his pubic bone until an aching cry broke around him.

Her breaths ragged, she clung for a long moment, her mouth open and eyes glazed, but then she sighed and fell back, her hands sliding from around him as he continued to thrust and at last gave himself over to the pleasure cramping his balls.

His explosion wrung a shout from him as hot spurts of cum filled the condom. He rocked between her thighs, trying to prolong the pleasure, but finally tumbled down, settling against her.

Her hands soothed his skin, raked his short hair. Her murmurs whispered in his ear. "Cross, Cross..."

The temptation to linger was there, but he suspected that she'd recover her pride quickly, and he didn't want to see the defensive jut of her chin. Not if he could make her smile instead. At least, at first.

He gave an exaggerated sigh and slumped against her.

TJ bit his earlobe. "You're crushing me, big guy."

"Best sex in forever," he muttered, "and you're complainin'?"

Fingernails dug into his armpits.

A grin tugged at his mouth. "I'm not ticklish." He lifted his head. "Are you?"

Her mouth opened, but she quickly clamped it shut, her eyes narrowing in warning.

Cross gave a chuckle then came up on one elbow, one hand free to roam, which it did, fingertips tweaking a nipple then sliding down her side.

She twitched, but her lips firmed into a straight line. "I don't like to be tickled."

"If you're not ticklish, why do you care?"

He snuck a finger beneath her arm and scratched.

Her arm clamped against her side, and she wriggled in earnest. "Don't tickle me. I'll pee."

Cross barked a laugh then rolled, bringing her with him, their bodies still connected. Her knees slid to either side of his hips, and she pushed up to rise off his cock.

He clamped his hands on her hips to hold her snug against his groin. "Why the hurry?"

She shrugged. "I came. You came."

"So we're done?"

"It's how I roll."

Cross grunted. The woman was a terrible liar. She wanted to put some distance between them because she felt vulnerable. "Were you always like this?"

"What do you mean?"

"Before Iraq. Were you always this quick to jump off a guy's dick?"

She froze, her face whitening. "What did you say?"

Cross locked his gaze with hers. "Was I too crude for you?"

"The other part," she said, her voice strained. "How'd you know?"

Before he'd brought her to bed, Cross hadn't been a hundred percent sure that he'd level with her. And he hadn't meant to blurt it out that way, but maybe it was for the best. It wasn't as if she could storm out of the house. She needed him to drive her back to the city. "We met there—a few months ago."

She shook her head. "I'd have remembered you."

"Apparently not."

She rolled her hips, trying to wriggle out of his embrace. "Let go of me."

"Not a chance. We're talking, Tansy Jo. We're gonna have a conversation about something that matters."

"Why does this matter to you?"

"Because you're eaten up with rage. You're beatin' yourself up over something that wasn't your fault."

Shock drained the rest of the color out of her face. "How the hell do you know that?" she whispered furiously. "Let me up! Now!"

"Tansy—"

She slapped his chest. "Don't call me that. No one but family calls me that."

"I like it. It's soft. Feminine. Like you are inside."

"I'm not. Not anymore," she said, scratching at his hands. "And I want off now."

Cross released her, holding out his hands in surrender.

She slid off him and the bed then ran to the bathroom, locking the door behind her.

Frustrated, he pounded a fist into the mattress.

Not well done, buddy. Fuck, why did I push?

But he knew why. He'd hoped she felt the same way he had when he'd slid inside her body—impatient for her to admit something special was happening between them. Something beyond the sex.

Cross knew why he'd blown it, why he'd lost control of the moment. He'd finally come home.

Chapter Seven

ஐ

Once again, TJ stood at the bottom of the steps leading to Unfettered. This time, a bouncer guarded the door with a clipboard in his hands.

Seven days had passed since she'd last seen Cross. Seven days during which she'd begun the battle to regain control of her life.

For one thing, she'd slept like a baby every night. Work had been exhausting, demanding, and at last, the sparkle in Marnie's eyes when she spoke to her was back. Her friend's relief had been palpable.

When Marnie had asked what had changed, TJ shrugged. "I got some help."

And she had. Making time to see her counselor, and at last opening up about the things she'd been unable to cope with on her own since she'd returned from the war. This time, she hadn't immediately flushed the meds she'd been prescribed, and she'd let him schedule her for more sessions.

The nightmares no longer plagued her dreams, but the memory of the event that had haunted her for so long was never far from her thoughts. She'd forced herself to face it, to follow the jagged path from the first terrifying moments to its devastating conclusion. To relive the event and accept that she couldn't change a thing.

And to finally start to make peace with herself. Not that she was ready to talk to anyone else about it. Not yet.

But she remembered everything. She remembered Cross.

TJ closed her eyes.

She awoke, gasping, inhaling smoke, and then began to choke. Which forced her to close her mouth and breath through her nose – a mistake because the smell of burned rubber, gasoline and something mustier and more frightening turned her stomach. She feared she'd vomit, but her seat belt gouged her waist as she hung upside down in the harness.

Something was in her eyes. She blinked but couldn't clear the viscous fluid. Panic swelled, and then she heard a sound beside her, an odd rhythmic gurgling, and she remembered.

The driver. PFC Figueroa. A bullet had ripped through his neck and he'd lost control of their vehicle, rolling it with her inside, bouncing her head inside her Kevlar helmet. She'd clipped her chin against something, causing it to bleed.

Blind, she reached for him, but her fingers sank into warm, sticky blood. She began to scream but quickly muffled her shouts and tried to staunch his blood with her fingers, but he bled out beside her.

Then strong hands reached inside, loosening her belt and dragging her from the vehicle. She fought her rescuer, slamming her fists against his cheek and chest until he subdued her. Only then did she realize the convoy was still under fire. He spread his body over hers to pin her and protect her.

Her rescuer had been Cross, and he'd shushed her, rubbing his thumbs over her eyes to clear away the blood until she could see. She owed him her life, but she'd spat and snarled and called him names until she'd shuddered and begun to cry. Figueroa had been a sweet-faced kid with a wife and young child awaiting his return. He was dead because of her. She'd sketched out the supply convoy's route based on the day's intel.

All this, Cross had heard while others continued the fight around them. He'd protected her, at last rolling from her but tucking her between him and the wrecked vehicle while he returned fire.

The sudden upsurge of noise around them, the shouts and staccato reports of weapons, made it impossible to hear exactly what he said, but he'd kept talking in soothing tones until she'd calmed and given him a nod that she was okay. Then she'd drawn her weapon from her holster and crawled on her belly to take up a position beside him and help lay cover fire for the men forcing their way inside the house where the shooter hid.

Perhaps she hadn't recognized him before because she hadn't been ready to remember. Now she needed to see him. To thank him. And to figure out whether he'd arranged their meeting at Unfettered because he felt responsible for her still or because something had happened between them, there in Fallujah. Something so profound it had shaken her to her core.

Climbing the steps, she took deep, cleansing breaths. The man with the clipboard eyed her face then scratched at the paper and stood to the side for her to enter.

The main room was busy—a woman with her hands bound behind her, tied in intricate winding of ropes and knots, sat on her knees before a man who circled her, touching her hair, a breast with the loving waft of a feather.

On another stage, a man was bent over what looked like a sawhorse, a ball gag in his mouth while a woman plowed his ass with strap-on cock.

Smiling faintly to herself, because she could never envision wanting to ream a man's ass. TJ passed them by, heading toward the door that led down the corridor and the room the Operator had told her to go to.

The door handle depressed without the need of a passkey. She opened it, searching the room for Cross, but stiffened when instead she found Tanner.

He was dressed in a dark tee, leather pants and cowboy boots. Had she met him in The Shamrock before she'd been with Cross, she would have been tempted. But now Cross held her hopes and dreams in his hands. Tanner was just another handsome guy with a crooked, killer smile.

"Come in, TJ," he said in his sexy drawl. "Cross'll be along in a moment."

Disappointment seeped through her bones, weighing her down. She'd hoped it would just be the two of them, her and Cross. That she'd meant more to him than just as a playmate, but he'd invited his buddy along again.

"Shall I prepare you?"

TJ shook her head. "I'd rather wait for Cross."

"I want to show you something." He invited her deeper into the room with a lazy wave of his hand.

She blew out a breath and approached, watching his expression. If he'd smirked even once, she'd have turned on her heel and run for the door. She couldn't take mockery, not even a gentle tease today. She was too nervous about seeing Cross again and angry with herself that it meant so much.

The last thing she *wanted* right now was trust in someone else's strength when she'd finally begun to believe in her own. But she *needed* Cross in ways she couldn't explain, not even to herself.

However, she walked closer, halting when she saw the ropes arranged on the floor. There was a pattern to their placement, but not one she discerned, and the ends of two of them were drawn up to curve over the tops of two pulleys in the ceiling.

She cleared the knot of tension in her throat. "This for me?"

"Depends."

"On what?"

"How much you trust Cross."

She shrugged, trying for casual when her stomach was beginning to knot. "What's he want me to do?"

"He wants me to bind you, and then pull you up."

"Suspend me," she said, her voice rasping now because she thought she understood why he wanted this.

Tanner nodded. "That's right." There wasn't even a hint of smile on his handsome face. Only something soft and a little sad in his blue eyes as she watched her.

TJ turned away and blinked at the moisture filling her own. But she squared her shoulders and began to strip. When she was nude, she faced Tanner.

His gaze never dipped, and he held out his hand. Then he led her to the center of the ropes and helped her to the floor. When she lay on her back, she watched the line of muted, recessed lights that ran the length of the room rather than anything Tanner was doing.

She sought that center of calm, the one that only pain had given her in the past. While he moved around her, binding her feet, her hands, wrapping ropes around her waist and thighs, she ignored the clamoring of panic building inside her chest. *Breathe. Cross will come.*

Cross watched the monitor as Tanner slowly built the cradle of rope that would suspend TJ gently from the ceiling.

"You're sure she's ready for this?" Dru asked beside him.

"I'm not, but she needs this and it has to be me."

"Do you think she knows who you are?"

Cross rubbed the back of his neck. "Yeah, or she wouldn't have ignored my calls all week." A week that had dragged while he'd worried that he'd blown it completely.

Dru's mouth quirked. "She didn't ignore this summons."

"It's neutral ground. She figures if things get too hairy, you or one of the staff will step in."

Dru turned, her usual professionally neutral mask gone. Concern darkened her eyes. "Are you in love with her?"

Cross swung away from her to stare blindly at the monitor again. "Head over fucking heels."

Tanner was finished and nodded toward the monitor out of view of TJ, whose head was supported by a leather strap beneath her neck. She couldn't move, not without pulling at the rigging and offsetting her balance to send her swinging.

Cross wanted her still. Her body. Her mind.

He crossed the hallway and entered the room, walking around her to gaze down into her eyes.

She looked frightened but stoic just the same. Her face was pale, her lips tense.

"Want that safe word now?" he asked softly.

"Will I need it?"

Cross smiled. At last she'd acknowledged that she trusted him. She'd trust his advice. "You'll need it, sweetheart. The same one. You remember it?"

Her gaze paused for long poignant moment. "All of it."

He nodded then tugged a blindfold from his back pocket. He dangled it in front of her face.

"That's necessary?" Her lips twisted. "You've already got me trussed up like a turkey."

Cross cupped her cheeks and stroked his thumbs across her skin to soothe her. "You know it is. But remember, I'm right here. I'm going to undress. Tanner's here to help but won't do anything I don't approve of. You'll be safe." Then without another word, he tied the blindfold around her head. "Can you see anything?"

"No Sir," she said in small voice.

"How do you feel?"

"Like I'm floating."

"The ropes are comfortable?"

"None are digging into my skin. He's good."

"That's why he's here, baby. Now's the time for quiet."

Her lips crimped as if she wanted to say something else but held it back. Satisfied, he nodded to Tanner, and the two of them quietly undressed.

TJ heard the rustle of clothing as the two men disrobed. The sound was soft but jangled her nerves anyway. When a hand glided along the outside of one thigh, she gasped.

Her folds were opened, a blunt, round tip pushed against her entrance and she tightened in rejection because the cock sliding inside her didn't feel like Cross'.

"Don't fight it. Just float, sweetheart," Tanner said softly.

Hands, Cross', molded her breasts, rubbing a warming oil into her skin.

"I wasn't sure this was right for you, having Tanner here again," he said softly. "I know you aren't comfortable, having me share you. Fuck, I don't like sharing you."

He paused to circle her nipples, the pad of his fingers gliding around and around. The tips tingled and hardened, but he was already moving down, rubbing her belly, and then the folds stretched around Tanner's erection as the other man slowly shafted her.

"But Tanner's more than a friend, Tansy Jo. He was over there with me. I trust him with my back. And you, sweetheart, like to be in charge even when you aren't. I had to push you past your comfort zone. Push hard."

"Why?" she asked, her voice more of rasping croak.

"To break you."

She shook her head, not understanding.

A finger soothed over her lower lip. "What I saw in the alley. It was fucked up. You were hard. Bitter. Sure that all you needed from that guy was for him to make you come."

Shame set fire to her cheeks.

"No, sweetheart," he whispered beside her ear. "I'm not judging. I made my own mistakes when I came back. Trying to get rid of the edge, the dirt. I found a card, the same one I tucked into your purse. I'd played at being a Dom before but hadn't understood what I needed from it. Not before you."

"What was it you needed?"

"Everything I ever played at, everything I ever experimented with, was preparation for you. To see you through this. To break you down then make you strong."

Something in his tone, something in the whispered harshness told her what she needed to know. This wasn't a game—really, truly wasn't about the sex. It was about them. What they'd survived. What bound them still.

She swallowed to wet her mouth. "I'm not sure what this means. What's happening between us."

"Do you trust me?"

She drew in a ragged breath and nodded. She trusted him, but that still didn't mean she was going to like this.

The cradle of ropes resumed rocking forward and back, pulling her off Tanner's cock then sliding it back inside. The motion was fluid, oddly soothing—like the hands once again caressing every part of her. Her frantic thoughts slowed, grew peaceful as she rocked again and again.

Her breaths deepened. Her body warmed. The rocking slowed then stopped. Tanner's cock slid free.

Hands cupped her head. Fingers combed through her hair. The scrape of Cross' beard abraded her cheek. "You remember where we met, don't you?" Cross rasped.

"In the bar?" she said, knowing it was a lie, but she didn't want to go *there*. Not now when she felt so relaxed. And certainly not when she was aroused and ready for sex.

"Now's not the time to be cute. You and I have a past. One I have to know won't come between us."

"I don't blame you. Not anymore."

"But do you still resent me?" he said, his voice tightening. "Do you still think I'm the bastard who let that kid die?"

She'd said that. No, *shouted* that while she'd beat him with her fists. She'd meant to wound, and apparently she had. "I'm sorry about that. I know you didn't. Figueroa couldn't have survived."

"Do you really know it, TJ? Deep inside?"

She hesitated. Suddenly, the sling tilted, lowering her head beneath her body then turning her upside down. The rope twined around her waist bit into her midsection, not painfully but reminiscent enough of that other time to send her into panic. Her body tensed and she tried to flail her arms and legs.

Tanner grasped her thighs.

"Baby, stop," Cross said, petting her cheeks, kissing her forehead. "Shhh," he said beside her ear, until at last she calmed.

Then something warm and wet trickled from her chin and across her cheek, seeping into her hair. Something thick, like blood.

TJ clamped her mouth closed but screamed behind her lips and bucked hard. Arms wrapped around her to hold her still.

"This what is was like inside that Hummer?" Cross whispered next to her ear. "Was this how you felt? Blind? Bound?"

TJ gave a ragged sob and began to cry. "Stop. *Stop it now.*"

His head shook, scraping her skin again. "I was there. I had you."

"I was supposed to stay with him."

"You couldn't save him." He cupped her head again and kissed her upside down. "He was already gone when I pulled you free," he said, his warm breath gusting against her mouth.

"You don't know that," she whispered raggedly. "His blood was still pumping beneath my fingers."

He kissed her again. "Baby, he was gone. I swear it."

A sob jerked her chest. "It was m-my fault."

"Not your fault," he whispered. "It was a sniper. An ambush. You were targets of opportunity."

"It should have been me."

"Why, baby?"

"I took the convoy down that street."

"You think you made a mistake? That you cost him his life?"

She shook inside his embrace. "Yes… No. I know it was just shit luck. I know that. But I still feel…"

"Like it wasn't fair you walked away?"

Tears stung her eyes, and she nodded. "I remember you," she said hoarsely.

"I'm sorry as hell it had to be me who pulled you out."

"I'm not."

Cross' hug tightened, and she sobbed again, shaking in the ropes. "*Fallujah,*" she whispered.

The sling lowered. Bindings loosened. And then she was picked up and laid atop a soft mattress. The blindfold slid away and she blinked, looking up to find Cross' face hovering above hers, tension digging lines around his mouth and between his brows.

He sat beside her, not touching her. She wiped her eyes with her fingers and touched the oil soaked into her hair, grimacing at the mess. "I bet I'm a sight."

"You're beautiful, Tansy Jo."

Her glance fell away. "What now?"

"Guess that depends on you," he said softly.

"You always told me you'd give me what I need."

"What do you need, sweetheart?"

She closed her eyes, drawing deep for courage. Then she opened them to meet his steady gaze. "I need you."

His smile was quick and one-sided. He cleared his throat. "Then you're in luck. I need you right back."

TJ rose on one elbow and curved a hand around the back of his neck to pull his face toward hers. The closer he came, the surer she was that the glitter in his eye was a tear.

His mouth slammed into hers, devouring her lips. His hands slipped beneath her and lifted her onto his lap. He held her close and gradually the kiss softened.

TJ sighed and drew back.

"You okay?" he asked in a ragged voice.

He'd been worried. She could see it in tension in his jaw. "I'm… I feel…new."

His jaw eased a fraction. A soft smile curved his lips. "Sure it's not just the blood rushing back to your toes?"

"I'll be okay. I have you." She leaned closer and brushed her mouth softly over his. When she leaned back, his smile deepened.

Reassured she hadn't made a complete fool of herself, she smiled. "Want to play?"

Her glance cut to Tanner, who stood with his arms crossed over his chest. He raised an eyebrow, and that charmer's smile of his quirked up one corner of his mouth.

"What do you have in mind?" Cross growled.

"Trust me?"

Cross' mouth eased into a grin. "With my life and my heart."

Cross watched as Tanner bent TJ over the spanking bench then deftly bound her hands behind her. He'd raised the padded bar beneath her waist, so she knelt with her back sinking in a lovely arc to lift her firm, round buttocks. The men stood behind her, admiring her smooth, white skin and the slick pussy that was engorged and a pretty pink.

"You did put dibs on her ass…" Cross drawled.

TJ groaned and her head sank between her shoulders. "You aren't going to leave me even an inch of pride, are you?"

"Pride's overrated. We're in the pursuit of pleasure."

Cross palmed two silver clamps and walked around in front of her, knowing she was eyelevel with his cock and would be distracted from his purpose. He reached beneath her and cupped a breast then stroked and squeezed it with his fingers before twisting the tip and pulling. He released it, enjoying her faint gasp and the way her lips pouted.

"You're going to be a tease, aren't you?"

"I never tease." He knelt in front of her and kissed her lips. Then ducked lower to twist one engorged tip and clamp it with a tweezer clamp with rubber tips. "Too tight?" he asked.

She blew between pursed lips but shook her head. Between the two clamped nipples, he connected a chain from which he hung a small fishing weight.

"Jesus!"

"Too much?"

She shook her head, but her expression lost a little confidence. He glanced toward Tanner and gave him a nod.

Tanner slicked up his cloaked cock with warm oil then trailed a finger between her buttocks. The moment he sank the finger inside her, Cross knew because her eyes widened and color bloomed on her cheeks. "You'll have a new safe word."

"I won't need it."

"Never say never," he murmured then leaned in to whisper it in her ear.

She laughed but shook her head. Cross straightened to stand directly in front of her and stroked his cock. His shaft was thick, felt like a steel rod in his hand, and it was bare because he wanted nothing between them—just the sensation of her mouth working his dick. Her idea.

He gripped his shaft and slapped her cheek with it. She opened her mouth like a baby bird, her tongue extended. He couldn't resist and let her use the tip to slide into his slit and taste the pre-ejaculate he squeezed out.

Her tongue fluttered then sank, rimming the slit. Cross scraped his feet across the carpet to come closer, lured by her enthusiasm. He let her suck the cap, her lush mouth surrounding him, her tongue swabbing the surface, stroking in wicked circles.

A snort drew his attention to Tanner, who pulled his finger from her ass. Tanner pointed his cock at her entrance then spread her hole with his thumbs and pushed against it.

TJ moaned deep in her throat and stretched to suck more of Cross into her mouth.

"Jesus, Tanner, let's get her off the bench."

Tanner laughed at his eagerness, but pulled out. Then he gripped TJ's hips and helped her up.

Cross slipped off the nipple clamps and strode to an armless, upholstered chair and sat. Tanner urged her forward, helping her to straddle his lap.

Cross gripped his cock and centered it between her folds then eased back, bracing his hands on the edges of the seat. "Tanner's gonna take your ass. When he moves, you'll move."

"Won't I need my hands for balance?" she said, not a trace of trepidation in her face. Just an eagerness to please and explore.

He shook his head. "Rest your pretty tits against my chest and show him your ass."

TJ leaned against him, hiding her face in the corner of his neck while Tanner came up behind her. He widened his legs to lower his hips then guided his cock into the cleft of her buttocks.

TJ shook her head. "Fuck," she whispered.

"Is he hurting you?"

"No… *Jesus.*"

Cross knew what she was feeling because Tanner's large cock was separated from his by only a thin membrane. He felt the other man push inside, crowding into her. Cross tensed his buttocks to lift her higher.

TJ moaned, the sound so thin, so strained he knew she was close.

"Don't need a pinch or a slap?"

She shook her head. "Don't think so. Full. Dammit, I'm so full. I'm gonna come."

"Look at me, sweetheart."

She lifted her head. Her eyes were moist. Her lips blurred and swollen.

He rubbed his mouth against hers then tilted his head to push his forehead against hers, his gaze boring into hers. "You're mine, you know. Sweet little body and soul."

Tanner leaned over them both and rode TJ's ass in deepening glides. "Just tell her you love her, man."

She laughed, but her eyes betrayed her doubt.

He arched a brow. "Think this isn't the real thing for me?"

"You're letting another guy do me."

"My best friend. For you, baby. Because you need this. Because you're ready for it."

Her nose wrinkled, a teasing light glinting in her blue eyes. "You think you know what I need."

Cross grunted. "Have I been wrong? About anything?"

"I…" She bit her lip. "This… You tore me down. Piece by piece."

"Was it a bad thing?"

She shook her head, releasing a single tear that streaked down her cheek. "You got to the heart of me."

Tanner increased the depth and speed of his thrusts, pounding, shoving her up and down his dick. Cross closed his eyes and kissed her hard then leaned back to watch her face again. "Can you take this? Take me the way I am? I like to play. Hard. Often."

TJ trembled against him, her lips blurring as they rounded with pleasure, sweat shining on her face. "You really love me?"

"Baby, ever since I took you to the dirt and covered you. You cried and fought, but in the end, you let me in. It was powerful, what I felt for you then. You haunted me. I would have looked for you, but my unit moved on. I'm not lettin' go of you this time."

"I'm not sure how I feel. I'm not all the way back yet."

"And that's okay for now. Just know I'm here for you."

Doubt cleared from her face, and she gave him a tender smile. TJ arched, her tight little buds scraping his chest as Tanner powered harder. He glanced up to catch Tanner's expression. His buddy was close but gritting his teeth to make sure he lasted.

"It's okay, Tanner. Baby's all right. She's right there, aren't you, sweetheart?" He plucked her clit then rubbed it hard.

She gave a little yelp then moaned, rubbing her head against Tanner's chest, her tits against Cross'. "Oh please, fuck! *Fuck!*" And then she stiffened between them and howled.

Tanner cursed then came, jerking them all until he pulled free and leaned against TJ's back to catch his breath. When he recovered, he kissed her shoulder, winked at Cross and left.

Alone now, Cross tugged on her bound hands to pull her upright. She gave a moan, but he knew she could take a little discomfort. It was his turn.

He pulled down on her hands again, forcing her back to arch. Then he bent and drew one pink-tipped nipple into his mouth. He'd take his time, torture her tits until she begged him for release.

Only TJ didn't know how this game was supposed to be played. He grinned as her cunt clasped his dick, the contractions measured and strong. He grinned against her breast then laughed. "You're not a very submissive woman, are you, sweetheart."

With her head bent back, she eyed him through narrowed lids, a challenge sparkling in her blue eyes. A tawny brow arched and she glided forward and back on his lap, grinding on his dick.

He pulled the loose end of the rope knotted around her wrists, freeing her, then lunged upward. Her legs wrapped around his waist, her arms encircled his neck. He walked her to the wall and ground her back against the smooth surface as he banged her hard.

No, TJ wasn't a sub. But she was his to mold. His to love. He'd keep her safe, close, and too damn busy to let any damn shadows from the past creep into their bed.

"I'm yours, Cross," she said, her voice soft but strong.

He aimed a glance into the corner where the camera monitored their lovemaking. He imagined Dru smiling then saw the little green light at the bottom blink out.

They wouldn't be back to Unfettered. Neither of them needed any safe haven other than the one they'd found in each other's arms.

CONTROLLING INTEREST

Francesca Hawley

Acknowledgements

℘

To Paris Brandon. You are an amazing crit partner! Thank you!

To my editor Mary Moran. Thank you for seeing a spark in my writing that appealed to you. I've learned a lot from you during the last couple of years and I've enjoyed working with you. I look forward to working with you for a long time to come.

Trademarks Acknowledgement

℘

The author acknowledges the trademarked status and trademark owners of the following wordmarks mentioned in this work of fiction:

Minnie Mouse: Disney Enterprises

Chapter One

ꙮ

"She did *what*?" Torin Stuart rose from his chair with a roar.

Mouse was entirely grateful that the lion's roar was directed at his late mother's attorney and not at her, but the attorney was unperturbed.

"Your mother left her controlling interest in your club Erotically Bound to Ms. Mozelle Vincent."

"But Mother *knew*..."

"Please sit down and allow me to finish reading the will in a proper manner, Mr. Stuart."

Tor ran his fingers through his bright ginger hair and glared at her briefly before sitting with a growl. Mouse kept her hands tightly around her purse. He'd been really kind in letting her stay in the townhouse his mother had set aside for her use, but with this news, he'd probably toss her out on her ass. Damn it. She thought she was done with being homeless.

"Ms. Vincent, shall I continue?" Mouse nodded. "Very well." The lawyer cleared his throat. "I leave my controlling interest in the amount of fifty-one percent in the club Erotically Bound to Ms. Mozelle Vincent. In addition, I will her the townhouse and all furnishings thereof in which she has been living for the last five years. The estate will pay property taxes for two years, but then, and I quote 'you're on your own'. Do you understand, Ms. Vincent?"

Mouse's jaw dropped. That townhouse was stunning. Huge and smack in the center of Washington D.C. with a multicar garage. It was located in the historic Capitol Hill district, just blocks from the Capitol building and Pennsylvania Avenue. The place was worth...millions.

"Ms. Vincent, do you understand the terms of the will regarding the townhome?"

"Yes, I own it and Regine's estate will pay the first two years of property taxes then it's my responsibility."

"Precisely."

"Is that all? Can we discuss my club now?"

The lawyer frowned at Torin over the top of his reading glasses, his bushy white brows extending over the frames. "I have not finished. Please remain silent until I do, sir."

Tor waved his hand with a sigh and the lawyer nodded. Mouse wanted to laugh at the byplay between the two men, but she was too shocked. What had Regine been thinking?

She had to have had an ulterior motive for doing this, God knew, she always did. Regine Stuart was always three moves ahead of everyone else…a master strategist. That was how she'd managed to be one of D.C. society's reigning queens. When Regine spoke, everyone listened…even the president.

"Ms. Vincent, please attend."

Mouse looked up as the lawyer admonished her. "Sorry." She shrugged.

"Finally, for—and again I quote—surviving six years in my employ as my downtrodden Jill-of-all-trades and for making my final years a pleasure instead of a burden, I will Mozelle Vincent twenty million dollars."

Ice filled her body before unbearable heat melted her emotions. Her jaw dropped, but she was so utterly shocked she couldn't move. Then she burst into uncontrollable tears. Throughout most of her life she'd hadn't had a pot to piss in, but then six years ago she literally tripped over Regine Stuart and her world had completely turned on its head. The lawyer rose and approached her.

"My dear, are you quite all right?" He awkwardly patted her shoulder and she nodded, still trying to cover her abrupt emotional response.

She hated crying. She hated losing control of her emotions. She hid whatever she felt behind a façade of calm, which was something Regine had always valued in her. And it was something they had in common. Even if the world came crashing down around them, both she and Regine could remain calm to pick up the pieces and move forward.

Mouse glanced at Tor, worried that he'd think she was being overly dramatic or that she was getting money she didn't deserve, but he seemed moved by her emotional display rather than scornful. When she could catch her breath, she cleared her throat.

"Don't mind me, really. Go on with reading the will."

"There isn't too much more." The lawyer returned to his desk. "To my household staff…"

Mouse stared at her perfectly manicured fingers as the lawyer finished. Those nails were a luxury she'd gotten used to with a steady paycheck and Regine's insistence that she look polished at all times. God, if she had walked past the Capitol building five minutes earlier or five minutes later six years ago, she and Regine never would have met. Regine had given her a chance when no one else would. Sometimes miracles really did happen.

"This concludes the last will and testament of Regine Stuart."

"Can we discuss my club now? Please…" Tor growled as he turned to her. "Mouse, how much do you want for it?"

The lawyer held up his hand as the remaining listeners filed out of the room, leaving Mouse alone with the lawyer and Tor.

"I'm sorry, Mr. Stuart. Your mother left explicit instructions. Mouse…rather Miss Mozelle is required to hold her interest in the club for a minimum of six months. Under the terms of the will, the two of you are required to work together during that time."

Tor opened his mouth then closed it again. He stood and began to pace. Broad shoulders, narrow hips and the most amazing ass she'd ever seen. Add a stunning body to his ginger hair and bright blue eyes and he was a package of mischief that made better women than her melt and get silly.

Mouse looked down at her hands out of habit. Ever since she began to work for Regine, she'd quietly had the hots for Tor, but putting that attraction to the test was unthinkable. First, she was sure Regine wouldn't have been keen on having her assistant flirt with her son. And second, and most important, Torin Stuart had been seen escorting tall, slender and decidedly beautiful super models around town—his lovers had most definitely *not* been chunky personal assistants with frizzy, flyaway, boring brown hair and dull brown eyes.

"Mouse… Mouse, did you hear me?"

She met Tor's blue-eyed gaze and felt the blush crawl up her neck. Damn.

"What?"

He sighed and rolled his eyes. "You've had a tough six years working for Mother. Just relax for the next six months then I'll offer you a great price for the interest in the club."

The lawyer cleared his throat, causing Tor to whip around. "Damn it, Thompson. What the hell is it?"

"Your mother required you to work *together* to manage the club. If any of the terms of her bequest are violated, the shares will be sold…but not to you."

"What?"

"If the two of you don't work together, or if you make an offer for her shares before six months have passed, which she accepts, then the shares will be sold to anyone *but* you."

"The shares belong to Mouse. She can sell to whomever she wants."

"No, I'm afraid not. If she goes against the terms of the will, she loses everything your mother willed to her."

God, she didn't want to challenge Tor about this, but she wouldn't go back to living on the streets. She just wouldn't.

She cleared her throat. "I'm sorry, Tor. I have to abide by the will."

"I thought you were different." He snorted, shaking his head. "But it's always about money."

"Says the man who's always had it," she retorted sharply.

Tor frowned at her. "Damn it, Mouse…"

She waved his words away. "I've been careful with my money, but I will not toss your mother's largesse down the drain as if it has no value. I just won't."

He ran his fingers through his hair. "I can make it worth your while."

She cocked her head at him, raised her brows and crossed her arms.

He opened his mouth to argue then closed it again, turning to the lawyer. "Okay, what did Mother do?"

The lawyer took out a handkerchief and wiped his forehead with it. "If Miss Vincent forfeits her inheritance by violating the terms of the will, you also forfeit your inheritance."

"Which means?"

"Your mother left you the bulk of her estate. *Both* of you must abide by the terms of the will or you *both* lose…everything. Your inheritance will go to charity instead."

"And my club?"

"The shares for your club will be sold by this firm to the highest bidder—but that bidder may not be you."

"Son of a bitch!"

"Yes, you are," Mouse muttered.

"You just called my mother a bitch."

Mouse laughed. "She was and she knew it. In fact, she considered it a badge of honor."

Tor chuckled. "You're right. She did." Their gazes met, and Mouse felt it right down to her toes. "I can stand it, if you can," he growled.

"Stand it?"

"Working with me at the club."

"Oh right. I'm sure I can manage. I was a good assistant to your mother."

His brows shot up. "You aren't the assistant anymore, darlin' Mouse. You're an owner."

Her belly tightened. She wasn't just *an* owner… "I'm your boss now. Aren't I, Tor?"

He winced. "It would seem so."

"It is so, Mr. Stuart. Ms. Vincent is indeed the primary owner of your…um…club." Mouse frowned as the older man grew flustered.

"What's the name of it again?"

The lawyer studied her and she gained the impression from the intensity of his stare that he was trying to decide if she was playing some game. She wasn't. She couldn't remember anything after she found out Regine left her the townhouse.

"The club is called," he tugged the neckline of his shirt and again mopped his brow with a handkerchief, "um…Erotically Bound. It is a rather special sort of club."

Tor smiled for the first time since the big announcement. "Special indeed. That's a genteel way of putting it."

"I don't understand. Is it a strip club or something?"

"Or something…" the lawyer muttered, glancing at Tor.

She shook her head. "It either is or it isn't."

Tor cleared his throat. "It's a private—*members only*—BDSM club."

Mouse blinked then she began to blush. "You mean like whips and tying people up?"

"Still interested in being my boss?" Tor grinned.

She straightened. "I can handle it. Can you?"

"For six months, I can be the submissive."

She put her hands on her hips and looked him up and down. "You? Submissive? I'll believe it when I see it."

His eyes crinkled as he smiled, and the warmth he always hid behind his tough exterior showed through.

"Smart girl."

Why did he have to be so damn hot? And why did she have to want him so much? She'd just received her heart's desire posthumously from Regine—a home to call her own and the money to live well. Why did she have to want more than that? Like receiving the fulfillment of a desire from a whole lot further south than her heart.

"Ms. Vincent, I have a message and a letter for you from Mrs. Stuart."

Tor turned to him. "Mother left a message?"

"Strictly for Ms. Vincent. I'm sorry, sir."

He lowered his head briefly and rubbed his hand over his face. When he looked up, it was as if nothing had happened, but she'd seen his pain at the rebuff. She wanted to ease it. Even though he and his mother had often been at loggerheads because they were so alike, Mouse had never seen a parent and child who understood one another so well. Regine knew who her son was and had loved him warts and all, and apparently the feeling was mutual.

"Right. I'm sure Mr. Thompson will give you all the particulars. I'll see you at the club bright and early on Monday morning."

"Morning? I thought clubs were nighttime places?"

He smiled. "They are. But we get the business done during the day so our guests can enjoy their evenings."

Tor winked at her, picked up his long coat to protect him against the late autumn chill and left her with the lawyer. Six months in close proximity to that man was likely to kill her, she thought, staring at the closed door. The behavior he'd shown today was unusual for him. Tor Stuart was typically the poster boy for phlegmatic Scotsmen everywhere, but every once in awhile, volatile emotions swept over him. Like those today. Jeez, normally he was so in control he was a little scary. Only his occasional fits of anger lurking under the ginger hair made him seem human.

Mouse sighed, turning to Mr. Thompson. "Well, what did she have to say?"

He walked over to his desk and picked up an envelope. Regine's stationary. She'd recognize it anywhere. Handmade paper in a soft, warm peach tone. Not too girly. Just classic, like Regine. He pressed a button against the wall and the landscape painting silently slid upward to reveal a flat screen and below it a player.

"Press here to start the recording." He pointed. "Open this envelope as directed during the course of the recording. I'll wait for you outside."

The lawyer handed her the envelope and slipped out of the room, shutting the door quietly behind him. Mouse closed her eyes. She wasn't sure she was ready to see Regine again. And which Regine would it be? The woman completely in control of herself and everyone around her or the woman in a pain only barely dulled by drugs as she'd been at the end?

Mouse stood and walked over to the player, pressing play before she sat down again. Suddenly nearly three feet of Regine filled her vision. Looking sleek and slender in a peach-toned designer suit with a matching hat to cover her bald head, which she always called her chemo merit badge.

"Alone together again, Mouse dear. Your hands are probably itching to begin taking notes," she chuckled, her voice still bearing hints of her Southern upbringing.

Mouse grinned. She'd be fine never taking notes again, but if Regine were really sitting here beside her, she'd find a notebook and her pen and be poised to take down her boss's every word. That was just how they'd been together. Regine was a hard woman to love sometimes, but Mouse had adored her. No one she'd ever known had such a deep well of emotions so carefully hidden from public scrutiny.

"Well, now that I'm dead..." Regine took a deep breath, looking away from the camera recording her. "God, that thought truly terrifies me." She returned her gaze to the front, and Mouse felt pinned beneath those pale blue eyes. "But I thank you for helping me through this. You've been my rock in so very many ways..." She trailed off and carefully wiped her eyes so as not to smear her makeup. Regine cleared her throat.

"Now I've gone all morbid and sentimental and it's your fault, dear. I need you here to help me with this bit, but since it's for *you* I won't tell you about it until I'm dead. Quite the catch-22 I've presented myself." She shook herself and straightened, folding her hands carefully on her lap.

"To business then. As much as I love you, Mouse my girl, your inheritance comes with a price, which you now know. I expect you to work with Tor at Erotically Bound for six months. A difficult task on so many levels. Open the envelope you were given but don't read the contents yet."

Mouse followed directions precisely and sat with a letter and business card in her hands but remained staring at the screen. "So okay. Now what?"

"Now what, you ask? I can almost hear you, dear." Regine chuckled, and Mouse felt a chill run up her spine. Shit, the woman had known her so well.

"Well, now I'm going to tell you a little story. There was a beautiful young woman who set out for New York, determined to be a model. After a few years in the business, she met a marvelous lawyer named James. They fell madly in love, moved to Washington D.C. together and had a son. They had a fabulous life until he was taken from her far too early."

Mouse cocked her head. That was the public version, but she'd never quite bought it as so many others had. Very few people were privileged to live such an easy, simple life.

"As you no doubt guessed long ago, that's just the PR spin we put on things. It was a Cinderella story and everyone loves those so much, don't they? The true story is a bit different. *Vastly* different, in fact."

Mouse looked down and smiled then realized she didn't have to hide her grins from Regine anymore. Not that Regine hadn't caught every one of them but Mouse had always tried to keep from laughing out loud.

"I know you're smiling, dear. You never could hide that irreverent sense of humor from me, especially when your humor was at my expense, as it so often was."

Damn, if she didn't know better, she'd think the woman was in the room. Mouse frowned. "Well, get on with it then, Regine."

"Yes, let's get on with it. Shall we?" Regine took off her hat, baring the baldness she'd hated at first then later embraced, both in private and public. Her last few years had been spent crusading to raise money for breast cancer research, and Mouse had been at her side the entire time. Organizing. Calling people. Making pitches. Writing press releases. In general, making Regine's life easier while she fought a losing battle.

"You need the true story so that you can move forward and make a difference in my son's life, as you did in mine.

"I come from a tiny town in West Virginia. My daddy was killed in a mine cave-in when I was seventeen and Mama was desperate, the way you were the day we met. She went to the richest man in town, the coal mine owner, and asked him to help. Within a week I was his mistress." Regine tilted her head, her eyes far off in remembrance. "I did what I had to in order to help my family—just as you have. I know you've sent money off every pay period to care for family in Ohio."

"So what's the point, Regine? Why the club?"

"Let me get to the point..."

"How the hell do you keep doing that?" Mouse got up and began to pace.

"Oh do sit down, dear."

Mouse fell back into her chair and stared at the screen. No way. Just...no.

The Regine on the screen was smiling faintly. "No, I'm not a ghost. I just know you very well. And the reason is because I'm a Dominant woman. A Domme. I know how to read people. Their nuances. It made me a very good mistress and a very good *Mistress* too. So good, my first lover wanted to leave his wife, but I said no. I told him it would destroy my mama if I broke up his family and asked him to help me get a start in New York. So he did."

"I became a model, but I also fell into the life of a professional Dominatrix. I was good at both, and that's how I met James. He was a submissive."

"No waaaay."

"Yes, he was. A man with so much control in his public life often enjoys relinquishing that control privately. And so he did, *to me*. I valued his submission more than all his money. Tor knows about and respects our relationship. When he realized he was a Dominant too, his respect grew. Greater respect arises out of understanding." She brushed her fingers over her hairless scalp, wincing slightly. "In fact, his respect was one of the reasons he started Erotically Bound. He wanted a safe place to play for those with a great deal to lose. I held controlling interest, but I was a silent partner. *You* will not be. In your hand is a list. Open and read it now. I'll wait."

Mouse unfolded it. There were specific tasks enumerated—from removing alcohol from the premises to mentions of individuals who should lose their memberships because they abused their privileges and didn't play safely, sanely and consensually with their partners.

"These items are merely guidelines. You have a mind of your own, so I want you to determine which of these are true and should be followed and which are false—to be ignored. Yes, some *are* incorrect. Only through observation and investigation can you find out if you fit this lifestyle yourself, but I think you do."

Mouse's gaze flew from the sheet of paper to the screen. "You're nuts. I'm not..."

"No, you are *not* a Dominant, Mouse. I know that. You're a submissive." Regine chuckled. "You and I have had a non-sexual D/s relationship for the last five years. Like James you are a perfect submissive and worth your weight in gold as such. I adore you just as much as you adore me. We understand one another. But it's time for you to find another Dominant. One who can share your life...*all* aspects of it. You have six months to do it." She put her hat back on and adjusted it to the perfect angle.

"Finally, don't underestimate Tor. He needs someone like you to shake him out of his complacency. That boy thinks he knows everything. He doesn't. And he doesn't trust easily, but he needs to be able to trust *you*. Show him your mettle. You gained your strength in the fires of our first year together. I honed you, now I set you free to find what you need and maybe what you need is my son."

Mouse felt heat rush to her face. God, she wished she could have Tor, but there was no way he'd be interested in her. He dated women like his mother. Classy and beautiful.

"Didn't I just say *not* to underestimate my son, dear?" Mouse jerked. Damn it. She wished Regine would stop doing that. "Tor doesn't choose based on looks, though it might seem that way based on his recent...conquests. No, he values people as I taught him to. By who they are, not what they look like. And remember, you may be a submissive but you're not a doormat—even if your name *is* Mouse." Regine chuckled. "Oh, and one final thing. Call the phone number on the business card as soon as you get home. Ask for Mistress Zarah. She'll be expecting your call and will answer all your questions. She has a few additional instructions for you. Then…full steam ahead. Tackle the club and teach my son a thing or two. He needs you desperately, just as I did."

Regine looked down briefly, when she looked back at the camera, tears streaked her cheeks. "I know you think that you were the lucky one when you found me and I lifted you out of the gutter, but the truth is *entirely* the reverse. You brought meaning back into my life when I had grown cold and cynical. And you have helped me face this disease with a grace I never would have been able to find without you. For that, you have my undying gratitude and love. Thank you, my dearest Mouse."

As the screen went black, Mouse began to cry again. God, she'd loved that woman. Regine had been a bitch on wheels, capable of terrifying everyone in D.C.—everyone *but* Mouse. She'd miss Regine horribly in the future because her best friend and surrogate mother was now gone. Mouse slipped the list and the card back into the envelope and stood. It was time to follow orders and make her former boss…and Domme proud one last time.

Chapter Two

ജ

Mouse unlocked the front door and looked around the entryway. *Her* entryway. The foyer was open with high ceilings and beautiful hardwood floors. She closed the door and locked it behind her before setting the alarm. How could this place really be hers? But it was. It was *all* hers! Yes! She walked with purpose to the kitchen and made herself a cup of tea with lemon then went into her at-home office. Mouse ran her hands over the cherry wood desk and settled into her chair with a shake of her head. She looked at the ceiling and closed her eyes.

"Thank you, Regine," she whispered, and hoped her mentor heard her.

She took the envelope out of her purse and pulled out the list and the card. She studied the business card. Who had such a plain business card these days? It was a simple and white with *1-800-DOM-help* in thick black letters. On the back, the words *Mistress Zarah* were written.

She had to do this but felt terrified. Working with Torin Stuart would be excruciating—a combination of sexual frustration and a sincere desire to strangle him. He was as opinionated as his mother had been, but he pushed all her hot buttons. She still remembered the first time she'd seen him.

He'd breezed into his mother's home and ignored Mouse as he threw open his mother's office door. She'd been in the midst of an important meeting, and for Mouse there'd been hell to pay for not stopping him. Even while he'd chuckled at her predicament and Regine verbally ripped her hide off, Mouse had wanted to drop to the floor and suck his cock until he shot in her mouth. She shivered. Her desire had raged on high ever since while he remained cordially distant. Lousy bastard.

She sighed and looked at her hands to find they were shaking. She clenched her fists. She *would* do this. Mouse dialed the number. It took awhile to connect, but then the line rang, precisely twice, before a man spoke.

"Thank you for calling 1-800-DOM-help. This is the Operator. How may I be of assistance?" Mouse swallowed…hard. She needed to speak. Just open her mouth and talk. "Hello? I can hear you breathing. How may I help you?"

"I was told to ask for Mistress Zarah?" Mouse rolled her eyes at her tentative squeaky tone.

"Ah, you're a special caller. I believe you were directed to me by Mistress Regine."

Her jaw dropped. How the hell had he known? "Um…yeah. I guess."

"Very good. Please hold while I connect you."

Mouse held her breath and released it in a huff when a smooth, deep-voiced woman answered.

"You sound happy to speak to me," she chuckled drily.

"Sorry."

"Mouse, right?"

"Um…yeah. How did you know?"

"You asked for me. No one else would do that. How can I help you?"

"If you know my name, do you know my situation?"

The deep, sexy chuckle made goose bumps rise on her skin. If she weren't straight, she could fall for this woman just by her voice alone. She must drive her submissives insane.

"I do. Regine was specific, and Tor would be a handful—even for a submissive comfortable in the life. I don't know what Regine was thinking to toss a newbie sub into a battle with him."

"Are you sure it will be a battle?"

She laughed again. "Hell yes. Regine and I have both made the suggestions on her list to him through the years but he blew us off."

"I thought Regine held controlling interest?"

"She did, but Erotically Bound was his baby so she didn't interfere. That and the fact that it's part of a franchise of a sort."

"It is?"

"Yes. Do an internet search, dear. You'll find clubs with the same name all over the continental United States."

"Oh."

"Well, we need to get you up to specs at the speed of light, so let's talk."

For the next few hours, Mouse learned about BDSM. How it worked and didn't work. What safe words were and when to use them. At the end of their talk, Mistress Zarah told her that first thing in the morning a package would arrive for her and that night she and Zarah would be visiting a local club called Unfettered. She wrote down the address Mistress Zarah told her and took a deep breath.

"Mouse dear, Unfettered is exactly how a club *should* be run. Look and learn so you'll have something to compare EB to. This club is…new to D.C. but I've been there before."

"Is EB so terrible?"

"No, it's an excellent club—but it could be better. That's your job. Make it the best it can be."

"I wish I knew what that meant."

"It will become clear in time. Memorize that list. Oh, and there will be a mask in the box. Wear it. Also, I won't call you Mouse. Hmmm, what name shall I give you?"

"My name is Mozelle."

"No, someone might know that. Ah… I'll call you Minnie."

"What?"

"Minnie. Short for Minnie Mouse."

"Minnie Mouse wouldn't be caught dead in a BDSM club."

"You might be surprised."

"Right. So how will I know you?"

"I'll wait near the bar for you. Arrive precisely at eight p.m. and don't be late, or I might have to punish you." Her throaty laugh gave Mouse another chill of arousal. What the hell?

"I don't belong to you, Mistress. So punishment isn't really appropriate."

"Maybe not, but you'll be under my protection. It will be easier that way because we don't want any roving Doms to hit on you…yet. I'll see you tomorrow evening, dear."

"Good night."

Mouse sighed as she hung up. This was the craziest thing she'd ever done in her entire life. She just hoped it was worth it.

* * * * *

Walking up to the front door of Unfettered terrified her. Not because of its location. After all, it was only a few blocks from her townhouse. No, her fear arose from what she'd learned by surfing the web after her call to Mistress Zarah. How could Regine possibly think this would work? Tor would never allow her to make the kind of changes on that list.

Mouse adjusted her gold leather mask and hoped she wouldn't meet anyone she knew as she tugged her coat tighter around her. Even though it wasn't yet winter, the cold wind blew up under her coat and her very short red leather skirt. She felt like a walking cliché festival in her mask, metallic gold bustier, red leather skirt and red spike heels.

After taking a deep breath, she approached the woman at the door, trying to ignore the big guy leaning against the wall flexing his muscles.

"Can I help you?"

"I…" Oh damn. One of her squeaks. That squeak was why Regine always called her Mouse instead of Moze, her lifetime nickname.

The woman smiled in a kindly way. "Do you have a name?"

"Yes, M-M-Minnie."

"Well, M-M-Minnie let me check my list to see if you're on it." She perused a clipboard and finally nodded. "Yes, you're meeting Mistress Zarah. As you go in, you'll see her at the bar. She's the tall lady in tight black leather pants who bears an uncanny resemblance to Melissa Etheridge."

"Oh. Okay. Thanks…"

"I'm Dru. And don't worry, I'm sure you'll have fun. Mistress Zarah isn't *too* tough on newbies—usually."

Mouse scuttled through the door and came to a halt just inside. She stood and stared, barely noticing as someone helped her off with her coat and handed her a coat check stub. She absently stuffed it into her clutch purse. She didn't know what she'd been expecting, but she didn't think this was it. The décor was gorgeous in a very sexual way. Dark, polished wood was everywhere. From the beautifully carved wood of the bar to the gleaming floors. The couches and arm chairs were covered in a deep burgundy leather. It looked exactly like a classy private BDSM club should look. Not cheesy and over the top, but rich and elegant.

She noticed the people at the bar and there was one woman who stood out. A circle of silence marked her and no one approached. Every submissive in the room eyed her with interest, and if they came anywhere near her, they bowed. Yup, black leather pants, black jacket and wavy light brown hair. Melissa indeed. Mouse took a step and paused. How the hell was she supposed to go up and talk to her?

"Hello, angel girl. Alone tonight?" Mouse jumped then looked up at a tall, reed-thin older man.

"I..."

"She's with me."

"Your new girl? You have taste, old friend."

Mistress Zarah chuckled. "She's my guest, but she is lovely, isn't she?"

"Indeed. Let me know if you decide to cut her loose."

"Her choice of partner is up to her."

He sighed dramatically. "Pity. Submissives need guidance."

"Only once they choose."

As he shrugged and walked away, Mouse sighed in relief. "Thank you, Mistress."

"Turn. Face me."

Mouse followed directions with a blush while Mistress Zarah surveyed her. "You'll do." She walked behind Mouse and poked her in the small of the back. "Stand straight. Head and shoulders up. Be proud of yourself. Dominants would love to spank that curvy full ass." Mistress Zarah's hands slid over her butt and gently squeezed.

"Um... Mistress."

"Hush. I'm enjoying." She strode back in front of Mouse. She ran her fingers over the rise of her breasts as they rose from the bustier. "Ah, Minnie, you have luscious tits too."

"Are you a lesbian?"

Mistress Zarah grinned. "Bi. I'm an equal-opportunity Domme."

"I see."

"You're straight?"

Mouse nodded. Zarah brushed over her nipples. "Yet these are at attention for me." She looked beyond Mouse and smiled. "Perfect. He's right on time for once."

"He who?"

"Master Torin."

"Oh my God…" Mouse shivered and ducked her head.

Mistress Zarah surveyed her. "Oh, now that's just not fair. I bet you creamed your panties, didn't you?"

"Mistress, could you please keep your voice down?" Mouse hissed, heat filling her cheeks.

Zarah chuckled. "Oh, I don't think so. But for your sake, I suggest you don't speak much when he comes over here or he might recognize your voice." She turned her head to look behind Mouse. "Ah, Master Torin. How are you, dear?"

He came around Mouse and gave Zarah a brief hug and a kiss on the cheek. "Well enough, considering."

"It's such a loss. We'll miss Regine terribly, you know that, don't you?"

"I do. Thank you." Torin turned and looked Mouse over from head to toe. "Very nice. Is she yours?"

"No, darling. A guest who wants to explore the dark side."

"As a submissive or is she a Domme in training?"

"Submissive."

Tor turned the full force of his gaze on her. Their eyes met briefly before she dropped her gaze to his shoes. Please let him not recognize her. Please.

"Yes, definitely a submissive," he purred. He lifted his hand and paused, glancing at Zarah. "May I?"

"The choice is hers."

"Do you have a name?" he asked, brushing a strand of hair off her forehead. Normally, she kept her bushy hair pinned severely back, but the letter that arrived with the clothes ordered her to let it fall around her face naturally.

She glanced at Mistress Zarah, begging for help. Zarah smiled. "Her name is Minnie."

"Minnie? Unusual."

"That's her name tonight. Who knows? Her name tomorrow might be Mickey."

Mouse glared at Zarah, who just laughed.

"Do you want to play with me, Minnie?"

Mouse's eyes flew to Tor's. Did he know? Surely not. And what the hell did he mean by play?

"Play?" she squeaked. Damn it. Why did she always have to squeak like a mouse when she was anxious? At least Tor was unfamiliar with her nervous habit because by the time they'd met, Regine had worked the squeak right out of her.

He chuckled, his fingers trailed along the bare skin of her arm from her shoulder to her wrist. Gently, he encircled her wrist and rubbed the vulnerable skin there with his forefinger.

"Yes, Miss Squeak. *Play*. That means you and I go someplace private and I give you a spanking you'll never forget. A spanking that will have you begging for more."

Mouse couldn't catch her breath as he lightly ran his fingertips up to her elbow. He leaned close and brushed his lips along the edge of her ear. She jerked when his tongue flicked against her lobe.

"Sensitive, aren't you?" he murmured.

"Yes."

"Yes, *Sir*."

"Oh sorry. Yes Sir." Her voice was barely a whisper.

He chuckled in her ear. His hand moved from her elbow to her waist while he tormented her by trailing the fingers of his other hand from her wrist to her shoulder. Then he brushed a finger along her shoulder and up along her neck.

Mouse couldn't stop the shiver that coursed through her at his touch.

"You haven't answered my question. Would you like to play with me?"

She closed her eyes at his purr. God, she wanted him. But what was she letting herself in for if she agreed to this? She opened her eyes and she saw Mistress Zarah grinning at her.

"The choice is yours. What do *you* want?"

She swallowed hard. "Aren't I supposed to be learning?"

"Yes, but there are many ways to learn. Observation…or experience. How do you want to learn?"

Mouse peeped up at Tor who had picked up a strand of her hair and was curling it around his finger. He seemed completely focused on her and she liked it. She liked having him look at her and her alone. No one in her life had ever made her the center of their attentions before and it was heady stuff. She didn't want it to end.

"Experience might be good," she whispered.

"Is that a yes?"

She licked her lips then nodded.

"I want to hear your consent."

"Yes." Damn it, she'd squeaked again.

He laughed. "Well, Miss Squeak, allow me to introduce you to a private dungeon." Tor reached for her mask but she caught his hand. His brows rose at her action. "What's this? Defiance?"

"No Sir," she whispered. "This isn't defiance, it's a limit. I want the mask to stay on."

He pursed his lips as he studied her. Her gaze dropped from the full force of his and again she shivered.

"Very well. What other limits should I follow?"

She opened her mouth to say something, but she didn't know what to say. Her gaze flew helplessly to Mistress Zarah.

"I'd say she would prefer no scat or water sports."

"What's that?"

"Feces and urine play."

"Eew, yuck." Mouse responded to Zarah. "People actually *do* that?"

"Some do, but I don't. So no worries there," Tor responded. "Needle or blood play?"

Mouse's gaze flew to Tor. "Blood? No. I don't think I'd like that…at all."

He chuckled. "Fair enough."

"This is complicated. Maybe I should just watch."

"There is pleasure in that, certainly, but you learn more by doing."

Mouse bit her lip and glanced up at Tor. "You don't mean out here. In public."

He smiled. "If you wish."

"No, I'd rather not play in public."

"Are you willing to go to a private room with me?"

She swallowed. Because she knew him, she trusted him. And she wanted this… She nodded.

"Speak, Miss Squeak," Tor ordered softly. "I want no confusion between us. The game is safe, sane and *consensual*. Consent is mandatory."

"Yes, we could go to a private room." She felt her face heating but was glad she'd gotten out the words…even if it was in a breathless whisper.

He patted her bottom and she jumped. "All right. Mistress, thank you for the introduction to this lovely girl."

"You're welcome, my friend," she purred, a faint smile on her face. "Have fun."

"Oh, we will." He chuckled, sliding his arm around her waist to lead her away. "One final thing. We're new to playing together, so we need to establish safe words."

Mouse glanced back at him. "Safe words?"

"If you wish to pause the scene, say yellow. Like the yellow caution light in traffic."

"And red to stop?"

"Yes, I think that will work well… For now."

Tor glanced over at the bar and pointed to a hallway in the back. The bartender nodded as Tor took her hand and led her past the public play area where a female sub was bound against a large wooden cross while a Master stood behind her striking her with a flogger. Her buttocks were red while she sobbed for more around the ball gag in her mouth. Tor paused, setting his hands at her waist.

"What do you think she's feeling?"

"Pain."

"But she's begging for more, isn't she?"

Mouse nodded.

"Why?"

She tried to look up at him but he shook his head. "Don't look at me. Watch the play." Returning her gaze to the couple, she swallowed hard. "So why is she begging for more?" he pressed her. Mouse didn't know the answer, and she hated not having an answer to give him. Maybe a guess…

"She's a masochist?"

He chuckled in her ear as he cupped her breasts. "Probably, but there's more to it than that. Any ideas?" She shook her head. "Out loud."

"No Sir. I don't know." She kept her voice soft, hoping he'd never connect Mouse, his new business partner, with Minnie, the submissive from Unfettered.

"Well, you're right about the pain. It definitely stings, but the heat from the blows will shift into pleasure after a little while."

"How?"

"Endorphins." His hands skimmed from her waist down along her thighs to the V between her legs. "I'd be happy to show you. Are you ready?"

The master in front of them changed from a flogger to a thick leather paddle. Mouse jumped as his first blow fell on the sub's ass, but she licked her lips as another blow fell, imagining herself in the sub's place with Tor behind her wielding the paddle. Tor's fingers slipped under her skirt to tease her pussy.

"You're wet."

"I am?" She closed her eyes, mortified by her voice…again.

"Yes, Miss Squeak. You're very wet." He pressed on her panties and rubbed her clit. Her breath hitched in reaction, her hips wiggling with excitement.

"Oh God." She was ready to come and he was still only rubbing his finger against the outside of her panties. What would happen when he bared it for his pleasure?

"I'm not God, but you can worship me later," he chuckled, "when you'll be on your knees with my cock sunk deep inside your open mouth."

Mouse's eyes closed in anticipation as the sounds of the paddling continued. Maybe Regine knew her a lot better than she thought. This whole thing was turning her on more than anything she'd ever experienced before.

Tor continued rubbing his finger over her tight clit. "Your sexy little wiggles are driving me crazy."

He withdrew his hands and guided her forward. Feeling almost mesmerized by the arousal pulsing through her body, she obeyed his direction, enjoying the heat radiating from Tor as he urged her onward. They turned down a corridor to the right of the bar and one of the doors slid open almost silently.

Inside was a room that looked surprisingly like an office. A large desk with a leather chair sat along one side of the room. Behind it ranged closed cabinets that probably held toys or paddles or something equally scary-sexy. On the opposite side of the desk was a straight chair. A leather couch ran the length of an adjoining wall while a leather bench and a wooden cross sat in the corners.

Mouse swallowed hard when Tor laughed behind her. "This is perfect, one of my sweetest fantasies is instructing an administrative assistant in her new duties."

He walked across the room and settled in the office chair, leaning back to put his feet up on the desk.

"So, Miss Squeak, can you take dictation?"

Mouse colored. Did he know? She was terrified that she was being made fun of here. "Some, I guess."

He opened a desk drawer and grinned. "Perfect." He pulled out a pad of paper and a pencil.

"Come take some notes. I need to plan out the evening and I want to remember the plan." He pointed imperiously at the straight chair across the desk from him.

Reluctantly, Mouse took up the pad of paper and pencil then took a seat. "I'm ready, Sir," she whispered.

She took notes through his rapid-fire dictation of what he planned to do to her. It started with her sucking his cock and swallowing his come before he bound her to the spanking bench and introduced her to the flogger and the paddle. Somewhere along the way as he dictated, her clit began to throb and her nipples tightened. Before long, she was staring at him with her mouth open instead of taking notes.

"Well, Miss Squeak. Read back my notes."

Mouse blinked and looked down, horrified to realize she hadn't maintained any sense of professionalism. She barely had two sentences written.

"Well? I don't want to wait all night, Squeak my girl."

"I…didn't get everything written down."

He raised his brows. "Really? How far did you get?"

Mouse read the notes back to him in a low voice, her face heating as she stumbled over his words about sucking his cock. She glanced up once to find his brows drawn down into a straight line of displeasure. Oh no. Not good.

"That's it? That's all you got?"

"Yes Sir," she whispered.

"Huh. Not acceptable. It would seem you need correction so you remember to follow orders properly."

"But..."

"No buts. You either do your job or you don't." Mouse swallowed hard, remembering the days when she and Regine had similar conversations during her first year on the job.

"Stand up and walk around the desk."

Mouse reluctantly followed orders, staring at her feet as she stood in front of Tor.

"Set the pad and pencil down."

Mouse obeyed. With nothing in her hands, her fingers twisted around one another.

"Reach up under your skirt and tug your panties to your knees."

Her eyes shot up to his. There was no compromise on his face. None at all. She followed his instructions and tugged the panties down and let them drop to the floor.

"Did I tell you to take your panties all the way off?"

She blinked. "No Sir."

"What did I tell you?"

"To pull them down to my knees."

"Then get them there. *Now*."

Mouse bent down to retrieve her panties, leaving them around her knees. Their gazes met again and a sense of embarrassment warred with a twisting of excitement from her belly to her pussy. He merely stared at her and finally her eyes dropped. For several minutes he just watched her. Her pussy throbbed and she felt her juices trickle out of her wet cunt. There was something naughty and sexy about standing before him like an errant schoolgirl in need of a spanking. Her breathing increased and she licked her lips.

"I want to you to walk over here, keeping your panties around your knees, and lay yourself over my lap."

"Yes Sir."

In what felt like more of a waddle, Mouse followed orders, hobbling a few steps then looking at his lap where his erect cock tented his trousers. Her gaze met his again, but his expression didn't waver.

"I'm waiting, Squeak. And the longer I wait, the longer I'll spank you."

Awkwardly, Mouse hobbled to him before she laid herself across his lap, shivering with excitement as his cock prodded against her lower belly.

"Good. Now, Squeak, flip your skirt up."

She reached behind her and tugged her skirt up to her waist. Her position was uncomfortable and surprisingly intimate. Tor's fingers tapped against her ass then slid down between her thighs.

"Spread 'em."

Mouse parted her legs and she whimpered when his fingers dipped into her tight, wet pussy. He buried the fingers of his left hand in her pussy. He adjusted her on his lap slightly.

"Your lack of attention left a perfectly good plan for the evening unrecorded. Now I'll have to play the whole thing by ear, and I don't prefer to do that. This is a serious infraction, Squeak. Do you understand?"

As the fingers buried in her pussy pressed and teased, she fought to follow what he was saying, but it was nearly impossible. She hadn't had anything inside her but a vibrator in a good long time, so having her favorite fantasy man tickling her cunt destroyed her concentration.

"I said, *do you understand*?"

"Yes Sir."

"What did I say?"

"I didn't record your plans and you don't like that."

"No, I don't. Each of your ass cheeks will receive five solid slaps for a total of ten. I expect you to count them as they fall."

"Yes Sir." Mouse shivered again at the tone of command in his voice.

He continued to finger-fuck her pussy and she closed her eyes…until the first blow fell. The crack against her left buttock sent fire spiraling through her and she gasped in shock.

"I said to count. Do I need to add more?"

"No Sir. That was one."

"Yes, it was." When the second fell, she squeaked in surprise. More fire covered her bottom. Now both cheeks were aflame.

"Two."

She clenched her ass against the blow, but it didn't come. And it didn't come. When she finally relaxed, the blow fell and then another.

"Three and four."

"Very good."

The heat from the blows was doing precisely what he said it would. It felt good. Heat built inside her. Arousing her. By the time she counted six and seven, her fiery ass was lifting in anticipation. She wiggled against him, spreading her legs more so his fingers could worm their way more deeply inside. Her pussy throbbed with excitement and she was panting.

Another blow fell and she whimpered with the pleasure of it, stretching against him. "Eight."

Between the fingers teasing her pussy and the blazing blows striking her ass, she was on the edge of an orgasm more intense than anything she'd ever felt before.

"What a naughty girl you are... All wet from your punishment."

"Yes Sir."

"Perhaps I should stop now..."

"No."

"No?" He chuckled.

"No Sir. Please don't stop. I earned the last two. Really, I did."

"Yes, you did." He landed another sharp blow to her ass. The fire shot directly to her cunt and clit.

"Nine. Oh God yes."

"I'm not sure you're being punished anymore."

"Don't stop, Sir. Please."

"You want another?"

Mouse squirmed in his lap. "Yes Sir. *Please...*"

He gave her the last blow. She sighed, but it wasn't enough to drive her over the edge into the orgasm she yearned for. He withdrew his fingers from her pussy.

"Ten." She could hear the wistful dismay in her soft whisper.

"Up."

"Sir?"

"Stand up. We've completed your discipline." Mouse struggled to stand, and finally stood to face him, bending to pull up her panties. "Did I give you permission to do that?"

"No Sir," she whispered.

"With your panties at your knees, I want you to lift your skirt so I can see how wet you are as a result of your spanking."

Mouse shivered, her clit throbbing. She lifted her skirt to her waist.

"What a naughty girl you are."

Tor reached up and gently parted her folds and Mouse sobbed with excitement. One long finger was drawn over her quivering clit, making Mouse fight the orgasm that threatened.

"You're fighting me."

"What do you want, Sir?"

"Obedience." Tor's fingernail scratched over her clit.

"Oh..."

Mouse quivered as Tor flicked his finger against her trembling clit. He tugged her cunt lips wider, baring the interior pink folds of her labia to his heated gaze.

"I think I'd like to taste the pink fruit."

"Taste?" Mouse squeaked. This was one of her deepest fantasies. Having Tor eat her out.

"Yes, I have a fondness for pussy. I could eat the soft pink fruit for hours. Do you understand?"

"Yes Sir." She was breathless. Excited. Uncertain. But she felt safe as Tor played with her.

Mouse's eyes drifted closed as he parted her further to put her erect clit on display.

He stroked her clit with the tip of his finger again, rolling it around and around over the taut nub until Mouse was jerking her hips and thrusting back.

"Oh God..."

"So close," Tor observed. "And I want to taste you when you come."

She opened her eyes, and at that moment, Tor's tongue flicked against the underside of her clit and she mewled as release shot through her. Her eyes closed again while he kept up his oral assault, Tor pulled her close to hold her up so she didn't collapse while he nibbled and sucked her. Wave after wave of pleasure shook Mouse. Although the fire filling her body this time was different from the spanking, it was just as potent, just as arousing, and just as devastating to her hard-won self-control. Finally his mouth released her.

Her eyes fluttered open when Tor growled hoarsely, "Oh shit, I've got to fuck you."

"Yes. Please!"

Tor swung Mouse over to the desk and laid her on it on her back. He tugged her panties off and threw them over his shoulder. She stared up at him as he unzipped his trousers and released his thick erection. God, she'd always wanted this. Wanted to have him out of control with need for her and buried in her quim up to the hilt. She spread her legs and bent her knees, offering herself.

"Oh fuck yes!" He pulled a condom out of his pocket and slipped it over his thick, hard cock.

"Don't wait, fuck me!" Mouse cried. He took a deep breath, pausing to stare at her.

"Just a minute, Squeak."

Tor glided behind the desk and seized her wrists while he pulled a long, soft rope out of a desk drawer. He looped the rope around her wrists then brought it down to the legs of the desk and tied the rope off. She tugged but couldn't get free. She ought to panic, but instead she felt moisture flood her pussy.

"Oh yes. Please…"

"I thought you'd appreciate that. I certainly will." Tor watched her wriggle with a widening grin. He reached into the drawer and grabbed something that he put into his pants pocket.

Tor moved back between her thighs and set himself at the entrance of Mouse's cunt while she watched, wide-eyed, ready and thrilled. She'd already had a screaming orgasm, but she knew that was a warm-up for what was about to happen when Tor fucked her.

As he wedged the head of his cock inside the entrance, he shuddered. "Damn, you're tight."

He pulled the top of her bustier down to bare her breasts, pinching the tight nipples then bending to suck on one. Mouse shivered, mewling and twisting in her bonds.

"Sweet, lovely Squeak," he growled, nudging himself forward.

While he pressed himself into her inch by inch, Mouse watched him fill her cunt, lifting her hips and opening for him. She threw her head back.

"Oh yes. Deeper. Fuck me deeper," she moaned.

Mouse twitched when he pinched her nipples again. She arched into the pinches and into the thrust of Tor's thick cock. "More. Please…more!"

He lifted her legs so her ankles rested on his shoulders. Mouse thrust up to meet him as he plunged into her pussy, closing her eyes. Suddenly she felt a bite on one of her nipples. Her eyes flew open, expecting to see him gnawing on her, but instead there was a clamp fastened tightly to one of her nipples.

Tor withdrew, and as he thrust back inside, she closed her eyes once more and she felt the bite on her other nipple. Now both of her straining nipples were imprisoned by clamps. She twisted, trying to loosen them, but there was no recourse. Her hands were bound and she was at Tor's mercy, but she enjoyed it. In fact, to her surprise, it felt good just to let someone else decide what would happen next.

Mouse sighed when he bottomed out again. "Yes, don't stop. Please…"

"Stop?" He chuckled. "Not a chance, Miss Squeak."

Mouse whimpered when she felt fingers teasing her clit. Tor rubbed her as he stroked in and out. Round and round, pressing on the tight bundle of nerves until she had trouble catching her breath.

"Keep it up. Ah, shit yeah. Your cunt is clenching on me... You're on the edge of coming again, aren't you?"

She groaned.

He tugged on one of the nipple clamps and she shrieked. "Aren't you?"

"Yes Sir."

Tor laughed. "I thought so."

With a groan, he tossed back his head and thrust his hips forward. Every plunge took her closer and closer to the edge of the abyss. Tor leaned down to kiss her damp forehead above the mask.

"Look into my eyes," he growled, and Mouse obeyed, unable to look away. The command curled around her, spinning a fire inside her body. "I want to watch you come."

"But..."

"Quiet. Just focus on the way it feels to have my cock driving in and out of your clasping cunt." He continued to rub Mouse's clit and teased her clamped nipples.

Mouse looked up at Tor. They connected in a way she never thought they would, their gazes locked as he drove deeper...faster.

"That's it, Squeak. Tighter. Clasp me. Feel the thrust of my cock while I pound into your cunt."

Mouse thrust harder, gasping as her muscles constricted...tensing in preparation. Her pussy throbbed and she fought to come. She wanted to find her release now...right now.

"Relax. Let it go," he growled. "Give me your orgasm. Share it with me."

Tor flicked and pinched Mouse's clit until finally she couldn't fight it anymore and gave herself to the Dominant who played her body so expertly. When she let go, her hips lifted from the desk and she threw back her head with a scream. It was too much…and not enough. She wanted Tor with her…

"Please come, Sir. Please," she whimpered as her belly quivered and spasms of pleasure jerked along every nerve ending in her body. As if it was her request that he'd been waiting for, he shouted and thrust deep—his body jerking as his orgasm took him over.

At the end, he collapsed forward, his damp forehead finally resting on her breastbone between her clamped nipples. She continued to twitch as residual shocks tormented her. He lifted his head and removed both clamps. She arched beneath him and another orgasm ripped through her body. He chuckled weakly as her cunt secured him inside her.

"Fuck, Miss Squeak, you're gonna kill me here." He sighed.

As she lay gasping, he untied her wrists.

"Ah, my lovely one, I could take you all night, but I think you've had enough for now. Perhaps we can find each other again…another time."

"I'd like that."

"We aren't done here, sweetheart." He lowered his head to press kisses to the curve of her neck. "Not by half."

Mouse shivered at the promise in his husky voice, wishing she could show Tor her face so he'd know who he'd just had sex with. But she couldn't. For the next six months they were going to be business partners, and Regine had always taught her that sex and business didn't mix. But at least she'd had her fantasy…if only for one night.

Chapter Three

ℰ

It was only as she stood in front of Erotically Bound at eight thirty a.m. on Monday morning that she realized she didn't have a key. Had he done this on purpose? She hoped not. It would be tough enough to look him in the eye after their adventure on Saturday night—especially since he didn't know his submissive playmate had been her. But if she knew he really didn't want her here *that* much, she'd be tempted just to throw in the towel.

Damn it. A walk around the building was her only course of action. Unfortunately, the service entrance in the back was just as locked as the main door. Mouse stomped back to the front of the building to glare at the mirrored glass façade. At least the wind wasn't whipping her coat around, but it was damn cold today. She didn't even have the phone number for the club. Shit, shit, shit! She pulled out her cell, deciding maybe a call to the lawyer would get her somewhere until she realized she still had Tor's cell number on speed dial.

In the last few months before Regine died, Tor wanted her to call if there was any change at all. Thank God, she hadn't dumped the number. She hit speed dial and waited. Two rings and he picked up.

"Mouse?"

"Yes."

"Where the hell are you? You're late."

She started to feel a swell of guilt fill her which she promptly squashed. "I've been searching for a way into the building for the last half-hour. I'm standing in front right now."

"Oh..." There was a pause. "Sorry about that. All the staff has a key and our service people don't start coming by until ten a.m."

"You want to come and let me in?"

The door opened and she sighed, hanging up the phone. Damn, he'd moved fast. Tor smiled at her, looking as hot as he had Saturday night. Hotter actually, since she now knew what an amazing cock he had. She felt heat rush to her face. He held the door open so she had to slip past him to squeeze through. Just brushing against him had her pussy wet. Oh dear. Maybe Saturday night had been a bad idea. A really bad idea. How was she going to work with this guy without giving herself away?

She looked away from Tor to take in the interior of the club and almost tripped over her feet. The exterior, with its mirrored glass and clean lines, was contemporary, but that was nothing on the rooms. Two walls were glass and let the morning light stream into the space. The ceilings were two stories high...soaring and slightly intimidating. The room was stark white with whitewashed oak floors. There were low white leather couches around the space. Along one wall was a curved bar with more glass and mirrors. The barstools were low with straight lines. Toward the back of the space was a large public play area. The toys were in white oak or chrome and mirrors were placed strategically around the play space. There was a sweeping wide staircase that went up to the upper level.

Normally, Mouse didn't really like contemporary design because it seemed cold to her. But this space really worked and it fit Tor's personality somehow. Not that he was cold, but that he was up-to-date...cutting edge.

"Would you like a tour?"

"Yes please."

"You can leave your coat on one of the couches."

Mouse did as he suggested then followed him to the public play area. Out the corner of her eye, she could see him watching her. In fact, he watched her closely, as though trying to determine what she thought without actually asking her. Mouse hadn't noticed at first, but a clear catwalk ran the full length of both windows on the front and side façades of the building. She pointed up.

"Don't those windows allow people to look in here and see what's going on? Kind of defeats the purpose of a discreet club, doesn't it?"

He smiled, obviously proud. "That was a great design. From the outside, the glass reflects like a mirror. From the inside, you can see out. Guests can stand in front of those windows buck naked and feel as if they're exposing themselves to the whole world, but no one outside can see them."

"Even at night?"

"Yeah. When we did renovations after purchasing the building, I stood outside to make sure and I still check periodically. Just to be sure. It's kind of like a one-way mirror."

They headed for the bar area and Tor introduced her to a man straightening the area.

"This is Wade, my bar manager."

"You serve alcohol?" Mouse tilted her head as she surveyed the wall of bottles behind Wade.

Tor frowned. "We do. Customers expect it."

"But the focus of the play is safe, sane and consensual, right?"

"Yes. What's your point?"

"Well, a drunk Dom isn't particularly safe or sane, and a drunk sub certainly couldn't give informed consent, could they?"

Wade laughed, looking away from Tor. "She sounds like Regine."

"Mother probably primed the pump. C'mon, we have more to see."

Mouse didn't move. It was only as he reached the stairs to the upper level that he realized she wasn't following him.

"Let's go, Mouse," he called.

"You didn't answer my question." She crossed her arms across her chest, determined not to move from her spot until he came back to explain.

He rolled his eyes and returned. "The members of this club expect elegance. We deliver."

"How does alcohol contribute to elegance?"

"It contributes to the ambiance. We serve nothing but the best."

"How does alcohol contribute to ambiance? Frankly, drunk people are the least elegant people around, and the ambiance they contribute is the sense of a place that's out of control."

She watched him take a deep breath and could almost hear him counting to ten before he responded.

"People don't drink to excess here."

"How do you know?"

"We enforce a two-drink maximum."

"How do you do that?" Tor growled, so she turned to the bar manager instead. "Well, Wade? On a busy night, how do you know that Mistress A has had only one drink but Master B has had his two drinks? Especially if the sub is going to the bar to get the drink for them?"

"Uh…" He looked uncomfortably at Tor.

"In other words, you don't know."

"We have discreet dungeon monitors keeping track of whether someone is behaving badly so you can just quit channeling my mother."

"Tor, just because it was your mother who commented does not mean she was wrong."

"Look, Mouse, why don't you just observe operations for a night or two to see how things go before you start suggesting changes."

She pressed her lips together to silence her irritation. "Fine I'll observe…*tonight*. We'll see how that two-drink maximum functions in reality."

"Right. Let's move on." He rolled his eyes and headed for the stairs to the upper level.

She followed. Mouse looked up the stairs as she started to follow Tor, and even as obnoxious as he was, she couldn't keep her mind on business. He had such a *fine* ass. She wished he would have gotten naked on Saturday night. That was the only thing missing from making that evening a perfect fantasy experience. He reached the top and turned to face her, only to catch her staring. He grinned when he realized what she'd been staring *at*. She looked away as she joined him on the upper level. There was an open space at the top of the stairs with a reception desk.

"What's that for?"

"We have someone on duty to coordinate the private rooms."

"Is that all that's up here?"

"No. We have a large public water bondage area up here along with locker rooms so people can keep a change of clothes on-site. In addition, we have small private dungeons for use by couples or small groups under five. We also have some large dungeons for private parties. One can accommodate up to twenty, the other will hold up to fifty."

"Do the dungeon monitors stand watch at private parties?"

He colored slightly. "They're *private* parties."

"But if someone is hurt here or something, aren't you liable even though it's a private party?"

"We have our members and their guests sign waivers."

Mouse thought about it and raised her brows. "Okay that covers your ass, but what if someone really messes up? This isn't a video game arcade. Someone could get seriously injured, and if they did, the club's reputation would be damaged and you could still be sued."

His face reddened and he gritted his teeth. She could tell he was counting again. She should *not* have been with him on Saturday—not when she had to work with him on Monday morning. It bothered her to press him about club operations because she could see it upset him. So how stupid was she? Their working relationship was already going south because she was addressing Regine's list and she hadn't even been here for an hour yet. He obviously wasn't going to handle *any* of her questions well.

"Mouse, I know my mother is behind this. So fess up. What's the deal?"

"It's a legitimate question, Tor. Your mother has nothing to do with it." Which was a lie, but she wasn't ready to deal with that yet.

"Nothing to do with it? *Bullshit.*" He shrugged his shoulders to ease some tension then went over to the reception desk. Tor moved behind and grabbed a set of keys. "Let's get this damn tour over with and then you can start finding fault elsewhere."

"Finding fault?" She frowned as he stalked past her and quickly unlocked the rooms along the main corridor and flipped on light switches.

"Yes. You don't like anything here and I know why."

"Why?"

"Mother. She disapproved and she infected you."

"She did not *infect* me."

"If you say so." He sighed and pointed. "The water play room is straight back behind the reception desk. Along the hallway on either side of the desk are a series of rooms with different themes. The party rooms are at either end of the floor." He tossed the keys to her, but she didn't get her hands on them before they hit her in the tummy and dropped to the floor at her feet. "Go ahead and explore, and I'll wait for you in the office downstairs."

As he all but ran down the stairs, she sighed. Regine hadn't made this easy…for either of them. He seemed to take every comment she made as a personal insult. This was a business, wasn't it? Shouldn't he want to improve it? She bent and picked up the keys. Maybe she was going about this all wrong. For whatever reason, this place was more to him than a business—it was like an extension of himself. So her criticisms of the business were like criticisms of *him*. And obviously he didn't like it. Damn. She wished she could start the day all over again, she thought as she began her very quiet, solitary tour of the second floor.

* * * * *

Tor slammed his office door shut, feeling highly satisfied at the ringing sound. But damn, he needed to calm down. A Dominant did not lose control like this, but that woman was getting under his skin. And it was even worse than it had been with his mother. When Regine spoke, he could blow her off as old-fashioned. Behind the times. But Mouse was new to the scene.

And while he was damn sure his mother had primed the pump in some way, he didn't think Mouse would parrot comments just because Regine told her to. She'd never been like that in all the time he'd known her. The number of times she'd talked back to his mother astounded him. Hell, *he'd* rarely talked back to his mother. He'd gone the route of avoidance by ignoring her. But when Mouse voiced her opinion, it was because she felt strongly, and usually Mouse had been right. And when she was right, Regine had caved. Mouse had a damn good brain and she used it. So if she was feeding him Regine's suggestions, it was because she agreed with what his mother had told her. Shit.

He leaned against his desk. Tor could count on one hand the number of people who could get under his skin enough to make him mad. His mother had always been number one on the list. But Mouse was right up there. The worst part was…he wanted her. He'd wanted her almost from the first time he'd met her after Regine had hired her, and six years was a fucking long time. Not only did he want her, but he *liked* her too. She was funny and smart. There'd been so many times she'd make some dry comment and have him laughing out loud.

And God, that had been a gift ever since his mother had been diagnosed with breast cancer. Mouse had been a rock. Always doing and saying exactly the right thing. She'd acted as Regine's protector—and his—during the darkest days. Mouse had even run interference for him the day his mother died, dealing with the press while he slipped out the back. He couldn't have faced the jackals that day, and Mouse knew it. He should cut her some slack about all this. She was new to it and she faced a steep learning curve. If only his emotions weren't involved, it would be easy.

"Damn," he groaned, throwing himself into his chair and putting his feet up on the desk.

His mind drifted back to Saturday night. Now *that* had been a good evening. Tor sighed, rubbing his face. If he was truly honest with himself, he'd been drawn to Miss Minnie Squeak because she'd reminded him of Mouse. Of the way he wished Mouse was…sexually submissive.

Tor closed his eyes and let himself remember the way the sub had wiggled on his lap as he spanked her. He pictured Mouse in her place and groaned as his cock rose to attention. He could just imagine pulling that dull brown tweed skirt up to her waist and reddening her ass. Fuck. He set his hand on his cock, rubbing through his pants. Imagining himself buried inside Mouse's tight, wet cunt while she begged her "Master" for more. Begged *him* for more.

He heard the door and opened his eyes. Mouse stood there, her eyes wide and startled as she stared at his crotch.

"Son of a bitch." He kicked his feet off the desk and slid under it to hide his erection from her shocked gaze.

"I… I'm sorry, Tor. Really. I didn't mean…" She started to back out the door.

"Get back in here, Mouse."

"But…"

He waved her apology away. Tor was a little embarrassed, but he wasn't going to apologize for jacking off when he was alone in his office.

"Come in here and sit down. Now."

She did his bidding and looked startled when she sat down without a word of protest. Tor smiled, his cock tingling because of her obedience. It was hot to have her obey him, but… But they had to deal with this thing with his mother and they had to deal with it now. He wasn't going to fight her disapproval for the next six months.

"We need to talk about the club, Mouse."

"Tor, look, I'm sorry. I meant to ask questions and offer suggestions about the business. I wasn't questioning you or your management of the place."

He leaned back. "The business is me. I'm the business."

"This business *isn't* you. It isn't a person. It's a *thing*."

He shook his head. How could he make her understand? "This was my first business right out of college. I had my parents' support and mother helped me with the funding, but it was *my* baby. It rose or fell with my management. *My* efforts. For you to come in here with nothing but disapproval…"

"I don't disapprove of everything."

"No? Just what do you approve of?"

"The location is awesome. I love the way it's decorated. The contemporary design fits the building. The place seems really cutting edge, you know?"

He smiled. "Thanks, but you dislike more than you like."

"Don't you want me to be honest?"

Tor frowned and looked down at his hands. "Yes. Actually I do. There are few enough people I know who'll be honest with me, even when it hurts."

"Well, let me be one of those people." She leaned forward and reached out to touch his hand. "Just because I ask a question or offer a differing opinion doesn't mean I think less of *you*. What I have to say is about the business. Not about you." She pulled her hand away and he wished she hadn't. He met her earnest gaze.

"I get that."

"And I want to be able to share my opinions honestly. I don't want to enforce things because I have controlling interest in this club. I want us to discuss things with one another, and if changes get made, we do it together. With consensus."

"I'm a Dom. I don't do consensus. I do command."

She laughed. "Well, Mister Dom, it's time to learn cooperation. Didn't your mother teach you how to share your toys?"

"I *never* share my toys." Tor grinned wickedly at her, flirting to see how she'd respond.

"Never?" She blushed, but there was definitely awareness there. Awareness of him.

"Well, almost never. But when I own something..."

"Or someone?"

"Or *someone*," he nodded, "then my toy belongs to *me*. And I *don't* share."

Color bloomed in her cheeks and he liked it. He liked the way she responded to his teasing and flirting. God, he wanted her, but he wanted Mouse combined with Miss Squeak's submissiveness. Now that would be the perfect woman for him.

She cleared her throat. "For the next six months, you have to share the club. So let's call a truce. For your sanity and mine."

"All right. But damn it—what kind of agenda did Mother put in motion?"

"Agenda?" Her voice squeaked.

Damn, that was fucking odd. And familiar. But no... He shook his head then turned his gaze on her. "Yes, agenda. What kind of laundry list did she give you?"

"List? I don't know anything about a list." Squeaky again, and he could see by her expression she was lying through her teeth.

"Mouse, if you want me to trust you, then quit lying to me."

She rubbed her hands on her skirt. "Okay."

"Okay, what?"

"She gave me a list. Regine said it was my job to weed out the truths from the lies."

He held out his hand. "Hand it over."

"I don't think I should."

"Damn it, Mouse, did she forbid you to let me see it?"

She tilted her head. Why did he have to love that? It was so...cute. And he hated cute. But he didn't hate Mouse.

"No. She didn't."

"So?" He held out his hand. The command worked. With great reluctance, she reached into her purse and tugged out a sheet of peach paper. His mother's handmade stuff. She held it toward him but then pulled her hand back as he reached for it. "What?"

"I'm going to let you look at it, but then I want it back. *Intact*."

He smiled. She knew him far better than he liked. Even though his mother had written it and he was feeling sentimental about losing her—shit, he missed her like hell—still, he wanted to tear the damn list into tiny pieces.

"All right. You get it back in one piece *after* I read it."

She handed it to him. He skimmed the list and realized that he'd heard all of these from his mother at one time or another.

"So, you're in favor of all of these changes?"

"I don't know yet. I've only been in the club for a couple of hours. Regine told me to read through the list and use my brain to decide whether these things are true or not and if I should push for the changes she listed."

He looked down at the list one last time before returning it to Mouse. "I'll consider some of these. But I'm not going to just do what you tell me because you tell me to."

"I realize that. Although you know I could force the issue if I saw fit."

Tor frowned. "I know that, damn it. Are you going to ram it down my throat?"

"No. I don't operate that way."

"Even if I do, you mean."

"I didn't say it, but if the shoe fits…"

"Wear it."

She nodded.

"Right." He held out his hand to shake. "This is going to be one hell of a roller coaster ride, partner."

She took his hand to shake, grinning. "That's Mistress to you, fella."

"We'll see about that, Mouse." He smiled. "We'll see."

Chapter Four

ꟸ

Tor paced in his office while he waited for Mouse to arrive at the club for the evening crowd. Working closely with her all day already had him on edge. She smelled good, and every time she'd accidently brushed against him, he'd had visions of burying himself inside her. He rubbed his hands over his face. Lock it down. Get under control. He needed to keep himself focused for tonight. They had a large private party scheduled in addition to their usual business, and Mondays tended to be busier than most of the other weekday evenings for them anyway.

It was as if the movers and shakers had a day back at the grind of power so they needed to unwind. Tuesday and Wednesday nights were usually dead and then things picked up Thursday and through Saturday. Or things *had* picked up on the weekend until Unfettered moved into town. He was sure the novelty would wear off for Erotically Bound's regulars, but still he worried. Maybe the club really needed some changes. God, what was he thinking?

He heard the door click and blinked. Mouse looked hot enough to eat. Just a hint of cleavage tantalized him from beneath her black suit jacket. As pulled together as Mouse was, he bet there was a matched set of black lace panties and bra encasing all her lovely flesh. She looked no-nonsense except for the blood-red lips he could imagine wrapped around his cock.

"You're late," Tor growled, trying his best to bring his libido under control.

"Are you always going to say that to me?"

"Only when it's true," His cock had tightened the minute he'd seen her. Damn, that black suit did amazing things for her. She looked all buttoned-up and he wanted to button her down. Right here, right now.

"Down, boy. You don't have to look at me like you wanna kill me, you know?"

"That's not the look I'm giving you. *Believe* me." He laughed drily. Not unless he killed her by fucking her to death, and if he died too… Well, what a way to go. God. He shifted his shoulders to loosen his tense muscles. "Let's go check out the crowd."

"It was already starting to fill up when I came in."

"Good. We could use the business."

"Unfettered causing problems?"

Tor frowned. "It's been quiet here lately, that's all."

"And you haven't been worrying about what might happen when membership renewal comes up?"

He glared at her. "No, I have not."

"Liar." She opened the door. "Let's emerge to greet our guests, *mon cher*."

"If you're not channeling mother, we might need to check for possession."

Mouse grinned. "No worries. I'm not Regine. I could never pull it off."

"You might be surprised, sweetheart."

He took her hand and tucked it into the crook of his arm before leading her out of the office and staff area at the back of the club to where the evening activities were already taking place in the public play area.

He loved the way her eyes widened as they strolled through the club. Tor introduced her to long-time members who relaxed in the main seating area near the front entrance. She sat down with them and began asking them about why they were members. What drew them. At first, several were put off.

"Tell me, young lady, why should I explain anything to you?" Master Marcus, who had held membership since the club opened, asked as he petted the soft hair of the submissive kneeling at his feet.

"Because I'm new to this world and I want to learn. Isn't that the point?"

"No vulgar curiosity?"

"No Sir. When Regine left me her shares in this club, she also tasked me with learning, not judging. That's what I want to do. I want to know what draws people to this life, yes. But even more, I want to know the draw for you of *this* club. Why here instead of another place?"

Master Marcus smiled slightly, surveying her from head to foot as she leaned forward earnestly. The older man glanced at Tor and raised his brows. Mouse looked between them and saw the way Marcus seemed to ask permission. She pressed her lips together and glared. Despite what Mouse thought, Marcus wasn't asking permission to speak freely about the club. No, Marcus was asking if Mouse was taken.

Though he knew he should shake his head, he couldn't help but nod to indicate she was claimed. Marcus sighed and returned his gaze to Mouse.

"Very well, my dear. What would you like to know?"

Tor left them knowing Master Marcus would quietly pass the word to the other Dominants not to approach Mouse with the intent of playing with her. If she played with another Dom or Domme, he wasn't sure he'd be able to handle it. Six years was a long time to wait for someone, but he'd waited. Not patiently, but he'd waited. Oh, he hadn't been celibate by any means, but his few relationships had been light. No commitment right from the start. He glanced over at Mouse and watched as she laughed at something Marcus told her. Shit. Obsession was a bitch.

Tor went to talk to Wade so he could get his mind off Mouse, even if it was only for a little while. He kept his eye on her as Marcus introduced her to other members and she questioned several submissives. A couple of submissives were here solo and she spent a lot of time chatting with them. He watched with pride as she politely asked the permission of the Dominant before questioning a collared submissive. She was learning fast.

"So, Tor, how is Regine's little protégée doing?"

Tor grinned as he turned to face Mistress Zarah. "Very well. I think we might survive the next six months without killing each other."

"In other words, she's remaining mute and letting you do what you want?"

"Hell no." Tor laughed. "She's a fucking pain in the ass."

Zarah raised her brows. "Since when do you enjoy sassy subs?"

"What makes you think she's a sub?"

"The way your mother described her, darling. The perfect assistant. Almost psychic about knowing what Regine needed before she needed it." Zarah turned to look around the room. "If your mother had been the least bi or lesbian, she would have probably taken the girl as a lover."

Tor's gut tightened. "What makes you say that?"

Zarah returned her gaze to his. "Because she adored Mouse."

"Are you sure you're talking about *my* mother?"

"Such a skeptic. Your mother was the most soft-hearted woman on the planet and you know it, Torin Stuart."

Tor grinned at Zarah. Yup, this woman really had known his mother well. Regine had looked like the hardest, toughest bitch ever, but inside she was a marshmallow. Soft and sweet. But someone had to crack the shell to get to the sticky-sweet middle. He wondered if Mouse had ever managed it. Probably…

Tor glanced over, noticing Mouse as she stared, open-mouthed at Master Drago at play. Drago was a law unto himself, but one of the best Dominants Tor had ever seen. He played rough, especially if that's what a sub wanted. And his current playmate liked pain…a lot.

Mouse continued to watch the scene as the sub screamed with the pain being delivered from solid, repeated strikes from a cane. Tor studied Mouse. This wasn't good. Something about the situation upset her. She looked repeatedly at the dungeon monitors as if expecting them to intervene, but there was no reason to. The sub wasn't calling out a safe word, and Drago was laser focused on what the submissive could take. Even so, Mouse's body language screamed at him. Then when she clenched her hands, he knew he needed to act.

"Tor, are you ignoring me?"

"I'm sorry, Zarah. I need to avert disaster."

He was hurting her and no one did anything. *No one.*

"No! Oh God, *no*!" the bound submissive screamed. Mouse flinched as the cane struck against the submissive's quivering buttocks. Where were the monitors? Why weren't they stopping this? Damn it, this is why they were here!

Mouse looked at the nearest big guy dressed in a black t-shirt and black jeans. He had a red scarf tied around his huge biceps to indicate his role as guardian. Some guardian. Utterly useless.

The black-haired master continued to strike the little submissive's ass. Stripes covered the trembling globes, but at least there was no blood. Not yet anyway.

"No… No… *No…*"

As each blow fell, her scream became louder. A *no* for each stroke. Yet everyone watched as if this were no big deal. Just like the way people used to ignore how her grandfather beat her mother. It didn't matter what she screamed or who she went to for help…they ignored her. Deacon Vincent was a good God-fearing man, and if he thought punishment was merited, then it was. Well, fuck that. No one was going to beat someone up while she screamed for help without Mouse doing something about it. Her fists clenched and she took a deep breath. Just as she lifted her foot, she was grabbed from behind.

She struggled as she was tugged away from the scene she'd been watching. Mouse twisted, relaxing only slightly when she realized she was in Tor's grip.

"Let me go," she hissed.

"No. Not until you calm down."

"Why the hell aren't the monitors doing something?"

"Because there's no need."

"She's no match for that huge guy."

"Neither are you." He kept tugging her backward as she fought to move forward.

She pulled out of his arms and whipped around, slapping him hard across the face. "How can you just stand there and leave her to be abused?" Tears streamed down her face and she noticed only as she lifted her throbbing hand to stare at it. She'd hit Tor. Good God, what was the matter with her?

Tor growled and shook his head. "That's it."

He bent and tossed her over his shoulder in a fireman's carry. She fought to get away as she realized he was carrying her to his office. No one stopped them.

Once in the office, he let her down but remained between her and the door. She put her hands on her hips to glare at him.

"What the hell's the matter with you, Tor?"

"The matter with me? Nothing's the matter with me. What's wrong with you?" He rubbed his hands over his face and took a deep breath. "What the hell happened back there?"

She paced back and forth. When he moved in her direction, she whipped around to glare at him. "She was screaming *no* at the top of her lungs. How much clearer did she have to be that she wanted him to stop?"

"In normal circumstances, I completely agree with you. But a BDSM club comes nowhere near normal circumstances." He walked over and gently took her hands to stop her from chafing them against each other.

"Why?"

"First of all, because no submissive would ever use *no* or *stop* as safe words."

Mouse could feel her face heat. Shit. He was right. She didn't want him to be…but he was.

"A submissive wouldn't use them and a Dominant would never allow it."

"Oh."

"Yes, oh. Second of all, never—and I mean *never*—interrupt someone else's scene."

"I thought that's why there are dungeon monitors. If they won't interrupt a scene, of what possible use are they?"

"*You* are not a dungeon monitor."

"So?"

"A DM has had training to handle him or herself. It's something I demand of anyone I hire to handle that job. They need to understand when there's a problem and when there isn't one. A novice should never go blundering into something they don't understand."

"But she was crying." Mouse shivered in memory. "And screaming too."

"I know that. But that particular submissive craves pain. It gets her into subspace and she was really close."

Mouse bit her lip. "It didn't look like that."

"I know. But you don't know her and the DMs who work here do. Take your cue from them. If you don't trust them, come find me."

"But that man was such a brute. He ignored her pleas to stop."

"Because he knows she craves pain. I'm not sure Master Drago even noticed you… Then again, he may have been watching your every move while simultaneously focused on the sub."

"How could he?"

"A top can become hypervigilant…hyperaware. Drago is probably that kind of top. But a Dominant also focuses their attention deeply and profoundly on the submissive. He was judging just how hard to hit her. Whether she was at a point where she wouldn't even think about a safe word anymore… There's so much that was happening that you didn't understand. That's why you should never disrupt a scene."

Mouse dropped into a chair and put her head in her hands. "This is too much for me. I don't know what Regine was thinking." She shook her head as she fought tears again. Her gut was still twisting in the aftermath of what she'd witnessed.

Tor crouched in front of her and took her hands. "Hey. What *really* happened back there?"

"You saw…"

"I saw. But it was more than wanting to pound Drago."

"Shouldn't I want to help someone who needs me?"

"Sure, but this was way more than that and you know it. That was a deep memory for you. What was it, honey?"

Mouse lifted her gaze, surprised to see Tor's eyes soften with concern. She shook her head and tried to pull her hands away, but he didn't let go.

"You were seeing more than what was in front of you. What did you *really* see?"

Mouse closed her eyes while Tor just waited. Could she tell him? It was so dark… Buried so deep…

"It's okay, Mouse. Share it with me and maybe you'll release some of the pain tied to it. Were you in an abusive relationship once?"

She shook her head. Thank God she'd never had a boyfriend who hurt her.

"Was it a friend of yours?"

"Not exactly."

"Who then?"

"My mother."

"What about her?" His question was soft but insistent. "Did your father abuse her?"

"Not exactly. It was my grandfather."

"Your *grandfather*?"

She looked up at the question in his voice and tried to pull away again.

"It doesn't matter. Let me go."

"Not yet. What did your grandfather do?"

"It was my fault. Mine." She tugged her hands away and stood up to walk over to the wall. But he followed, gently pressing her back against the wall with his arms around her.

"What happened?"

"I was five and I was disobedient," she said, and settled into his protective embrace.

"Your mother was living with her parents still?"

Mouse nodded. Those years were awful. She didn't know how she remembered her first five years with such clarity, but she did.

"How old was she?"

"When I was five?"

"Yeah."

"Nineteen."

"She had you at *fourteen*?"

Mouse lifted her gaze, glaring at him. "Yes. But it wasn't her fault. He raped her."

"Who? Your grandfather?"

"No." She shuddered. "The minister. Mama had gone to stay overnight with her best friend. The minister's daughter. When she got up in the middle of the night, he was awake and took her to his bedroom. He raped her."

"Where was his wife?"

"He was a widower."

Tor growled, brushing her cheek with his fingers. "Did the bastard go to jail?"

"No." Mouse snorted. "No one believed my mother. At first they thought she'd been with some boy. Until I looked so much like that horrible man. Then they blamed *her*. Said nasty things. Said she must have seduced him." Her gaze met Tor's. "A fourteen-year-old doesn't seduce a man in his late thirties. My mother was no Lolita."

"So when you were five, what happened?"

"I'd been playing with my ball in the dining room and it got away from me and broke Grandmother's china cabinet."

"So why didn't they spank *you*?"

"They should have. I wish they would have."

"But?" Again he stroked her cheek.

Tor leaned forward and set his forehead against hers and she sighed. "Grandfather said I was too young for a proper beating. So Mother would take my punishment so I'd learn my lesson."

"Oh Mouse, honey. I'm sorry."

"She leaned over the dining room table and they planted me right beside her so I'd have to watch her be beaten and know that I was the reason she was being punished. I'd have to see that, *but for me*, she would've been fine."

"That sucks."

"Yeah. He flipped up her dress and she took down her panties. Then he pulled out a switch and began to whip her." She shuddered. "It was horrible. At first she was silent. She just took it. And that made him mad, so he hit her harder."

"Where was your grandmother?"

"She was holding me…forcing me to witness it because it was Grandmother who had demanded that Mother be punished for *my* sin of disobedience."

"God."

"God had very little to do with it, even if Grandfather was a church deacon."

"Yeah." He brushed a strand of hair off her forehead. "How long did he beat her?"

"Too long. Her buttocks were quivering and she started to cry. But he didn't stop. When the switch started to cut her and she was bleeding, I added my apologies too. Screaming and hoping I could make it stop."

"But it didn't."

"No. Finally I screamed at him and threw myself between the switch and her. I still have the scar on my back."

"Jesus." Tor shook his head and pulled her into his arms, gently cradling her close.

"It ended up being a good thing."

"Did the police arrest them?"

"No, but seeing them abuse me the way they had her made something click. Mama grabbed me and dragged me upstairs even though she could barely walk. She packed some bags and we left her parents' home and never went back."

"Oh Mouse, honey. I'm sorry." He kissed her forehead and she sighed.

"We lived on the streets for a while…until she got a job. Later, when I was ten, she met someone special and they got married. My step-father loves her and their kids. He's a good man."

He tilted his head back to meet her gaze. "So when you saw Drago working over that sub, you remembered your grandfather beating your mother."

Mouse blinked then slowly nodded. "Yes, I guess so."

"No guessing needed. It happened. But you need to learn that a club like this is designed to be a *safe* environment."

"But she said *no,* Tor."

"And no isn't a safe word, remember?" Reluctantly, she nodded. "And one other thing. If you hadn't been living in a past moment, you would have noticed that each time she cried out no it was because he paused." Mouse shook her head. "Oh yes, it was. He'd strike then pause. She'd cry out no and he'd strike again. Then pause."

"But he kept hitting her."

"Yes, because the no meant *please don't stop* and Drago could see that. He understood that because they've played together before."

"Are they a couple?"

"No. I'm not sure he'll ever find a permanent submissive."

"Why?"

"Long story. Suffice it to say, Drago is an excellent top. Careful. Concerned. And completely focused on whatever a submissive needs from him when they're working together. All right?"

Mouse sighed and nodded, sagging into Tor's embrace. "I'm sorry. I just…"

"Didn't understand. Yeah, I know." He brushed her tears away. "So why didn't the other scenes bother you?"

"It was how small the woman was and the way she cried, and yet he just kept hitting her." She shook her head, curving herself against his chest. He stroked her hair and the small of her back soothingly. "Something about the position too…I guess the way she was bent over reminded me of the dining table."

"So the other scenes down there didn't bring this up for you?"

"No. And neither did what I saw at Unfettered. Not really."

"Unfettered?" He continued to stroke the small of her back and she closed her eyes, relaxing into him.

"Yeah, Saturday night. The public stuff seemed fairly mild, I guess."

"Would that be when you wore a gold mask?"

The quiet question brought her out of her calm and she lifted her head to look up at him. Oh no. No. This was just so bad. He didn't look mad. But he didn't look happy either. In fact, she couldn't read him at all.

"Um…why would you think that?"

He tugged her hair out of the bun she'd bound it in and it escaped in kinky waves around her face. His fingers stabbed into her hair, stroking through it as if he loved the texture. She stared up at him, wide-eyed.

"Let's see. Some odd squeaks you made this morning and this hair. And the comment you just made about visiting Unfettered on Saturday night. I'd say—case closed. Wouldn't you?"

"Circumstantial evidence."

"Oh, I don't think so." He cradled her face. "Why did you do it?"

This wasn't going well and she still couldn't tell if he was pissed or not. "I wanted to learn."

"So you picked me?" He stiffened, pulling away from her.

"No. Not exactly."

"Well, what? Exactly?" He put his hands on his hips.

"I didn't know you'd be there until Mistress Zarah looked past me and said you were right on time for once."

"I see." His eyes narrowed. "And if I hadn't pieced this together, would you have ever told me?"

She bit her lip, knowing the answer was no. When she opened her mouth to speak, he withdrew from her—she could almost see it— as he waved her words away.

"Don't lie." He backed toward the door and she felt cold. Alone. Bereft. "You wouldn't have ever told me, would you?"

"Probably not," she whispered.

"I see. Right. I'm glad I was a good fuck and gave you a nice intro to BDSM. I hope you enjoyed it." His face was tight and his eyes were cold as he glared at her.

She reached out toward him but he shook his head. "No. Don't pretend it was important to you."

"But it was."

"Sure it was, Mouse. Sure it was. Look, I've got a business to handle. Get yourself together and come back out."

"But I made an idiot out of myself."

"All the more reason to come back to the party. Once Drago is free, you can apologize to him."

She blanched. "I don't need to do that. Nothing happened."

"Apologize, Mouse. Knowing him, he'll expect it, and if you don't, it will reflect poorly on the club. And that's what this is all about, isn't it? You want the money mother left you." He pulled open the office door and walked out, slamming the door shut behind him.

"Well, fuck," she groaned, falling into a nearby chair.

Tor stood in the hall, taking deep breaths. His fantasy girl on Saturday night had been Mouse. He'd fucked her and it had been…amazing. Just fucking amazing. He groaned as he recalled the experience and his cock stiffened painfully. If he'd known it was her, he would have spent all night enjoying her. Shit.

He sighed. Mouse had been sweet, sexy and so surprised by her reactions that it had been a pleasure to tutor her. He shook his head, wanting to smash his fist into the wall. *Something* about the submissive had reminded him of Mouse, but he dismissed it. Now he wished that he hadn't.

But what good would it have done him to know who she was? While it meant something to *him* to know his submissive lover had been Mouse, it obviously meant nothing to her. If it had been important to her, she would have told him. *Should* have told him. Instead, she played innocent. Pretended that he never put her over his lap to spank her or that he'd never been inside her hot, wet cunt. He growled.

Shit, had she done it just to secure the damn inheritance? He took another deep breath. No. He'd known her for years and that was one thing he knew about her. She might want the inheritance, but he didn't think she'd lie and steal to get it. It just wasn't part of who she was because she could have robbed his mother blind if she'd really been of criminal intent. Instead, she'd been Regine's guardian—standing between his mother and the rest of the world. Especially at the end.

Tor groaned as the prospect of six months of this distance between them suddenly loomed like a hurricane on the horizon. God help him if Mouse took another Dominant as her lover. God help them both.

Chapter Five

ຣ

Mouse was on her way over. *Now* what? Two months of butting heads with her was getting old. Damn old. He glared at her as she approached. For a moment she quailed then a determined expression stiffened her expression and she tilted her chin. Why did she have to be so fucking cute? Life wasn't fair.

"Sir?" A soft melodious voice asked. "Master Torin?"

He blinked and glanced down. Drago was shopping for a new play partner and Torin was serving as an aide de camp. "Yes, Michele?"

"I've been very bad…" she purred. "Please punish me."

He was torn between humor and irritation. The only submissive he'd wanted for two months was the most elusive one alive. Mouse. Celibacy sucked. He couldn't make himself take anyone but Mouse, but he couldn't *have* her.

"Tor, can I talk to you?"

He turned to frown at Mouse. "No." He turned to look back at Michele, but Mouse didn't move. In fact, he could hear her toe start to tap in irritation. He sighed and turned his gaze back to her. "Make it fast."

"I have a suggestion."

"Oh Lord no." he groaned. "Not another one."

"Very funny." She sniffed. "I think it would be a good idea to begin offering classes for our members."

"Classes?"

"Yes. Beginners classes…you know like etiquette."

She nodded and smiled sheepishly at Master Drago. He winked at her. Fuck. Drago winked at his Mouse. He clenched every muscle in his body to keep himself in check. If he launched at Drago, the other man would wipe the floor with him.

"I'll think about it, Mouse."

"And also how-to classes. You know intermediate and advanced level. It's important for new Dominants and submissives to find mentors, and we could facilitate that."

He opened his mouth to tell her no when Drago smiled at her.

"Miss Mouse is very astute, Tor. I've suggested you offer classes in the past, if you'll remember."

Tor clenched his teeth in an approximation of a smile while he fought to stay in control. "I'll consider it. The problem will be finding someone to do the scheduling. It takes a person with knowledge of the lifestyle and the ability to twist arms."

"I can do it," Mouse said.

He glared at her. "It takes someone with a strong will to bring something like this off."

"You don't think I can handle the job?"

"Let's just say, I have concerns." Tor felt like a bastard when her eyes grew moist with unshed tears.

"I'll volunteer to be your first sacrificial lamb, Miss Mouse. I'd be happy to teach a class."

Tor winced when Drago turned his dark eyes toward him. The censure in Drago's gaze hit Tor in the gut. The two men had been friends for years, so disapproval and disappointment from his friend struck Tor hard. He cleared his throat, opening his mouth to speak, but Mouse got in first.

"That would be awesome," Mouse enthused, setting her hand on Drago's muscular forearm. Tor clenched his fists at his side.

"And are you going to be his bottom for this class?" Tor didn't recognize his own voice as jealousy ripped through his gut like a poisoned arrow.

She blinked and looked up at Drago, a little afraid. The two of them had made peace when Mouse had apologized after almost interrupting his scene, but Tor knew the big man still scared her a little. Mouse swallowed hard.

"I guess so," she squeaked. Her eyes flashed up to Drago. Tor came damn close to shouting *no* at the top of his lungs, but he didn't. "Unless Master Drago would rather work with someone else, and I'd understand completely." Mouse finished rapidly, color staining her cheeks.

Drago studied him for a minute or two, and he gave Tor a grim smile before turning back to Mouse. "Miss Mouse, I'd be honored to be the first Dom to lead you through a public scene if you trust me enough."

She smiled shyly at Drago. "I do. Thanks."

Mouse turned a triumphant smile on Tor, and he wanted to kill them both. He'd never learned to share what belonged to him, and Mouse was his. Damn it—she was *his*. The idea of Drago training her in any way, shape or form was impossible, but he didn't have a choice. He'd all but dared her to do this and now that he'd made his bed he'd have to fucking lie in it—even if it was filled with glass.

* * * * *

"It's time, Miss Mouse," one of the staff called through her office door.

She shivered—torn between terror and determination. Drago had been great helping her to plan this class, but he still intimidated her. He was just so big…six foot four and ripped muscles from top to bottom. Of course he wasn't all bulked up like Arnold Schwarzenegger, but he still felt massive to her. Maybe it was just his presence that filled the space wherever he was. Maybe it was the dark hair and unfathomable dark eyes. Whatever it was, she didn't *quite* trust him. Didn't *quite* feel safe. Yet she knew he would never hurt her. Knew it gut-deep. So what the hell was her problem? Her problem was that she'd rather have Tor. She sighed.

Not only that, but she was scared. Scared of Drago. Scared of putting herself out in public. But Tor had thrown down the challenge and she was damned if she wouldn't face him down. She straightened and marched to the door as if she were headed for her own firing squad. Scared or not, she *would* do this.

* * * * *

Tor tensed when Mouse appeared. He'd been hoping…praying that she would cancel. He didn't want to watch her with Drago, but he had no intention of leaving. He wasn't completely certain that she could handle the stern man, and Masters rarely let their submissive play with someone without supervising, at least this one didn't. Although he hadn't admitted it to her, Tor felt as if he were Mouse's Master.

She strode forward to stand beside Drago. Gingerly, she knelt on the pillow he'd placed by his feet and bowed her head. The big man caressed her hair, which hung loose and wild, then he met Tor's gaze. When Tor just matched his stare, Drago nodded once and began the class.

"Good evening, everyone, and welcome. Tonight's class will cover introducing a novice to the BDSM lifestyle and public scenes. I am Master Drago and my submissive this evening is Mouse." He eyed the audience. "She is new to this lifestyle and newbie submissives need to be protected by those of us with experience. Teaching you about that will be one of the goals of this class."

As Drago continued to outline the goals of the class, the females in the audience—and a few males—sighed as he spoke. If Mouse weren't involved, Tor would grin at the way his friend could sway his audience using only his deep voice. But Tor's concern right now was Mouse and she looked tense.

His gut tightened when she looked up once to meet his gaze before quickly looking back at Drago's feet. Fear. He saw fear in her eyes. It tore him up because this whole damn thing was his fault, but unless she safe worded, he couldn't intervene. God damn it.

Tor barely heard Drago's words as he watched the scene unfold because his attention was devoted entirely to Mouse. When her ass was shown off to the crowd so Drago could explain where it was appropriate to deliver blows and where it wasn't, Mouse went a brilliant red.

He loved her ass, but he knew she had some body image issues, so this had to be torture for her. Tor was torn between admiration for her strong spirit and a desire to cover her until she was truly ready for this kind of play. Drago assisted her onto a spanking bench and bound her then set his hand on the small of her back. She flinched. Her buttocks clenched in anticipation of blows soon to be delivered as the Dominant described proper spanking technique before delivering blows to her ass. She jumped with every blow but remained silent.

Shit, this wasn't right. With him, she'd relaxed into the spanking and eventually lifted her ass for more. With Drago, nothing. She just knelt on the padded bench…waiting. Why the hell didn't she safe word? When the master picked up a large leather paddle, Tor's gut tightened. She couldn't handle that. Not now. Her endorphins hadn't kicked in and she wasn't enjoying this at all. Fuck.

As Drago drew back, the world seemed to flow into slow motion. He saw the paddle swing forward to connect with Mouse's quivering buttocks, and for the first time since this started, she made a noise.

"Oh God," she squeaked.

Tor closed his eyes briefly, opening them when Drago asked, "Are you all right, Mouse?" She nodded vigorously. "Are you ready to continue?" Again she nodded.

Another blow fell. Another gasping squeak. Again Drago checked on her and had her consent to continue. Tor grabbed the chair he leaned against, but holding onto it wasn't enough truly to anchor him because he desperately wanted to stop this. But it was *her* choice. Submissives gave their trust and consent to a top, and Mouse indicated she wanted to continue. Another blow. This time he heard a sob. Shit.

Safe word, Mouse. Please, honey. It's okay. He wished he had the right—the privilege—to protect her. Wished he hadn't been such a fucking asshole two months ago. She lifted her head and her hair fell away from her red, tear-streaked face. Her eyes destroyed him. Accused him. She glared at him as if to say *See? I can do this! I'm worthy, you son of a bitch.*

Clarity struck him straight in the chest. She was doing this solely to prove him wrong, and that was a bullshit lousy reason to let someone beat her ass. Not when she wasn't into it. Another blow fell against her ass and she continued to glare at him as the tears streaked her face and she bit her lip to endure the pain.

Tor knew that nothing would induce her to stop now. She wouldn't safe word even if Drago took a whip to her. He might not have the right as her Master to stop this, but as a dungeon monitor he fucking did and this was done. Right now.

As the next blow fell, he stepped in front of it, taking it in the gut. Drago raised his brows and straightened.

"Would you care to explain why you disrupted a scene between a Dominant and a submissive? You know that's against the rules."

Tor took a deep breath. He set his hand gently at the base of her spine and she relaxed for the first time since she'd marched out here. "This submissive is refusing to safe word and it's my fault."

"You think she'd safe word if you weren't here?"

"Yes. She's not into this at all. You can see the tension in every line of her body."

"Are you suggesting I'm abusing her without her consent?"

"No. You have her consent, but she doesn't know what she's doing right now."

"She's not in subspace, so she's completely cognizant of her surroundings."

"I agree that she's not in subspace, but her reasoning is gone because she's out to prove she can endure this."

"Prove it to whom?"

"Me. 'Cause I've been a fucking asshole. I'm stopping this now."

"By what authority?"

"First as dungeon monitor…" He paused and looked at Mouse's red ass. He brought her skirt down to cover her butt. "And second as her Master. *If* she'll have me."

Drago's brows rose, but he smiled slightly. "I recognize your authority…in *both* roles. Let's cut her loose."

The crowd began to murmur, moving around as if to break up. Drago stood, glaring at them all and they froze. "This class is *not* finished. Remain seated while we take care of Miss Mouse."

Tor released her hands while Drago took care of her feet. Tor helped her stand and she almost fell, leaning heavily on him. He pulled her close as Drago wrapped a soft blanket around her then Tor led her away.

Mouse leaned against Tor and sighed as he helped her walk away from the public play area.

"I could have done it," she whispered.

"You did it, Mouse," he murmured in her ear. "And you don't have to prove anything to me. I'm sorry I made you think you did."

She glanced up at him as he helped her into his office and shut the door. He looked grim. Had she pissed him off…again? He tugged her gently toward a low, white leather couch that ran the length of one wall of his office. He eased her down onto the sofa, but the minute her butt hit the leather she whimpered and struggled to her feet. He frowned.

"What?" he asked. She grimaced and he nodded, his expression lightening somewhat. "It hurts too much to sit?" She nodded, rubbing her sore ass. "C'mon over here." He waved her over to his desk. He reached into his drawer.

"No more paddling please."

"None planned." He pulled out a tube of something. "This should take some of the sting out. Bend over, honey."

Mouse bent over and put her hands on his desk for balance. He walked behind her and flipped up her skirt. She stood, whipping her skirt back down. Tor raised his brows.

"Honey, your gorgeous ass was just on display to nearly all our members and I was there. Remember? I've seen your ass before." He leaned forward to kiss the tip of her nose. "Hell, I spanked it not that long ago."

Her face heated. "I know, but…"

"Let me take care of you." He cupped her face in his big hands. "Please, Mouse."

She took a deep breath, reading his expression. The entreaty in his eyes made her blink back tears and she nodded.

"Turn around and bend over again then I'll rub some of this on you. It should help ease the pain."

She obeyed, wincing when he lifted her skirt. He gently slathered ointment on her butt cheeks. First it was cool, and then the sting started to numb out. She sighed with relief.

"Why didn't you safe word?"

She frowned and remained silent while he continued gently to massage the ointment over her ass. Damn, even with the numbing effect of the lotion, her pussy began to respond to his touch. Shit. Why did it always happen anytime they were in proximity? It wasn't fair.

"*Mouse…*"

"I don't owe you any explanations."

"That's open to debate. But rather than declaring war on one another, I'm asking and I'd really like an answer."

She sighed and stood up, turning to face him. Mouse lifted her chin to glare up at him. "Because I wanted you to know I could do it. Okay?"

"It's not okay because I never want you to feel like you have to prove anything to me. I believe in you. Even when you piss me the hell off."

"You do?" She turned her gaze back to his.

"Yes, I do."

He closed the distance between them, pulling her into his arms, a warm and tender expression on his face. Mouse had caught the expression a couple of times during Regine's last days. When he wasn't on guard. When he thought no one was looking. The look was love. He couldn't be looking at *her* like that.

"I've spent the last two months behaving like a bastard."

"Yes, you have."

He laughed at her quick agreement then grew serious again. "Did you ever wonder why?"

She shrugged. "I challenged you about how to run this club."

"Nope. None of that mattered to me, honey. Well," he paused, "at first it did. But not later. I acted like an ass because you hurt me and I refused to tell you."

"Hurt you? How did I do that?"

"Because if I hadn't guessed that we'd been lovers, you never would have told me."

"I figured you'd prefer it that way."

"Well, you were wrong."

He dipped his head and gently took her mouth with his. Her arms snaked up along his shoulders and her fingers curled into his thick ginger hair. Their tongues twined together. Learning each other as they hadn't done two months ago. She loved the way he delved into her as if he owned her. As if he never wanted to let her go. When he lifted his head, she clung to him and Tor smiled.

"I like that."

"What?"

"That you don't want to let me go because I feel the same way." He traced his fingertips across her brow and over her cheek.

"You do?" She closed her eyes when her voice came out in a squeak.

"Yes. And, damn, I love that little squeak." She chuckled, dropping her gaze from his. "Would you come home with me tonight, Mouse?"

"You mean like…sleeping over?"

"No, not sleeping over because we won't be making popcorn and watching movies."

"I *know* that." She slapped his shoulder, laughing.

"Well?"

She nodded.

"I need to hear it."

"You mean you need my verbal consent?"

"Yeah."

"Okay." She took a deep breath. "Yes, Torin Stuart, I'll spend the night with you."

Chapter Six

ꟸ

When Tor drove through the automatic gates and up the curving drive in front of Regine's Georgetown mansion overlooking the Potomac River, Mouse felt as if she was coming home. She'd always loved this place.

"Are you living here now?" she asked as he parked.

"Yeah, I moved back because I couldn't imagine selling it. I grew up here. I've made a few changes, but it'll still look familiar.

Mouse stayed in the warm car while Tor came around to open her door. He held out his hand to help her out of the low-slung vehicle, and she laughed as he tugged her into his arms for a kiss. His arms enveloped her and she relaxed into his embrace. This felt like coming home too.

Reluctantly, he released her. "Let's go inside where it's warm." He held her hand and led her to the front door, which opened as soon as they reached it.

"Good evening, Mister Torin."

Tor shook his head. "Didn't I give you the evening off, Simon?"

"I was in the kitchen when the gate opened." The butler shrugged then smiled at Mouse. "Good evening, Miss Mozelle. It's a pleasure to see you again."

"Thanks." Mouse blushed as she saw the approval in Simon's eyes.

"You can go to your apartment, Simon. We'll be fine on our own."

The older man's eyes went from Mouse to Tor and back again then he smiled. "Very well. Have a pleasant evening."

Once the butler was out of sight, Tor signaled for her to turn around. "I'll take your coat."

She let him ease the coat off and hang it in the coat closet near the door.

"You look stunning, honey." Her face heated as his eyes surveyed her, noting her bare shoulders and short skirt. "I love your curves." She shrugged and he moved in close, tipping up her chin so she was forced to meet his gaze. "I think you're gorgeous just the way you are. Beautiful and sexy."

"If you say so…"

"I do." He took her hand again. "C'mon, let's go up to my suite."

The space was huge, with large, east-facing windows. In the distance, the Capitol building glowed, dominating the city.

"Wow. What a view."

"Yes, it is," he murmured, coming up behind to nibble on her neck.

Mouse shivered but leaned back against him, tilting her head so he could reach her more easily. His warm hands curled around her shoulders while his breath tickled her and his lips sent chills up her spine.

"Oh Tor…"

"What, honey?" He nipped her earlobe and Mouse sighed.

"That feels good."

He chuckled. "That's the plan. I want you to feel very good."

Tor gently turned her around to face him. "How does your ass feel?"

She laughed. "Much better, thanks."

"Still sore?"

"A little."

"So no spanking—*tonight*—but that still leaves us a lot of play possibilities if you're up for it."

"I'd like that."

He dipped his head to take her mouth in a kiss. Mouse wrapped her arms around his lean waist, opening for his kiss. Their tongues tasting and twining. This was what she'd wanted from the moment they'd met.

Mouse reached up to unbutton his shirt. Teasing the buttons open one by one. As each opened, it revealed more of his muscled body, so she followed her fingers with her mouth, licking his warm skin. She smiled when he groaned and his fingers wound into her hair, encouraging her.

"Do I have permission to continue, Sir?"

"Hell yeah," he groaned.

She chuckled. Kneeling in front of him, she tugged his shirt from his pants and finished unbuttoning it. He peeled the shirt off and dropped it beside her. Their eyes connected and the fire in his blue eyes made her gasp, her pussy dampening.

Mouse unfastened his belt then slowly lowered the zipper of his pants. She took his erection in her hand with a sigh. A pearly drop of pre-come coated the tip of his long, thick cock, so she stretched up to run her tongue over him. He threw his head back with another groan.

"God, that feels good, Mouse."

"I'm glad," she purred. "I want to give you pleasure, Sir."

"You're succeeding brilliantly."

She licked the head of his cock, swirling her tongue around the straining knob. From the first moment they met she'd wanted to suck him. Having him in her mouth was so much better than her fantasies. Mouse cupped his balls and stroked him while she sucked his cock, watching his reactions. Every time he shuddered… Every groan he made combined to give her a sense of power unlike anything she'd ever felt before. And a sense of purpose too.

He gently pulled back, stopping her so she frowned.

"Aren't I doing it right?"

Tor smiled. "Honey, if you did it any more right, I'd come all over you."

"I might like that."

"So would I, but we've got a long night to enjoy, and I don't want this to go too fast." He held out his hand and she took it. "Stand up." She followed his orders, staring up at him. Mesmerized by the command in every line of his face. "Now turn around and watch us in the mirror across the room."

She faced away and found them reflected in an old-fashioned standing mirror. Tor lowered her zipper then stepped close so she could feel his body heat pressed against her. He let her dress drop to the floor.

"Reach down. Push your panties off and shimmy out of them."

Mouse did as directed while he continued to tease and torment her tight nipples. The panties fell to the floor at her feet so she stood in nothing but her high heels.

"Step out of your dress and panties then kick them to the side."

Mouse took a gasping breath but followed his orders again.

He groaned in her ear. "You are so fucking hot."

"Really?"

"Really. Now take a wider stance then lean back against me again."

When she obeyed, he sighed. "Beautiful. Your hard little clit is peeking out at me from between your swollen cunt lips." He reached one hand down to flick at her clit.

"Oh Tor…"

"You like that?"

"Yes…"

Her eyes fluttered closed as he continued to tease her—stroking her clit and pinching her nipple. Mouse spread her feet farther apart. His forefinger rolled over her clit as if it were a perfect pink pearl inside an oyster.

"Oh…that feels so good. Please don't stop." She sighed at his deep-throated chuckle.

With his other hand, he palmed her breasts, pinching first one nipple then the other. She gasped when he cupped her pussy and one of his fingers slipped inside her. Teasing in and out, making her hips roll in response.

Mouse grasped his thighs. Holding tight to keep from collapsing in a heap. The crisp hair on his chest teased her back while he pressed his hard cock against the small of her back.

She whimpered when he slid a second finger inside her wet pussy while he continued to stroke her clit with his thumb.

"Oh yes. Please…"

"Do you want to come?"

"Yes, Master. Please can I come?" His hands paused on her and her eyes fluttered open to meet his gaze in the mirror. Her breaths rushing out in gasps.

Tor lifted his hand from her breast to cup her chin, turning her head gently he took her lips with his. She opened for him, soft cries escaping into his mouth. With his other hand, he intensified his stroking of her pussy. Three fingers plunged in and out while he kept up a steady pressure on her quivering clit. Tweaking it, stroking it. Her clit tightened painfully and she thrust into his hands.

"Oh God, yes. Please, Master… Please don't stop."

Tor growled, nipping at her lips. Her belly fluttered. She thrust her pussy onto his fingers, twisting her hips while she sobbed against his mouth.

"Come for me, honey. Let go."

She cried out as waves of pleasure hit her body. Her nipples tightened painfully as she shuddered. He continued to pump his fingers, drawing out her pleasure while she clung to him. Finally, he eased off, his touch growing gentler. She turned her face toward his neck. She sighed happily when he rubbed his chin against her forehead.

"That was a lovely sight. Watching you lose yourself in my touch."

"I'm glad it pleased you." She kissed his neck, resting against him in the afterglow.

"It did." He cradled her close. "Mouse, did you mean it?"

"Mean what?" She lifted her gaze to his.

"You called me Master." His voice was soft, caressing her, but her face heated. She knew that calling him her master was a big deal. When she met his gaze, he looked so very serious.

"I'm sorry." She started to pull away, but before she could, her feet tangled up in her dress and she started to fall off her heels. He caught her and eased her onto the bed, following her down. He trapped her under his weight and grasped her wrists, lifting them above her head to hold them in place. She stared at him, tears gathering in her eyes.

"Why apologize?"

"I know it's important when a submissive calls a Dominant her Master. I shouldn't have done it without being invited." She looked away, taking a deep breath and blinking tears away…unsuccessfully.

Tor pressed a kiss to her cheek then lifted his head. "Mouse, look at me."

Reluctantly, she met his gaze again. "Yes?"

"When we were at the club and I interrupted your scene with Drago, do you remember what he asked me?"

"What authority granted you the right to intervene."

"And what was my answer?"

Mouse stared up into his blue eyes and racked her brain. She hadn't really been thinking too clearly just then. "Um…"

She frowned. What had he said? Then she blinked as it clicked in her brain. "That you were my Master?"

"That I was your Master…*if* you'd have me."

"Oh." She blinked as tears slipped out of the corners of her eyes. "Oh my."

"The submissive chooses who to give herself to, and I'd very much like you to give yourself to me. But it's ultimately up to you, Mouse."

"You really want me?"

"Very much. If you want me too, because it's a big commitment."

"Why?"

"Because I want you to wear my collar."

She shifted her hands and realized he still held them against the bed. He released her and she wrapped her arms around him to hold him close, pressing a soft kiss against his lips.

"Is that a yes?" He smiled down at her, the corners of his eyes crinkling in the sexy way they always did when he laughed.

"Uh-huh," she nodded, tracing the dimple in his cheek with her finger. "I'd like nothing better."

"Good."

He laughed and covered her face with kisses, kissing away her tears, making her giggle. His eyes darkened as he looked down at her breasts.

"Mine. All mine."

"And you don't share your toys," she teased.

"No, I don't. Not ever."

She ran her fingers along his strong jaw. He could be so pugnacious sometimes. Argumentative even. But then there were times like right now, when he was gentle. Loving. She traced his lips, smiling when he nipped her fingertips.

Mouse arched in his arms, feeling a different kind of power exchange when he groaned as she teased his bare chest with her tight nipples. She felt as if she were in control of him...for just a moment. Then he reasserted himself by cupping her ass in one hand and cradling her breast with the other. He dipped his head to run his tongue along the edge of her areola. She sighed, closing her eyes. Giving herself into his keeping, certain that he'd protect her. Care for her. She felt truly safe for the first time in...years.

"I want to feel you inside me." He raised his brows and waited. For a minute she didn't know what he was waiting for, but then she understood. It was all about consent and making a request. She smiled up at him. "*Please* make love to me, Master. Please fill me with your hard cock now that we *both* know who we're making love to."

"I think I can grant that request and happily too." His face relaxed and he returned her smile. She loved the way his gaze lingered on her body and hunger filled his eyes. "And I think we'll start with binding you." He kissed her neck, his breath teasing her ear. She shivered. "Does that work for you, Mouse?"

"Yes, Master. I think that would be wonderful."

"Yeah, so do I." Tor grinned.

Chapter Seven

ꙮ

He'd been in committed relationships with submissives in the past, but he'd never given his collar to anyone before because it had never felt right. But this was. Tor studied her wide eyes. He could see that Mouse didn't realize how seriously he viewed her acceptance of his collar, but she'd learn. *Tonight.* He loved this woman and he wanted to spend the rest of the night showing her that love before he finally whispered it in her ear when they were both sated and exhausted. Then he wanted to spend the rest of his life loving and protecting her.

Tor leaned back, releasing her arms. She began to sit up with him, but he gave her a look, which she read correctly, lying down again. He winked at her. How thoroughly should he tie her? Would she accept being bound tightly? Lovingly? Then he remembered her fascination with the *Kinbaku* rope bondage expert Mistress Kimika. Bondage would please Mouse as much as it did him. Tor studied her from the tip of her wild curls to the bottom of her soft feet.

"What's wrong?" she asked, folding her arms over her chest and pressing her legs together. She was withdrawing, almost as if she thought there was a problem with *her*. Time for a little honesty.

"I'm considering the best way for our night to continue and how much binding to use on you."

"How much binding?" She tilted her head. "You mean you'd do more than just tie me to the bed?"

"Much more, if you'll let me."

"Are you talking about...um...*Shibari*?" Her face colored. She licked her lips, pressing her thighs together.

"In *Kinbaku*, it's the journey as much as the destination that's important."

"*Kinbaku*?"

"The traditional term for *Shibari*. And it's the tying that's the seduction."

She looked up at him, rubbing her thighs together again. "Is it?"

Tor swallowed, his cock tightening with anticipation. "Yes." He leaned forward to trace his thumb along her cheekbone. Her eyes were wide but trusting, and few things were as sexy to him as the trust of a submissive. *His* submissive. "You really are beautiful, you know?" he murmured.

"You don't have to say that."

He met her gaze again. "No, I don't. I'm saying it because I mean it." He leaned down and brushed her lips with his. When she attempted to deepen the kiss, he lifted his head.

"Now what should you say if you want to stop?"

"Red."

He nodded. "And if you're uncomfortable or uncertain?"

"Yellow."

"Correct. Are you certain you want to continue, Mouse? You'll let me bind you?"

Now was the moment of truth. Would she go forward? She bit her lower lip and stared at him. Considering him. He wanted to touch her. Caress her. But this decision had to be all hers. He wouldn't coerce her in any way—not even with her own desire—or his.

"Yes, Master. I want this. I trust you."

"Thank you, sweetheart," he whispered, his voice rough with emotion. "Let me find us some rope."

She nodded. His stomach twisted as her trust radiated from her. God, she *was* beautiful like this, and every time he looked at her, she grew lovelier.

Mouse watched him clear the floor of their clothes and enter his large closet. She licked her dry lips as she listened to him move things around.

He made several trips to the bed, leaving lengths of rope secured by something looking like a chain stitch and a pair of safety shears. He crossed the room to a small refrigerator and brought back two bottles of water. He handed her one.

"Drink some of this." She took it and looked at him. "You need to stay hydrated. Drink." Mouse opened the bottle and drank some of the water. "Now stand up beside the bed." He held out his hand and she took it, smiling as he helped her stand.

Mouse contemplated the possibilities. She should be scared, but instead her clit started to throb as she grew moist.

"This is turning me on," she whispered, surprised. Just thinking about it aroused her. She could only imagine how incredible it would be when he'd finished tying her.

"I know." He caressed her briefly. "We'll start with something fairly simple tonight."

He walked to the side of the room to kick off his shoes and socks then peeled off his pants before returning to her. He was hot—as hot as she'd imagined. His wide shoulders and narrowed hips were knit together with firm muscles which were lightly covered with ginger hair. Mouse longed to run her fingers over him…from head to foot. But she didn't, instead waiting for his orders.

Tor picked one of the ropes from the bed, loosening the chain stitch that kept it looped together then he took a slow deep breath. Closing his eyes, he ran the entire length of the rope through his fingers and then he turned the rope over and went back in the other direction before slowly opening his eyes. Something about him had changed. His focus had narrowed on her, putting him utterly in the moment. His gaze struck her to the core, making butterflies collide in her tummy and her nipples tighten.

"Come here, Mouse."

Her breath hitched at the command in his tone. Without a word of dissent or sass, she approached. He brought the rope over her head so it lay against her chest like a very long necklace. She looked up at him.

"Are you ready, love?" he asked.

"Yes, Master."

"If you change your mind, use your safe word."

"I understand. May I caress you while you tie me?"

"Not tonight. I need to concentrate."

Mouse nodded. If she couldn't touch him, at least she could look at him and feel his fingers as they manipulated the rope against her skin. He stared at the rope where it rested along her breastbone.

"I'm going to tie a series of knots down the rope."

"Pearls?"

"Yes. Very good."

She dropped her gaze, only for it to be captured by Tor's impressive erection. While she stared at his cock, he reached forward and took the rope in his hands. He created one knot at her breast bone just slightly above her breasts. As the rope slid along her skin, she shivered. It was soft, caressing her as it moved. He tied another knot just below her breasts then another high on her abdomen and one low on her belly. Each touch of his fingers or the rope teased her. Sensitized her, so she was almost painfully aware of him. The rope now hung down along the center line of her body in front of her.

"Now we reach a special knot," he purred.

He crouched in front of her with his hard cock straining upward along his abdomen. She wanted to suck him so badly, but her only task right now was to obey, so her hunger remained unanswered, her clit swollen and throbbing. Tor looked up at her and their gazes locked. He grinned.

"I think you'll like this one…at least at first."

He took the two strands of loose rope in his fingers, pulling it against her. His fingers slid between her pussy lips, pinpointing her clit. She jumped at his touch then he rubbed the hard nub lightly, making her squirm and her pussy dampen. He withdrew his touch, tying a knot before he drew the rope between her thighs.

"Widen your stance."

She obeyed, still watching him. He pulled the rope up in back so it was drawn between her swollen pussy lips in front and between her ass cheeks in back. The knot he'd tied rode just above her clit. She might survive it if she didn't move too much.

"That doesn't look quite right." He parted her labia so he could see where the knot fell, making her face flame. Tor's stare made her feel naughty…sexy. His brow crinkled as he studied the knot's placement. "Nope. It's a little high, isn't it, sweetheart?"

"No, it's fine."

He glanced up at her, grinning. "Oh no, Mouse. I'm not going to let you off easy on this one. I want you wriggling every time that knot presses against your clit."

"If you move the knot, I'll be wriggling nonstop."

"Exactly." He eased the knot enough so he could slide it. "Reach behind you and hold the rope for me while I adjust this."

"Yes, Master."

He chuckled when she sighed. The rat. Yet, as the knot pressed tight to her engorged clit, Mouse shuddered. God, it felt good. The adjustment he made to the placement of the knot had her longing to reach down and move it. The pressure was constant, making her breath quicken.

"Very nice. Now turn around." Mouse obeyed, releasing the rope when he took it out of her hands. "Pull your ass cheeks apart." She gasped but complied. Her face heated as she imagined how she looked to him while he surveyed her ass. The swipe of his finger against her tight asshole made her jump again, emitting a little squeak. He laughed and stroked her again. This time she didn't jump. Instead she bit her lip, closing her eyes as he gently caressed her. She pushed back toward his probing finger, yearning for penetration.

"Yeah, you like that. Don't you, sweetheart?"

"Yes, Master," she murmured.

She continued to spread her buttocks, wondering what the hell he was up to when his touch was withdrawn. The rope pulled tighter again and she gasped. He stood up behind her, pulling the rope up along her crack. She groaned. There was a knot in the rope pressing against the tight bud of her asshole. Mouse shifted, wanting to move the tormenting rope. Even a little bit. But he read her like a book.

"Stay still, Mouse." She obeyed, letting go of her ass. "Did I give you permission to let go?" His voice was soft, but there was a hint of stern menace that sent a shiver of excitement curling through her.

"I'm sorry, Master." She reached behind her to part her buttocks again, waiting for his next play.

His fingers brushed the base of her spine and she couldn't suppress her whimper. Then she felt his breath against her shoulder. He tied another knot, this one rested against the sensitive curve of her lower back. His fingers brushed mid-back as he tied another knot then he drew the ropes upward and connected them with the rope resting at the back of her neck before tying a final knot. Tor pressed closer until she felt the moist tip of his cock brush her ass, resting between her buttocks. She sighed, leaning back against him, enjoying the feel of his chest hair teasing her shoulder blades. Mouse pressed her ass against him so his cock rode along the crack, using the knot to tease him too. What was sauce for the goose was definitely sauce for the gander.

He groaned softly in her ear. "You may let go of your ass now, pet."

She obeyed, continuing her slow tease. He set his hands on her shoulders and leaned forward, his lips trailing along the side of her neck. Her breath hitched as she tilted her head to allow him better access. Her eyes drifted closed. She'd never been more present with a lover…or more aroused. It was as if he knew just what to do to tighten the coils of her arousal. He moved with her and she sighed as his cock rode up and down between her buttocks.

"How do you feel, Mouse?" His soft question brought forth only a wordless moan. "No, sweetheart. Words. How do you feel right now?"

"Turned-on."

He chuckled. "I'd guessed that. What about this turns you on?"

She forced her eyes open as his hands lightly stroked down her arms then back up to her shoulders. "The way you've focused on me. Like I'm the center of your world."

"You are."

She pursed her lips, fighting the desire to say, "Yeah, sure I am."

"Mouse, turn around and look at me."

Reluctantly, she turned around to meet his gaze, wiggling as the knots teased her clit and ass. She blinked as she met his gaze, reading absolute sincerity. He meant what he'd said.

"You really feel that way?"

"Yes, pet. I do."

He lowered his head, taking her lips. She opened for him. Allowing him inside. His tongue twined with hers. Tasting her. Teasing her. Then he lifted his head, lightly biting her bottom lip. Tugging just to the edge of pain before releasing her.

"Open your eyes, Mouse."

Only then did she realize that she'd left her eyes closed. She had to force her eyelids to open. But when she did, it was worth the effort. His expression was gentle. Loving. As if she was the most precious thing on earth. As if she was his most prized possession.

He lightly trailed his fingers along her cheekbone. "You're lovely…and you're mine," he breathed. Mouse smiled.

"Yes, I am."

He reached behind her to catch the strands of rope he'd left hanging from the knot. Tor carefully checked to make sure there was play in the rope running vertically along her body. Evidently he was satisfied.

"Are you ready to continue?"

"Yes, Master."

"Good. So am I."

He pulled the separate strands of rope under her arms, running first one line and then the other through the vertical strands of rope between the pearls above and below her breasts. As he pulled the ropes through, the vertical strands parted to form a diamond.

"Turn around."

She obeyed and he did the same along her back. He directed her to turn to the front again. Once more, he pulled the rope between the pearls, only this time it was between the knot under her breasts and the one along her upper abdomen. Again he turned her, running the individual strands between the vertical ropes along her back. She sighed when he rotated her to the front. The slow rhythm of the tying hypnotized her and she swayed slightly, loving the way the rope enfolded her body. It was like a hug. A hug that encompassed every inch of her torso. Finally, he turned her to face him once more, pulling the ropes through the knots between her upper and lower abdomen. Then he tied off the harness.

Mouse looked up at him. "Are we done?"

"No, sweetheart. Not yet. But we're going to pause for a moment so I can do this…"

He gathered her into his arms, using the extra rope he held to tug her close. She loved being controlled this way, sighing as he wrapped his arms around her. The extra length of rope in his hands brushed against her buttocks and legs. Teasing her senses. Tor dipped his head and took her mouth.

When he kissed her, she felt…safe. Protected…owned. She lifted her arms to his shoulders to clutch him. She wanted them to merge. Become one. But she didn't know how.

With his tongue, he teased her lips apart. Their breaths mingled and combined, beginning the process she longed for. Mouse breathed him in, sharing her breath with him. Tor nipped her lower lip gently before dipping his tongue into her open mouth. She met his kiss with enthusiasm and hunger, groaning when he twined his tongue around hers.

Reluctantly, Tor lifted his head. She tried to prolong the kiss, but he stopped her, smiling when she looked surprised. Mouse was so incredibly beautiful wrapped in his ropes. For the first time in his life, he knew what it felt like to truly *own* his submissive. Other dominants had told him he'd never forget his first time, but he hadn't believed them. They were right about the intensity of it. However, he knew that for him there wouldn't be a second time…or a third. There would only be this time with this one woman whom he'd waited his whole damn life for. Tor wanted this night to live in her memory forever as their *real* first time together.

"You look so serious," she murmured, tracing his jaw with her small fingertip.

"I want tonight to be wonderful for you, Mouse."

She tilted her head. "It is—just because I'm with *you*. Don't put so much pressure on yourself, Master."

He chuckled. "Hey, I'm supposed to take care of *you*."

"It's mutual, and I like it that way."

"Me too." He laughed because he realized it was the truth.

Tor cupped her soft breast, smiling as she shivered and arched into his touch. He rolled her nipple between his thumb and forefinger, pinching gently. She moaned, licking her lips, and he increased the pressure slightly.

"Oh yes," she groaned.

She lifted her leg along his thigh. He caught it in his free hand, reinforcing his control by refusing to let her tempt him to fuck her right now. He held her leg tight against his thigh. She canted her hips closer to his straining erection, but he didn't let her connect. He was in control here and he hadn't finished her bondage yet. Tor wanted her entirely under his control before he let himself finally penetrate her tight cunt.

He released her nipple and she sighed, opening her eyes to stare up at him. Tor smiled, trailing his fingers to her other breast. Mouse wordlessly arched toward him, silently begging for him to tease the nipple he hadn't previously caressed. Instead, he brushed his fingers over her rib cage and down to her belly. She gasped, lifting her pelvis toward his roving hand. He ignored the invitation by continuing downward, skirting her quivering and swollen clit in favor of her sensitive inner thighs.

"Please…" Her soft sob tightened his cock.

So responsive to him. God, he loved the way she moved. The way she begged. She *was* the right woman for him…the right submissive. He couldn't ask for more.

Chapter Eight

ഗ

Mouse sighed when he stepped back. She wanted to follow him, but his expression told her to stay right where she was, so she waited.

"Climb up on the bed, sweetheart."

She scrambled up, hoping that he'd climb on with her and slide into her wet cunt. Instead, he surveyed her for a moment before picking up another rope. She swallowed as she realized he wasn't done with her yet. Oh God, what did he have in mind?

"Sit facing me."

She obeyed. As she moved, she was forcibly reminded of the knots he'd tied in the rope. The pearl resting against her clit rubbed while the knot between her butt cheeks pressed against her asshole. Both knots teased her. Heating her body… Making her belly tighten as she fought against losing herself in the pressure and the pleasure.

"Now, bend your knees and bring your legs up—bend them toward your chest."

She drew her legs directly toward her, leaning her forearms on her knees. She shivered as the change in position tightened the rope, drawing the knots firmly against her. Increasing the pleasure.

"Honey, I want your legs spread. I'm going to tie you in an open-leg crab position."

Mouse closed her eyes. Helpless. He really intended her to be helpless. And she wanted it. Oh God. She *really* wanted it.

She reluctantly opened herself for him to look at and enjoy. "Place your hands outside your ankles."

"Master?"

"Yes, pet?" he asked as he climbed onto the bed with the rope in his hand.

"Could I place my hands to the inside of my ankles?"

His brows drew down as he considered. "Why?"

She bit her lip.

"Just tell me. Always be honest with me."

"When we make love, I'll be able to caress you."

He smiled. "With the hands to the outside it would be harder, wouldn't it?"

"Yes, Master."

"Very well, I'll grant your request."

"Thank you."

He chuckled. "We'll both enjoy it. Now place your wrists to the *inside* of your ankles, sweetheart."

Mouse obeyed him. Tor leaned forward and ran the rope around her waist, knotting it, then he drew one strand down to her left knee. Mouse watched him wrap the rope around her thigh and down to her shin, securing it. The way she was tied forced her to remain with her legs bent. Finally, he took her left wrist gently, adjusting the space between her wrist and ankle as he looped the rope around both.

"Keep your wrist and ankle an inch or two apart."

"But then I'll be able to move."

"For now, but not once I finish."

He leaned forward and lightly brushed her lips with his. "Relax, pet. You'll enjoy this."

"I know, but it's all so new to me."

"Yes, you've been watching for two months, not doing…haven't you?"

"That's right."

"I'm glad. Seeing you with another top would've killed me," he murmured. Mouse blinked and met his gaze. He looked serious.

"Really?"

He continued to tie her wrist to her ankle, looping around the strands of rope, taking up the slack she'd left with more binding before securing the rope with a knot. Finally, he looked up to answer her question.

"Yes, sweetheart. I've wanted you to belong to me for so long that I would not have handled it gracefully."

"Gracefully? You've been a bear for two months. I'd hate to have seen you grumpier than you were."

He chuckled. "I don't like to be hurt."

She lifted her free hand and cradled his chin. "I am sorry, Tor. I didn't mean to hurt you."

He held her gaze, smiling slightly. "I know." He kissed her palm. "We've both learned a lesson. No lies. Ever."

"Not even at Christmas or birthdays?"

"Not even anniversaries."

She smiled. God, she loved this man. Mouse didn't know what the future would hold, but she prayed it included the rest of her life with him.

Tor moved to her right side and made the same ties there. When he was done, she was immobilized. Her legs were bent and spread with her wrists bound against her ankles. All the while the knots he'd tied earlier teased her clit and ass. She sighed as he leaned back to enjoy the view.

"God, that's fucking hot," he growled. "And now I can torment you and there's not a damn thing you can do about it."

"Unless I use my safe word."

"True. But given the torment I plan, I doubt you'll be using that safe word any time soon. I think you'll enjoy every minute of this."

He went to the bedside table and picked up the bottle of water and opened it. He lifted it to her mouth.

"Drink."

She obeyed, surprised her mouth was dry. How the hell had he known that?

"Are you warm enough?"

She nodded. He frowned. "Maybe. I'm going to turn up the heat just a bit."

He crossed the room to do just that. When the heat kicked in, she realized she *had* been cold. Her respect for him as a Dom edged up a notch. She blinked as she realized that except for the night at Unfettered, she'd never seen him top anyone. Maybe he really had wanted her and her alone…

"I'm going to grab us some toys for play. Call out if you need anything. All right?"

She nodded, but he waited. Staring at her.

"What?"

"Words, honey. I want to hear you speak."

"Yes, Master. I'll call out if I need anything."

"Much better."

She watched him return to the large walk-in closet to rummage around. He returned with a feather, a flogger and a vibrator. Oh shit. He smiled down at her.

"This position isn't working for me anymore." He told her as he joined her on the bed.

Tor eased her onto her back which put her legs in the air—like a turtle on its back. Vulnerable and open.

"Oh yeah. I like that," he growled.

He reached between her spread thighs to stroke her damp pussy.

"You're so wet, the rope will definitely need a wash after this." He laughed.

"I'm sorry." Her throat grew tight. She felt as if she'd done something horribly wrong, but she couldn't think what it was.

Tor studied her, still stroking her wetness. "Don't apologize. I like your pussy wet and ready for me."

"But I'm making a mess..."

Mouse gasped as tears sprung to her eyes. She turned her head so he wouldn't see. What the hell was the matter with her? She was happy, but she was crying, for God's sake.

He leaned over her. "Mouse, I'm not your grandmother or grandfather. To me you're a *miracle*, not a mistake."

She gasped, her gaze flying to his. Tears dripped down her cheek. He gently wiped them away, smiling at her.

"I love you, Mozelle Vincent." He lay down between her open legs to kiss her, still stroking her face gently.

"You do?"

He nodded. "I was going to wait to tell you until you were falling asleep in my arms later tonight, but you need to know now. And I need to tell you. You mean the world to me and I want you to know it."

"Oh Tor..."she breathed. "I love you too."

God she wanted to embrace him for understanding. It was suddenly too much and she burst into tears, shaking her head at her own stupidity. But instead of chiding her, Tor cradled her close, kissing her while she cried. Feeling the weight of him against her made her feel protected...loved. She fought to stop the tears, but she couldn't.

"Just let it run its course," he murmured, holding her close and kissing her forehead.

"I'm sorry," she finally blubbered.

He chuckled softly. "I should have expected bondage to draw out some unexpected emotions."

"I feel like such an idiot, and I'm ruining everything." She met his gaze, humbled by the love she saw there.

"Never. You aren't an idiot. BDSM is primal and it touches the core of us. Remember how you reacted to Drago the first time you saw him with a sub? Well, this is reaching something deep inside you too."

"I wanted this to be special," she groaned miserably.

"It is. Deeply special." Tor kissed her again. "I'm honored that you trust me this much, sweetheart." He brushed her hair off her forehead. "You know, I think the flogger can wait. In fact, everything can wait."

"But I want to please you, Master."

"You please me just by being here. By trusting me. We've got the rest of our lives to play together. Right now, I just want to make love to you."

"Yes…please."

"I'm glad we're in agreement then." He chuckled, lowering his head to take her mouth.

Mouse relaxed, sighing into his kiss. Even though she couldn't embrace him in the traditional way, she drew her thighs into his sides, caressing him with her fingers as he kissed her. He lifted his head, meeting her gaze—a slight smile on his lips.

"So beautiful." She shook her head. "Yes, you are. The rounded curves of your body. Your wide eyes." He stroked her wild hair. "And I love these curls. The way they cling to my fingers." He dipped his head to kiss her again. "You're perfect, just as you are."

Mouse blinked, staring into his eyes. "You mean it, don't you?"

"Yes, I do."

He lowered his head, dropping soft, teasing kisses along her neck. She closed her eyes, reveling in feeling truly accepted for the first time in her life.

Tor nipped at the soft skin of her neck and she arched under him. Mouse brought her legs even tighter against his side, clutching him as she tilted her hips temptingly. Inviting him inside. He ignored the invitation, instead kissing his way to her collarbone then down to her breast. She shivered when he breathed against her nipples, making them tighten in reaction. But she wanted more. She needed his mouth to take her. Own her.

"Oh yes. Suck me...please," she moaned, lifting her breasts. Again offering herself to him.

Instead, he nibbled his way around the soft mound. Biting gently at times, licking at others. She wiggled under him, trying to get him to focus on her nipples. But he had his own plan for the night.

As Tor trailed his hands down her body, across her belly and between her thighs, she moaned. God, she wanted his touch. She needed it, but he continued to tease. To tempt. A fever rose in her.

"Tor... Please..."

He chuckled then bit her neck. "Who am I?"

"Master. I'm sorry. I'm still getting used to this but, for God's sake, touch me."

He nibbled her jawline while his palms skimmed over her sides. "I *am* touching you."

"You know what I mean."

"I do. But we're doing this my way. That's what it means for you to submit, sweetheart." She twisted in his arms, but it did no good. "You can struggle all you want, but you're not going anywhere right now."

She glared up into his bright blue eyes and growled at him.

"First weepy. Now angry. What else will you show me tonight, love?" He brushed the back of his hand softly along her cheekbone, amusement making his eyes crinkle.

Mouse sagged under him and took a deep breath. "I just want you. Is that so bad?"

"No. But just relax. Let it happen. We have all night. Hell, we have the rest of our lives. Let's take our time."

Reluctantly, she nodded.

"Good." He tilted his head. "I'll be right back."

When he rose from her and got off the bed, her chest tightened. Was he going to leave her? Punish her?

"Master? What are you doing?"

He glanced back, smiling slightly. "You'll see."

He went into his closet and came back directly with a blindfold in hand. Tor climbed up beside her. "Lift your head, Mouse."

"But..."

"No buts. *Lift your head.*"

She obeyed and he pulled the blindfold over her head and adjusted the soft black velvet so it completely covered her eyes. This was a new sensation and she wasn't sure she liked it. If the rope bondage made her feel helpless, this made it more intense because now she was utterly dependent on him. Mouse could feel him beside her on the bed, but she couldn't see what he was doing. Couldn't anticipate his next move. She just waited.

For a couple of minutes there was silence. She could feel Tor shifting on the bed, but she didn't know what he was doing. Her belly fluttered and she paused, trying to listen, but by the time she thought of using her other senses he'd quit moving around.

"Master?"

"Yes, love?"

"What are you doing?"

"Making love to you."

"You aren't even touching me."

"I will be," he chuckled. It was a low, sexy sound. She hadn't really appreciated that before.

Something brushed her nipple, but it wasn't his finger. She shivered as it happened again. What the hell was it? A scarf? It was soft…there it was on her belly. Mouse twitched. Then she felt it against her inner thighs. Her pussy lips. She gasped when she felt it against her other breast. Her belly again.

"What *is* that?"

"Guess."

"I don't know, Master. Really."

Instead of responding, he caressed her again. As it brushed her waist, an involuntary giggle erupted from her. Damn. It was the feather. She felt it against the ball of her foot and she jumped. She tried to pull her foot away from the feather, but her movements were too restricted.

Mouse giggled again. Then the teasing sensation was gone. He trailed the softness against the back of her thigh. The curve of her buttock. Each touch of the feather drew forth a mixture of giggles and twitches. She wanted to be annoyed, but every time she moved, the knots he'd placed so carefully worked to torment her clit and ass.

"Oh God," she cried.

Again the feather moved over her tight nipple. Lingering there to tantalize her senses. Tracing along the edge of her areola. Grazing her nipple. Over and over until she went from trying to escape the feather's caress to seeking it. Arching under it.

His hand brushed against her belly. Her abdomen tightened. Then he caught the rope in his hand, tugging gently. Drawing the knot against her clit. She moaned as her pussy dampened and her clit throbbed. He tugged again, this time she felt the rope pull against the bud of her ass too. Pressing into her.

"Beautiful," he whispered as she whimpered and rolled her hips. "Do you know how hard you make me, Mouse?"

"No. I can't *see* you," she cried.

"But I can see you, and I like what I see."

He took the feather away, leaving her panting. She heard a click and then the sound of a whirring motor.

"Oh no..." she wailed.

"Oh yesss..." he growled. She tensed, waiting to see where he'd rub the vibrator.

Mouse shivered as she felt a vibration near her nipple. She shifted, but still it didn't touch her. Yet she still felt it. Almost as if Tor was holding the vibe just above her, disturbing the air space just above her taut nipple. She arched, but still he didn't touch her. Then the sensation was gone and she groaned.

Suddenly, she felt it again. This time near her clit. She tried to lift her hips to reach the vibe without success. Yet she could almost feel it as the vibrations sent waves of awareness surging through her pussy. She raised her pelvis, seeking release.

"Master, pleeease..."

"Not yet, love."

While she sought the vibrator, she squeaked as the feather tapped against her painfully erect nipples. No amount of twisting eased her need. It only left her gasping and sobbing.

"Please..."

"I love the way you beg."

While she was distracted by the torment of the feather, he ran the vibrator along her inner labia. She arched into the vibrations, raising her hips in search of more.

"Yes. Oh God. Please give me more."

He took her at her word and pressed the vibrator against the knot over her clit, making her jerk at the intense surge of pleasure. It was electric. Like a live wire completing a circuit.

She thrust into the vibrator. God, she was so close. Mouse rocked her hips against the vibe while Tor continued to stroke her nipples with the feather. She strained upward.

"Oh yeah. Don't stop. God..."

Then it was gone. No feather. No vibrator. She rocked and twisted, her frustration dragging a scream from her.

"Damn it, don't stop now! I was going to come."

"I know."

He shifted on the bed. Was he finally going to fuck her...please God? She heard a swish of air then she yelped as the slap of a flogger struck her pussy.

"What are you doing?"

"You told me not to stop, sweetheart."

"I was talking about the vibrator, not a flogger."

"Next time you'll need to be more specific."

Again he struck with the flogger and she gasped. Mouse tried to close her legs, but he caught one to keep her spread for him. The light blows continued, and as Tor developed a rhythm the heat from the flogger against her pussy and lower abdomen transformed from pain to pleasure. She moaned and started to lift her pelvis to meet the blows. Searching for them.

"Oh God."

"Don't come yet."

"But..."

"I'm not done with you yet. Don't come."

But she couldn't stop herself from moving with the flogger. Then he paused and she sighed with relief...until he brought the vibe back to her pussy. He rubbed it over her clit and labia. She sobbed when he worked the vibe between the strands of rope and eased it inside her wet cunt. It was diabolically clever because he could use the rope to anchor the vibe inside her. When she thought he couldn't torment her any more, he flogged her again.

"Oh please…"

Mouse groaned, raising her hips as much as she was able so she could meet the downward stroke of the flogger. All the while the vibrator took her closer and closer to an orgasm more intense than she'd experienced in her entire life. He turned the vibe up and pushed it a little deeper inside her then returned to flogging her.

"Please can I come? Please?"

Her body was slick with sweat now. Tor drove her closer and closer to orgasm with each blow of the flogger. God, this was so good. She twisted, not knowing whether she wanted to escape the sensations surging through her or beg for more. It was so much more than she'd ever expected. More than she'd hoped.

"Do you want to come?"

"Yes. Oh please… Please, Master."

"Please what?"

"Please can I come? Please?"

One minute she was riding the steady throb of the vibrator and the rhythm of the flogger, and the next, he'd stopped flogging her. Then he pulled the vibe out of her pussy.

She screeched. "*No!*"

Then she felt his fingers pulling at the strands of rope covering her cunt. He tugged it apart and the knot pressed against her clit and she whimpered.

"I think you'll like this, love. I know I will."

She gasped as he eased his cock into her wet pussy.

"Yes please, Master. Please fuck me."

The penetration felt like slow motion. She froze on the knife edge of orgasm, but she wanted this more. She wanted him to fill her. Fuck her until she broke into a million pieces that only he could reassemble.

"Oh God, that's so fucking good," he grunted as he settled deep inside her and moved over her.

She brought her legs in and clutched at his hips, sighing as he kissed her. She was wide open. Vulnerable, but she couldn't imagine anything else. This was what she'd been missing all her life. Belonging to someone. Tor lifted his head and licked droplets of sweat from her neck, nipping at her chin. She sobbed as he withdrew. Then with painful slowness, he drove back into her.

"Ah, yeah. The ropes are like an extension of your sweet cunt."

She pressed kisses to any part of him she could reach as he withdrew and entered again. Her movements were limited, but she gave as much to him as she could. She clenched on him as he withdrew and opened for him hungrily as he surged back into her.

"Harder. Please, Tor. Harder!"

He grunted and his thrusts picked up speed. They moved together like professional dancers. Trained to move as one. She gasped as the knots continued their job, one tormenting her clit and the other pressing tightly into her sensitive asshole. She bucked under him.

Faster. Faster. She met him stroke for stroke, accepting his forceful kiss. Reveling in it and twining her tongue with his while he thrust inside her.

"Yes. Oh God, I'm going to come."

"Hold on. Not yet."

"Please…"

"No." He breathed into her mouth. Somehow he picked up speed and she met him. Accepting anything he wanted to give her. He sucked her nipples then reached up to pinch. Twisting slightly.

Mouse arched under him as he pounded into her, unable to stop her rising climax this time.

"Master, I need to come. Pleeease."

He groaned. "Come for me, sweetheart. Give yourself to me…now."

She obeyed, screaming as her pussy pulsed around him. He held on for only a few strokes before he too shouted and spasmed with pleasure. They shook together…becoming one in a way Mouse had never expected. Pleasure rolled through her. Tearing her apart and remaking her. When they collapsed together, she felt like an entirely new person. And this woman was well and truly owned by her lover, and she liked it. Liked being owned.

The only sound she could hear in the bedroom was their harsh breathing as they gasped and groaned in the aftermath of their shared release.

Tor lifted his head from her shoulder and removed her blindfold. She blinked her eyes and met his gaze. His adoring gaze.

"I love you, Mouse. I asked you to wear my collar before. Now I'm asking if you'll marry me too."

She opened her mouth to speak, and suddenly she was crying again. He gathered her close.

"I hope these are good tears."

She nodded, trying to form words. But nothing came out.

"So is your answer yes?"

He lifted his head to look into her eyes, gently wiping away tears.

"Yes, Master. I love you and I'll marry you."

"Good. You'll belong to me in every way a woman can belong to a man. I promise I'll cherish you for the rest of our lives—both as my wife and as my submissive."

She smiled up at him. "And I'll cherish you. I'll even obey you…when it's appropriate."

He threw back his head and laughed. "I'd expect nothing less, Mouse my love."

MISTRESS MINE

Samantha Cayto

Dedication

This story is dedicated to Desiree Holt, a wonderful woman, a fabulous writer and a dear friend. She inspires me.

Special thanks to Michelle Polaris, my soul sister.

Trademarks Acknowledgement

The author acknowledges the trademarked status and trademark owners of the following wordmarks mentioned in this work of fiction:

Catwoman: DC Comics, New York

Dr. Pepper: Dr. Pepper/Seven Up, Inc.

Star Wars: Lucasfilm Ltd., San Francisco

Time-Life: Time Warner Inc., New York

Chapter One

ꟷ

"If you don't stop mooning over your ex, I'm going to resign as your wingman."

Trey Boudreau lifted his gaze from the beer bottle to glare at his friend, Mike. "I'm not mooning over Gina, and who the hell says 'mooning' anymore?"

Mike rolled his dark brown eyes and shook his head. "I figured you being from the south and all it was a fitting expression. And yes, you are mooning over Gina. You haven't stopped staring at your drink all night. Either you've developed an unhealthy attraction to malted beverages or you're obsessing over your ex-wife. Either way, it makes being here pointless. Look, if you're not interested in hooking up with any of the fine, and I mean fine, women in this club, we may as well head back to my place. No point in spending seven bucks on a bottle of beer if you're not going to snag some bodacious booty at the same time."

"Oh my God." Trey put his head in his hands. This night was a disaster. He should never have let Mike talk him into clubbing. They were too old for this kind of meat market, and he wasn't interested in "hooking up" with any woman. He wanted to find what he thought he'd had with Gina, a woman to spend the rest of his life with. He still wasn't sure what had gone wrong. How did a ten-year-old marriage simply die? Sure, he had spent many of those years deployed overseas, but unlike other marriages killed by war, his had ended well after he'd taken a civilian job. He was still reeling from the aftershocks.

Mike's big hand landed on Trey's shoulder and gave it a comforting squeeze. "Come on man, it'll get better. Maybe you're pushing it too soon. I have to tell you, though, that I can't say I'm sorry Gina shoved you out the door."

Startled by the admission, Trey raised his head to frown at his friend. "I thought you liked Gina."

Mike shrugged and tossed a couple of peanuts in his mouth. "Sure, I liked her. She was a nice girl, just not your type."

"Not my type?" Gina had been the perfect type for Trey, sweet and caring, always eager to please him in some way. Biddable, his grandmother once called her. Coming from Granny, it had sounded more like an insult than a compliment. Then again, his Granny hadn't been sleeping with Gina. Trey had, and a more attentive lover a man couldn't ask for. Gina had been willing to do anything he wanted, pliant and accommodating and passive as hell.

Shit, when he thought about it, and he had a lot lately, his sex life with Gina had been boring. When he'd first been back from a deployment, he couldn't get enough of her, like a man fresh from the desert downing lukewarm water. After a while, though, he'd start to crave Dr. Pepper, or beer, or Christ, a shot of bourbon. Then he'd deploy again and the thirst built up to a point where he forgot the tedium. Once he was home for good, working for the FBI, he was with his wife every night or gone only for a few days. Always the one to initiate lovemaking, he hadn't been able to work up an interest very often. Their sex life had petered out. He'd thought he was the only one missing it. Gina hadn't said anything or done anything about it. Obviously he'd been wrong about how she had felt because she was the one to ask for a divorce. She had demanded it, actually, the most assertive he'd ever seen her.

Trey took a long pull of his beer, draining the bottle. "Crap, you may be right. I know I let her down in the bedroom. I let us both down."

Mike raised his eyebrows. "They say the first step toward recovery is admitting you have a problem."

"Fuck you," he replied without any heat. Mike was a good friend and Trey knew he'd been a lousy one these past few months. Standing up, he added, "Let's get out of here. This is a waste of time until I figure out what I'm looking for in a woman."

Mike joined him and tossed a few more bills on the table for a tip. "As long as we're talking about it, I may as well tell you what I think you might be looking for."

"Bring it on." Trey doubted very much his friend had an insight that he, himself, lacked in his own sex life.

"Remember Major Bradford?"

Trey's stride hitched for a half-second before he replied. "Yeah, I remember her. So?"

"So, tell me your dick didn't get hard every time she came into view."

He waited until they were outside the club, the cool peace of the Boston night a welcome relief to the noisy crush of the club. "Come on, man, you're talking about a superior officer."

"Who is not here and we are no longer in the army. Be honest. A woman like that, tall, strong, commanding and mature. She was hot in a way all those young junior grades could never be."

Trey stopped his body mid-squirm because honestly, he remembered the major in the mess hall one day when a mortar hit. She had been on her feet barking out orders before the dust had cleared. He'd had no problem following her orders when she so obviously knew what she was doing. And, yeah, the sight of her had aroused him each and every time their paths had crossed after that incident. Thinking of her made him hard that very moment. Hence the urge to squirm. He didn't want to admit it to his friend, though. His reaction didn't seem right somehow.

"I like to be in charge," he countered, striding down the sidewalk.

Being a taller man, Mike had no trouble keeping up with him. He also had no compunction about challenging Trey's resistance. "Sure, you liked being in charge of your squad, you like being in charge of an investigation. We're talking about the bedroom."

"You think I don't like being in charge when having sex?" Even as he sputtered out his indignation, an image of a woman looming over him while he lay spread-eagle on a bed popped into his mind. It wasn't the Major, either. The face was covered in shadows, a mystery woman. His dream woman? His heart skipped a beat before picking up speed. He licked his suddenly dry lips. "You don't know what I want in a sex partner."

"I didn't say I knew for sure. All I'm saying is you had the sweet, traditional young woman right? The sex got stale, the marriage ended. Maybe you should try a different kind of woman, a different kind of sex life. You can't know unless you try."

Trey slanted his eyes toward his friend. "You got someone in mind?"

"Hell, no. I'm just flapping my gums here. I have no idea who might be a good fit for you. I do know that club hopping is not going to work. We've run this particular flag up the pole a bunch of times and no one is saluting."

Amen to that. Except his cock was locked and loaded at the idea of a forceful, mature woman. Maybe he needed to unleash those deep, dark fantasies that had been lurking in the back of his mind all his life. The way Mike talked about it, giving up control in bed to a woman wasn't a crazy idea for a guy like him, an alpha male by anyone's definition. He'd always believed that guys who gave women the whip hand, so to speak, in bed were wimps. Trey had never seen himself as anything other than strong and in control. But, if Mike, another strong man, could speak so reverently about a dominant woman, perhaps Trey had been wrong to deny himself. Maybe, too, it was time to seek out a more mature woman, someone who knew what she wanted and wasn't shy about going after it. The only problem was how would he find a woman like that? The army might be full of them, but he wasn't in the army. The FBI might have its share, too, although working and fucking never mixed well when it involved the same people.

Ah, best to put the whole thing aside for now. He didn't need to find a woman right away. It had been less than a year since Gina had kicked him out. His right hand worked fine. He could take care of himself for a while and when his right hand got tired, he had his left one to fall back on. The internet contained all sorts of possibilities, too. Perhaps when he got home, he could surf for what he hadn't yet dared. Stifling a pretend yawn, he said, "I'm too tired to figure it out tonight. Let's see if we can grab a cab."

Mike shook his head and followed Trey as he stepped off the curb.

* * * * *

Trey groaned deep in the back of his throat, unconcerned about being heard alone in his own apartment. It had taken hardly any effort at all to find the images that had only fleetingly been allowed in his imagination all these years. Here in the vastness of the internet he found women, tall in their fuck-me heels, clad in black leather, holding crops and floggers, some with strap-ons cinched around their waists, all forcing men to do their bidding. The sight of the false phalluses made him queasy, though, so he stayed with images of bondage and pain. Most of the women appeared to be a bit older than he, and those were the images he focused on, too. There was something so right about a man being dominated by an older woman. The men, naked and vulnerable, were standing, kneeling, or lying down, some tied-up, some not, but to a man, hard and willing. Their expressions told the story. While they grimaced in pain, there was another look layered beneath the surface. Worship, rapture, peace, it was all there to see and envy.

There were so many pictures and videos, he couldn't stop with just one. His mind reeled at the possibilities while his cock strained to be free. With one hand on the mouse, he undid his pants and yanked his rod out of its confines. The head was already slick with pre-cum. He couldn't remember the last time the strength of his arousal made his cock almost painful to touch. As soon as his fingers wrapped around the hard length and squeezed against his glans, he felt ready to erupt. A couple of jerks and he'd be done. He choked it back. Too soon. He wanted to savor the moment. God, it had been so long since he'd experienced such intense pleasure. Playing idly with his erection, he scrolled through the offerings of a particular site and clicked on a free video. It welcomed him into a world of forbidden delights.

The woman appealed to him with her long, dark hair pulled into a high ponytail. Large breasts spilled over a tightly cinched black bustier. Her bare pubic mound peeped out from the bottom of her bustier, as did her firm, round ass. Her legs were long and shapely, set off by her high-heeled boots. With her bright red lips pursed, the Dominatrix sauntered around a kneeling man. His arms were secured behind his back and a ball gag filled his mouth. His eyes were down, submissive, waiting. Every few seconds, the woman slapped the riding crop she held against her thigh. The sharp crack made the man flinch, but his cock remained rigid, swaying in front of him, ready to serve.

"God," Trey whispered into the quiet, his gaze transfixed on the screen.

With each ominous whack, his cock jumped, too. It was also ready, ready to thrust, ready to burst. There was nowhere for it to go, though, except past his teasing fingers. And, yet a guy could imagine what it would be like to be inside the scene that played out in front of him. He tightened his grip, pulled and tugged at the taut skin of his hot cock. More pre-cum spilled over. It slicked his way while his fingers picked up speed. The woman slapped the crop against her thigh faster. Trey panted as his climax built, crested and, when the crop came down suddenly against the willing man's ass, it crashed.

He doubled over, deaf and blind with the intensity of the orgasm. His body rocked as spurts of cum ejaculated over his hand. He grunted and pounded his free hand against the table. Long seconds ticked by before he caught his breath and leaned back in his chair. He let his hand drop against his thigh and was only vaguely aware of the sounds of both pleasure and pain coming through his computer.

Trey was spent and content in a way he hadn't been in years, maybe hadn't been ever before. He knew now what he was looking for in a woman, and the realization both relieved and disturbed him. He wanted a woman to command him and to hurt him. Biddable women like Gina had been all wrong for him because he was the one who was destined to be submissive, at least in bed. Cracking his eyes open, he watched while the woman reddened the man's ass. Not even necessarily in bed. On the floor, tied to a rack…shit, anywhere as long as a strong woman put him there. She needed to be older, too. With maturity came authority, and he believed in authority.

There was only one problem, he realized with a groan. He had no idea where to find this woman. No idea at all.

* * * * *

As Trey drained his second cup of coffee, the last of the cobwebs cleared from his mind. It was already early afternoon on Sunday. He had slept in longer then he was used to, exhausted from the marathon jerk-off session that had lasted well into the wee hours of the morning. A sense of guilt tried to creep into his head. He batted it away. It was not in his nature to obsess and whine over the way things were as opposed to how he wished them to be. Like it or not, he was a sexual submissive. It didn't make him less of a man and it didn't make him weak. He had a bronze star that told him and the world what kind of man he was. He was working his way up the ranks of the FBI, too. He had nothing to prove to anyone, least of all himself. The one issue, the big issue, was finding the right woman. The internet could help him hook up. It made him uneasy, though. The internet was so impersonal, and potentially dangerous as he knew all too well being in law enforcement. You never knew what someone was really like until you met them face-to-face. Still, what choice did he have?

Pushing himself up from the table, he set about cleaning his apartment. Sunday was always cleaning day unless he was out on an assignment. When they were married, Gina had done all the housework. Another thing for him to feel guilty about. He was determined not to devolve into the stereotypical bachelor with a constant mess under foot and mold growing in the bathroom. The first thing he tackled was his clothes dropped on the floor where he had disrobed after his first mind-blowing orgasm. He checked the pockets of his pants as he walked to the corner that housed the washer and dryer. He pulled out a card. Frowning, he studied the unexpected find.

It was a simple white business card with a black back. The front of the card merely said "1-800-DOM-help" and nothing more. Trey stood still, staring at it for long seconds before swearing.

"Son of a bitch!" He dropped the pants into the washer and picked up the phone.

Mike answered on the second ring. "What's up, man?"

"You asshole."

"Huh? What'd I do?" His friend sounded genuinely confused.

Trey didn't buy any of it. "I found the card you slipped into my pocket. And, by the way, how creepy is that for you to stick your hand so close to my dick?"

"Are you having some kind of psychotic break or something? Because dude, I have no idea what you're talking about."

The guy sounded so sincere, Trey started to have doubts, but how else could that weird card have ended up in his pants? He took and let out a deep breath. "All I'm saying is that it's pretty strange that you were talking about ball-busting women last night and all of a sudden I find this card in my pocket about Dom help, whatever the hell that means."

"Dude, you've got a card for what, a hotline?"

"I don't know. It's a number, is all. You telling me you didn't do this?"

"I swear I know nothing about a card. Sounds like someone from the club last night slipped it to you, maybe when we squeezed by people to get out."

"Maybe." Trey couldn't keep the skepticism out of his voice. It didn't make any sense. Who else besides Mike had any idea of Trey's submissive inclination? It didn't matter. "Okay, I guess I have to trust the guy who covered my ass in Kandahar."

"Damn straight." Mike paused. "So, what are you going to do with the card?"

Suspicion pricked again. "I'm throwing it away. Why, what do you think I should do, call the damn number?" The pressure of facing his sexual orientation took its toll. He couldn't keep the anger and frustration out of his voice.

"No, no," his friend soothed. "I didn't say that. Who knows what kind of weirdo might answer. I don't want to have to dumpster dive for your body parts."

Trey squeezed the bridge of his nose, pulled himself together. "Yeah, right, sorry, dude. I need to chill. Enjoy the rest of your Sunday. I'll see you tomorrow."

"Same back at you."

Trey ended the call and stood still, staring at nothing for long moments. He did need to pull himself together. It's not as if he'd realized he was a cannibal or anything. He didn't need to hook up with a woman right away, either. There were limitless fantasies to be lived through the images on the internet. The night before had proved that. But he couldn't let sex get in the way of duty. Ignoring the lure of his computer, he tossed the card in a trashcan and went back to cleaning. A couple of hours later, he decided the place was clean enough and sat down at his desk.

As soon as he reached for the mouse, his hand touched the business card. Eyebrows raised, he picked up what he was sure he had thrown away. "What the fuck," he muttered. Maybe Mike was right, he was having some kind of mental breakdown. Could he have subconsciously picked this thing out of the trash? Was it possible he never threw it away in the first place, only thought he had? Well, those were the only two options. Either way, the possibility of the woman of his dreams only a phone call away intrigued him. He spent a few more seconds wrestling with his saner half before picking up the phone and dialing the number.

A male voice answered on the first ring. "Thank you for calling 1-800-DOM-help. This is the Operator. How may I be of assistance?"

Okay, not what he was expecting. It was like calling Judy at *Time-Life* for a magazine subscription. A bit stunned, Trey didn't know what to say.

"How may I be of assistance?" The man persisted in a calm, yet firm, tone.

"I'm not sure." Having found his voice, Trey still didn't know how to respond.

"Are you a Dom or a sub, sir?"

"I-I am a sub, a submissive looking for a Domme." Wow, as hard as it was to admit it, saying what he was and what he looked for out loud lifted a weight that had been crushing him slowly to death. "I'm not sure how to go about finding the right woman," he added, emboldened, now.

"I understand. I see that you are calling from Boston. Please write down the following address. You will find a club called Unfettered at that location. You will find what you need at the club."

Trey stared at the address. If accurate, it put the club inside what was known as the Leather District. Nice touch, he supposed, although the name of that area of Boston was tied to old factories, not fetishes. It surprised him to learn that Boston had a BDSM club at all. Massachusetts laws frowned on even consensual sadism. This had to be a very private club, and if it wasn't, the last thing he needed as a law enforcer was to be picked up in a raid.

"Um, can I go there without an invitation?"

"You just received one."

"I see. When is it open?"

"Whenever you want it to be."

Trey was skeptical. "Tonight?"

"Do you want it to be open tonight?"

"Yes." *Maybe.*

"Then it will be open tonight," came the mild retort.

"Okay. Thank you."

"You're welcome."

The line went dead before Trey could ask anything more. He stared at what he had written down the same way he had stared at the card earlier. It all seemed so unreal. Yet, the idea of going to the club made his heart beat faster, part fear, part arousal, a testament to his ambivalence. His cock had no such qualms. It was hard and pulsing with need. Shit, he had to go. He had to at least try this lifestyle. So what if he didn't know what to expect? So what if the club might prove weird or even dangerous? He was a combat soldier and an FBI field agent. He walked into the unknown and the dangerous all the time. Like all those other times, this was a matter of doing what was right, a matter of life and if not death, at least a matter of happiness. His happiness for the rest of his life. If he didn't at least explore this side of him, he would die regretting it.

Resolved to try the club that very night because, hey, the guy said it would be open tonight if he wanted it to be, there remained one question left, one that he had never pondered before in his life. "What the hell do I wear?"

Chapter Two

ꝏ

Juliette Coyne stood inside Unfettered's reception area and took a furtive, deep breath to steady herself. It was a Sunday night, for God's sake, a quiet time with few people lounging about. It was in fact the perfect time for her to test getting back in the lifestyle with a new sub. Any man hanging out at this time of the week looking for a Domme would be eager and perhaps not too experienced. The guys already active in the life were probably home recovering from taxing Friday and Saturday night scenes with their Dommes. She reminded herself that she had no expectations. She was merely there to check out the new club a friend had recommended. She wasn't even sure who had slipped her the hotline card. All she knew was that it ended up in her purse and the man who answered her skeptical call had led her to this place.

It certainly had promise. The reception room was spacious and comfortable looking with its large, chairs and low lighting. Several halls branched off the main area to what could only be the play chambers. Her clit tingled at the idea of what she could do in a new dungeon with a new sub, although she hadn't come to play necessarily that night. She had dressed in street clothes, in fact, wearing black slacks and a casual jacket of the same color. Her blouse was red satin, yet modestly cut to expose only a hint of her breasts. Even her shoes were fairly sensible sling-back pumps with two-inch heels. The only outward sign of her sexual orientation was the black and red suede flogger dangling from her left wrist. It was a beautiful tool, hand-made with alternating colored lacing up the handle. It was her favorite, notwithstanding the rather delicate nature of suede.

Holding it, allowing it to swish gently against her leg, centered her and reminder her that she was a Domme. It was long past time for her to shake off the effects of her last sub, Tom. He had been a pretty, young and clever boy who had topped her from the bottom with subtle brilliance simply because he could. The secret power play had given him greater satisfaction than a true Domme/sub relationship would have, and she had trusted him enough to miss what was happening before he messed with her head and her confidence. She closed her eyes to block out the sudden memory of the worst of it, the night she had begun to doubt her ability to dominate and to do so safely.

"Red!"

The safe word tore out of Tom's mouth, piercing Juliette's cloud of pleasure. She froze, the dildo strapped around her hips seated fully inside her sub's ass. "What, what's wrong?" she demanded, her heart racing with fear. This was the third time in a month that Tom had used his safe word. What had she done wrong? She had been so careful before introducing pegging to their play.

"Take it out," he begged. "It hurts too much. Please, Mistress."

As carefully as she could, she eased out of him. Her fingers caressed his ass cheeks in a motion meant to soothe, while her eyes looked for blood or any other sign that she had damaged him unintentionally. God, there was no worse offense for a Domme than to be careless with her sub. If she had truly hurt him this time, there was no forgiveness, at least she would not forgive herself. She sighed with relief when she saw nothing wrong and released him from of his restraints.

Tom collapsed in her arms and hugged her tight. "I'm so sorry, Mistress. I try to submit to you always, but I'm not strong enough to take everything."

His words of contrition clawed at her heart and her conscience. It wasn't his job to endure more than he could handle. It was her duty to give him only what he could. She had screwed up, again. What was wrong with her?

Gently brushing aside a trickle of tears from the corner of his eyes, she said, "No, I'm the one who is sorry, so sorry. I'll take better care of you, I promise, if you'll let me."

"Of course, Mistress. I want you, I trust you."

She had missed that night the look of triumph that she knew he must have sported. Instead, she had scaled down their play, questioning her own moves, asking him at every turn if he was okay with what she did. Bit by bit, losing her confidence, losing her own joy in dominating. It had taken her months to catch the cocky, furtive grin he wore whenever he got his way, to realize how she was being played. Confronting Tom and breaking with him had been easy, fueled as it was by her rage. Many months more were needed, however, for her to recover her confidence. She was a good Domme. She knew how to take care of a boy properly. Tom had been an anomaly. She told herself that and she believed it, mostly. There was a part of her still that was unsure. Finding a new boy to play with, an older one, though, more mature, perhaps to introduce to the lifestyle would banish the last of her lingering doubt forever. She wasn't looking for a guy to commit to. This was all about having fun.

"Good evening." A woman who could have been Juliette's sister given her slender build, long black hair and blue eyes, stepped in front of her and greeted her with a smile. "Welcome to Unfettered. I'm Dru, the manager."

Juliette looked down at the other woman because even with short heels, she towered over the petite manager. "Thank you," she smiled back. "I'm Mistress Juliette."

Dru inclined her head. "I can assume, then, you are looking for a boy to play with this evening."

"Perhaps. I'm in the market for someone untrained." Someone who hopefully wouldn't have had a chance to develop bad habits and manipulative ways. "I don't suppose this club sees many of those."

"As a matter of fact, there's someone here tonight who would fit the bill." Turning slightly, Dru nodded her head toward a man sitting at the far end of the bar.

Juliette had missed him in her first glance of the room. His age from that distance was hard to determine, although he appeared to be in his early thirties. Damn, younger than she by a good seven years or so, although not as young as Tom had been. Thirties was okay, she reasoned, a mature decade for men. His hair was short and dark. He was dressed in jeans and a dark colored t-shirt and what appeared to be sneakers. As slouched over the bar as he was, his legs still looked long, implying height. His body certainly appeared lean and hard. His gaze was focused on the glass in front of him, his expression neutral, conveying a sense of "I don't give a fuck". To most people, the man screamed alpha male, and therefore, Dom. She knew better. Her body went on high alert at the sight. Her nipples hardened against her shirt and wetness seeped into her nether lips.

She grasped her flogger, her fingers itching for action. "Are you sure he isn't waiting for someone?" Her voice sounded breathless to her own ears. She glanced at Dru and the other woman smiled.

"I didn't say that. He's definitely waiting for a woman to help him be the man he is." With that cryptic response, the manager turned and walked away.

Juliette stared after her, waging an internal battle. When she had left her condo, she had told herself she was only going to check out the place and the people. Wade in a little to test the waters. She was not prepared to start something with a new boy. Still, the man intrigued her. Strong, overtly masculine, the kind of man who liked to be in charge, except that when she commanded, he would obey. She suppressed a moan at the thought. Nothing aroused her passion as much as a powerful man submitting to her will. She couldn't pass by this opportunity. If she let him go, some other Domme would snatch him up in a flash. It didn't have to be forever. Hell, it didn't have to be more than this one night. She had to take this first step before her fear made it impossible to take any step at all.

Determined to move on with her life, Juliette sauntered toward the bar.

Trey sensed the pair of eyes boring into his back before he became aware of soft footsteps coming toward him. His gut tightened along with his cock, although he couldn't tell why. Somehow he knew he was about to get what he had been looking for since entering the club. Not knowing how a submissive went about hooking up, he opted for the obvious choice of sitting down and waiting for a Domme to come to him. It seemed like the right thing to do, except now that someone approached him, he felt a little like a cornered animal. Slowly, he turned on his stool and looked behind him.

Surprise hit him first. There was a woman coming his way, her gaze locked on his. But this wasn't the kind of woman he had expected in a fetish club. Her clothes were casual business attire, her long hair pulled back in a braid of some sort. Other than a hint of shiny red beneath her jacket, there was nothing overtly sexual about her. Somehow the simple attire made her more commanding, more interesting. And then there was the matter of the flogger she held. Mesmerized, he stared at it swinging in time with her gait. Blood pooled farther into his groin, his cock swelled to an even harder length. He fought to steady his breath as he watched her come closer and closer.

The woman stopped in front of him and cocked her head. "Stand up."

The order surprised him. No, "hi, my name is" or any other pleasantries to break the ice. No effort to discern his interests. Shit, maybe his submissiveness was obvious to this woman. He was new to all this, though, and he wasn't sure he liked being ordered about without so much as a by-your-leave. The woman continued to stare at him, an unreadable expression on her face. She clearly expected him to comply, so he did. No point in coming to the club if he wasn't willing to give it, whatever *it* was, a try.

Sliding off the stool, Trey stood in front of the woman, looking down at her. She was tall, maybe five eight, but at six three, he was taller. Having the height advantage put him more at ease. The way the woman looked him up and down, as if assessing his worth, made him want to squirm. He fought to remain still. He had his pride, after all. Let her look. He knew she wouldn't find him wanting. When her scrutiny slid to his groin and lingered there, he suppressed a grin. He definitely had a package to be proud of.

Her gaze swept up. He stared back and made his own assessment. Fair was fair, and man, was she ever fair, make that pretty. Light, creamy skin with deep blue eyes set in an oval face. There was a hint of fine lines around her eyes showing maturity. He figured she was about forty. Perfect for him. He wanted experienced and he wanted a woman he could talk to when they were done fucking. Her pale pink lips pursed.

"Eyes down."

What? No way. He wanted to get a good look at her, too, before they started to play. When he continued to look back at her, she tsked. "Sorry, my mistake." She turned to walk away.

Shit! "No, wait, please," he blurted out before he could question the wisdom of it. Reaching out, he touched her arm briefly before snatching it back. Way to look like a predator or a loser. Besides, the big bouncer, Hayden, had stepped into view when Trey called out. The man was not going to allow any trouble. Trey held up his hands in surrender, but the other man didn't look away again until the woman nodded.

She pivoted back with raised eyebrows. She slid the strands of her flogger idly through one hand. Silently she stared until he did as she had commanded, he lowered his gaze to the floor. "Good," she said in a clipped voice. "Now, hands behind your back."

This time, he hesitated only a second before complying. At least the stance was familiar. He acted as if he were at parade rest. "I'm sorry," he said, not sure that speaking was the right thing to do. "I'm new to all of this. I'm going to need a lot of patience I'm afraid."

Her shoes came into view. "I'm a very patient woman, but if we're going to play together, you're going to have to give me control and you're going to have to trust me."

Trey swallowed audibly. It was hard to breathe, his chest was so tight. But his balls were tight against his body, too, a testament to how aroused he was. "It's going to be difficult for me. I'm used to being in control."

"I know," she replied in a silky voice that raised the hairs on his arms. "I can tell that about you. It's what I find appealing." She ran a single finger down one of his arms. He shivered at the touch. "So much strength. I'm going to enjoy your submitting it to me. You are going to submit to me, aren't you?"

"Yes, ma'am." His reply came out in a low tone, almost a whisper. The blood was churning within him so hot and fast, he could barely speak.

"Ma'am is fine, so is Mistress, or even Domina, if you'd like. My name is Juliette, and if you are very good, I may let you call me that. Now tell me your name."

"Trey."

His voice was as smooth as sipping whiskey with a hint of southern in the tone. The sound of it electrified her body. Her blood raced to swell those parts of her that evidenced her arousal. She wanted to grab him by the belt and shove him into a room to start his training. It was the most excited she had been in months. Yet, caution stilled her movements. On the surface, this was exactly the kind of man she searched for.

His response to her in the few seconds they had interacted told a different story. He was reluctant to submit to her. Even standing as she had commanded, he appeared a warrior ready to take command himself. Not surprisingly, he showcased military training, his back ramrod straight. Given the shortness of his hair and the perfection of his hard body, she figured he was either still in the military or newly mustered out. Either way, the notion sent her desire into overdrive. Military men had always been her fantasy.

In a very deliberate way, she scrutinized him, drinking in the delicious details of his body. The biceps and triceps were marvelously cut. His tight t-shirt hugged impressive pecs and gave a hint of tight abs. And, then there was the lovely bulge of his jeans. His cock was a hard ridge pressing against the worn material. She'd seen countless men both clothed and unclothed in her life, and she knew a large cock when it saluted her. Her tongue flicked out to lick her dry lips at the thought of freeing him to her touch. Her breath quickened and her lizard brain screamed in frustration at her. What was she waiting for?

What indeed? By his own admission, this man, Trey, was used to being in charge. He was new to the Dom/sub lifestyle. The fact that he was in the club meant he was looking to pursue his true nature. But his reluctance to respond to her commands warned her that he might not be able to truly give up control. If she ended up in another power struggle such as the one she'd had with Tom, she might never recover her place as a Domme.

Juliette took a deep breath to steady herself. She was being a ninny, jumping ahead to a point in time that might never occur. Tonight didn't have to mean anything more than having fun, trying out someone new. So what if he turned out to be a controlling shit? She'd walk away and find someone else. She tightened her grip on the flogger for a few seconds to dispel some of her nervous energy. Then she got down to business.

"Is there any alcohol in that drink?"

"No, ma'am, it's soda water. The bartender said no alcohol if I wanted to play."

"Good. Follow me," she commanded in a clipped tone.

Walking toward the hallway to the play rooms, she gave thought to what kind of room and what kind of play she intended. Something simple would be best this first time. No need to freak the newbie out with some medieval dungeon scene. She didn't intend to do more than introduce him to restraint and perhaps a little pain. Her flogger twitched in her hand as if it had a mind of its own. Yes, a good plan. She didn't check to see if Trey followed her. If he hadn't done so, he was out of the game before it even started. She could hear the soft tread of his sneakers behind her in any event.

Dru intercepted them before they reached the hall. "Everything all right?"

"For now," Juliette confirmed. She liked how the staff checked up on them. It meant the club wasn't simply a flashy place to make some money. These people understood the lifestyle which meant they understood safe play. "I'm looking for a simple set up. Could you please recommend a room?"

Dru smiled and turned to point at the first door on the right. "I think that one will fit the bill."

"Thank you." With a nod, Juliette continued. Trey followed. Opening the indicated door, she peeked inside and saw what had been promised, a simple, small room with a large leather chair, a padded bench, and manacles hanging from one wall. Dimly lit, painted in an off-white color and with a brown stone floor, it was a tad boring, but that was okay. The surroundings would hopefully put her new boy at ease.

Stepping inside, she held the door open and beckoned Trey. He still had his hands behind his back and his eyes down, but damn, there was nothing subservient about the guy. He looked confident and in control of his surroundings. If he was nervous it didn't show, except when he passed her, she could see that one hand gripped the other so tight, his knuckles were white. Not so confident after all. Good, in a way. It wasn't that she wanted him afraid, of course. Fear wasn't the objective, trust was. If being in this room with her made him uneasy, it indicated his agenda didn't include controlling her. At least she hoped it did.

And she could stand there all night, analyzing Trey and their situation to death. Or she could go about breaking in her new boy. Resolved to stop fretting and start playing, Juliette shut the door and flicked the switch that would light up the sign she had seen next to the door. The room was now "occupied" and no one would bother them, unless of course things got out of hand. That wouldn't happen. She wouldn't let it. She understood the magnitude of what she did, the responsibility that came with being a Domme. If all went well, Trey would put his body in her hands. She would take good care of it. She would take good care of him.

Trey had stopped a few feet into the room, waiting for her to tell him what to do. Good boy. She sauntered past him, letting her hips sway with the sensuality coursing through her body. She flicked the flogger against her leg, letting the gentle sting heighten her passion. As eager as she was to play, ground rules needed to be established first. Sitting down in the chair, she settled back and crossed her legs. The flogger rested on her lap.

"Come here and kneel in front of me." She watched him approach her and couldn't hold back a small smile of satisfaction.

Chapter Three

ཉ

Trey kept his steps slow and measured even though he wanted to hurry. It was that damn pride again, he supposed. He didn't want to appear too eager to do this woman's bidding. Of course, the hard ridge of his cock leading the way was an obvious indication. He didn't know what to expect and that uncertainty was perversely incredibly arousing. Being in this room with a woman who would take control away from him made him as hard and horny as a teenager. He was having trouble catching his breath and his balls ached with the need to release. It was as if he were coming off a deployment, not a guy who had jerked himself off multiple times less than a day past.

He was careful to keep his eyes down, yet he could feel her cool gaze on him as he stopped in front of her and slowly sank to his knees. The stone floor was hard and the mild discomfort only increased his arousal. Holy God, how had he missed his need for submissiveness and pain? Having taken a furtive look at the room, he knew that while it was Spartan, it contained enough for him to be initiated into the dark and exciting world of BDSM. Then there was the flogger. Lying on the woman's lap—dare he think of her as his Mistress?—it was elegant in its simplicity. He wondered what it would feel like slapping against his skin. His cock jerked. It was obviously ready to find out.

"You may look at me."

That voice, so soft, yet firm, with a hint of a Boston accent. When he raised his gaze, she looked back at him, an unreadable expression on her face. If she was as turned on by all of this as he was, he couldn't tell. There were so many questions he wanted to ask her. He struggled to remain silent.

This was not a briefing of an assignment. He didn't need to know everything, only what she decided to tell him. She was in control, not him. He didn't have to worry about anything at all. Not his job. He willed himself to relax, loosening his grip, letting his shoulders slump down.

His Mistress nodded. "Good, you're starting to understand that in here, you may let go. What we do, what will or will not happen is for me to decide. You have no duty here save obeying me. Simple. Relaxing, is it not?"

Trey took a deep breath and let it out slowly. "Yes, yes, it is. Mistress," he added on. Remembering to show her the proper respect should be easy for him. It was no different from being in the army.

Lifting one foot, she placed the toe of her shoe lightly against his erection. A grunt escaped his lips before he could stop it. She smiled. "You don't have to hide your pleasure. I like seeing you hard. Do your balls ache?"

The question caught him by surprise, but he smiled back at her and answered truthfully. "Yes."

"Would you like me to undo those pants, reach inside and curl my fingers around your cock? Do you want me to squeeze and pump your hard flesh until your balls empty themselves all over my hand?" To emphasize her words, she pressed her foot more firmly against his package.

This time, the intense pleasure doubled him over. He moaned long and low. "God, yes," he replied, trying to control himself, trying not to come in his pants like a virgin. The foot pulled away. Recovering his breath, he kneeled straight again.

"Well, you can't have what you want, I'm afraid. You can only have what I decide to give you. I'll warn you right now that you will not be coming in this room. It's too soon for that."

Trey closed his eyes briefly at the disappointing news, then focused on what his Mistress said next. "If you and I decide to go ahead and play together, then we'll do a little restraining and light flogging, just to break the ice. I'm willing to train you as a new boy." She paused. "You did mention you are new to all of this, didn't you?"

"Yes, ma'am."

"But you're also used to being in charge in the rest of your life?"

"Yes, ma'am. I was in the army for eight years as an officer. Now I'm with the FBI."

She blinked. "This isn't a raid or something, is it?"

He chuckled. "No, ma'am. This is a man exploring what he's looking for in a woman, in a lover."

"What you want is a woman to dominate you."

It wasn't really a question, yet he answered it anyway. "Yes, ma'am."

"A woman to discipline you."

He closed his eyes once more, picturing what it was going to be like to have the suede flays hitting his back, his ass, his cock and balls. Biting his lip for control, he nodded.

"Because in your life, you're always in control. You're the one with responsibility, and it's a matter of life and death. People are literally counting on you for their very lives. It's difficult and it's stressful. You need some place, some time when you don't have to worry about making the right decision or the wrong one. You need someone else to take control, tell you what to do and beat that stress right out of you."

To have it said so plainly was like a minor miracle. He could hardly believe he had spent so much of his adult life burying this obvious truth. For a moment, he was overwhelmed emotionally. Opening his eyes, blinking back tears, he said, "You understand."

"Of course I do." Her voice was soothing. "You don't have to worry about a thing in this room. I will take good care of you. That's a promise. But it will only work if you trust me. Do you trust me, Trey?"

"I-I don't know," he answered truthfully, afraid he might ruin everything, but determined not to lie to this woman.

"An honest answer. I appreciate that. You don't know me, so how could you know if you can trust me? I have to earn that trust and it starts tonight, if you are willing."

"I am."

She paused. He caught a hint of uncertainty in her expression. "I'm older than you."

He nodded. "I know. I like that. It makes it easier for me to trust you."

"Good." She uncrossed her legs and leaned in closer to him. The warmth of her body played on his arousal. He wanted to touch, yet didn't dare. He needed permission, even a novice like himself understood that. "Now pay attention. Here are the rules. You do what I tell you to do immediately, no questions unless I give you permission to ask them. You stop thinking the moment you are in my presence. You watch and listen and obey. I will control you and your body and I promise to take good care of you. I won't demand anything more of you than I know you can handle. But you have to leave the alpha man outside. You have to relinquish control. Will you do that?"

Trey sighed heavily. "I'll try."

She shook her head. "There is no try. You do it or you don't."

He stared back at her and saw the confidence and resolve in her eyes. If this was ever going to be right for him, he had to jump in with both feet and make a commitment. "I understand, Yoda, I mean, Mistress." God, what was the matter with him, cracking jokes at a time like this?

Her hand reached out but instead of the slap he braced for, she merely patted his cheek. "You don't have to check your sense of humor at the door." Standing up, she added, "Come."

Juliette led her new boy over to the manacles on the wall, not completely sure the scene was going to play out the way she wanted. Trey had been truthful, and that had merit, and yes, the reference to *Star Wars* had been funny. Still, he was going to have trouble giving up decision making. Not that anyone could jump into a BDSM lifestyle without some reservation. She needed to take things slow and steady, fight the urge to ramp things up to her own speed. It would help her, too. Her nervousness and doubt were enemies to her goals.

"Take everything off," she ordered, shutting down the more analytical part of her brain and going into automatic Domme mode.

Trey's hesitation was almost undetectable. She let it go and concentrated instead on the tantalizing show he gave as he took his clothes off. It wasn't that he performed a striptease or anything. The efficient way he pulled off shirt, sneakers, sox, jeans, and underwear had its own satisfaction. A man of action, his movements were smooth, elegant even. He was obviously used to doing a quick strip as a former soldier. If he was self-conscious about being naked in front of her, he didn't give any indication.

For her part, Juliette remained passive as she saw the magnificent body unwrapped for her pleasure. At least she gave no outward signs of how desirable she found him. The sight of his upper body alone with all its finely sculpted muscles had her pussy quivering. Already hard, her nipples tingled and ached within her bra. The urge to rub them against Trey's smooth chest nearly overwhelmed her. Her fingers clenched against her beloved flogger, a distant second to their desire to clasp and squeeze the high, taut globes of his ass. She had to bite her lip to hold back the gasp when his dark, rigid cock sprang free. Her new boy was a damn fine toy. When he was done stripping, he stood silently before her.

"Stand closer to the wall, facing it," she ordered with a weaker voice than she would have liked. Chastising her softness, she took him by the wrist and secured it to one of the manacles. She crossed behind him to do the same thing with his other arm and pulled the restraint tight. His arms extended fully above his head, yet he could still stand comfortably on the flat of his feet.

Now that he was contained, she gave into the temptation to touch. When she ran the fingers of her free hand across his shoulders, his body shivered. Good. She liked that he enjoyed it. Despite the warmth of the room, fine goose bumps rose up from his skin. She detected them as she petted him down his back and over his ass, his firm squeezable ass. He gave little reaction except a small murmur of pleasure when she copped a feel. But when her fingers wandered over to explore the crease between the globes, his body jerked from her touch. His breath hissed out and not in a good way.

Juliette circled toward his side and studied his face. His lips were set in a tight line. "You don't like ass play, do you?" she ventured.

He shook his head once. "No, ma'am. Sorry, I'm not comfortable with the idea of taking anything up there."

Juliette cocked her head. "Well, most men are a little leery at first. We'll work on it."

Trey said nothing, although his expression spoke volumes. "Like hell we will," was how she read it. Doubt crept back in. She couldn't go through another relationship where everything was a battle. This man might be more straightforward than Tom was, but still, it gave her pause.

"Stop it." She was looking for excuses to end this relationship before it even started. Of course an alpha male would worry about yielding his asshole to a woman, or anyone, really. She was getting ahead of herself again. So she let it go and ran her hand down the smooth terrain of his chest. Almost hairless, his skin stretched tautly over finely sculpted muscles. She dipped her fingers in and out of the valleys of his abs, careful not to touch his cock. His breathing turned ragged from this simple attention, and his eyes drifted shut. His

nipples jutted out, begging to be tweaked. With thumb and forefinger, she pinched and tugged each in turn. He gasped. His eyes flew open before narrowing in obvious pleasure.

Juliette was delighted at how responsive her new toy appeared. She returned to standing in back of him. Instead of touching him more with her hands, she used the flogger to caress his back and buttocks. She weaved the soft flays across the expanse of his skin in a way designed to sooth and lull. When the muscles in his shoulders relaxed, she flicked the flays at him to lightly sting. He showed no outward reaction to the low-key pain, so she continued the game of petting for a while and flogging. Each time she snapped the flays against his body, she increased the force, until finally his body jumped. A gasp flew out of his mouth and Juliette smiled at the sound. It had been too long since she had known this pleasure. Her simple cotton slacks molded to her labia from the wetness seeping from her core.

"How are you doing, Trey?" she asked coyly.

"Thank you, ma'am. May I have another?"

She chuckled at the response. The guy did have a fine sense of humor. There was nothing inconsistent with laughing and BDSM. It was supposed to be fun, after all. "You let me know if it gets to be too much."

"Do I need a safe word, ma'am?" he asked, his voice thick with passion.

"You can have one if you want. Personally, I don't use them." Not any more, not after Tom, but she didn't explain that to him. No need to spook him with her emotional baggage. "I'm careful to monitor your condition. Subs have a way of getting so into the zone, into sub space it's called, that they don't have the good sense to ask their Domme to stop. It's my job to take care of you, so I'll decide when it's time to end our play. If you feel at any time that you can't take what I'm doing, then ask me to stop."

"It's that simple? Aren't you worried I'll say stop too quickly?"

"I trust you to say it only when you really mean it." Otherwise they were doomed before they started.

He took a deep breath and let it out in a rush. "I won't say it. I'll take whatever you choose to give me, Mistress."

The last word alone nearly sent her over the edge. God, how she loved having a man in her control again. "I'm glad to hear it. The lesson will continue." Juliette went back to the petting and flogging for a few minutes more before beating his ass in earnest. Setting a horizontal figure eight in motion, she flayed his ass cheeks, occasionally whacking her boy with extra force to see his fine body jerk. He couldn't withhold his grunts of pain any longer and those sounds morphed to more of a yell when she hit him hard enough. A fine red glow covered his skin.

The rhythm of her effort was hypnotic, mellowing her, setting her arousal at a constant high. The muscles of her left arm, so used to the movement, moved without conscious control. She could have worked her boy's ass all night, but the need for vigilance overrode her pleasure. Stopping the beating, she touched his forehead. A fine sheen of sweat covered his brow and his palms were cold and clammy. Although his eyes were closed, his mouth was open to accommodate his heavy breathing. He hadn't said as much, yet she knew he had had enough.

Juliette unbuckled Trey from his restraints, careful to avoid touching his cock. It hadn't lost any of its hardness during the flogging, testament to how much he enjoyed the pain. She wished she had packed a few items after all, like a cock ring to make sure he didn't come. Oh, well, next time. And as she rubbed his arms to help the blood flow, she knew there would be a next time. He remained passive while she ministered to him and his eyes opened a bit to stare at her. He gave her a small, knowing smile before shutting his eyes again. He was a happy man at that moment, to be sure. Pride swelled her chest. She had done it, she had taken the first step back to the way of life that gave her joy. And orgasms, lots and lots of orgasms. In fact, she wanted one before the night ended. Unfortunately, she had a firm policy not to let a boy touch her the first time out. Boundaries needed be established and denial was good for a sub. He would learn to yield his pleasure, all of it, to her command. She had no rule about touching herself, however.

"This way," she ordered walking back to the chair, a firm grip on one of his arms. Although he seemed steady enough, she never took chances. It could take a while for a sub to come down from wherever they went when in sub space. She wouldn't let either of them leave the room until she was sure he could manage on his own. When they arrived at the chair, she gently pushed him toward it. "Sit down and rest."

He looked up at her with a quizzical expression for a second before remembering to lower his gaze. "I'm fine, Mistress, really."

She smacked his left ass cheek with the palm of her hand, making him grunt. "I said, sit!" He did as ordered, although he sat gingerly on his reddened backside. His hands he rested in the tops of his thighs, too close to his erection by her reckoning. "Put your hands on the arm rests. Do not touch your cock. Look at me," she ordered. When his eyes flew up to meet hers, she added, "Watch me and don't move a muscle."

She stepped back a bit and slipped off her jacket, letting it slide to the floor. Shifting her flogger to dangle from her right wrist, she lifted her left hand and opened her blouse, one tiny button at a time. Her gaze stayed on Trey's face, watching him watch her. As she revealed her lacy, black bra, his eyes widened and a small smile played across his lips. She left her shirt tucked into her pants, but slipped her hand under the gaping front to cup her right breast. Her nipple pressed against its confines, hard and needy. She rubbed her finger around it and hummed as a tingling sensation radiated out to engulf her entire breast.

Her sub's gaze zeroed in on her movement, mouth open enough to show gritted teeth. His fingers clenched at the fabric they rested on, while his cock bobbed with the small thrusts his hips made. His harsh breathing mingled with her own to fill the room.

"Be still," she admonished, flicking the flogger around her thighs in emphasis. The delicious sting added to her growing arousal. Her sub complied instantly, a very quick study, indeed, although she could see he was practically popping out of his skin. Excellent.

Her own need drove her to move more quickly. She let go of her breast and popped the clasp on her pants, widening her stance to keep them from falling to the ground. She brought her first two fingers up tease her lips before sliding them into her mouth. She swirled her tongue around the digits to moisten them, not because she needed to. God knew her pussy was dripping wet already after such an arousing scene. No, this show was for Trey, designed to drive him wild even though she forbade him release. She moaned past her fingers, while thrusting them in and out. Trey's body quivered as he watched.

Slipping the fingers out of her mouth, Juliette lowered them to the waist of her panties. Past the elastic and into her curls they went. Her slick folds welcomed them with heat, demanding attention for her clit. The first touch of her swollen nub was almost enough to send her over. She had to force herself to go slow, to tease and build the pleasure. Her breath came out in pants; her eyes wanted to close to savor the sparks of pleasure shooting up her core. She made them stay open so that she could see her sub's face when she climaxed.

It hit her hard and sooner than she wanted. The explosion rocked her body, ripping a cry from her throat. The flogger snapped across her thighs, peaking the pleasure higher, stronger. She moaned and rocked her hips against her hand. Her fingers pressed against her clit, digging into her flesh, driving her up again. The second orgasm, less intense, more diffuse, bathed her body in pleasure. Throughout it all, her gaze remained locked on Trey's, and his remained locked on hers. His body, heaving with every breath, stayed otherwise still, as she had commanded, under her control.

Chapter Four

ᘓ

Juliette watched her new boy slide his pants slowly over his stiff cock and winced. It had to hurt and she considered briefly easing his pain. She let him be, though. Denial was a good training technique for a guy new to submission. It built emotional strength and would make him eager for their next play date. She was certainly looking forward to it. Trey had given her powerful pleasure and he hadn't even touched her. It was the way he had taken to the lifestyle, accepting the pain she gave him, following orders. If ever a man had been tailor-made to be a submissive, it was this one. When he finished dressing, he assumed the submissive stance without being told.

As a reward for herself as much as for him, she went to him and lifting his chin with a finger, gave him a chaste kiss. At least, she'd intended to give only a small sign of approval. His strong, warm lips parted and followed her when she withdrew, pulling her back in. She slanted her head to accept his invitation because God, she had missed this simple comfort. It was effortless to slip her tongue inside his mouth and taste his heat. Her sated and sleepy clit woke up, ready to tackle the hard, straining bulge that stood mere inches away. It would take nothing to lean just a bit farther forward and clasp his hot body to her own.

Too soon. She was doing what she always did, jumping in with both feet. She didn't know this man, couldn't know what kind of sub he'd make with such a short session under their belts. If she had learned nothing else from Tom it was to take things slow and build up the intimacy before giving too much of herself. Reluctantly, she released his mouth and stepped back. The disappointed look on his face tugged at her heart and made her smile.

"That's enough for one night," she said sternly.

"If you say so, Mistress." He clearly wasn't convinced, but then he didn't need to be. It was her job to make the decisions.

"I do," she replied. Giving the room a once over to make sure it was as clean as when they had come in, she turned and walked out. She smiled and said goodbye to Dru who hovered by the front door, a Cheshire Cat grin on her face. The bouncer held the door open for them, wearing a similar expression. It lifted Juliette's spirits even more to know others had witnessed her successful comeback into the lifestyle.

The September night was nice and cool. Few people were hanging about this part of Boston on a Sunday. She stopped at the curb and looked at Trey. He joined her, still holding his submissive pose. It spoke well of him that he was able to keep his role even in the "real" world. But play time was over and he wasn't hers permanently, so she released him from his obligation.

"You don't have to submit any more tonight," she informed him, although she hated to stop. When he raised his eyes to hers, she forgot her disappointment. She almost forgot her name. Inside the club, she hadn't noticed his sexy hazel eyes much because she had been so intent on making him submit. Now they pinned her, made her heart stutter. They told her he wanted her, he needed her. She stepped back to ease the intensity of his gaze.

"Well, it's late. Did you drive?" That was it, keep it mundane, ignore the fire his look had started deep in her belly.

He blinked a few times before answering. "Yes, I'm parked a few blocks that way," he said pointing behind him.

"Oh, well, I'm in a lot this way." She pointed in the opposite direction.

"I'll walk you to your car."

"Thanks, but it won't be necessary." The night wasn't quite as cool anymore and if she didn't distance herself from this man, she might become the first verified case of spontaneous human combustion.

Trey shook his head. "Sorry, but it is. This is no place for a woman to walk alone at night. Shall we?" He gestured her forward, one hand hovering near her back as if to steer her down the sidewalk. It was that possessive yet gentlemanly way men had of helping a woman along. The Domme in her bristled at his manner. The primitive part of her, though, melted at the gesture. Besides he was right, she'd be stupid to refuse the escort.

They walked in silence the couple of blocks to the little, mostly empty lot where she had left her car. Taking keys from her pocket, she unlocked the door and slid inside the driver's seat. Trey stood by the open door, his arm resting on the frame. "Will I see you again, Mistress?" His voice was low and thick.

She swallowed hard. "Juliette. Out here, Juliette is fine, and yes, you will. Are you free tomorrow night?" So much for slow! The question was out before she could stop it. She held her breath, waiting for a reply.

"Yes, I am," he answered, then frowned. "Oh, maybe not. My current assignment might go later tomorrow than planned."

She shoved her disappointment away. Of course the man had a life. Work came before play, and his work was more important than most. "That's right, you're with the FBI?"

"Yes, ma'am, Special Agent Trey Boudreaux." He didn't offer his hand to shake which was just as well given what they'd done minutes ago. It would be too weird to step back to formality.

"My last name's Coyne," she replied and reaching inside the console beside her seat, took out a business card. "Let's say we meet back here tomorrow night at the same time. If you can't make it, please call my mobile number and we can reschedule. If you decide you want to, that is." There it was, her insecurity. She hadn't had it all her life, only since Tom, the rat-bastard.

Trey raised his eyebrows. "Oh, I want to. If I have been even a little bit unclear about how much I've enjoyed myself this evening, Mistress Juliette, please allow me to rectify it right now." He gestured toward his still hard cock pressing against his pants. Then he looked at her card and frowned. "You're an accountant?"

Juliette stiffened at the question. "Yes, why, do you have something against bookkeeping?"

Trey chuckled and slipped her card into his pocket. "No, I guess I figured you'd have a more, uh, athletic career."

"You mean because I like to beat men?" She saw where he was coming from. He shrugged and looked back at her sheepishly. Now, she chuckled. "Like everyone else, I have my quiet, boring side. Anyway, being good with numbers helps me keep track of how many times I strike your ass." She gave him a sly smile.

He closed his eyes and moaned. "You are killing me."

"Good." She pulled her door shut, started the engine and rolled down the window. "Now, Trey, you will be a good sub and keep yourself nice and hard for me until we meet again."

His eyes widened. "You mean I can't give myself any relief?"

She deliberately made her voice hard. "I mean that you, your body, including your magnificent cock, belong to me for the next little while. You will not touch yourself or rub yourself or let anyone else do it. You will stay ready for me and only me. Is that understood?"

"Yes, ma'am, and so we're clear, there is no one else who is touching my body right now. I'm all yours."

Juliette's breath hitched at his declaration, but she didn't let him see how affected she was. "Damn right you are," she concurred and peeled away before she lost control and pulled the man into her car.

* * * * *

"Eight." The word burst past Trey's lips as pain shot through his body. His Mistress wielded a crop this second night of play. It gave a sting more potent than the flogger as it concentrated on a smaller portion of his body. Because she made him count the strokes, there was no chance, either, to relax into the rhythm of the beating. The drifting peace of the previous night eluded him. Instead, his body was inflamed with pain from the bite of the crop and the tiny clothespins digging into his nipples.

"Nine," he groaned as the crop slapped against his ass once more. He yanked reflexively against his bonds. Once more, they were in the stark room, his wrists manacled above his head. Nude, exposed, and under the control of a woman he hardly knew, he had never felt more alive. It was not unlike the heightened awareness that he had experienced when in battle. This situation, however, made him feel safe and secure, as well. His raging hard-on came not only from the adrenaline rush, but also from the stimulation of the pain. There was no question that he was a submissive and a masochist. His cock had been in various stages of hardness since the previous night. Every pinch, slap, poke and prod from his Mistress made his rod harder, his balls more achy and his slit weep with pre-cum.

"T-ten." That was it. He had done it. Ten strokes and he would get a reward. He didn't know yet what it was. He wasn't worried, though. His Mistress would tell him what she wanted him to know when she wanted him to know it. All he had to do was endure and obey. It was Heaven on Earth.

"Good boy," his Mistress cooed, her cool fingers wiping across his brow. "Time to get you down. First we'll remove the clips. Take a deep breath, darling, this will hurt much more than they did going on."

Sharp agony ripped through his chest when first one clip came off and then the other. Trey yelled and gulped in air. He gritted his teeth against the pain, then he hardly noticed it. The effect was muted by warmth that gripped his cock below the base of the head. His Mistress squeezed and tugged his erection with one hand, while the other kneaded blood back into his nipples. He moaned long and low, his head thrown back, his fingers curled into fists. But there was no relief for him yet. Instead of continuing her cock massage, his Mistress stood up and released his wrists. He grimaced and swayed as she lowered his arms, rubbing the muscles. Her smaller body bolstered his until he was steady on his feet once more.

"Time for your reward," she whispered, her breath tickling his ear. "Follow me."

Juliette turned and walked over to the chair. Her body hummed with arousal. Trey had taken a good amount of pain, had been a good little sub and now he would know how much she appreciated his behavior. Turning again, she watched him approach. His steps were steady, a good sign that he was strong and she had been careful enough with him. Without being told, he kept his gaze down, another good sign. He learned quickly and well. He stopped a couple of feet from where she stood. His cock beckoned, and it took all of her resolve not to reach out and clasp it again. Instead she gave herself a few seconds to imagine what it would feel like to straddle this man and slide his hot, hard length into her pussy. It would stretch and fill her and she would welcome it with slick warmth and a tight squeeze.

God, if she thought about fucking Trey long enough, she'd come right there. It was too soon for such intimacy in any event. That didn't mean she couldn't enjoy other parts of his body. Toeing off her shoes, she said, "Remove my pants."

Trey jumped slightly at the command as if she had whacked him hard with her crop. She didn't need to order him again, however. He closed the gap between them and with slightly shaky hands, undid the clasp of her pants. They both watched them pool around her ankles before he knelt down and lifted first one of her feet and then the other to free her of the material. He stayed kneeling, waiting for the next command, his gaze fixed on her pubic mound. She knew the small triangle of red silk was wet from her juices. She smiled when he licked his lips. She snapped the crop against his cock for the pleasure of seeing of his mouth pop open in a yelp.

"Naughty boy," she chided. "I can tell you want a taste of me." She gave a mock sigh. "I suppose I can indulge you, but you're going to have to work for it. Pull down my panties." She paused, grabbed a fistful of his hair and yanked him back when he raised his hands to comply. "With your teeth."

He arched his eyebrows, then put his hands behind his back and leaned forward. She kept her hand in his hair to steady them both and stared at the wall behind him as his mouth descended to the top of her thong. His warm breath tickled her skin before his lips kissed it just long enough to give his teeth purchase. The cloth pulled away from her and was tugged down, exposing the swatch of wet curls. The coolness of being exposed only worked to heighten her arousal. Her fingers dug into her boy's scalp. His gasp uttered through a mouthful of silk made her pussy clench. When he had managed to drag her panties past her knees, she stepped out of them to finish the job. Her need made her impatient.

Releasing Trey, Juliette turned and took off her jacket. Spreading it on the chair's seat, she turned again and sat down, her legs spread wide in invitation. "Come to me, my pet, on your knees and show me what that handsome mouth of yours can do."

Trey gripped his wrist so tight, it was a wonder he didn't break something. His ass was on fire from the beating he had received only minutes before, yet his erection had never wavered. If anything, it had grown longer and harder. Now he was staring at his Mistress' pussy, plump and pink with a hint of dark curls. The glistening flesh winked at him and beckoned. His cock pulsed with the need to push inside those welcoming folds and find release. It took all his strength and discipline not to grab his cock and pump the ache right out. But he didn't have permission to do that. His orders were to crawl to that heavenly place and worship it with his mouth, his lips, his tongue and God, his teeth. This was a mission he knew he could accomplish.

His gaze fixed on his destination, he knee-walked the few feet. Before he could lean into the chair, however, his Mistress grabbed a fistful of hair and held him back. The sting of his scalp made him grunt with pleasure even as he resisted the urge to push forward. He didn't like being stopped. He didn't like having to wait for a taste of this luscious woman.

"Easy," she commanded. "You're here for my pleasure, not yours. To that end, you will make sure that at no time does your cock touch this chair. You will not get yourself off while you pleasure me. Understand?" Her fingers tightened their grip.

Trey grimaced at the words as much as the discomfort, but he responded the only acceptable way. "Yes, ma'am."

"Good." She released him and settled back, eyes closed.

It wasn't easy to do as told. He had to brace his legs apart to achieve the right leverage. Even then, he didn't dive in right away. He wanted to, oh, how he wanted to. He decided, instead, to tease them both by starting with little flicks of his tongue on the inside of her right knee. Her skin was as soft and smooth as her panties. It was warm, too, and even that far away from her cunt, her scent teased his nostrils. He breathed in deeply while he licked his way up her inner thigh. With his eyes closed, he pictured where he was headed, still wanting to race to the finish. His cock was off-limits, but his Mistress had said nothing about other parts of his body. As he leaned in farther to plant kisses near her junction, his nipples rasped against the lining of her jacket. Never before had he or anyone paid particular attention to them. The clamps had heightened their sensitivity. A jolt of pleasure hit him low in the belly.

Trey moaned and was rewarded with an echo from his Mistress. Her legs moved restlessly while he switched to attend her left one. A hand descended on his head and fingers ran through his hair. There was no grabbing this time and he perversely missed the bite of pain. Still, it encouraged him, told him he pleased her. He would have been happy to nuzzle her thighs longer, but when next his face lay inches from her pussy, her hips bucked a little in invitation. Never one to turn down a lady, Trey slid his tongue between her folds and gave one long lick up her slit.

"Oh, God," she sighed and now her fingers clenched his scalp.

He smiled as he buried his face between her legs, lapping and sucking at her juicy clit. It had been literally years since he had tasted a woman and never had one been so delicious. Sweet and salty, wet and warm, his Mistress was a treat. He licked and nibbled at her swollen flesh, making her writhe ever faster. Her legs closed in on him, her heels dug into his back, urging him to go faster, harder. Keening moans filled the room. She pressed her body so tightly into his face he could hardly breathe. And, yet he stayed firm, taking her clit between his lips and sucking the climax out of her. She doubled over, clasping his head in both hands. He released his hold only to use his tongue once more, lapping her with short strokes to bring another release. She had no time to catch her breath before he sent her over again, and he would have kept going if she hadn't shouted and shoved him away from her.

Trey caught himself with his hands, sitting with his fiery ass on the cool stone floor. His Mistress was collapsed against the chair, eyes closed, legs akimbo. She was the perfect picture of a woman satisfied to bonelessness. He stared at her with a measure of pride. He hadn't known such utter satisfaction before, even while his cock remained hard and aching. If only Juliette would grant him some relief.

As he thought it, her eyes opened to sleepy slits. "Your turn, precious." His cock jerked at her words and he shifted back to a kneeling position, hands clenched behind his back. His breath quickened at the notion of finally getting off. "You're right handed?"

"Yes, ma'am."

"Then grip your cock with your left hand." He did as order and shuddered at the feel of his own touch. Not as good as his Mistress', but after so many hours of restraint, any hand would do. He pumped his hard flesh upward.

"Stop!" He froze. "I didn't say you could jerk yourself. Be still. You will move only when I tell you to and stop immediately if I say so. Otherwise there will be no orgasm for you tonight." Trey shuddered at the effort to obey, a fine sheen of sweat popped out all over his body. He had never been so aroused.

"Very well, you may work your cock—slowly. You will not come until I tell you to. Is that clear?"

Trey nodded. "Yes, ma'am." The words were little more than grunts as he stroked himself slowly and carefully. Enough pre-cum leaked out to slick his movements, but his flesh still burned with need. His balls, pulled tightly to his body, ached for release. The tremors of a climax climbed up from the core of his body, threatening to erupt from his cock. His body shook from the effort to hold back. He didn't have permission.

"Hold for me, Trey." His Mistress' voice was low and seductive. "I know you can wait for my command. I won't make you do anything more than you can. Do you believe me?"

"Yes," he managed to bite out.

"Do you trust me?"

Trust? Did he trust her? Yes, she could take care of him. She was taking care of him. Oh, God, he needed to come. His answer was more grunt than word. "Yes!"

"All right, then, now."

The last word was barely out her mouth before he let himself go. With a roar, Trey climaxed, semen spurting out of his engorged cock. His fist clenched and yanked the orgasm out of his body. He doubled over, his other hand squeezed his balls, more pain and pleasure mixing. He became deaf and blind to everything except the spasms of his cock as he milked that last of the cum from it.

And, then a hand descended on his head, petted him, and he knew he had just had the best sex of his life.

Chapter Five

ꙮ

"I said don't move!" Trey grimaced with satisfaction as he ground his knee deeper into his squirming prisoner's back and snapped cuffs in place. The little shit howled like a kid who'd dropped his ice cream cone, but he was well and truly trussed. The guy had to know the FBI had compiled enough information to send him and his friends away for the rest of their wretched lives. Terrorists be damned, it was still good to put away old fashioned mobsters who preyed on Americans every day. Trey stood up, hauling his catch of the day with him. Mike jogged over.

"Holy Christ, what's put the spring in your step?" Trey quirked his eyebrows. "The way you climbed that fence and brought this mother down, you were in fine form my friend." Mike slapped him on the back. "Man, bringing down the Moss gang makes this a beautiful day."

"For some people, maybe," grumbled the prisoner.

"No one asked you, asshole," Trey snarled, but he was grinning like a fool. The takedown was wrapping up early enough for him to meet Juliette. God, his cock throbbed. It had remained hard all night and most of the day. The temptation to make it go away had been strong, ignoring the urge had been pure torture. Still, he hadn't touched himself because his Mistress had ordered him not to—again. The very thought that a woman now controlled him, or his body anyway, turned his arousal up to an eleven. It was hard to wrap his mind around the fact that he had actually taken the step to become some woman's toy.

Had he really gone to a strange club, sat around waiting for a woman to pick him up and then when one did, followed her into a room, let her string him up and whip his ass? Yes, his ass was telling him with its faint sting, he had. And, he had done it again two nights ago. It had been amazing. The beatings had been not only arousing, but calming. The stress had fled his body, leaving him satiated and refreshed the next day. Except one part, of course, remained needy. His erection had begun the moment he had laid eyes on Juliette and hadn't flagged with the pain, or with the glorious experience of going down on her or even jerking himself off at her command. He licked his lips and swore he could still taste her. He grunted as he shoved the prisoner into the back of a car. Both the guy and Mike stared at him. He slammed the door and smiled back at his friend.

Mike gave him the once over, but Trey had strategically crossed his hands in front of him. Still, the guy was no fool. His eyes narrowed. "You've been awfully cheerful all day and for the better part of the week, come to think of it. Damn, boy, are you getting yourself laid again?"

"No, sir, I am not," he answered in all honesty.

His friend didn't seem convinced. "Something's up with you." He beckoned with his fingers. "Give."

With a grunt, Trey moved away from the car and with a flick of his head, asked the other man to join him. He wasn't sure what to say, but this was his best friend, a man he had fought alongside and was still fighting alongside albeit in a very different sort of war. Besides as safe he had felt in the club and with Juliette, it would be wise for someone else to know where he was going.

How to tell his friend, though? It wasn't exactly small talk. *Hey, great news, I found my inner submissive! Want to go have a beer in celebration?* No, that approach might give his friend a heart attack, although frankly he couldn't think of a more acceptable way to broach the subject. Damn. He pinched the bridge of his nose before taking a deep breath and just spitting it out. "Remember that weird card I found in my pocket last Sunday? Well, I called it, went to this club in the old Leather

District, met a woman and let her work me over. I enjoyed it enough to have met her twice."

Mike stared back at him as if frozen in time for a few seconds. Blinking hard, he said, "You're not joking. I can tell when you're joking and you're not."

"No, I'm not." Trey grinned and shrugged.

His friend rubbed a hand down his face. "So let me get this straight. You went to a strange club and let a strange woman, what, beat you?"

"With a suede flogger. She has crops and paddles, but the flogger is her favorite." He waited a beat. "And mine."

"Uh-huh. What color is it?"

"What difference does that make?"

"Just answer the question."

"Red and black. Beautiful really. Looked handmade."

"Uh-huh," Mike said again. "And, this woman, does she look like Catwoman, or something?"

"No, actually she looks like an accountant, which is what she is."

"An accountant? An accountant beat you with a beautiful, handmade, red and black suede flogger?"

Trey blew out a long breath. "You sound like you don't believe me."

Mike held up his hands in surrender. "Oh, I believe you. Only a psycho could make up that kind of detail and I know you're not a mental case. It's the weirdest goddamn thing I've ever heard, but I for sure believe you. I have one final question. Do you really like it?"

In answer to the question, Trey unclasped his hands and spread his arms wide. His friend glanced down at Trey's crotch, as intended, and winced. "Oh, man, you're going to make my eyeballs bleed. I do not need to see that. A simple yes would do."

Chuckling, Trey clasped his friend on the shoulder. "Come on, I want to finish up the paperwork and get going. I have a date tonight."

"With the sadistic accountant?" When he nodded, Mike continued, "Are you going to get laid tonight?"

"I don't know. That's for my Mistress to decide." As he said it, his muscles relaxed a fraction. He didn't know what would happen that night, but he didn't need to know. It wasn't his decision, wasn't his problem, to decide. Relinquishing control was liberating. Soon he could stop thinking, stop worrying, and the mere thought of it gave him a measure of peace he hadn't known in a long time.

* * * * *

Juliette entered Unfettered and already felt at home. The club was a little bit more lively than it had been the other nights. There were a couple of dozen people milling about. A few of them tried to catch her eye immediately, but she was looking for one man only, and there he was. Trey sat on the same stool as she had ordered, drinking what she knew to be soda water, again as she had ordered. She wanted his mind clear for what she planned. She hefted her gym bag higher on her shoulder. This time she had come with more advanced toys to play with. Their scenes together had been successful thus far, and she deemed it time to step things up, make them more intimate.

She made her approach slow and quiet and was pleased when he turned to see her even before she arrived. Her pleasure increased tenfold when he stood up and assumed his submissive pose. Yet he hadn't done so quickly enough for her to miss his expression. Hungry, that was the right description for it. It was as she had hoped when dressing for the evening. Gone were her business casual clothes. Instead, she wore a sleeveless black suede minidress, cut low to accentuate her breasts. Her high-heeled boots were red suede, the ensemble a deliberate homage to her precious flogger. She had dressed to entice and incite. The thick bulge of her boy's jeans confirmed she'd succeeded.

She didn't bother to say anything, merely turned on one sharp heel and strode toward the play rooms. Of course, Trey followed her, that was a given. After a quick consultation with Dru, Juliette entered a room farther down the hall from the simple room they had used the previous nights. This new chamber was set up like a bedroom, a simple one, but it served her intent very nicely. The dominant piece of furniture was a dark, steel-framed canopy bed with a flat top and a St. Andrew's cross at the foot. Perfect, given that she'd decided to first beat her boy and then fuck him. Perhaps it was too soon for that type of intimacy, yet she couldn't resist. Just seeing the man again had sent her body into overdrive. Panty-less as she was, her inner thighs were already wet from her juices.

Juliette went to place her bag on a low table by the wall. "Strip." She didn't turn to watch him, although she wanted to very badly. Instead, she opened her bag and pulled out a few toys. She took a couple of yoga breaths for calm before turning to look at Trey. It was her long experience as a Domme that kept her from giving any outward signs of pleasure. She perused her naked sub, standing with legs braced, head down and hands clasped behind his back. His cock jutted out from his body, hard and dark from engorgement. Her pussy clenched at the sight. Her nipples tightened and tingled. What she wanted was to go to him, drop to her knees and swallow that magnificent rod whole.

What she did was scoop up a couple of her toys and saunter toward him. It was hard to do, but necessary. It was her duty to be in control. He needed to know he could trust her to be careful. If she gave into her impulses, he would be right to worry she couldn't be trusted to stop if necessary. So she took it slow, stopping in front of him, gently taking his hard length in a firm grip and yanking. A harsh sound, part groan, part gasp, erupted from his mouth.

She cooed to soothe him, yet kept her grip tight. "Have you been a good boy, Trey, and left your cock alone?"

"Yes, ma'am." The struggle to speak clearly was obvious. The poor boy was in pain, and he was going to be in more soon enough.

"Go stand against the cross, facing me," she ordered, following him as he complied. She didn't bother to truss him up for what she had planned. He had already proven himself to be stoic, so she judged he'd be able to stand still while she applied her toys to his body. "First things first," she said briskly. "I've seen stronger boys than you coming spontaneously from a good beating. We can't have that now, can we? This simple harness will keep you nice and hard until I say otherwise."

As she spoke, Juliette snapped a soft leather cuff around the base of his cock and wrapped its split strap down between his balls to separate them. When she snapped the two tongues of the strap to the cuff, Trey's package was secured high and tight against his body. His breath became more labored. The taut skin of his cock darkened. She ran a finger up the length of it and flicked the glans just to see him jerk. He didn't disappoint.

"Good," she purred. "Now a little bit more pain to add to both of our pleasure." She had brought her more elaborate nipple clamps this time. She leaned over and laved his right nipple with the tip of her tongue. Not many straight men appreciated the sensitivity of their own chest. It delighted her when he uttered a low curse.

His response morphed into a full blown "Holy Fuck" when she removed her tongue and replaced it with the clamps, tightening them into his aroused flesh.

"Wait until I take it off," she warned sweetly. "Remember the pain will be far worse." She repeated her ministrations with his left nipple, but she wasn't done yet. Grabbing a handful of the clothespins, she applied a few along the underside of his restrained cock. Engorged as it was, little skin was available to pinch, making the pain that much more intense. Trey shook and stuttered out low moans as she worked her way down the shaft. He howled when she moved to his balls, head thrown back. Moisture leaked from the corners of his eyes. Juliette thumbed away the tears with a murmur of comfort and stood back to admire her handiwork. Despite her sub's response, she knew the restraints were quite mild. They were plenty for what was only their third time at play, however. It was hard to believe they had known each other for such a short time, she was so comfortable with him already. "Turn around, spread you legs and place your hands on the cross by the shackles."

With a shuddering breath, he obeyed her, keeping his body far enough from the cross so that his cock didn't touch it. The cross was made from the same dark steel as the bed frame, with bars that were a couple of inches wide. She secured his ankles first into cuffs lined with a soft material, then she did the same with his wrists, pulling everything tight so that he couldn't move his arms and legs. He said nothing while she moved his body into position. His breath, though, became more labored and the hairs stood up on his body.

With him at her mercy, Juliette allowed herself the pleasure of touching him some more. She ran her fingers lightly down his arms and across his shoulders. The muscles bunched under her touch. "Relax," she whispered into one ear and was pleased when she felt the tension drain out of him. She kept going to pet and cup the taut globes of his ass. She was tempted to slip a finger into him, but didn't. She remembered his reaction from the first night. Pegging would be something she would need to introduce slowly. She would do it, eventually. It was the ultimate surrender for a straight man and unless he surrendered to her fully, there was no future for them.

She was getting ahead of herself, again. For now, there was so much fun for them to have. She retrieved her flogger from her bag and returned to stand behind him. Without warning, she went to work on his shoulders, beating first one side and then the other. Each time the suede tails hit, he uttered a gasp or a groan. She moved down to his ass quickly, careful to avoid slapping the flogger against his kidneys or around his hips. Instead, she went for the meat, setting a figure eight motion that soon sent her into the zone. Rhythmic, hypnotic, she could do it all night. She bet her new boy could take it all night, too, but that would be far easier and less fun than what she was capable of giving him.

She paused her stroke a fraction of a second before landing a hard slap against one ass cheek. Trey yelled out. The wetness of her labia increased. Her clit and nipples throbbed to the beat of her flogger. She let go another stinging stroke, made him cry out once more, and her own breath whooshed out of her lungs. She was hardly straining herself, yet her lungs felt as if they needed more air. She picked up the rhythm, hitting harder, ratcheting up the tension. Trey grunted now with each blow, his arms and legs tugged at their restraints. A fine sheen of sweat coated his back. He neared the breaking point.

Recognizing as much, Juliette gave one last, hard blow and stopped. She ran a hand over her head and yanked a bit on her braid, reveling in the bite of pain. Time to give them both relief. Putting her flogger away, she went to her boy and wrapped her body around his from the back. Heat poured out of him and into her. She sighed and clasped the area beneath his balls and tugged up to make him groan. She rubbed her own aching body against his to make herself moan. Then she moved her hands up to his chest and fingered the clamps, twisted them back and forth.

"Shit!" Trey forced the word.

"Mmm, isn't it wonderful?" she purred, rubbing against him even more to make her clit sing. She stretched up on her toes and first licked, then nipped his ear lobe. "You've been such a good and brave boy, I'm going to let you fuck me now."

Blood roared through Trey's body. It drowned out virtually every other sound except for Juliette's voice, his Mistress' voice. She was going to let him fuck her now, her words. He hadn't dared hope the evening would include getting inside her luscious body. He tried to stay strong as she released him from the restraints. It was hard, his body was alive with the pain she had given him, yet numb, too. He swayed a little when his arms were freed. But she was there for him, giving her body in support, massaging the blood back into his hands. She led him over to the bed and pushed him gently down. Sitting, his face was level with her magnificent breasts. Soft, round flesh swelled over her neckline. The urge to taste overwhelmed him and he leaned forward. A sharp tug of his hair brought him up short.

"Uh-uh," his Mistress admonished. "I did not give you permission."

He nodded once to show he understood, his throat suddenly so dry, he didn't think he could speak. He remained passive as she positioned him down on his back and secured his ankles and wrists once more with shackles at each bed post. His arms and legs were stretched taut again enough to make him ache. His arousal had never been so great. He didn't doubt that without the cock harness, he might very well have come already. He loved the idea too, as he always had, of the woman being on top and in control. Never before had a woman done it without his urging. The freedom of not having to worry about what to do added to his pleasure in an indescribable way.

"Trey, look at me."

The sharp command jerked him out of his thoughts. He turned his head toward his Mistress, and once his gaze locked with hers, she stripped down to join him. Her movements were slow, calculated. First she lowered the side zipper of her dress, then let the top slide down her arms, down past her breasts. His breath hitched when he saw her hard, dusky nipples freed. He licked his lips. Would she ever give him a taste? God, he hoped so. As the dress dropped down to the floor, his attention shifted to her plump mons and the swatch of curls he was already acquainted with. His stomach clenched when he realized she had been panty-less during his beating.

His Mistress smiled at him. She held up one finger as if to silence him and wagged it. His gaze now fixed at that point, he watched her run the finger down between her breasts, past her stomach and through her curls. A low moan escaped him when the finger dipped between her folds and disappeared. Her hand moved up and down. His hips bucked in sympathetic rhythm. She took a piece of her lower lip between her teeth and moaned back at him.

"Fuck, fuck!" he panted. His cock strained ineffectively within the harness. It felt as if it would burst. The ache in his balls spread up his body.

His Mistress pursed her lips and blew him a kiss. "Okay, sweet boy," she cooed.

Taking her finger away from her clit, she stepped out of her dress and dug into her bag. Out popped a condom in her hand. Trey almost wept from relief. Finally! She sauntered over to him and climbed up on the bed. Kneeling beside him, she took her time giving him what he desperately wanted. Her fingers played across the tops of those damnable pins torturing his aroused flesh. He gritted his teeth against the pain. When she pulled the first one off, a howl ripped past his lips.

"Oh, yes, my darling," his Mistress crooned. "That's what I like. Let me hear how much pain you're in. It makes my pussy weep. See how wet you've made me already."

Trey's gaze lowered to drink in the sight of her glistening mons and slick inner thighs. So transfixed was he by her obvious arousal, he barely noticed his own agony and the ensuing cries of his own voice as she freed his cock and balls from the remaining pins. He panted like a dog when she was done, yet his gaze never wandered and his mind focused on the promise of sliding into all that wet heat beckoning him.

Juliette teased the underside of his cock and squeezed his balls for a short while. He hissed and bucked throughout the playful assault. Small grunts passed his lips until she undid the straps and freed his package. He sighed, then growled when finally she unwrapped the condom down his length.

His Mistress studied her handiwork for a few seconds before looking into his eyes. "Shall I straddle you now, Trey? Shall I place your cock against the entrance of my cunt?"

"Yes, please, Mistress." It was a strain to speak. He wanted to howl again instead.

"Very well." Her tone was soft and matter-of-fact, but there was an underlying breathlessness to it. She was not as cool and in control as she wanted him to believe. The knowledge added to his heat. He wanted to have that effect on her.

She did as promised and with her legs clamped firmly against his thighs, she poised him at her entrance. "Shall I slide your cock into my pussy? I'm very hot and very wet, you know. And tight." To emphasize her words, she squeezed his rod with her fingers.

He bucked up, trying to push inside her. "Yes, God, yes. Please, Mistress!" He was beyond caring how he sounded. This waiting was the worst kind of torture.

Without further warning, Juliette impaled herself on him. His cock shot up inside her welcoming cunt, instantly caught in the promised hot, wet and tight embrace. "Don't come!" she ordered.

That he complied was a minor miracle. It took all his strength. He clenched his teeth, closed his eyes and concentrated on the pain of his back and ass against the synthetic bedding. With slow rocking movements, she rode him. Each time she took him back into the depths of her body, the walls of her pussy clenched tight, milking his cock as she pulled up. Her hands rested against his abs, fingertips pressing into his taut flesh. Her rhythm picked up, her body riding him higher and higher. His climax built, threatened to spill over, and then he felt her grip him like a vice, heard her cry out. Past the roaring of blood in his ears, he heard her shout for him to come. He burst inside her and at that moment, the clips were pulled from his nipples. Agony shot through his chest. He yelled, pulling at his restraints, as pleasure and pain warred within him, fighting, joining, taunting each other to new heights.

As the orgasm faded, his body relaxed. His breath came out in harsh pants. Eyes mere slits, he looked at his Mistress. Her head thrown back while she milked the last of her climax, she looked wild, a goddess, the perfect woman for him. His eyes slid closed again.

"Yes," he whispered.

Chapter Six

ʚɞ

Trey's hand shook a bit with fatigue as he brought the cup of tea to his lips and took a sip of the scalding liquid. He and Juliette sat in a mostly empty restaurant in nearby Chinatown, waiting for a light meal. His Mistress had surprised him and beaten him to the punch by asking him out once she had deemed him recovered enough from their scene to leave the club. He had turned the tables on her by first making sure the scene was done and then by telling her he considered this a date, his treat, of course. He could see the internal debate by her expression before she had relented and let him have his way. The decision hadn't diminished her power and control in his mind, and he assumed not in hers either given that she was there sipping serenely at her own tea. He wanted time outside the dungeon to get to know her. She wasn't simply his Domme. She intrigued him, and he wanted more than being each other's playmates.

It was no different from any other date he'd ever been on, except that his body ached from their play and his cock ached despite it. Of course, sitting across from a woman sheathed in such sexy clothes would do that to a man. Resting his elbows on the table, he continued to sip his tea and enjoy the view. He couldn't help but grin.

Juliette narrowed her gaze, a teasing smile played across her lips. "What?"

"What what?" he replied.

She leaned over, chin resting on her palm. "You look awfully smug."

He ducked his head down and looked at her from under his lashes, suddenly shy. "I'm just a guy who's been well worked by his Mistress."

"Hmm. I'll give you that. Is it weird to be out like this after what we've done?"

"A little," he conceded. "But I can honestly say I've never felt more relaxed." Despite his current state of arousal, there was no denying that allowing a woman to control his orgasms made them stronger and more satisfying.

"Good. I'm enjoying our play, and it always works up an appetite, so I'm glad for the dinner. And, it's nice to have time to get to know you outside play."

Her words echoed his thoughts so precisely he couldn't help blurting out, "I like you." He groaned. "Damn, that sounded lame."

"No, it didn't," she was quick to assure him. "I like you, too." Color infused her cheeks and she looked down in a very unDomme-like fashion.

Her shyness charmed him. They were quiet for a few minutes, each concentrating on their tea, before he ventured a question of his own. "May I ask you something?"

"Of course."

He didn't ask anything right away because their dishes arrived. They both tucked into them like starving wolves. When the worst of his hunger was appeased, Trey asked, "When did you first realize you were a Domme?"

Juliette swallowed her mouthful. "Oh, I guess I had an inkling as far back as grade school. I always loved ordering the boys around." She shrugged. "In college, I met a guy who introduced me to the lifestyle, although he was looking for a sub. We both realized pretty quickly we were a mismatch." She took a sip of her water. "He mentored me, taught me how to be a good Domme." Her mood turned pensive. "I lost sight of myself for the last few months."

Trey leaned forward and rested his arms on the table, food forgotten for the moment. He'd seen something in her eyes, heard something in her voice. She had been hurt. The realization made him mad and protective. He might be a submissive sexually, but he was an alpha male nevertheless. "What do you mean? What happened?"

She shook her head. "Nothing, really." When he remained staring at her, she shrugged again. "I made a poor choice in a sub last year. He was young and very pretty, and apparently I have a weakness for those attributes." She gave him sly smile and passion flared in his otherwise sated belly. Sighing, she looked away. "He was clever, too, a manipulative sub." Her gaze returned to him. "You've heard of topping from the bottom?"

He pursed his lips. "Maybe."

"In a true Dom/sub relationship, it's the sub with the real power. You give to us control and trust. It's a powerful position and a humbling experience for the Domme. Some subs, though, aren't really giving the power up. They keep the control in a subtle way that a Domme should recognize and squash or break off the relationship. I thought I could spot that kind of thing. I was wrong."

He heard the bitterness in her voice and anger, not just at the guy, but at herself, too. Again, the need to protect her, soothe her, reared up. "You did spot it," he pointed out. "You're not with the little bastard any more are you?"

She smiled wanly at him. "I guess that's true. I did realize what was going on, although by the time I had, I had lost confidence in myself. The night we met, I was trying to ease back into the scene."

Without thinking it through, Trey reached a hand over and clasped hers. "I'm very glad you did. You are a wonderful Mistress."

She laughed. "How would you know?" she teased, lacing her fingers in with his.

They were simple things, this touching, this banter, all over a delicious meal. It told him there was more to them than simply sex. "I promise to be a good sub for you. I trust you completely."

"Good," she replied, raising his fingers to her lips and planting a quick kiss on them. "I can't take another sub like Tom. I need a sub who submits to me completely."

"I won't let you down." He said the words and meant them even though a small part of him worried he would. He couldn't let that happen. She deserved nothing less than his total surrender.

"I'm going to put your vow to the test in the next couple of weeks," she warned.

He quirked his lips up in response. "Bring it on."

* * * * *

Juliette wrapped her lips around the head of Trey's cock and tickled the underside with her tongue. He grunted his pleasure from around a ball gag. They both felt comfortable restraining his voice after a couple of week's worth of playing together. The blowjob was a reward for all the pain he had taken that evening. His chest, back and buttocks were covered in red stripes from the crop she'd used. Tight clamps pinched his nipples, while a weight pulled his balls down taut. His cock was only newly freed from its restraint and she intended to make him come with her mouth alone. But only when she gave the command and she wasn't going to for a while yet.

She felt fierce tonight. She had needed to work off the annoyance of the call she had received earlier. Damn Tom, anyway, for using a number she didn't recognize. He had tried to call her a few times before after she dumped his manipulative ass, but she had ignored his calls when his number came up. She had been at work, happily biding her time before meeting up with Trey, when she answered her phone. The sound of her ex's voice did conflicting things to her. Her body had grown excited in an instant reaction from happier times. Her brain, however, got mad. The bastard had no right to contact her. She had made that clear enough.

Yet, he had begged and pleaded for another chance, had told her how miserable he was without her, how sorry he was for being a bad sub. He had changed, he claimed. He promised to be her good and obedient boy if only she would let him back into her life. It almost worked. They had a long history together and part of her not only had loved him, but loved him still, or at least loved the idea of the man she had thought him to be. It was hard to resist him, but thoughts of Trey had helped. More, she'd heard the undertone of his voice, that coaxing, weaseling way he had of getting her to do his bidding. That had done it. She'd shut him down fast. Still, it bothered her. It was easy for the self doubt to snake its way inside her and because of it, she had come into play loaded for bear. Only her great experience as a Domme had kept her temper in check.

Her new boy had paid for her old boy's call nevertheless. His chest heaved with sharp breaths as she swallowed his cock deeper into her mouth and down her throat. Her fingers grasped his striped ass and dug in while she sucked and laved his climax out of him. His body tried to buck against her face, but the strap around his waist held him tight to the two sides of the wooden frame she had tied him to. She knew he couldn't hold on any longer, and knowing the frenzy of desire she had built in him excited her even more. Her nipples were painful peaks pressing against her bustier and her exposed pussy ached to rub against her boy's leg for relief.

When she felt his cock pulse with his release, she sucked hard and pulled his balls down farther with one hand. Trey yelled in pain, in pleasure, and semen burst inside Juliette's mouth. She took it all, again a reward for his strength and obedience. The salty, warm cum slid down her throat, and it kicked her own need for climax up another notch. As soon as the last of her sub's spasms subsided, she released his cock and stood up. She studied Trey's face and saw utter contentment. His eyes were closed and he took great gulps of air through the gag.

She released the strap and pulled the ball out of his mouth to give him a kiss. He moaned in surprise as she slipped her tongue inside and gave him a taste of himself. With her high heels, they were of similar height, so she had no trouble plastering her body to his and rubbing her engorged nipples and clit against his hot skin. It would have taken very little to orgasm with just that contact, but she had other plans. It was time for her to conquer his body completely.

Releasing his mouth, she sauntered over to her bag of toys. Doubt tried to creep into her mind, and she batted it away. They had played enough. He could take this. He trusted her, and she trusted that he had given himself to her completely. She would possess his body tonight, and he would submit like the good sub he had become in such a short time. With only a second's more hesitation, she pulled out her black leather harness with the flesh-colored dildo already fitted through the hole. She grabbed a bottle of lube as well and turned to face her sub. His eyes were open and there was a look of concern on his face. He stared at what she held and licked his lips.

"You can do this for me," she said in an encouraging tone. "You will do this for me," she added more sternly.

He opened his mouth, then closed it again and looked straight ahead. Juliette went around to his back and slipped into the harness where he couldn't see her. The vibrating bullet was already inside the harness's front pocket. All she had to do was slide her fake cock into Trey's very real and inviting ass, and the bullet would massage her clit. She could already feel the sensation through memory alone. First things first, though. Her sub had a virgin ass and she couldn't just shove inside him without causing the kind of pain that was not fun.

The orgasm she had given him helped ease his body, relax his muscles, but arousal would help her cause as well. It would take patience and she had it. She took long minutes to caress his body, to tease the most sensitive spots. She tweaked his nipples, rubbed his cock, and massaged his balls. His body was rigid, on guard, at first. Eventually he let go, hanging from his restraints, eyes closed. When his cock once more stood erect, she put a dollop of lube on her finger and slid it between his ass cheeks. The moment she touched him there, he jerked.

"Stop," she admonished. "It displeases me when you act as if I won't be careful with you."

"I'm sorry, Mistress," he replied in a strained voice. "This is hard for me."

"Of course, it is. If it weren't, there wouldn't be as much pleasure for either of us. Relax. I promise you'll like this. Remember your role is to trust and obey." She circled his anus with the tip of her finger for a few seconds. Despite her efforts and admonishment, he was tense again, his ass cheeks clenching tight, trapping her finger. She was going to have to distract him better. Reaching around his body, she twisted one of the nipple clamps at the same time she slipped her finger into his asshole.

Trey yelled, but it worked. Her finger slipped inside and she held it there. "See, not so bad."

"Yes, Mistress." He didn't sound very convinced.

She wiggled the finger around and pushed it in and out. His sphincter clamped down, not giving way, forcing her to press hard. She squirted more lube onto it and the second finger and eased two fingers inside. Her sub grunted in pain and it wasn't good pain, either. She knew the difference.

Juliette held the fingers still and planted kisses on his shoulder. "Relax and push out," she told him in as soft a voice as she could manage given the height of her passion. So close to her goal, her body was revved up with nowhere to go.

Trey took a deep breath and let it out in a hard whoosh. "I'm trying, Mistress. I just can't seem—" He stopped and then, "No! Take them out. Now. Stop!"

The words were like a slap to her face, echoing her time with Tom. She pulled her fingers out quickly and took a step back. Her own breathing came out in harsh pants as she fought for control. Damn, she was disappointed to the edge of mad, mad at him and mad at herself. She had chosen wrong again. Trey wasn't ready to submit to her totally and while another woman might stick around to see if he would change, she couldn't. She wouldn't. She did not need another controlling sub.

With jerky movements, she stripped off her harness, returned to her bag and tossed it in. The lube joined it and she cleaned her fingers with exaggerated care while she brought her emotions under control. Her passion had fled. Her body sagged with sudden fatigue. Tears pricked her eyes, but she didn't let them fall. Stupid to have become so infatuated with a man after only a couple of weeks. She tossed on a wrap around skirt, zippered her bag shut with a vicious tug, took a few deep breaths and turned to Trey.

He watched as best he could from where he remained immobilized. Wordlessly, not looking at his face directly, she went to him and released his restraints. She was a careful Domme, so she made sure to rub the circulation back into his arms before unbuckling his waist. She could feel his eyes trained on her. When she bent to free his ankles, he spoke.

"Mistress, I'm sorry." His voice quiet, he sounded sincere. It didn't matter, she knew from bitter experience how deceptive a sub's words could be.

She straightened and looked into his eyes. Because he had a troubled expression on his face, she forced a smile to her own. No need to be cruel and no need to let him know how disappointed she was. "It's all right," she assured him. "This was an experiment. We had two good weeks, but I'm not the right Domme for you and you're not the right sub for me."

"What? No," he replied, alarm in his voice. When she turned from him, his hand shot out and grabbed her upper arm. A hard look from her led him to let her go. "Please,

Mistress," he continued, following her. "It's just that it's too soon from me. I'm not ready for that. I need more time. Damn it, Juliette, I'm not like that other guy."

Juliette walked to the door and stopped. She could feel the heat of his body, though he kept a respectful distance. Part of her wanted to stay, to work him some more, fuck him hard and forget the ass play. A bigger part of her told her to go. She couldn't risk another sub topping her from the bottom. Her confidence couldn't survive it. She looked at Trey over her shoulder.

"We agreed that I would be your Mistress. Your job was to trust and obey. You're obviously not ready for that, and frankly I'm not willing to find out if you are ever going to be ready." The look in his eyes had her softening her tone. His upset was genuine. "You're a strong man, Trey, and a commanding one. Maybe you're not cut out to be a sub. Maybe you should find a nice woman out there in the club who wants to be dominated."

He shook his head hard. "No, that's not me. I'm not a Dom. I thought without ever articulating it that I was. I know better now. You've showed me what I am." He stepped closer to her. "I'm a sub. I'm your sub, Juliette. Please give me another chance."

She wanted to. Oh, how she wanted to, but she didn't dare. "I'm sorry," she whispered. With a deep breath to hold back the tears that still threatened to come, she gave one last order. "Sit down and wait here for thirty minutes, or longer until you're steady. I'll ask Dru to make sure you're okay to leave the club. Don't try to follow me."

Unable to bear the look of the sadness in his eyes, she turned and bolted from the room.

Chapter Seven

ꕥ

Mike heaved a big sigh for the second time in a minute, and once again Trey ignored him. He knew his friend wasn't having any fun and frankly, neither was he. Some stupid impulse had led him to cajole the guy into club hopping, but his heart wasn't into it. No surprise there. This was the wrong type of club for him now, and the women sending him flirty signals weren't the right kind of women. He knew it. Mike knew it. No wonder his friend was sighing and drumming his bored fingers on the table top.

"Okay," Trey admitted, knocking back the last of his beer. "This was a mistake."

"Damn straight it was," the other man replied. "You going to tell me what happened with the flogging accountant or what?"

Trey shook his head. "Doesn't matter."

"The hell it doesn't. Let's get out of here. I can't hear myself think, let alone talk."

Despite not wanting to talk about the debacle the other night with Juliette, Trey followed Mike out into the waning evening. The street was full of people hustling from one place to another, but it was cooler and quieter than the club had been. It didn't lift his spirits, though. He was miserable since his Mistress had dumped him. It felt as if a heavy weight pressed on his chest, squeezed his heart, shortened his breath. No amount of work or play eased the tension. He hadn't been this bad when Gina had dumped him. How could a woman he barely knew affect him this badly?

Mike hustled across the street and plopped down on a park bench. He gestured toward the place next him. "Sit down and tell Uncle Mike all about it."

"Suck my dick, Uncle Mike," Trey replied without heat. Instead of sitting, he braced one foot against the bench seat and rested his chin in his hand. "Sorry, man, I don't think I'm up for talking about it."

"Yeah, I know, you'd rather suffer in silence, but I have to tell you, I have never seen you so fucked up and distracted. I'm worried about you, dude."

Trey traded his chin for his forehead and groaned. "I'm okay, I'm just an idiot, is all." The memory of his failure loomed up as it had repeatedly for the last few days. He couldn't stop thinking about how he had chickened out. The look on Juliette's face when she gave him his walking papers haunted him. He had failed her, failed himself. Goddamn, he wished he could do it over. The thing was, though, he couldn't be sure he could go through with it. The thought of being fucked in the ass, even by a woman, raised insecurity he barely had acknowledged before.

"By that I assume you mean that you screwed up something with the accountant and she tossed your sorry ass out of the dungeon."

Trey barked out a laugh. "Yeah, something like that." It was all about his ass, and what made him feel as if his ass was some kind of sacred ground? Hadn't he talked Gina into letting him fuck her in the ass? It had been sweet, and he had taken good care of her, going slow and easy. He knew the drill and Juliette had been taking equally good care of him when he had broken. Maybe it was him. He had seen lots of videos on the net of men being fucked by women. They seemed to enjoy themselves, that was for sure. Of course, one couldn't believe everything on the internet. Did other straight men really like being pegged?

Trey arched a brow at his friend. "You really want to help me?"

Mike shook his head. "No. I love wasting my Saturday night sitting in a park shooting the shit with another guy instead of hooking up with a fine woman. It's a quirk of mine."

Trey rolled his eyes. "Okay smart mouth. Here's a question for you. You ever let a woman do you in the ass?"

Mike's eyes popped open for a second before he looked away and squirmed. "Um, wow, when you decide to open up, you don't mess around." He slanted his gaze back to Trey. "Is this what screwed the pooch for you, she wanted to peg you?"

Trey took a deep breath. "I took the beatings and the clamps and the orders and I was in heaven. I promised I could take anything she dished out, but when she went for my asshole, I balked. I told myself I would submit. She trusted me to, and I was determined. But when push came to shove, so to speak, I panicked." Standing up, he groaned. "She said I didn't trust her enough and wasn't prepared to submit to her entirely. She's not into a power struggle. She said..." He stopped.

Mike stood up, too. "She said what?"

"Argh! She said maybe I'm a Dom, that I really do need to be in control. It's not true, I swear it's not. I thought I was. I thought I needed to be the alpha male all the time. When I was with her, though, at the club, at her mercy, it was fantastic. I could relax in a way I hadn't in years. I didn't have to worry about a thing except obeying." He stared into his friend's eyes. "I know it's hard for you to understand, but it's liberating."

Mike rubbed a hand over his face. "I can't say I understand it. I do know that I've seen the effects on you of being with this woman for the last couple of weeks. You were more relaxed, happier, than I've seen you in a long time. Maybe more than I've ever seen you. I can also say that while I've never had the full experience, I have had a female finger or two inside me and it rocked."

"Yeah?"

His friend grinned broadly. "It rocked my orgasm big time. The prostate is your friend. And, there's nothing gay about it, if that's your worry."

"I guess maybe it is, which is just dumb on so many levels."

Mike clasped his shoulder. "Go back to the club and find your accountant. Get down on your submissive knees and beg for a second chance."

Trey gave his friend a feral grin. "Yeah, you're right. That's exactly what I'm going to do, and I'm going to stay on my knees until she decides I'm worthy of another chance." His grin faded. "If she ever does decide." If she didn't, he thought, then it was his own fault and he would accept her judgment as his Mistress. But he would at least show her how contrite he truly was and pray for an opportunity to redeem himself. Then he would pray for the strength to follow through.

* * * * *

Dru greeted Juliette as soon as she entered the club. Perhaps the manager could sense her unease at returning to the place. God knows she had warred with herself for hours before coming. There was a risk of running into Trey, and while she told herself it was unimportant, that returning to the club was necessary to keep from losing her confidence all over again, she knew deep down inside that part of her wanted to run into her newly ex-sub.

The manager smiled. "I wasn't sure you'd come back."

Juliette blew out a breath. "Was it that obvious Trey and I crashed and burned the other night?"

Dru cocked her head. "I could tell something had gone amiss. I can tell you're too good a Domme to run out on a sub post-play like that."

"Yes," she replied, grimly and ashamed. "That was not well done of me."

"It's okay, he was fine, physically anyway." She paused. "Do you need to talk?"

The idea of opening up to this virtual stranger gave Juliette pause, but then what did it matter? This woman might understand how she felt and God knew there really wasn't anyone else in her life she could talk to about what had happened. "Yes, actually I could use a sympathetic ear."

Dru beckoned toward the bar. "Come on then, let's grab a soda."

Once they were seated and sipping on their drinks, Juliette related how she had a crisis of confidence after her last sub and then how Trey had seemed to be another guy who couldn't really submit. "I seem to be on a losing streak where subs are concerned," she confessed.

The other woman shrugged. "I understand about your old submissive. Some guys really get off playing the sub while holding the whip hand, so to speak. It's an old story and a lousy one. It can really mess you up. I'm not so sure I'd put Trey in that category, though."

"Do you think I pushed him too hard to soon?"

"Maybe. Let me ask you this, if it hadn't been for your previous experience, would you have been as upset with him freaking out about ass play?"

Juliette sighed and rested her head against the back of her chair. "I don't know. I've wondered about that ever since it happened. Perhaps I overreacted. No," she amended, fist pounding the armrest. "I did overreact. Damn, it was another manifestation of my lost confidence. I know that. I've started to call Trey a half dozen times, but I stop because I don't want to take the chance. It will be safer to find a more experienced sub, someone who knows his limits."

"Safer," Dru agreed. "Not as fulfilling, though. There was real chemistry between you two. We all noticed it."

"Really?" She couldn't say why exactly, yet hearing it gave her a feeling of warmth. She'd thought there was something special beginning with Trey. If other people had noticed then she must have been right. Before she could pump the manager for more advice, her attention was drawn to the front door. Out of the corner of her eye, she saw a familiar form. A gasp erupted past her lips before she could stop it.

Dru turned to look and arched her brows. "Someone you know?"

"Tom," Juliette spit out. "My ex, my ex before Trey."

"Ah, the manipulative one. Shall I have Hayden escort him out?"

Juliette hopped off her chair. "No, I'll take care of this." Her stomach was already churning as she strode toward Tom. He was dressed in a provocative way, tight leather pants molded his excellent, young body and cupped his impressive package. A black sleeveless t-shirt showed off his arms. She noticed a new tat adorned his right biceps. His blond hair was shorter and sculpted into spikes. As he sauntered into the main reception area, his gaze swiveled back and forth. It stopped, he stopped, when he spotted her. His face lit up in a broad smile.

Despite her anger, Juliette's body reacted to the sight of her old lover with glee. Nipples hardened against the silk of her corset, and her clit tingled. She ruthlessly tamped down the longing and scowled when she reached him. "What are you doing here, Tom?"

"Hey, Mistress, you look fabulous."

"Don't call me that! I am not your Mistress."

His grin faded. "I know, but I want to change that. I found a card lying around for this place and thought I'd give it a try." He dropped his gaze and softened his tone. "I have to confess I kind of hoped to run into you. You won't take my calls." He looked up at her from under his lashes.

She felt the familiar tug of desire once more and her hand twitched at the memory of playing with this man. It would be so easy to fall back into the old pattern of wrestling for power with Tom. But she knew it would be a mistake. Not only was she done with power plays, she'd had a taste of another man, a better man, honestly. When she pictured Trey next to Tom, there was no contest. Trey exuded power and confidence, whereas Tom oozed smarmy charm. Yes, the guy was beautiful, but how had she been so blind? Real pleasure came from dominating an alpha male. Match the two men up, and Trey would blow away the other. She could imagine it easily, and then she didn't have to. The door opened and in he walked.

If the sight of Tom had heated her body, Trey's presence sent her senses into overdrive. She inhaled sharply as if kicked in the gut. He wasn't dressed as provocatively as Tom, yet he was ten times as sexy. His worn jeans outlined cock and balls. His button down shirt opened up just enough to show a hint of his chest and the sleeves were rolled up his strong forearms. His gaze homed in on her immediately and the look of sheer delight on his face nearly brought her to her knees. And then he spotted Tom and his expression turned hard. His obvious displeasure at seeing her with another man thrilled her more than she wanted to admit.

When he reached them, Trey dropped his gaze and stood with his hands clasped behind his back. "Mistress Juliette, may I speak with you please?"

Tom shot him a thunderous look. "The Mistress is otherwise engaged," he spat out.

Her old sub's reaction jolted her. "I decide whom I talk to," she said sternly.

Tom immediately struck a submissive pose. "Forgive me, Mistress."

"I am not your Mistress," she retorted and before Trey could say anything, she turned on him, too. "I'm not yours, either."

She could tell Trey wanted to dispute the statement, but he wisely kept silent. Tom, on the other hand, was not so smart. "Come on, Juliette, give me another chance. We were good together."

"No, we were not." Her temper was rising and it felt good because it replaced the hurt. She stepped closer to Tom and said, "You were a manipulative little shit and I will never play with you again. Now get out of here. I've already told the manager about you, so your reputation precedes you. You won't find another playmate at this club."

Tom opened his mouth, still not ready to capitulate. Before he could get a word out, though, Trey leaned into him. "You heard the lady, beat it or I'll kick your disrespectful ass out." Trey topped his threat with a lethal looking grin. It caused Tom to lean away from his adversary.

Juliette was torn. That purely girly part of her was once more thrilled at Trey's alpha male response, but the Domme in her knew that she couldn't let him get away with being in charge. "Trey!" She made her voice sharp, commanding. His startled face turned to her. "Do you see my bag over there on the floor by the bar?" When he nodded, she continued. "Go stand next to it and wait for me."

His gaze flicked from the bag to her and to Tom, the war inside him obvious. It raged for only a few seconds before he nodded again. "Yes, ma'am."

Juliette watched him leave, a deep sense of satisfaction and hope welling up inside her. She knew it had taken a lot for a strong man like Trey to leave in circumstances like these. But he did it and his compliance spoke volumes. She turned her eyes to Tom. "Get out and don't try to contact me again. It is over. Do you understand?" The bouncer, Hayden, watched by the door, waiting for her signal to intervene. It turned out not to be necessary.

Tom sighed. "Okay, I get it. I'm sorry."

"So am I." She watched him walk out the door. When he was gone from her sight, she turned it on Trey. Desire burst through her as she saw him standing, waiting, waiting for her.

Chapter Eight

ꕥ

Trey clasped his wrist with a bone-crushing grip, his gaze fixed on a spot on the floor. The urge to look up, to see what was happening between Juliette and the Eminem wanna-be warred with his discipline. It was make or break time, and he had to show his Mistress once and for all that he could follow orders. God, it killed him. Nothing pissed him off more than another guy preying on a woman. He had wanted to protect her by kicking, literally, her old sub to the curb. Walking away instead had been important. He had to show her he trusted her to make the right decisions, for her and for him. It was hard, though. The top of his head threatened to blow off from the effort to remain in place. Finally he was rewarded by the sound and sight of her high heels coming into view.

He sensed more than saw her body lean into his. "Pick up my bag and follow me." Her voice was soft yet no less commanding for it.

He let out a breath he hadn't even realized he was holding, bent to pick up the bag and kept his Mistress in his sight. He still thought of her as that even though there was some chance he would not be forgiven, a chance he might let her down.

Fuck that! This time, he would submit no matter what.

She stopped briefly to speak with the manager before leading him down the hallway past the point they had ventured before. They entered a room filled with all kinds of restraining apparatus. He had mere seconds to take it all in before his Mistress called him over to one corner. She stood beside a padded bench that could have been in any gym, except this one had restraints where weights would have been.

"Put the bag down here," she said pointing to the floor beside her. When he had done as she commanded, she told him to strip.

As he moved quickly to comply, he saw she did the same. Off came her silk bustier and short skirt. Underneath she wore a lacy garter belt that held up her black fishnet stockings. Those things plus her heels she kept on. He watched in confusion as she straddled the bench and lay down on her back. She held up her arms. "Secure me."

"What?" Trey shook his head. "I mean, I'm sorry, ma'am, I don't understand."

"Really? I'm quite sure my words were plain enough." Her voice was cool and dismissive. As erect as he had been since first seeing her, he became even harder. "Put the straps around my wrists." So saying, she stretched her arms up toward either side of her head. "Are my orders clear?"

Trey swallowed hard. "Yes, ma'am." His voice was rough to his own ears. Holy shit, what was she doing? "May I ask a question?"

Juliette sighed heavily. "You want to know why I am taking the submissive role. You're mistaken. I'm not a switch and I'm yielding up nothing to you. This is to show each of us how much we trust the other. We need this if we are to get past what happened. You will bind me and you will play with my body. I will tell you how to play with it, and you will do exactly what I tell you. Then you will do what I tell you to do with your own body. You will do all this even though you have the freedom not to and I am physically powerless. You will do it because you want to obey me and you trust me enough to do what I say. I'm right about that, am I not?"

His chest rose and fell in harsh breaths as his arousal increased. What she ordered him to do both frightened and intrigued him. He wasn't worried about hurting her because he knew he had the self-control to be trusted with her body. Yet, he also knew she might very well order him to hurt her simply to show her level of trust in him. Could he really do it?

Could he obey an order to harm his Mistress? The answer was obvious. If he didn't then there would be nothing left for them. She wouldn't be his Mistress if he didn't obey her completely, totally. He had to let go. No more thinking, no more worrying. With a deep breath, he released the last of his reservations and did as commanded.

He took each of Juliette's delicate wrists in hand and restrained them. When she told him to pull the straps tighter, he did, wincing only slightly as he pulled her arm muscles taut. When he was done, he stood up beside her and waited for the next order. He tried not to look at her beautiful breasts on display, rosy nipples pointed up at him. Nor did he gaze at the thatch of hair nestled between the straps of her garter belt. Perhaps it was only his imagination, but he swore he could smell her sweet arousal. He kept his sight fixed on the wall beyond her head and clasped his hands in a tight fist.

His Mistress cooed. "Good boy. Now go into my bag and find the wooden box. Inside it are several metal rings. Take them out and slide them one at a time down your awesome cock. They'll keep you nice and hard for me."

Trey did as he was told, happy to have something to do that didn't involve hurting his Mistress. There were five rings in the box, and going down on one knee, he slid them past his cock head and onto his shaft. It was excruciating, the cool metal against his heated flesh only served to heighten his desire to come. But the rings also did their job, choking the path his semen would have to take. When he was done encasing himself in the restraints, his breath labored and sweat beaded his skin.

"Excellent." The simple praise made him grin. The next command erased it. "There's a butt plug and a tube of lube. Get them out."

Trey found the items and held one in each hand. The cone-shaped plug with the narrow neck caused him to swallow hard. Whether the item was for her or him, he didn't like it. Still, he would place it wherever he was told and knew enough already to apply a liberal amount of the lubricant on it.

"Good," his Mistress said when he was finished. "It's for you. You understand it's not a dildo. Its purpose is merely to enhance your pleasure. It will stimulate your prostate and when I let you come inside me, it will be like nothing you've ever experienced before."

Her words alone sped up his heart and made him moan. His cock pulsed in its confinement and his asshole tightened. He looked at the plug, shiny with lube, and wondered how he would take it inside. But he knew already. He had done this before to someone else and could do it to himself. Reaching around his body, he pulled at one ass cheek. He relaxed his sphincter and pushed out as he slid the cone in. There was a bite of pain before it settled in, filling him, stimulating his already aroused body. He sighed heavily and looked at his Mistress. She smiled back at him.

"Not so bad, is it?"

"No, ma'am."

"Good. Now come and enjoy my body. Play with me." With a deep breath, she turned her head to face the ceiling and closed her eyes. "Start with my breasts. Touch them, lick them, bite them." She said the last word with a growl.

His whole body jerked with the urge to grab her and feast. Instead, he took his time, worshipping her as she deserved. Kneeling fully beside the bench, he leaned over to cup her breasts in both hands. They were soft and lovely, yielding to his gentle pressure. When he rubbed his thumbs over the hard nipples, his Mistress moaned and arched into his hold. Encouraged, he replaced one thumb with his lips, tugging the nub into his mouth, laving it with his tongue. He repeated the motion with the other breast before sucking and tugging and grating the engorged flesh.

Juliette bucked and writhed. "Yes, like that. Show me how much you want me, how much you missed me."

"Mmm," he murmured against her hot skin. Releasing her, he stared at the wet pucker of her areola. "I did miss you. I want you so badly. I'll do whatever you say."

"Of course you will," was her breathless reply. "Time for you to straddle the bench. Face me and move that clever tongue of yours down south."

Trey didn't need to be told twice. He hated to abandon her breasts, but the chance to taste her pussy again was not to be ignored. He stood on stiffened legs, the movement sending a jolt of pleasure inside his ass. Clever woman, his Mistress, giving him the gift of the plug. He could understand now why straight guys craved being pegged. His equally stiff cock bobbed in front of him, eager to play, yet still side-lined. Easing himself across the bench, he stared at his destination.

"Not yet," Juliette admonished. "I mean for you to tease me up to it." He wanted to groan in frustration. "Place your hands on my thighs and inch them upward. I want gentle pressure, a light touch."

Trey obeyed, placing his hands on her thighs just above the stockings. Here, too, her skin was creamy soft and warm. His thumbs made lazy circles on her flesh as he crept upward. He never took his eyes off his goal. The folds of her labia winked at him, wet as they were with her juices. When he inhaled deeply, he could smell her. She was ripe for the taking, her hips undulating as his fingers moved higher and higher. When his thumbs met in the middle, he flicked them up between her lips and caressed her clit with alternating strokes.

Juliette cried out and bucked her hips. "Don't let me move! Hold me down and use your tongue. Now, Trey, make me come."

His hands clamped down on her hips, pressing her firmly back against the bench while his head dipped down to her mons. His tongue darted between her folds and tasted the sweet salt of her arousal. Her clit was waiting for him, swollen with her need. When he touched it, she cried out again and strained against his hold. As commanded, he held her down tightly, keeping her body still as he used tongue and lips to rip the orgasm from her. She screamed and thrashed against all the restraints holding her back. Her body shook with the orgasm, all the more intense because there was nowhere to release it other than inside. He knew the feeling, knew how wonderful it was. He lapped and sucked, determined to give her every last drop of pleasure, before she commanded him to stop.

Breath heavy, his body flushed with his own arousal, Trey reluctantly pulled back and stared down at his Mistress. Her chest heaved and her body glistened with sweat. God, she was beautiful. He wanted her more than ever, but the damn rings and her own words, or lack of them, kept him in check. So he sat and waited, praying for patience.

"Take off the rings and replace them with a condom." The order came quickly, between pants. Juliette's eyes remained closed.

Trey hesitated, afraid he heard only what he wanted to, then mentally kicked himself into gear. Without leaving the bench, he reached down to grab the bag and the box inside it for the rings. It was agony once more to move the metal over his tortured flesh. The promise of release made him rush, and he bit back a cry when he snagged the sensitive lip of his cock head with the edge of one of the rings.

"Careful." His Mistress had opened her eyes to mere slits and watched him. "I want the erection inside me, and you are not to come before I tell you."

"Yes, Mistress," he bit out as the last of the rings came off. It took no time to cover himself with the condom. He faced her, eyes down, waiting for permission.

"Scoot closer to me. Put my legs over your thighs and place the tip of you cock outside my pussy. Don't put it in yet."

He did as commanded and nestled his body against hers. His body vibrated from the effort it took not to slam his cock home. But he didn't have permission, so he waited, and waited, and waited. His palms rested on her thighs. His fingers squeezed her before he could stop them. Instead of admonishment, his Mistress chuckled.

"Okay. Slide it in, slowly." His cock entered her hot, tight pussy. He half moaned, half sighed at the feeling. "Stop." Gritting his teeth, he did. His cock pulsed, his balls were pulled tight against his body, aching for release. He worked hard to steady his breathing, holding onto control with a tenuous grip, but he was doing it.

"Now, my dear sub. Slam it home!" He did, even before the words were completely out of her mouth. He pushed his cock to the hilt, lifting her legs higher as he did so. "Yes, that's it," she encouraged him. "Lift me up, push harder, push faster."

Complying was easy, fantastically easy, and oh so exciting. Lifting her legs up and pushing them back toward her chest, Trey dove deeper into Juliette's willing body. Clasping her thighs closer to him, he levered himself up with straining quads and calves to thrust as she had commanded. Harder and faster, he drove them both higher and closer to climax. His sphincter clamped down on the plug that filled him and urged him to greater heights of pleasure. His body hummed and vibrated with the need to come. He grunted against the strain of holding it back. Eyes closed, jaw clenched, he worked his Mistress's body, felt her release, heard her scream.

Juliette's cunt gripped his cock, taunting him to join her, yet no command came. She thrashed against his hold and with a keening cry, came again. God, he howled his frustration, felt his control slip, and just as he meant to beg for release, permission came. So did he. Blood roared in his ears, the room spun around his tightly shut eyes. Intense pleasure burst inward from his ass and out of his cock, right into his Mistress's sweet, grasping pussy. He held onto her body and pumped himself dry. When he was done, he quickly rid himself of the condom and slumped over her body, head pillowed between her breasts. Her heart beat quickly against her chest. He heard it, felt it and reveled in causing it. Her labored breath matched his own. He could have easily stayed where he was all night, but there was one thing he craved still.

Lifting his head, he asked his Mistress a favor. "Please let me release you so I can feel your arms wrapped around me."

Her eyes were closed and remained so, but she nodded. He wasted no time in freeing her from the restraints, careful to massage her arms as she had done for him. His reward was having those arms embrace him, allowing him once more to place his head between her breasts.

Juliette could have stayed in that position forever, the heavy weight of Trey's satiated body pressing her to the bench. But her back was starting to protest, so she patted his ass. "Time to get up." He lifted his head and gave her a sloppy grin, one that told her everything she needed to know. Her sub had enjoyed his little sojourn as a Dom, and more importantly had enjoyed having his ass plugged.

He sat up, pulling her gently into his arms and kissed her, his lips and tongue giving testament to his gratitude. When he finally let her go, he said, "I hope that wasn't too insolent, Mistress. I couldn't resist the urge."

She traced his lips with her finger tip. "I'm willing to let it slide given how well you obeyed me this evening, both in here and out there."

Trey frowned. "It was hard, I have to admit. I didn't like leaving you with that little shit and I didn't like restraining you."

She ran her fingers through his tussled hair, unable to keep her hands off her sub. Had she really let him go? What an idiot she'd been. "I know it was hard, but you did it because I demanded it of you." She took a deep breath and let it out harshly. "And it was something I knew you could handle.

That's part of my job as a Domme, knowing what you can handle, and knowing what you can't." She pressed a simple kiss against his mouth before hugging him close. "I'm sorry about the other night. I let you down. I knew you weren't ready to be pegged. I should never have pushed you so hard and fast."

Trey held her in a tight grip. "No, I'm the one who is sorry. I should have trusted you more. I promised to obey and I'm the one who let you down."

Juliette frowned against his skin before pushing him away. She ignored the startled look on his face and disentangled her body from his. Standing with all the grace of a newly born foal, she rounded on her sub and barked out orders. "On your knees, boy, right here, right now!" She pointed to the floor in front of her and watched her sub push off the bench with a speed and fluidity that had her smiling inwardly. Outwardly she kept her expression stern. When Trey knelt in front of her, hands behind his back, eyes cast down, she laid down the law.

"I'm only going to remind you one more time. When we play together, I'm the one in charge. It's my responsibility, my privileged to make the decisions for both of us. I let my past with Tom influence how I treated you and that's what I'm apologizing for. I should never have let that happen, and I promise you it won't happen again. You needn't give the matter another thought because it's not your job to think. You obey, that's it. And, when I decide it's time for you to take it up the ass, you will. Are we clear on this?"

A grin popped out on his face and disappeared quickly, but not quick enough that she didn't see it. "Yes, ma'am."

"Excellent." She suppressed her own grin. "Now I'm in the mood to redden that plugged ass of yours. Get up and face the bench, bend down and put your hands flat on it. Don't you dare let your cock touch anything."

He was already erect, ready for another round. Maybe she'd give him some relief, maybe not. She had all night to decide, maybe all week. Hell, if she allowed, she could picture spending the rest of her life with this man. But she was getting ahead of herself, again. For now, she thought reaching into the bag and pulling up her favorite flogger, it was time to play.

Epilogue

ꟾ

Trey was a fool, an idiot, an imbecile. Christ, there wasn't a good enough word in the English language to describe a man who had been stupid enough to resist the sweet mixture of pleasure and pain he felt at that moment. His Mistress, Juliette, thrust into his ass with increasing vigor. She had been so gentle and careful at first, but now he urged her on, pressing back against her thrusts as much as his restraints would allow. His cock jutted out, unrestrained, yearning for release. He could almost come from the pressure on his prostate alone. He closed his eyes and grunting against a ball gag, surrendered to the sensations bombarding his body.

His Mistress dug her nails into his hips, her breath hot and heavy against his neck. She would come soon, he knew her so well. After six months of play, how could he not? How could he not love her? He had said the words right before she had stifled his voice with the gag. She had smiled and repeated them back. Then she had told him she would show him how much she loved him by fucking his ass. Words that would have terrified him such a short time ago, only served to quicken his blood, heighten his arousal, and stretch his cock. He had been ready, finally, and she had known it because she was his Mistress. She had command of his body and his orgasm. God, when would she give him his release?

Her body trembled against his. A keening cry tore from her lips. His voice joined hers as his body longed to do. With a final lunge, she filled his body and reached around to grab his cock in her hot grasp. She squeezed and yanked and ordered.

"Come for me, baby, come with me."

His body exploded, jerking against the restraints, shoving back against the hardness invading his ass. He was wild, mindless, out of control with the intensity of coming. Yet his Mistress held him close. She let him fall into the abyss sure in the knowledge that she was there for him, keeping him safe. When the last of the tremors died down, he hung limply. He grunted in dismay when she pulled out, leaving him feeling vaguely empty. When she released the gag, he gave her a sloppy grin.

"Can we do that again?"

She rolled her eyes. "In a few days, once I'm sure you're not too sore."

"I like being sore."

She groaned as she released his arms. "You've become quite the pain slut."

"Mmm," he concurred, pulling her into his weak arms, hugging her close. "And, a pegging slut, if tonight is anything to go by. All thanks to you, Mistress. I'm just sorry we couldn't do this at Unfettered."

Helping him stagger out of her spare room, Juliette sighed. "I know what you mean. It would have been poetic to consummate this last act where it all began." She frowned as they entered her bedroom. "Weird how it closed up so quickly. The building looked as if the club had never been there."

"Weird," he agreed. They sat on the edge of her bed, his ass stinging in protest. His cock twitched. Man, would he ever get enough of this woman and what she did to his body? Looking into her beautiful eyes, so full of concern for him, he realized he wouldn't. He reached up and cupped her chin with his palm, gazed back at her. "It doesn't matter. You've got the beginnings of a fine dungeon right here. Maybe we can do some shopping online this weekend and pick up some more, um, furniture."

Her face lit up. "That's a lovely idea."

He lowered his eyes, afraid he might be going a little too far, yet unable to stop himself. "Maybe you could clear out a dresser drawer and make a little room in your closet, you know so that I can sleep over and go to work directly from here?" He raised his gaze and let out his breath.

Juliette still smiled. "An even better idea."

"I haven't overstepped my bounds, have I, Mistress?"

Entwining her arms around his neck, she kissed him sweetly. "You could never do that, and I won't ever again be worried that you would even try. You are a man made for submission, and I'm the right woman to put you there and keep you there." She pulled him in for another kiss.

Relieved, relaxed and trusting, Trey once again relinquished control.

EMERALD DUNGEON

Kathy Kulig

Dedication

To the authors of the 1-800-DOM-help series, for their support and knowledge.

To all my readers for their kinds words and support.

Trademarks Acknowledgement

The author acknowledges the trademarked status and trademark owners of the following wordmarks mentioned in this work of fiction:

Disney: Disney Enterprises, Inc.

Velcro: Velcro Industries B.V. Limited Liability Company

Chapter One

ஐ

"The park's closed today," the gentleman at the visitor's desk said in a slow Irish drawl. He scowled at his computer screen then scribbled notes on a piece paper without looking at her.

"I'm not a tourist, I'm Dana Brennan. I was hired as a musician for the show."

Glancing up from his work, he gave her a quick once-over and frowned. "What happened to you, miss? You're soaking wet." He stood and approached the counter from the other side, giving her a closer look. "Didn't fall into the bog now, did you?"

"Bog? No, I had a flat tire on my drive over. It was raining."

"Changed it yourself now?"

She nodded.

He smiled, clearly astonished. He was a man of indeterminate years with white hair, a weatherworn face and blue eyes that held humor one moment and were severe the next.

"I'll get you your key so you can get into dry clothes. I'm Will Donegal, the proprietor of Rathmore Castle." He opened several drawers until he held up a key. "Here you go, Ms. Brennan. The cottages for the performers are to the right of the castle." He handed her the key with the number six on it. "You be an American? First time in Ireland?"

"I'm an American, but I've visited before. My cousin lives in Dublin. She told me about the job."

"I'd come and show you the cottage, but I best be staying here. Being it's Monday, the park is closed, but tourists still wander in."

Her spirits fell. "Darn. I was hoping to check out the castle. It's magnificent."

"It is that now, isn't it?" His eyes brightened and his back straightened, then he turned serious again. "You'll have plenty of time to explore the castle when it's open."

"I will. Thanks." She sighed. "I'm supposed to meet Jack. I understand he's the one who hired me." They'd talked on the phone and emailed for months. She had all the music he'd sent her memorized for the show. She couldn't wait to meet him. Her curiosity was driving her mad. Would his looks match her fantasy image of him? Jack's voice had a slow, rugged sound. Maybe it was the Irish accent that had kicked her libido into gear or that she hadn't had anything more than a casual date over the last six months. Knowing her luck, Jack probably looked more like the proprietor.

"Jack's around," Mr. Donegal said. "His cottage is at the edge of the forest, number two. And best you don't wander into that forest alone. You could get lost in the bogs."

"I'll keep that in mind." Get lost? She used to go backpacking in the Shenandoah National Park alone and she never got lost. She thought better not to mention that. "I had a large package shipped. Do you know if it's arrived yet?"

He pondered her question for a moment. "Yes, it's here. Delivered two days ago."

"Where is it? How did it look?" She clasped her hands to her chest, preparing herself for the worse.

He gave her a puzzled look. "Why, it looked like a box, a rather large one at that."

"I mean was it damaged?

"Don't think so."

"Good. Can I pick it up now, please?"

"Jack took it. Said it was your harp. Probably took it to the castle for the show."

"And the castle is closed," she reminded him. Her heart leapt with relief and disappointment. By the look on the proprietor's face, he wasn't going to leave his post so she could get her instrument.

"Ah, I love the folk harp. 'Tis a lovely sound. I shall look forward to hearing you play."

"Thank you, Mr. Donegal."

He caught her gaze and gave her a slight nod. "If you follow the drive, you'll come to a fork. Bear to the right. You'll see the cottages. There's a meeting tonight at seven in the castle for the entertainers. You can get your harp then."

She thanked him again and left the visitor's center with its quaint thatched roof and miniature windows with flower boxes, like something straight out of a fairytale. Despite her disappointment in having to wait to practice her music, she was excited about her summer job. Her parents had frowned on Dana's decision to take a leave of absence from a well-paying management position in a security company for a part-time, minimal-paying job as an entertainer in a medieval show. They were both high-powered executives and thrived on long work hours and stress. How could they understand that the stress of Dana's job had been wearing on her life? Work usually slowed down in her company over the summer, so her boss had agreed to the leave as long as she returned by September first. She deserved this break. At thirty-three, this was the first reckless thing she'd ever done.

The midday sun dried up the earlier rain and the air smelled of dew, cut grass and flowers. For a Maryland girl, June in Ireland was on the cool side. She climbed into her rental car, which looked more like a fishbowl on a roller skate, and drove along the gravel road toward Rathmore Castle. As she reached the fork in the road, she stopped the car. Across a large field toward the right were a dozen thatched-roofed cottages similar to the visitor's center. The left road led straight to the castle.

As she gazed up at the massive structure, a slight tremor went through her. Mostly, she was shivering from cold. The rain had soaked through to her underwear and the cool air had chilled her to the bone. But the tremor was more than that. She couldn't imagine her good luck at working in such a beautiful place, but what if her parents were right and taking this time off would somehow hurt her position at her old job? She found herself hoping to go back to her old routine. Why did she think she could make a big change in her life? That wasn't her.

Dana swung the car toward the cottages and stopped in front of number six. After unloading her luggage, she dragged it all into her unit and dropped it on the bed. The cottage was small but very neat. A tiny kitchen with a table for two was at the front, a bed and dresser in the middle, then a seating area with loveseat and coffee table. On one wall was a fireplace. Her teeth were chattering at this point and a hot shower beckoned.

She showered and changed into jeans and a tee shirt and slipped on a lightweight hooded sweatshirt, leaving it unzipped. Grabbing her room key and stuffing it in her sweatshirt pocket, she gave her unpacked suitcases a weary look as she left her cottage.

When she tried Jack's door and got no answer, she accepted the grim fact that harp practice would have to wait until after the meeting that evening. The castle loomed in front of her. A drive into town for groceries would wait. How could she pass up exploring the grounds of a five-hundred-year-old monument? Closed or not, she had to take a closer look. She had all afternoon to shop and unpack. Walking toward it, she admired how the dark stone structure rose well above the trees and at each corner were tower-like turrets. The view from the top must be amazing.

After working in a security company for thirteen years, force of habit had her scanning the castle walls for security cameras or spotlights. No cameras, minimal lighting, no motion sensors. She hoped the park had a better system in place inside, considering the castle was supposed to have fifteenth- and sixteenth-century furnishings.

Why did the castle have to be closed today? Just her luck. She walked up the drawbridge and tried the door and sure enough it was locked. *Crap.* Maybe it wasn't so easy to break into a castle.

Walking around the building, she ran her hand along the rough stone. Five hundred years old. What would it have been like to live here centuries ago? What was it going to be like to entertain here? She hadn't practiced in over two weeks since she'd shipped her harp. Even though the audiences for the dinner shows would be small, her stomach knotted up as if she was about to perform at a huge symphony hall.

She was three-quarters around the building when she discovered a small alcove and a wooden service door at the end of the narrow walkway. Dana tried this door and it opened. She shook her head. *Very poor security.* She should mention this to Jack and make some recommendations while she was here.

A narrow curved stairway led up. The castle was huge and she preferred to know the layout of the place since the first show would be in a couple of days. One flight up opened onto a great hall. A few tapestries hung on the walls between giant windows and heavy dark chairs and one table took up one wall. They'd need more tables to seat guests. There must be another room.

Dana crossed the hall to another doorway that led to a different stairway and was about to climb, when she saw a flickering glow from the darkness below. *Fire?* Could the castle be on fire? Wiring or the furnishings could be. She trotted down the circular stone stairs.

Darkness crept in around her except for the golden, flickering light from the basement. Walking through another doorway, she thought she heard voices but she wasn't sure. The hairs on the back of her neck stood up.

As she rounded a stone partition, the room brightened. Flames flickered within a half dozen wrought iron sconces, a fire burned in a small stone fireplace. The room smelled of sweet burning wood and damp stone. At the far wall two people hovered in shadows. Dana remained in her circle of darkness at the bottom of the stairs, unable to take her eyes away from the sight.

The woman was naked, her wrists and ankles bound with straps that hung from the ceiling. Her arms and legs were spread wide in a V shape. As Dana took a closer look, she saw the woman was cradled in a narrow hammock rigging that supported her back and bottom. Her pussy and anus lay open wide and metal clamps were attached to her nipples. Dana winced at the distended tips protruding from the tight clamps. The woman was also wearing a blindfold. The other person, wearing a hooded robe, was male. She could tell by his bare legs and feet. His back was facing Dana.

A rush of heat, then cold crept through her. Wrapping her arms around her waist, her first instinct was to escape and call for help. Then she stepped back and searched for a weapon, planning to do some damage to the guy if the woman needed help. Instead, Dana froze at the bottom of the stairs. Attacking this man was not a good idea if the woman was a willing participant. She would watch long enough to make sure the woman was okay.

There were people who got into this kinky stuff. Why this woman would allow this man to do these things, Dana couldn't fathom. "More, slave?" the man in the robe asked the woman.

The woman nodded. "Yes, Master, if it pleases you." His fingers stroked the narrow thatch of dark hair between her legs, avoiding the glistening folds of her pussy. The woman squirmed and tried lifting her hips.

Dana managed to breathe in teaspoon-sized portions of air. People did this for fun? It didn't look like fun. Was the woman in trouble? Should she stop this? Go for help? *Move, dammit.*

"You want me to touch your clit, don't you?"

The woman whimpered and arched her back. "Yes Sir."

"But I hadn't given you permission to move." He continued to tease her, his fingers trailing along her inner thighs, across her ass and back up to the thatch of hair.

The woman moaned in pleasure. "No Sir. You didn't. I forgot."

His hand moved to her breast and adjusted the nipple clamps until she let out a little yelp and sharp intake of breath. "I'll have to punish you for forgetting."

"Yes Sir."

He swung a flogger in the air several times. The woman's chest rose and fell quickly as if anticipating the blows that would come. Dana held her breath. The robed man struck her ass and she cried out and jerked against her bindings. Her feet pointed and legs tried to spread wider.

"Yes, Master, again. Please."

Biting her lip, Dana clamped a hand over her mouth. Good lord, the woman *was* enjoying this.

"Not just yet. You're being an ornery slave today." He chuckled as the flogger swatted her bottom and the underside of her thighs.

Dana's blood chilled with the sharp crack of leather hitting the woman's bare skin. As he hit her again and again, the woman slumped in her restraints, her head hung to one side. He approached her and brushed her long dark hair from her face and kissed her forehead tenderly. Whimpering, the woman leaned into the kiss. Dana stared at the couple shamelessly. She should leave quietly but couldn't pull herself away.

"Good," he said. "You ready for more?"

The woman nodded and leaned into his hand. He walked over to the wall and pulled an object out of a tote bag then came back to the woman.

"You remember the safe signals with a gag?"

"Yes, Master. Three quick grunts or open and close my hands."

"Yes." He bent down to kiss her. "Now open." A ball gag was secured in her mouth. He tied the straps around the back of her head. Now the woman couldn't scream if she needed to.

Dana was unable to shout or run. Should she trust this man or do something?

"You're such a pain slut, my love." The man stroked her hair then he swung the flogger in a circle. Turning to the side, the man faced Dana, and she noticed his robe was open. He was naked underneath. His hard cock jutted out from the draped fabric. "I think you like pain as much as coming."

The woman made a mewling sound as she nodded.

"You want to come, don't you?" His hand slipped between her legs, then he plunged a finger inside her.

She nodded and moaned, trying to raise her hips.

"No, stay," he ordered, pulling his hand away. He then swung the flogger and swatted straight across her breasts.

The woman gave a yelp as much as she could with a gag in her mouth.

Dana bit her lip as heat flowed through her followed by a throbbing in her pussy. Lord, she was wet and getting turned on by this. The man lapped at the woman's clamped nipples, then took a swollen tip between his teeth. The woman jerked against her restraints. "Too painful?" he asked.

She shook her head and arched her back, offering her breasts to him. He bit harder this time and the woman cried out beneath the gag. Dana's nipples hardened too and her pussy was sopping. How could she stand that kind of torture and appear to beg for more?

"Are you ready to be fucked?" he asked as his hand dipped down to her slit.

She nodded, writhing in her restraints.

"I'm going to fuck you, but I want to taste you first."

The woman let out a groan and looked up at her right hand. She had her pinky finger sticking up. He looked up. "You're signaling you're on the edge?"

She nodded.

"Good. I'll go slow." He cracked the flogger in the air. The sound made the woman and Dana jump. "But don't come until I give you permission. I still wish to taste you so you must remain in control."

The woman nodded slightly and whimpered. Stroking her breasts, the man then moved his hand lower, circling her pussy. His mouth positioned between her legs and Dana could see he was blowing across her clit and labia. The woman groaned. Dana held her hand over her mouth.

Obviously, these were lovers, strange as it was, and she needed to get out of there before they saw her. Slowly, she took a step back and another, but somehow managed to trip over her own feet in the darkness. Stumbling, she fell back against the wall. The movement and noise caught the man's attention. He jerked his head toward her.

Taking a step closer, he frowned and studied her for a moment. He didn't make any move to hide his cock or the flogger he held out at his side. Sliding the hood back off his head, he let the robe hang off his shoulders, giving her a view of his face and body. Straight black hair fell past his shoulders. Dark, intense eyes lingered on her breasts, then he locked his gaze with hers with an intimidating smile. "You like to watch, I can tell."

The woman hanging from the straps moaned.

"It's all right. We have a visitor, my love, but I don't think she means any harm." His eye narrowed. "Do you?"

Dana shook her head. "No. I saw a light. I thought it might be a fire." As if that explained why she was in the castle when it was closed to the public.

"Except you pulled my lady out of her sub space." His smile was grim. "Never interrupt a session."

She wasn't sure what he was talking about. "I didn't mean to disturb you. I wanted to make sure…" She was going to say make sure the woman wasn't tied up against her will, but she'd figured that out the first minute. Then why hadn't she left sooner?

"That something ominous wasn't going on here?" He laughed. "I can see your nipples through the bra. You like to watch. It's in your eyes too. My lady likes to be watched. You can stay if you wish, but you can't interfere and you must remove your clothes."

The throbbing in her pussy was almost painful at the thought of his suggestion. Her panties were soaking wet. This was turning her on, and scaring the hell out of her too. "I think I'll go. Sorry to disturb you."

He looked annoyed. "Suit yourself."

She backed up the spiral stone steps. As soon as she couldn't see him anymore, she turned and ran the rest of the way. Running across the main hall on the first floor, she found the door to the outside, yanked it open and raced toward the front of the castle where her car was parked.

A fine misty rain cooled her heated face but her body was on fire. She kept glancing behind her, expecting to see the naked man in the black, hooded robe chasing her. As she came around the front turret, she crashed into him.

Dana screamed and tried taking several steps back. Strong, muscular arms enclosed her.

"Easy now, miss. Are you all right?"

She looked up into calm, blue eyes that held concern, not the intense annoyance of the man in the castle's dungeon. "Let go of me." She pushed at his chest. Despite the cool air, he wore a short-sleeved shirt that showed off decent-sized biceps.

He released her and she took a step back. "You running from a ghost?" the guy asked, smiling. Not the man in the black, hooded robe. He was taller, his hair shorter and he was wearing jeans, not a robe, thank God.

She held a hand to her chest while she sucked in air, trying to catch her breath. "Who the hell are you? You scared the daylights out of me."

"I'm Jack."

"Jack Murray?"

He nodded, smiling with a glint of mischief in his eyes. "And you are..."

He was much better-looking than she'd imagined him. During months of email she'd made her own fantasy image. Thick, dark hair was combed back but a wavy lock fell low over his brow. He was a few inches taller than she was and about the same age. "I'm Dana. I just got here."

"Dana, hello." His eyebrows went up. "Got here. From where?" He was giving her an odd look, probably trying to figure out what she was doing running from behind the castle.

She hesitated. Glancing over her shoulders, she half expected to see the naked guy, robe flowing behind him as he chased after her. Her heart still pounded.

Jack looked past her as if he too expected to see someone.

"Dublin. I drove in from Dublin." She'd rather get as far away from the castle right now. What if that guy came out and saw her? But Jack was the one who'd hired her or recommended her for the job. She took a deep breath and let the air out slowly, willing herself to relax. She glanced back again. If the robed guy was chasing her, he would've been out by now.

She turned back and met Jack's eyes and her stomach did a twirl. Actually, he was damn hot, no question there. God, she didn't need the inconvenience of a summer fling, not that he'd be interested. Even if he was, it wasn't worth the trouble or pain. Imagine the awkward moment when she had to return to the states.

"Something wrong," Jack asked.

"No, I'm fine."

He gave her a look of disbelief and the corner of his mouth quirked in a grin.

"Did the other harpist have her baby?" she asked.

"Don't think so."

"The job is still mine through the end of August?" There was something about Jack that was very appealing—the easy way he talked, the spark in his eyes. In his emails he'd mentioned he wasn't married, but didn't say if he had a girlfriend. Their chats had occasionally gotten a little personal, but mostly they were business friendly. She glanced at his left hand and confirmed he wasn't wearing a wedding ring. Not that all men wore wedding bands.

He smiled and she wondered if he caught her checking him out. Her heart gave a little leap. She didn't believe in love at first sight but she did believe in instant attraction. Either the man was charismatic or her hormones were strung out after the bizarre scene she just witnessed.

"Yes, through August." He looked over her shoulder, and she spun around to see what he was looking at.

Had the man in the robe finally come out?

"Someone with you?" he asked.

She shook her head. "No, no. Just looking around the castle."

"Ah, 'tis quite a fine, old place. I can show you now if you like."

"No!"

He grinned. "Another time, perhaps."

"Yes, thanks. I should get to my cottage and unpack. I thought I'd drive into town for groceries then take a walk in the forest." She didn't want to ask for her harp now. Mr. Donegal said it was in the castle.

"Lots of bogs in the forest behind the cottages. Careful if you decide to go on that walk. Stay on the trails."

"Thanks for the tip," she said with a hint of sarcasm. Did they think she was from the city and never took a walk in the woods?

"You'll be wanting your harp?" he asked.

Dana panicked. She wanted to say yes, but she didn't want to go back inside the castle.

"I'll bring it to you. It's in my cottage."

Chapter Two

ꟹ

After Jack brought Dana's harp to her cottage, he drove into town to work at the store. Later, as he crossed the meadow toward home, haunting harp music drifted from Dana's place. The melody he recognized as one of the songs from the show. Standing now on the gravel walkway in front of her porch, he was mesmerized by the smooth precision of her music and the sensual flow of the notes. An accomplished player, not an amateur.

She was as beautiful as her music. She should be performing in a large symphony orchestra, not a small medieval dinner show.

While he listened, the stress of the afternoon eased from his shoulders. It had been a disappointing day. Another loan application turned down. He was running out of options. The thought of returning to his old job in the wool mills wasn't appealing. The last seven years he'd been running his uncle's store, pulled it out of near bankruptcy and now his uncle planned to sell it. The money from the sale would be his uncle's retirement. If Jack was the new owner, his uncle could continue working part-time. But if Jack couldn't get a loan to buy the store, his uncle would be forced to look for another buyer and would lose his part-time job. His uncle couldn't afford to hold a loan for Jack.

The music stopped and Jack found himself holding his breath. Was his private concert over? Why would she come all the way to Ireland for a summer job? Nothing in their emails had given him a clue as to why.

The music began again, a difficult classical piece for as much as he knew about music, not part of the show. He was a singer, not a musician. Closing his eyes, he got lost in his private performance. His mind wandered and easily imagined Dana playing the harp naked, then incorporating a pattern of rope bondage for that scene, allowing only her hands and arms free to play.

Someone who was that skilled at an instrument had to be regimented and disciplined. A master of her harp, had she ever allowed anyone to be her Master in the bedroom?

Dana reminded him of a sub he once knew at the club Unfettered. Usually focused and in control in her normal life, but under the careful attentions of a Dom, she would surrender to her sensual side and completely let go. During their many chats online, he wondered if Dana had picked up on his Dom nature. At first emails were business related, discussing the dinner show and where she'd be living, then progressed to friendly teasing and a little suggestive chat.

His cock hungered for the opportunity to train a sub, to have her surrender her physical self to him. There was something very enticing about bringing a novice into the lifestyle. She'd either be curious enough to ease into it or be scared off. Jack couldn't deny who he was—a sexual Dominant looking for a woman willing to take on the role as his submissive.

Unfortunately, the troupe couldn't afford to be without a harpist. His priority was to help Donegal, the owner, find a temporary harpist, to replace Jane while she had her babe, not find a new slave for himself. The summer was their busiest season and he didn't have time to hire and train someone new.

"Taking a nap are you, Jack?"

Jack shook himself out of his musing, opened his eyes and looked at Damon. The fellow troupe member and friend studied him with devilish dark eyes.

"Nah, listening to the new girl play. She's good, isn't she?" Jack answered.

Damon, the violinist, tilted his head toward Dana's cottage. His long dark hair was damp, and a large duffle was slung over his shoulder. "Yeah, she is. Is she coming to the meeting tonight? She needs to get her costume," Damon said.

"I don't know. She didn't say."

"You met her then. Is she cute?"

"Very." Jack couldn't stop himself from smiling.

"Ah Jack. I know that look. You'll be wanting to tie her up and do unmentionable things to her." Damon narrowed his eyes. "But don't scare her off now. We need a harpist for the summer."

"I know," Jack groaned. He could listen to her play all day.

"You could go to Unfettered and find a willing lady."

Jack shrugged. "For the night, yes, but I want more. A woman in my life, not just a one-night partner. I'd like what you and Shannon have."

Damon nodded. "I understand. Shannon and I are going to get something to eat before the meeting. Want to join us?"

"I'll pass, thanks. I think I'll check on the harpist." He gave Damon a wink.

* * * * *

"Dinner?" Jack asked, an easy smile greeting her at the opened doorway to her cottage.

"Jack! Hi." Dana's stomach gave a bit of a flutter. She knew he was probably looking at her opened suitcases with clothes piled all over the bed. Once she'd had her harp, she'd given up unpacking to practice. It'd been over two weeks since she'd played. Usually if she went more than a day she started climbing the walls. "What?" Sometimes when she played her harp she'd get so disconnected from the world. It took her a second to understand what he was asking. "A little early for dinner, isn't it? I was going to find a market in town for groceries. I can cook something here."

His eyebrows rose. "It's twenty minutes to town. I doubt you'll have time."

"I have all afternoon." She checked her watch. It was nearly five p.m. "Oh my God. I was playing for four hours." She suddenly realized she was hungry. "I guess I'll have to go after the meeting."

Jack shook his head. "Bet you didn't have lunch either."

She didn't answer.

"Follow me," he ordered, walking off her porch, not waiting for her to answer.

"Hang on, let me get my sweatshirt." Dana sorted through the clothes on her bed and found her sweatshirt and put it on. She slipped the room key in her pocket and felt a piece of paper. Her grocery list? She pulled out the paper but it was a business card. On a crisp white card was typed in black ink: 1-800-DOM-help. Weird. She didn't remember anyone giving her a business card. She turned it over and nothing was written on the back. The idea that someone must've slipped it in her pocket was unsettling and a little annoying.

"Dana?" Jack called from her porch.

"Coming." She ripped up the card and tossed it in the trash, then rushed out of her cottage. "Where are we going?" she asked Jack.

He didn't answer and kept walking. She hesitated for a moment then decided to see what he had in mind. Jack had to go to the meeting too. Maybe he knew a local place where she could get a quick bite. Grabbing her purse, she closed and locked her door, then ran to catch up to him.

"Are you going to tell me where we're going?"

"Jack's place."

"And why are we going to your place?" she asked. He gave her a sexy grin and her pulse kicked up a few beats. The sexy voice she remembered hearing on the phone certainly matched the rugged good looks of the man before her. Following him gave her a nice view of him from the back, from wide shoulders, to the tight ass in snug jeans to boots.

He glanced over his shoulder and shot her a dark look from blue-gray eyes. "Trust me." His smile was warm and sensual. His cottage had the same layout as hers—the kitchenette was at the front of the cottage, the bed with a red patterned duvet and a loveseat in the back. It was neat and organized except for several boxes stacked in one corner, a laptop computer on the small dining table and a bicycle propped against a wall. A wide window overlooked the forest behind the cottages.

In the kitchenette, he took out pots and pans, sliced brown bread and removed an enormous amount of food from the refrigerator.

"I don't want you to go to any trouble," she said.

"Soup and sandwich is no trouble. It's dinner. Have a seat. It won't take long. But this kitchen is too small for two people." He handed her silverware and pointed to one of two chairs at the small dining table.

"Thanks, Jack."

After he finished cooking their meal, he brought out bowls of steamy vegetable soup with warmed roast beef and melted cheese sandwiches. The creamed soup was flavored with herbs and the bread tasted homemade. "Good?" he asked.

"This is great. You didn't bake the bread, did you?"

He laughed. "No. I'll take you to the market in the morning and show you around town, including the bakery."

"That's really nice of you." She glanced around his cottage. "How long have you been doing the show?"

"Couple years. It's a part-time job. I also manage my uncle's store."

"What do you sell?" She was devouring the soup and sandwich. Have to love a guy who could cook.

"Woolens and leather goods."

"I'll have to stop by and check it out. I'm sure I could use a sweater in this weather. Ireland's summers are cooler than I'm used to." Something about the way the man was looking at her made her squirm in her seat. Not in a bad way. He had the most gorgeous blue eyes, sensual, intense but at the same time calming. "Not the season for leather though. Too warm and too much rain."

Jack smiled. "Leather never goes out of season." The look he gave her spread heat and longing through her. It was a very bad idea to get involved with someone considering she was going to leave in three months. "Leather goods provide our largest sales in the summer." His voice lowered. "Some of our clientele have special requests."

The way he said it made her feel strangely aroused. Her nipples tingled and hardened and her pussy throbbed. "Should I ask?"

He shrugged. "Fetish wear and bondage equipment. More soup?" He got up and spooned another serving of soup into his bowl.

She swallowed. "No, thanks. I've had enough."

His gaze locked with hers as if he was testing her, waiting to see if she'd react to the comment about leather goods. This reminded her of a business deal. Was he playing games with her? If he was, she wasn't going to let him rile her. "Interesting. And what's your best-selling SM device?"

Smiling he said, "Floggers, then various restraints. A lot of people enjoy pain."

"Mmmm." She said it in a tone as if they were talking about the weather or a favorite movie.

"What do know of the SM scene?" He was serious, the teasing tone gone.

She took in a breath. Images of the couple in the castle's dungeon flashed in her mind. Heat flowed through her like warmed honey. Her pussy felt wet and achy. "Not a lot. I read some about it. Curious, I guess."

He smiled. "Fantasized then?"

She choked on the last spoonful of soup. "Wow, this conversation got personal. From groceries to bondage to sexual fantasies." Her voice was shaking and her whole body was on fire. Exhilarated by the topic, she pressed her thighs together as her pussy clenched and pulsed. Damn, this man had her worked up now, and she'd only just met him. "Why didn't you mention this in your emails?"

"You mean about working in a store?"

She laughed nervously. "I mean about the SM products you sell."

He shrugged. "I didn't want to scare you off. We needed a harpist and your cousin highly recommended you."

"I don't scare too easily." She smiled. God, was she flirting? Yes, she was flirting and wasn't he her coworker?

"What does scare you?" He shot her a self-satisfied grin.

Her mind went to the couple in the dungeon. Had they brought leather items from Jack's store? Was she scared by what she'd seen? Or intrigued? This time she shrugged. "I'll have to let you know."

"I'll count on that," he lowered his voice and heat flowed through her. "We should go to the castle."

"What?" she breathed. Dana's heart fluttered as she thought about Jack tying her up in the dungeon.

"The meeting is starting in a few minutes. What did you think I meant?"

"Nothing."

* * * * *

After Jack introduced Dana to everyone, he walked her though her parts. Why was she so nervous? She knew the music. She met the other minstrel players, singers and actors.

"Damon and Shannon will be up later. They're bringing the costumes from town," said Jack. "There'll be a rehearsal at eleven tomorrow and a dress rehearsal at two. This is mainly for the benefit of our new member, Dana. She knows the music. I've heard her play. She'll do fine in the show tomorrow."

"Tomorrow?" Dana squeaked. She thought she'd have a couple days.

"Is there a problem?" Jack asked.

"No, looking forward to it." She swallowed. Dana glanced at Jack, giving him a worried look. Not much time to practice. Talk about getting thrown to the wolves. Returning her gaze, he gave her a reassuring smile with a slight nod. He must know what she was thinking. Did she have that panicked look in her eyes?

"You'll be fine," he whispered in her ear.

"That's all I have for you," Jack said. "Any questions?"

Everyone shook their heads. "Except for the costumes," Thea, a woman with long reddish hair said. There were eight people in the troupe, four women and four men, minus the couple who was missing. Thea was the flute player, her boyfriend, Kevin, played the uilleann pipes, which sounded a bit like bagpipes, and two dancers. "I hope it's soon. We all have plans tonight."

Jack nodded. "I know. Hang here for a few. I'll give Dana a quick tour while we wait for Damon and Shannon." He held out his hand, pointing the way to a spiral staircase. "After you."

Dana followed Jack up the shadowed staircase. He pointed out several rooms that had once been bedrooms, a chapel, guest rooms and servant quarters. Then the stairs opened onto the roof. A gust of cool air penetrated her sweatshirt and she shivered. "Wow, what a view."

"You can't see much in the dark."

"I'm glad to be here, Jack." She could feel him studying her and the butterflies were flitting around in her stomach. "Why did you bring me up here?"

She heard him let out a breath. "I want to know what you were so afraid of before. Why you were running from the castle earlier?"

She wanted to tell him, but she was embarrassed and confused by her reaction. She wasn't afraid, not anymore. Mostly she was turned on. How could she tell him this? A previous boyfriend had tied her up a couple times for fun during sex, but it wasn't anything like what she saw in the dungeon. "I can't."

"Don't you trust me?"

She let out a half laugh. "Jack, I don't know you."

"We've been talking for months."

"It's not the same."

"Take the chance. I can be trusted."

The sound of voices far below caught her attention. Dana looked over the stone wall and noticed most of the entertainers walking across the meadow carrying costumes.

"Shannon and Damon are back," Jack said, looking over the wall. "Maybe you'll tell me later."

Back down the stairs, Dana entered the grand hall again and it was empty. Then at one end she saw two people hunched over the large table with medieval clothing draped on top.

"Hey, you two. What kept you?" Jack asked.

The guy spun around and Dana gasped. "The dry cleaners had a time finding all the costumes—" He took a look at Dana and smiled. "Hello, there." By the way he looked at her, Dana knew he recognized her from the dungeon. "Look who's here, Shannon. Our visitor from earlier." The woman with long, dark hair turned around and gave Dana an up-and-down look, her mouth pressed together as if trying to hold back a smile. Her fingers played at the cleavage of her low-cut sweater.

"Welcome to Rathmore Castle," Shannon said with a teasing grin. "Next time maybe you'll stay longer or join in?"

"I don't think so. Sorry I disturbed you." Dana couldn't stop herself from remembering Damon naked in the black robe, or Shannon strapped up, legs spread. Her face felt flushed and her nipples tightened.

"Am I missing something?" Jack said.

"You'll have to get the details from Dana." Damon grinned. The man didn't look embarrassed at all. "My guess is we have a sub smoldering beneath that demure surface. With the right Master—"

Shannon punched him in the arm. "Stop it." She turned to Dana. "Ignore him. He's shameless, but harmless."

Dana glanced toward Jack's questioning look. "I'll tell you later." She wasn't about to go into details in front of this couple.

Jack nodded, his face expressionless.

Picking up a forest-green velvet dress in her arms, Shannon brought it to Dana. "This should fit you according to the measurements you sent us."

"It's beautiful. Thank you." She glanced at Jack. "I should go and practice. See you all tomorrow."

"Would you like me to walk you back?" Jack's expression turned serious.

"No," she said a little too forcefully. "It's been a long day." That brought a snicker from Shannon and Damon. She didn't acknowledge them, just descended the stairs out of the castle.

Back in her cottage, she tried playing her harp, but even that didn't help calm her. Images of Shannon and Damon in the dungeon haunted her mind. She could hear the flogger striking Shannon's ass and thighs and see the inflamed flesh, while her anus and pussy were exposed for Damon to fondle. Shannon had appeared to be in ecstasy. Was that type of sex really pleasurable? She'd had a few good lovers but had she ever experienced extreme ecstasy? Would Jack do something like that?

Everywhere her body tingled as she fantasized about standing in the dungeon naked, Jack restraining her and striking her with the flogger until her skin was red and raw. Then stimulating her clit, thrusting his cock inside her pussy. She groaned out loud. Enough, she was torturing herself.

From her sitting area she looked out the window onto the forest. Yes, she did have the same view as Jack. Dim light from the cottages illuminated a narrow path that led from the meadow into the trees. Light seemed to be coming from deep within the forest, or was it her imagination? She hadn't noticed houses back there.

She went outside to look. Sleep was far from her reach at the moment. Too many life-changing thoughts were spinning around inside her head. The air was dead calm and scented with pine and mossy bog. The silhouettes of tree branches appeared frozen against the twinkling star-filled sky. Scanning the forest, she no longer could see lights, nothing but trees. It must have been a trick of the eyes. Walking along the edge of the meadow, she listened for night creatures. Nothing. How odd. In Maryland at night, she'd hear crickets, cicadas or frogs. Then she heard voices.

Across the open field between the castle and the cottages were a half dozen cloaked figures heading right for her. They looked like monks or something out of a medieval horror story, some of them carried lanterns. Druids? Hoods covered their faces. Dana stepped back into the shadows from the cottages and froze, blood pounding in her ears. As they passed, the hood of one of the cloaked figures slid back. It was Shannon. Another cloaked figure covered her again. Was that Damon? Then she heard women's voices, giggling and whispering. It was the entertainers from the show. All of them. Was Jack with them too?

They all rushed by, not seeing her hidden in the dark. Entering the forest without flashlights, they moved as if they had night vision goggles. How could they see where they were going? "Shannon? Shannon!" She called out to them but they didn't answer. She thought she heard someone call her name so, ignoring Mr. Donegal's and Jack's warning, she strode into the forest.

Chapter Three

ঌ

Dana followed the lamplights of the robed people who darted through the forest. When she could no longer see them, she used their voices as a guide. But the voices shifted from far to her right one moment then far to the left. She was getting disoriented in the dark. The ground was mucky and smelled of damp, rotting leaves. She'd walked off the trail dozens of yards ago, but the lights from the cottages glimmered through the trees so she wasn't lost.

A shriek of laughter to her right sent her running in that direction again. Her feet stuck in mud, she turned and tried to back out but sank in deeper. The squishing sound from her feet blotted out the faint voices. Giving up on her pursuit, she tried backing out onto dry ground. Losing her balance, she slipped and fell into mucky water over her head. She struggled to the surface and screamed.

Spitting and sputtering the sour-tasting water, she swam to the muddy bank and tried climbing out, but the bank was overgrown with slick, wet grass and it was like trying to crawl up wet satin. Each attempt sent her slipping back into the water. Then strong hands gripped her wrists and dragged her up onto dry ground.

When she got to her feet, she expected to see one of the robed people. "Let me go!"

"Dana, what're you doing out here?" Jack said, still holding onto her. He wasn't wearing a robe, just jeans and a tee shirt.

"I fell in the bog. What does it look like? What are *you* doing out here?" She pulled free of him and planted her hands on her hips. Grass and muck hung from her arms, legs and clothes. She hated to think what was in her hair, what she smelled like.

"I heard you scream from my cottage. Come on. You need to get a hot shower and I'll show you how to start a turf fire in your fireplace so you don't get pneumonia."

Standing on her cottage porch, Dana dug around her soggy sweatshirt pockets for her key. Not there. No key. But she felt something else. She pulled it out and stared at another white business card. 1-800-DOM-help was clearly marked. The card wasn't even wet. A chill went right down to her bones. "Holy crap."

"What's wrong?" Jack asked.

He'd think she was crazy. She crumpled up the card. "I lost my key in the bog."

Jack started to laugh. "You didn't leave it in your room?"

"No, I didn't leave it in my room," she snapped. "It was in my sweatshirt pocket. Now what do I do? Can I get a spare at the office?"

"Sure." Jack laughed. "Tomorrow. The office is closed. Donegal's gone home for the night." He continued to laugh.

"It's not funny. Can't you break in or something?"

"Nope. Donegal would have my head. And I'd be paying for any damages."

Dana sighed and leaned against her door, defeated. "Terrific." The card was probably a joke, and she couldn't be bothered right now. But how did it get in her pocket?

"Dana, stay with me. I'll get a key in the morning."

She thought for a moment, trying to figure out her options. She didn't have any. "I could check with one of the other girls in the troupe..."

"They won't be back for hours."

She gasped. "They were the ones in the robes? Are all the entertainers involved in whatever is going on in the woods? Are they doing some kind of pagan ritual?"

Jack pressed his lips together. "I'll explain it to you when the time is right but now you need yourself a shower to warm up. I'll give you something dry to wear."

She hesitated again. What choice did she have? The keys to her rental car were in her cottage and so was her purse with her money. She couldn't even consider finding a place in town for the night.

"I'm being blunt here," Jack added. "Y'are shivering and you're smelling like a swamp. You'll be safe in my place. That be a promise."

"Okay," she said through chattering teeth.

As Jack led her into his cottage, she trembled more from the cold seeping into her bones than worry about spending the night in the one-room cottage. They'd been chatting by email for months so they were friends. Why shouldn't she trust him? The heat and attraction between them since she'd arrived couldn't be denied. She wondered if Jack felt it too.

Jack gave her towels, then a sweatshirt and sweatpants to wear. She stuffed the business card in the pocket of the pants. Maybe she'd try calling tomorrow and find out what it was about.

"I don't have a washer but I'll dunk your clothes in the sink with soap to get the bog smell out."

"Thanks." Dana's feet and hands were numb.

"Get yourself a hot shower now. I'll put the kettle on for tea and start up a fire."

Much later, Dana was sitting on the floor in front of the fireplace, mug of hot tea in hand while Jack soaked her clothes including her panties and bra. Once finished with his task, he brought over a blanket and covered her shoulders, then sat beside her, rubbing her arms. "Y'are still shivering." The heat of the fire and Jack's touch penetrated her body and was making her horny. Without her underwear, her body felt ultra-sensitive beneath Jack's baggy clothes.

"A little, but I feel much warmer. What kind of wood are you burning in the fireplace? It has a sweet scent."

"It's not wood, it's turf, organic material cut from the bogs."

She stared at the blazing briquette. "Why not use firewood?"

"Not many trees. Lots of turf."

"It smells good and it's warm." She pulled her wet hair away from her neck and shivered.

"Hang on." Jack got up, went into the bathroom and returned with a comb. "Turn your back to the fire." He sat cross-legged behind her and ran the comb gently through her hair, lifting sections as he did, allowing the heat from the fire to dry her hair.

"Feels nice," she said, closing her eyes.

"You'll feel warmer once it's dry." He used his fingers to hold her hair away from her neck. Sensations skittered over her skin, tightening her nipples. As he continued, her body relaxed. The pleasurable stoking of her hair, the gentle caresses along her neck made her pussy wet and achy. She trembled a little, feeling her body come alive beneath his touch. Her clit throbbed. She was so aroused, she had to control the urge to turn around and pounce on him.

"It's going to curl wildly without a hair dryer to smooth it out," she said. Now the fire was too warm. She let the blanket fall from around her, and as it did, his oversized sweatshirt bared one of her shoulders. Her breasts swelled against the soft fabric, her nipples clearly protruding and sensitive.

"I like it curled. Beautiful and soft. Smells like my shampoo now instead of the bog."

She play-punched his thigh, which was pressed against her hip. He laughed. Even though her hair was nearly dry, his fingers still combed through the strands and brushed the nape of her neck. God, it felt so good. Leaning into him, she wished his hands would slide from her hair and neck and move inside the shirt to her breasts.

It took all the willpower she had not to grasp his hands and guide them to her breasts. The attraction was so strong. She'd sensed the sexual teasing during their chats on line, nothing too obvious. He'd maintained a friendly professionalism, but she suspected there was more. How much did she know about him?

Her cousin knew him, went to college with him. What was she worried about? Why did she have to overthink everything in her life? Couldn't she be impulsive, spontaneous and indulge in some fun for once? Wasn't that the point of her taking this job? Putting her tea mug down, she slowly spun around and faced him. His hands dropped from her hair and rested on his knees.

There was no mistaking the lust in his blue eyes. His lips were slightly parted, ready to kiss her if she wished. He was letting her lead. If she wanted him, she could have him. All she had to do was give him a little encouragement. The sense of sexual power was such a rush. Her pussy was soaking his sweatpants. That thought got her even more aroused.

A muscle twitched at his jaw, a slight smile formed at his lips. "How are you feeling?"

"Good." She rested both hands on his arms. "And thanks for rescuing me and giving me a place to hang for the night."

"My pleasure." His voice was hoarse. He breathed deeply as his gaze dropped to her mouth then her breasts. Obviously, he wanted her. Why wouldn't he try to kiss her? She was so aware of him, thinking about how his muscular body would feel against her damp skin.

The heat from the fire only added to her lust. She couldn't stop herself from what she did next. Her hands slid up his thighs, to his waist and moved along his sides. Jack let out a soft moan and shook his head.

What a fool she was. Had she misinterpreted his desire? "I'm sorry, Jack. Guess I got a little carried away." She jerked her hand back and tried scooting away.

He let out a long breath. "I offered you a safe place to stay."

"I know." She watched him stare into the fire as if withdrawing from her. Shadows danced across his face and an uneasy feeling twisted in her gut. Picking up one of those briquettes, he tossed it on the fire and jabbed it with a poker. Sparks shot up into the chimney. "Anything wrong?" she asked.

"You were frightened today by something. What was it?"

The question slammed into her as if he'd dunked her back into the bog. She swallowed. "I'm not sure if frightened is the right word. At first I was, maybe. Curious, confused, intrigued. I'm not sure how I feel."

He nodded. "Want to tell me about it?"

Studying his face, she saw concern and warmth in his eyes. "Yes, I do want to tell you. I haven't been able to stop thinking about it. That's why I followed those people into the forest."

"What happened at the castle this afternoon?" He took her hand.

She felt like she could trust him and it didn't seem like such a big deal now. "It's kind of embarrassing. I went into the castle, even though Mr. Donegal said it was closed. I was curious and wanted to look around, maybe find my harp. I saw a light flickering in the basement and thought there was a fire so I went to check it out."

"You found the dungeon." His mouth twitched into a slight smile.

"Two people were having a…sex."

"Really?" He held her gaze as if he was studying her response to the event. "Is that what scared you?"

"No, I mean, at first I thought the woman was in trouble because she was naked and tied up, hanging by her hands and feet. But then she seemed to be enjoying it quite a bit. And a man in a robe was whipping her." Dana shivered.

"Guess you've never done anything like that."

"No!" With Dana's abrupt answer, Jack glanced into the fire again.

"When you realized the woman was having a grand time, you took off?" He met her gaze so intensely, her heart leapt in her chest.

"No."

"No?"

"I couldn't stop watching. The woman was obviously in ecstasy. I don't think I've ever experienced that. And I thought I'd had a couple decent lovers in my past."

He chuckled. "Damon did say he thought you were getting turned on by watching."

"Damon told you I was there?"

"Yep."

"And you let me go through all the gory details?" She felt her face flush, her pussy tingling, from the memory and from sharing it with Jack.

"Yep."

"Why?"

"Why do you think?" He grasped her arms and pulled her closer.

"You wanted to hear a good sex story?" She grinned.

Smiling, he shook his head. The smoldering look he gave her sent her heart fluttering. "I wanted to know about you. How you felt about that situation."

"Why?" But she had a feeling she knew the answer.

"To see how familiar you are with that lifestyle."

"Not very, I'm afraid. You?"

His look was so intense, she had to hold her breath. "I'm a Dom. I've been in the lifestyle for years."

"Oh." Breathing again. His admission frightened her a little but she was more excited by it. The business card came to mind. 1-800-DOM-help. Could Jack have put the card in her sweatshirt? He didn't seem the type to do sneaky things. "That's interesting. I'd like to hear more."

Had he been wondering about her during their flirty conversations online? Could he be fantasizing about torturing her the same way? All she knew of this lifestyle was from an erotic novel she'd read. Now that she thought about it, the story had shocked her then but also turned her on. She had been too embarrassed to talk about it with the boyfriend she'd been with at the time, but those fantasies had drifted into her mind during their lovemaking.

"Good answer," Jack said. Before she could say another word, he slipped his hand around to the back of her neck and lowered his warm lips to hers. The slow, gentle kiss teased her mouth then he moved to her ear. Her fingers dug into his hips, wanting more, so much more. Turning her head, she drew his mouth into a kiss again.

He moaned and parted her lips with his tongue. The intensity and heat surged through her body in sensuous waves. Hooking his arm under her knees, he pulled her across his lap and deepened the kiss. They both gasped for air.

She could feel the hard ridge of his engorged cock pressing against her thigh. Skin, she wanted bare skin against her. She wanted him. Boldly, her hands slid under his shirt, across his hard abdomen to his chest and felt his arms tighten around her. Then he grasped her breasts, first through the sweatshirt, then yanked it off, tossing it aside. His mouth captured one nipple and sucked it, rubbing the tip with his tongue, leaving raw nerve endings tingling.

Jack's clothes were so loose on her, it wouldn't take much for her to wriggle out of them. The thought heightened her arousal, making her clit throb. Images of the extreme sex scene in the dungeon played over and over in Dana's mind. This was a side to her sensuality she must explore. Wrapping her arms around his neck, she met Jack's gaze. "Teach me. I want to understand what this is all about."

He closed his eyes and took in a breath, then looked at her for a long moment. "It's not for everyone."

"That's what I'd like to find out."

Abruptly, he pushed away from her, stood and walked into the kitchen area. She stared at the fire for a moment, deciding whether or not to press him. Finally, she got to her feet and went into the kitchen. "I struck a nerve. Can you tell me why?"

He nodded. "A woman I was involved with was curious about the D/s lifestyle. It wasn't for her and she left. It was hard on both of us."

"Well, you know ahead of time this would be a brief arrangement. I'm only here until the end of summer. Haven't you had a casual affair before?"

"A few at the clubs."

"Then we both know what to expect."

"Perhaps." But he didn't sound convinced. What was wrong with a summer romance and sexual exploration between two adults? She'd leave Ireland with fond memories of her hunky liaison, and he might remember her as his sexy American fling. They would remain friends after. Wouldn't they?

Then a jolt of excitement and part fear struck her. Would he tie her up like Shannon? Part of her wanted to try that and part of her was terrified of the thought. "Are you going to take me to the dungeon?"

"No."

Her insides wanted to scream at him in disappointment even though she didn't know if she was ready for that. "Why not?"

He let out a long breath. "Because there are things we should discuss first. Limits for one. I wouldn't want to do anything to make you feel uncomfortable working here."

"Then we can take it step by step. I promise to let you know if something makes me feel uncomfortable." To Dana that seemed reasonable.

Jack nodded and stepped closer. Cupping her chin with his hand, he gazed deeply into her eyes. Dana held her breath. "In the middle of a scene, you may not know what you can and can't handle. I need to know you well enough to recognize a situation that's become too intense for you, and anticipate your needs. I don't want to hurt you."

If ripping off her clothes would prove her desire for him, she'd do it. But throwing herself at him wasn't going to convince him of her hunger for exploring the kinky side of herself. "I don't know, Jack. I may not like a D/s lifestyle. I won't know unless I get a chance to try it out. I'm not afraid to find out if this kink is my kink. If you were an asshole, you'd be dragging me to the dungeon and hanging me upside down right now."

He smiled. "Don't tempt me."

"I'm serious. You're concerned about your partner's needs. That's good. How would we start?"

"Another term in the lifestyle is sub or slave. There is a difference, but I won't go into that now," he added. "We'll begin by you calling me Master."

Her stomach did a twirl and her nipples puckered. "Yes, Master."

"Good." The hoarseness in his voice sent a jolt straight to her pussy. God, she wanted this badly. Dana had to know if she was capable of experiencing pleasure through pain. "The music I play on my harp may be sweet and delicate. That's not who I am."

He stared at her with a serious intent that made her breath catch. He was so handsome. His powerful shoulders and chest muscles tensed in the firelight. "Not too many women would chase after robed figures into a forest at night. Pretty ballsy."

"I saw Shannon and figured the others were the entertainers. I was curious."

He rubbed his forehead and sat down at the table. Was this his way of saying no? "Trust me, I'll tell you when a scene is too intense," Dana said. "We only have the summer to explore this. Why waste time?"

He shot her a dark look. "And what happens after the summer?" His words had a sharp edge.

She wanted to kick herself for that. "I have to go back to my old job by September first. Otherwise, I'll lose it. Do you want to spend the rest of your life wondering about what if?" She hesitated when he didn't answer and walked over and plopped down on the bed.

Walking out of the kitchen area, Jack brought with him a ladder-back chair and placed it in front of the fire. "Stand up," he commanded. "Your first lesson begins now."

Chapter Four

ℬ

Jack was reasonably sure he could handle a summer fling. His gut told him it was a bad idea, having had more than his share of brief relationships in his younger days that had ended in disaster. For months as they chatted online, he'd fantasized about Dana as his sub in a D/s scene and here she was asking to be a willing participant. How could he refuse? He removed his shirt and tossed it onto the bed.

"Are you going to tie me up?" Dana asked as she stood, crossing her arms over her waist. Her words made Jack's cock grow hard.

"For now, no. Stand in front of the chair and place your forearms on the seat. You may grasp the back if you like." She did as instructed, giving him a nice view of her smooth, round ass.

"Like this?" she asked as she bent over and did as instructed.

"That's fine. Keep your legs straight but spread them." Immediately, she complied. "Good. You're comfortable? Warm enough?"

She nodded.

"Respond to my questions with, 'Yes or no, Master'. There's no right or wrong way to do BDSM. Whatever is satisfying, meets the needs of the couple and is consensual." He walked slowly around the chair, getting her used to his presence, and stroked her shoulder, nothing sexual yet.

"Yes, Master."

"A submissive may surrender to her Master but she controls the scene. If something becomes too intense for you, say the word 'slow', and I'll stop or slow down with what I'm doing." This time he slid his hand over her buttocks to register her response. He heard an intake of breath and noticed her wriggle her ass. "If you want to end the scene completely say, 'butter'."

"I understand."

"Dana, I always practice safe sex. And trust me never to hurt you." Moving his hands over her back, he slid them around to her breasts and got a moan from her. She also arched her back and closed her eyes. "Working with a virgin has its own unique charms."

She giggled. "I'm not a virgin, Master."

"To this lifestyle you are. And I did not ask you a question." He swatted her on her ass and she jumped, but didn't protest.

He went to his closet and brought out a few implements: a rope, if he decided to tether her, and a suede flogger.

Was he making a mistake testing her this way? What if she decided the whole scene made her uncomfortable? First Damon and Shannon in the dungeon, then the group disappearing into the forest in robes and now him. What if she freaked out and decided to pack up and leave Ireland? The troupe would hang him. They didn't have the time to hire and train a new harpist especially with their busy season coming up.

It would be a lousy thing to do considering the troupe had helped him out by letting him stay in the cottage so he could save money to buy his uncle's place.

Playing sexual games with a curious novice was setting himself up for disaster. Turning back toward the closet, he put the flogger, straps and ropes back. Then he sat onto the bed. "Dana, you can get up. This wasn't a good idea. It's late. You can sleep on the bed. I'll take the sofa."

"But I didn't say slow or butter. Why did you decide not to…"

He rubbed his forehead with his hand. His cock was still hard but he hoped she didn't notice. "Because we've only just met today." He grabbed a throw blanket and attempted to lie down on the sofa, which was a loveseat. No matter what position he tried, he couldn't get his large body to find a comfortable spot.

"Jack, we've been chatting for months online. Don't tell me you had no idea there was flirting going on between us."

His mouth twisted in a half grin. "Yeah, you're right. We did have a few personal conversations."

"A few? One night you asked me what was my most sexually adventurous encounter."

"No way. I didn't ask... Oh yeah, I guess I did." He rubbed his face with his hand.

"You were fishing, trying to find out if I had been involved in a D/s relationship before." Dana stood and placed her hands on her hips, frowning. "I thought you were flirting."

His sweatpants hung low on her hipbones and threatened to slide off. And he knew she wasn't wearing any underwear. *Oh brother.* He stared up at the ceiling.

"Look at you. You can't sleep on that. I'll sleep there. You sleep in the bed," Dana said.

"No. I'll take the floor."

"And freeze your ass off." She took a breath and lowered her voice. "Jack, we're not a couple of teenagers. I thought we were friends. We don't have to have sex just because we're in the same bed."

He craved to hold her through the night, nuzzle his cheek against her breasts, curve his body against her round bottom, listen to her breathing while she slept. But to do so would be torture. To feel her close throughout the night without fucking her would drive him mad. If he had a D/s scene with her, he might be able to relax and get some sleep. He doubted he'd be getting much sleep.

He'd turned his back toward the bed, so he couldn't watch her but she hadn't crawled into bed yet. She walked across the room and at first he thought she was stirring the fire. Instead she came out of the closet with the flogger, straps and a rope.

She laid them out across the bed then walked over to him and knelt in front of the loveseat and bowed her head. "Please, Master. Show me. I want to learn. I want to understand why I was scared by watching Shannon and Damon and at the same time so turned on. I can't bear the thought of leaving Ireland at the end of summer without understanding these feelings. Every time I think of them, I get horny."

A knot formed in his chest. *Oh hell. She was a sub and didn't even know yet.* He'd have to take extra care with this one. It scared the hell out of him. She might realize this wasn't for her and panic in the middle of a session. He didn't want to do anything to hurt her. He'd never been with a sub who was so green.

She let out a huff, spun on her heels and marched over to the bed. She picked up the leather cuffs and started strapping them around her wrists. "Dana, don't."

She gave him a pained look and unhooked the cuffs. The firelight made her smooth skin glow and he noticed her nipples were hard. Her breasts were beautiful. Not huge, but perfectly shaped. Struggling with the wrist restraints, she managed to secure them to her wrists with the short length of chain dangling between the cuffs. Picking up the flogger, she walked over to Jack and knelt before him again, head bowed, and raised the flogger to him. "Please, Sir, I need to know."

His breath caught as he gazed at her naked from the waist up, wearing his baggy sweatpants that barely hung on her hips. Far from the exotic fetish wear he would see women in at the club Unfettered, but so sexy. He stood and took the flogger from her. "You need to know what, slave?" It took a conscious effort to keep his voice firm and in control.

She let out a long breath. "I need to know if pain gives me pleasure."

He closed his eyes and took a breath. *Oh hell. She's definitely a sub.* His cock twitched in response and rose to attention. Willing himself to remain in control, he pointed to the chair. "Get into your original position."

"Yes, Master."

Heart racing, he had to remind himself, even if she was receptive, she wasn't a seasoned sub. "Remember your safe words?"

She nodded.

"Answer me, slave."

"Yes, Master. I remember the words." His hands stroked her buttocks, her back and moved around to cup her breasts. Then down each leg and up, barely grazing her pussy. She shivered a little and didn't resist. He hadn't removed the sweatpants yet. It wouldn't take much to slide them down. Once he felt the muscles in her back and shoulders relax, he picked up the rope and tied her arms and wrists to the chair.

He checked to make sure it wasn't too tight then picked up the flogger. Her eyes looked up expectantly at him. "Eyes downcast, slave."

"Yes, Master." He took a number of practice swings and hit the bed, watching Dana jerk at the sound. Then he let the tassels hit her back in light strokes. She arched and moaned. As he moved over to her buttocks, he increased the power of his hits. She let out a couple of yelps but nothing she didn't seem she could handle.

"Painful, slave?"

"Not much, Master. More, please."

"Very well." He yanked down the sweatpants without giving her warning, drawing them to her ankles. She gasped but didn't struggle or protest. The flogger swung in circles again and swatted her butt cheeks on one side, then the other. He alternated the hits in a steady rhythm until her moans became shrill, then he brought her back down. He smoothed her reddened cheeks with his hands.

She was panting now and wriggled her ass as he touched her. No whimpers of suffering, only moans of pleasure. Moving to the back of the chair, he raised her chin, but she kept her eyes downcast as he requested. Her mouth was open, but she was breathing normally.

"Are you with me, slave? Look at me."

She locked eyes with him. "Yes, Master. I'm fine. I'm with you. More, please."

He had to smile at that. "Are you wet?"

"Yes, Master."

"How wet?" His hand parted her labia and he slipped a finger inside her channel. Withdrawing his finger slick with her juices, he circled her clit and felt it harden and swell. "Very wet and aroused. More?"

"Yes."

"Yes, what?"

"Yes, Master?"

"Good. Legs spread wide." Her ass twitched so nice for him and when she opened her legs, he got a good view of her pussy. Swinging the flogger like a pendulum, he brought it up between her legs hard enough to make her body jerk. But his lovely slave didn't protest or move away. Her breathing deepened and sped up as he struck her pussy harder.

Moaning, she flinched with each strike.

"You could come like this?" he asked.

"Yes, Master."

"Hold back, don't come until I say. Understand? I must give you permission to climax. Your pleasure is within my control."

"I understand. God, it's so good."

"Tell me when you're close."

"Now. I'll come if you continue like this, Master."

He stopped stimulating her with the flogger and rubbed her ass and back. "You did well, slave."

"Will you make me come now?" Her voice was shaky.

"No. This is the end of your first lesson. It's time for you to rest."

"But..."

"Your pleasure will exceed your fantasies if you can surrender to me." He untied her, brought her to the bed and cradled her in his arms. As much as his body wanted more of her, to make love, he'd wait. Control and trust made a brittle foundation in a new D/s relationship, especially when the sub was inexperienced. Best not to overwhelm his sweet slave. Besides, he'd promised her a safe place to stay the night.

* * * * *

The next morning, Dana woke to the smell of bacon simmering in a frying pan and brewing coffee. Stretching under the warmth of the covers, she gazed over at Jack as he prepared breakfast. Jeans hung low on his hips and he was shirtless and barefooted. His hair looked as if he tried to smooth it down with his fingers, sections were still mussed from sleep. *God, he looked hot.* She was still horny from last night, especially since she'd gotten no release. But she did say she was curious about the D/s lifestyle so she had to go along.

The chair she'd been tethered to stood in front of the cold fireplace. Memories of their bizarre night seemed like a dream now except for her tender bottom. The thought sent a rush of warmth straight to her pussy and her clit throbbed. Yes, pain did give her pleasure. The whole experience was strangely exciting but also unsettling. She didn't know how she felt about the need to be dominated. Was this something she could do in a relationship all the time? Or was she trying something new, just to say she did it? Like parachuting. A thrill-seeking thing. Once she'd done it a few times, she could say she'd had the experience but it wasn't something she'd care to do regularly.

This type of lifestyle required trust. But how could she trust Jack if she didn't know if she could trust herself? She'd taken a break from her well-paying job to be a musician in Europe. A responsible thirty-something didn't do that. That was what her parents told her anyway. "Morning," she called out to Jack. "Smells wonderful."

He turned around. "Morning. Sleep well?"

She got up, not shy about being naked, and enjoyed the up-and-down look he gave her. "Slept good, considering." She smiled as she rubbed her bottom with her hand.

"Sore?"

"A little, but in a good way." She found his discarded sweatshirt and pants and slipped them back on.

"You seemed to enjoy it. Did you feel I pushed too far?" He speared the browned bacon strips in the pan and drained them onto a paper towel, then poured off the grease into a can.

"No, I was fine. I'm ready for the next lesson."

He stirred beaten eggs into the hot pan with a spatula. "Good." His voice became husky. "After the show tonight meet me in the dungeon."

Her stomach clenched. "Where I saw Damon and Shannon?"

"Yes. Wait for me there immediately after the show. And I want to find you completely naked when I arrive. Understand?"

"Yes, Master." After they finished eating, Dana helped clean up and straighten the bed.

"Your clothes are still wet and they still smell like the bog," Jack said. "I'll take a run up to the office and get another key for your cottage. You can wait here."

Dana looked down at Jack's clothes. "Thanks. It would be a little obvious walking around in your sweats."

"Be right back." He pulled her into his arms, gave her a kiss, then released her. "Looking forward to tonight."

"Me too."

When the door closed, Dana folded up a throw blanket and placed it on the end of the bed. She picked up the flogger, wrist straps and ropes and opened the closet to put them away.

Inside the closet was a long, black robe. Like the one she saw the other entertainers wearing last night. She gasped and stepped away from the closet and shoved the door closed.

Jack was part of this secret group too. What was this all about? What would've happened if she hadn't fallen into the bog? What if she'd caught up to them and stumbled into whatever they were doing?

Images of bizarre sacrifices came to mind. She'd seen one too many creepy movies. Walking to the back of the cottage, she peeked between the curtains out the window, trying to see into the forest. She couldn't see anything through trees and shrub growth. The sky was clear and the paths into the woods could easily be seen. She wouldn't fall into the bog in the daylight.

She didn't know much about pagan practices but had a friend who was Wiccan. If the entertainers were a pagan group, she had nothing to worry about unless they were practicing black magic. A black robe didn't mean they were practicing black magic. She laughed at herself but it was a forced laugh.

The door to the cabin swung open and Dana jumped. "It took some persuading, but Donegal finally gave me the key. He couldn't believe you went into the forest at night after he warned you."

"What did you tell him?" She hadn't gotten the nerve to ask him about the robe yet. He was grinning and his eyes sparkled with mischief but not evil. There couldn't be anything evil about him, could there?

"Mr. Donegal is very superstitious. I'm afraid I told him you saw someone walk into the woods and you thought it was Shannon. You followed her. I wasn't lying. He assumed you saw a ghost. He asked me to keep an eye on you and protect you from anything supernatural. 'The forest is haunted,' Donegal says."

"Haunted?"

"No, it's not. I've lived here all my life. Never seen a ghost." Jack handed her the key. "He told me to tell you to stay out of the forest."

"Thanks for the key. See you later." She rushed past him, suddenly wanting to get far away from that black robe.

"You okay? Aren't I taking you to town?"

"Oh, right."

He gave her a puzzled look. "Go and get changed. I have a surprise for you."

* * * * *

Jack gave Dana a tour of the old town and pointed out grocery stores, pubs, restaurants and other shops. She couldn't wait to go exploring and browse through the quaint shops. Before their stop at the grocery store, he brought her to an older part of town where the streets were narrow and the store windows were decorated with flower boxes or hanging baskets. The smell of baked bread and smoked meat wafted in the air. "I'm getting hungry again," Dana said. "Something smells good."

"This is where I got the brown bread for your soup." He pointed to a bakery. "Next door is a good place for meats. My uncle's place is around the corner. I'm trying to get a loan to buy it."

"Your uncle can't hold a loan for you?"

"It would be a hardship for him. He wants to retire. And the place needs some work." Jack opened the door to a shop with a sign that read "Keagan's Wool Shop".

The store was quite spacious inside with several racks of woolen sweaters, coats and wraps. Wooden shelves lined the walls filled with neatly folded colorful knits. "Look at all the beautiful things." Dana strolled around the room, touching the soft knits. "I always thought wool sweaters would be scratchy. These are so soft."

He pulled out a gray tweed wrap and covered her shoulders with it. "Like it?"

"It's gorgeous. It's like a gray cloud with bits of purple in it. I'm sure I'll be back to shop here."

"My uncle will love to see you. This one's a gift."

She was about to argue with him, when a gentlemen came out from a back room. "I heard that. I'll be taking that out of your paycheck," the man said with a wink. He smiled at Dana and had the same mischievous sparkle in his eyes as Jack only this man was about seventy years old.

"Uncle Lee, this is Dana. She's from America and our new harpist."

Lee held out his hand and shook Dana's. "Nice to meet you. I love your shop."

"America? A long way to come for a job," Lee said. His voice held a note of disapproval.

"My cousin lives in Dublin and she heard about the job. She and Jack went to college together. I'm here just for the summer."

"Ah, so you're a student?"

"No, I took a temporary leave from my management job in a security company. I'll be returning to my position at the end of summer."

Lee's face scrunched up. "A manager? You left a good job? Aren't you a little old to be acting like a rebellious teenager?" His voice was tight. Dana didn't know what to say.

"Uncle," Jack cut in. "Maybe she had a good reason to leave."

"When you're young, you can be reckless and have a traveler life, drifting from place to place, job to job like a gypsy. When you're an adult, you stick with a job even if you don't like it. That's how you stay off the streets."

Jack was about to argue but Dana jumped in.

"No, your uncle has a point. If I had a family, I probably would've made a different choice, but sometimes taking a risk opens up opportunities. I don't want to look back on my life and wonder what if, or if only I had…" She glanced at Jack then at Lee. She obviously wasn't scoring any points with his uncle. "I might be making a mistake, but we learn from mistakes and become stronger from them." She should shut up before she dug herself in deeper.

"It's foolish." Lee's face was red. He headed into the other room then glanced back at Jack. "Look around if you like. I have the kettle on if you'd like some tea. Got a letter today. You were turned down on that last loan."

Jack swore under his breath. "Did they give a reason?" He held up his hand. "Forget it, I don't want to know. They're all stupid reasons. Out-of-town banks say the tourist trade has dropped off and a shop in this area is too much of a risk. Local banks say they remember my wild, reckless days in college and don't think I'm a responsible businessman. That was thirteen years ago. Other reasons mention the leather and specialty items are not appropriate merchandise. Certain months of the year we make more on those items than the woolen goods." Jack shook his head. "I've sold everything I own, given up my apartment to buy this place and it looks like it's not going to work out."

Lee frowned. "If I took out part of the loan."

"No. You've been trying to retire for seven years. You've worked hard all your life. I'm not going to have you sacrifice because of me. You could get a buyer for this place and live comfortably. If I can't buy it in three months, then it goes on the market and I find another job."

"Don't worry about it, Jack. There's time." Lee glanced over at Dana and gave her a nod. "I'll get the tea."

After Lee went into the other room, Dana turned to Jack. "I'm sorry if I upset your uncle."

Jack groaned. "You didn't. He doesn't understand. Things were different in his day." He took her hand. "Come on, I have something to show you."

"Is this the surprise?"

"Yeah."

Jack showed Dana into a room separate from the clothing section. It had a sign that said "Adults Only", which he pointed out to her. Opening the door, he led her through and kept an eye on her expression. He wanted to see her response when she viewed the various items and devices.

Upon scanning the room, Dana studied the display of leather fetish wear and extensive selection of bondage accessories and implements for a sadomasochist's dream. "Wow, this is amazing." She walked around and felt the leather floggers, held up a leather vest and frowned at the mask and ball gag. A few contraptions she examined for a long time. By the look in her eyes, she appeared more fascinated than shocked. He was relieved at that.

"What do you think?"

"It looks like Disneyland for the sadomasochist."

Jack laughed.

"I think I'd need an instruction manual on most of this stuff."

Jack agreed. "A lot of it does come with instructions and warnings." She didn't seem offended by anything in the room, but in the back of his mind he had his concerns. He picked up a flogger and swung it in the air and gave her a wicked grin.

"I like those, I discovered."

"I know." His smile faded. "Something my uncle said made me think. Why did you leave your job? Is coming to Ireland a rebellious diversion?"

She picked up a braided cat and ran her fingers through it. "The security business is a job I've had since high school. I went to college for electrical engineering and business. My parents are supportive about me playing the harp but not as a career. I always dreamed of playing in a large symphony but it would never pay like my management job. My cousin knows I love Ireland and has been urging me to spend the summer with her for years. When she told me about the medieval show, I knew this was my last chance to follow a dream."

"So you'll be going back," Jack said.

She let out a breath. "Yes, that's what I had planned."

"If you had the opportunity would you consider staying here?"

She didn't answer right away. "That would be a hard adjustment. I'd be so far away from my friends and family."

He nodded. "And what about this part of your life?" He held up some bondage straps. "Is this a lifestyle you're considering after last night or is this a rebellious phase like leaving your job?" He tried to keep his tone light but could hear an edge to his voice. He'd gotten involved with a woman before and after a year, she'd decided she didn't like the lifestyle and went back to her vanilla sex life. It had taken a long time to get over her. And now he was considering getting involved with another novice. Dana's arrival had set off a rush of emotions he hadn't anticipated. If he had any sense, he'd avoid her.

"I think it's too early for me to make that decision, Jack."

"Fair enough." Was he willing to set himself up for another fall, knowing at the end of summer, she would leave?

She moved up to him, her lips a breath away. "But I am getting wet and horny standing in this room, so that must count for something. Right?"

His cock hardened at her words. "It certainly does." He would probably hate himself by the end of summer but he couldn't resist a willing submissive as beautiful as Dana. "I think you're ready for the next step. The dungeon."

* * * * *

When Dana got back to her cottage, she pulled out the crumpled-up business card and punched out the number on her cell phone. She knew it wouldn't connect to anything anyway. She was in Ireland, 1-800 numbers wouldn't work from her phone as far as she knew. She'd call, and then she'd know the card was a prank of some sort and wait until the prankster decided to make himself known.

But after she punched in the number, it started to ring. She plopped down on her bed and someone answered. "Thank you for calling 1-800-DOM-help. This is the Operator. How may I be of assistance?" It was a man's voice, no accent, calm and formal.

"Hello?" Dana was tempted to hang up but then she wouldn't know what if it was a prank or not. "What's this all about?"

"I see you received one of our cards?"

"Yes. This is a prank, right? Who gave it to me?" She was wasting her time.

"This is a help line. If you received a card, you must need help in your relationship."

She sighed in frustration. "No, I don't need help. Besides, I'm not a Dom."

"Ah, you're a sub then, my mistake, hold on. I can connect you to someone who can help you with your Dom and your D/s—"

"No, do not transfer me," Dana raised her voice. "I don't need any help in my…whatever you said. Everything is fine."

"That's good to hear. Maybe there's something else that's troubling you?" The man seemed genuinely concerned and Dana felt her throat tighten.

"No, everything is fine." She hung up and ripped up the card.

Chapter Five

ꝟ

"Let the banquet begin," Jack announced. With his words medieval-clad servers brought out platters of soup and warm brown bread to each table for the first course while Dana and the other musicians performed a lively renaissance melody and Jack and Shannon sang a duet. They both had incredible voices.

When he'd said he was one of the singers, she had no idea how gifted he was. In her opinion he could be singing in a Broadway show. He looked so handsome in his period costume, the brocade tunic cinched with a leather belt. The tights he wore, she remembered laughing at earlier. Jack's comment had been, "Something wrong, my lady?" The thought brought a smile to her, and she caught Jack winking at her now as if he knew what she was thinking.

Or was he thinking about later, after the show? Earlier in his cottage, he'd instructed her not to wear panties under her costume. This, he said, was a simple test of her subservience and only they would know. After the show, he said he would meet her down in the dungeon for a more intense session.

Heat traveled through her body and her nipples tightened beneath the green brocade dress. The corset-like bodice pressed her breasts in rounded mounds above the lacy trim. Moving her arms while stroking the harp was restraining not to mention difficult for breathing.

Under the long skirt, Dana spread her legs and held her harp in the proper position between them. But without wearing panties, her chemise brushed over her bare pussy, making her more sensitive and wet each minute. And by the added movement of her playing, her clit swelled. She wanted

Jack's hand between her legs, touching her slit, rubbing her clit. Her pussy throbbed as she plucked each note in the song.

Jack glanced her way, a slight smile on his lips. Could he tell she was turned on? Would he do the things to her that Damon did to Shannon? Heat traveled to her face and she could hardly focus on her performance.

Halfway through the dinner, Shannon sang a solo and Damon played the violin. No other musical pieces or singers participated. The other entertainers stood and moved to the side of the room.

Jack graciously took Dana's hand and led her offstage for the performance. While they were aside he whispered into Dana's ear. The movements he did in a theatrical way so that it appeared to the audience his conversation was part of the show. "You're naked beneath your dress?"

"Yes." Dana followed his lead for the sake of the audience. They were acting like two peasants carrying on a little mischief while the lead performers entertained the Earl's guests in the castle. Although the guests could not hear the real conversation.

"After the show," Jack whispered in Dana's ear, "take that door down to the dungeon and close it behind you. There's a sign on it that says 'No Admittance, Staff Only'. When all the guests have left, I'll meet you there."

"Okay, I'll wait for you in the dungeon. It's safe?" Her pulse was racing now because many of the guests were nearly finished with their dinner.

"Yes, it's very safe. No one will disturb us. The others have plans tonight. There's a turf fire already in the fireplace so you'll be warm enough."

"Warm enough for what?" Her voice was shaky and she felt a little afraid.

"A lounger is in front of the fire. Wait there. After you've removed your dress and all your underclothing." He patted her bottom, then gave it a squeeze.

She gasped, glancing shyly into the crowd. There was a snicker in the audience, and Dana covered her mouth. Leaning into Jack, she whispered, still trying to play a part and hide her anxiety. "You want me to be completely naked before you come down?"

"Yes. If you're not naked, then I'll know you're not ready for the dungeon scene."

"No, I want to do this."

"Good. Then, my lady, after the banquet, your dungeon awaits." He took her hand and led her back to her harp for the final performance of the show.

After the show, Dana waited for the guests and entertainers to leave the hall then walked down the spiral staircase in her medieval costume. She felt like she'd stepped back in time for a moment, as if she was a maiden sneaking off to meet her knight.

When she entered the dungeon, she smelled the sweet woody scent of a turf fire blazing in the large fireplace. Even though the room was lit by sconces on the walls, the stones were dark, probably layered with centuries of soot. A straight-backed chair stood by the bottom of the stairs and a lounger was placed in front of the fire. The lounger looked comfortable but the rest of the items scattered around the room looked like devices straight out of a Dark Ages torture chamber.

The hammock swing with all its chains and straps hung from eye hooks in the ceiling. Another slanted bench with various pads and straps stood next to the swing. A table contained numerous items like floggers, handcuffs, dildos, condoms, a pitcher of water and a few other things she couldn't identify. Hanging from a hook on the wall was one of the black robes. Her body began to shake. Her pulse thrummed in her ears. *This was going to happen.*

With shaky hands she unbuttoned her dress and let the bodice slip from her shoulders. The cool air whisked across her skin and her nipples instantly puckered.

Bare from the waist up, Dana approached the angled bench with the straps. She knelt on the pads and rested her forearms on the other side of a raised cushion. Ah, now she got it. This was used for either spanking or fucking from behind. Her chest tightened. Would Jack try fucking her ass? That was not something she was fond of. She could always use the safe word if she didn't like what he was doing.

Dana was so hot she didn't care where he fucked her. On this restraining bench, in the swing or on the lounger by the fire. All of it was a little frightening but she was more turned on than she'd ever been in any other relationship. Her pussy was soaking and throbbing. In the shower this morning, she'd shaved herself smooth and her tender skin was tingling. On the table she found a set of metal clamps with a chain. Nipple clamps. Shannon had worn these when she'd interrupted their encounter.

They looked like they would hurt. Picking them up, Dana tried to pinch them onto her hardened nipples. "Ouch!" she cried out and the clamps dropped onto the table. She tried again and got one clamped. The pain was sharp but after a moment she got used to it. She attempted the other, but it kept slipping off.

"You're not naked," Jack said from behind her.

Dana yelped and spun around, the nipple clamp dangling from one nipple. "Jack." He had his brocade costume draped over his arm and was wearing the white silk shirt and jeans. The shirt was open at the neck a few buttons. Damn, he looked good. "You changed."

"I guess you're not ready for the dungeon." His voice held a tone of disappointment. "Get dressed. Maybe another time." He turned and started back up the stairs.

"No, Jack, wait. I was distracted by all the devices. I was trying the nipple clamps. Without much success, I might add." She laughed, trying to lighten his dark mood. "I guess I need some instruction." She let the clamp hang from one nipple as she gazed up into his eyes.

He came back down into the room. "A slave who doesn't follow her Master's orders is asking for punishment," he said firmly.

"Then I suppose I deserve to be punished." Her voice was edged with defiance. The thought of punishment didn't frighten her at all even though her body was shaking. She hoped he would use the flogger on her again to relieve the ache that inflamed her. "But what if someone had come down here before you did and I was naked?"

"What if they did? Some women like being watched."

An odd answer, she thought. "I don't.

He smiled. "You're safe here."

"Yes, you said." She relaxed a little, glancing around at the other contraptions in the room. "I'm still new at all this. How about you show me how this works? It looks like fun." She pointed to the slanted bench with the pads and straps.

Pressing his lips together, Jack tensed his jaw. He placed his costume on a straight-backed chair by the door. Then he moved closer to her, removed the nipple clamp and tossed the item on the table. Lifting her chin, he gave her a gentle kiss. "This isn't a game. It's true a sub or a slave has all the power, even the control of a scene. One word can slow or stop what's happening at any time." His lips were a breath away from hers. The warm, moist heat of his mouth and tongue drifted over to her ear and down her neck.

"I understand that," she breathed, her eyes closed as she indulged in his touch. His hands skimmed over her breasts and the pads of his thumbs rubbed her already raw nipples, which made her clit throb. "Not a game," she echoed.

His hands moved lower and finished unbuttoning her dress and chemise and let them drop to the floor in a pile of green brocade while his fingers slid up her thighs and over her hipbones, gliding toward her pussy but not touching her sensitive flesh. God, she wanted him to pleasure her there. She resisted the urge to beg for it. He was the Master and she the sub.

"It's more like a dance when two people try to lead. You're tugging each other in different directions on the dance floor. When one person leads, and you both hear the beat of the music, the dance is like magic. Does that make sense to you?" He drew her close and she felt the warmth of his hard body through his shirt.

"Yes." One arm held her possessively against him as his other hand worked her pussy. "That feels good." Dana arched her back and wriggled her hips.

Then he slipped a finger deep into her cunt. She gasped as a jolt of intense pleasure shot through her. "You want more?"

"Yes, more, Master."

His thumb circled her clit and her knees buckled. If he kept moving his hand and finger in just that rhythm, she could come. "That's incredible."

"Your clit is swollen and your pussy dripping. I bet I could make you come like this. Am I right?"

"Yes." She gripped his shoulders to keep from falling.

"Am I your Master?"

"Yes." She rocked on his hand, fucking his finger. When she moved just right, he'd hit her G-spot at the same time. "Please, Master, let me come."

To her disappointment, he withdrew his finger from her cunt and slowed the stimulation of her clit. "Not without my permission. As your Master, I control your pleasure. I'll tell you when you can come. When you do get close to an orgasm you tell me the word, edge. I'll know to slow down, or give you more, depending on my mood."

She nodded as the peak of her orgasm faded. Damn it, she'd been so close.

"We'll go at this slowly."

"I don't know if I can go slowly," Dana argued. "What if I were to come without your permission?"

"Your punishment would be more severe." He turned to the slanted bench. "You need a bit of punishment for not following my order before." He stroked her buttocks in a gentle caress. Was he trying to let her know he wasn't cruel with his gentle touch? His words were firm and they made her pulse kick up a few beats. She longed for the punishment almost as much as she ached for the release of an orgasm.

What was wrong with her? Was this normal?

"Yes, Master. I need to know." Her voice almost broke with emotion. She took a breath and tried to relax. But how could she if she was naked and he wasn't? Her bare pussy was getting more soaked by the minute.

"Need to know what, slave?" A grin twitched at the corner of his mouth. His hand brushed her hair back so tenderly her throat tightened.

She swallowed. "To see if I can feel the intense passion that Shannon seemed to feel while she was in that swing."

He smiled. "I think you will. If you trust me. But you'll need to communicate your needs during and after a scene. If I'm about to do something you're not sure about or you can't handle, use the safe words to slow or stop."

"I'll remember. 'Butter' to stop. And 'slow' to slow things down."

"Tell me when you like what I'm doing too."

She glanced over toward the stairs leading to the great room but she didn't mention her hesitation.

"We won't be disturbed here."

She wasn't so sure but she wasn't about to argue with him. She wanted him so badly she didn't care anymore if someone did come down those stairs. Her body was on fire, and she wanted him now. "Thank you, Master."

"Clasp your hands behind your back." She did and watched as Jack unbuttoned his shirt, yanked it off and tossed it on the chair. Then he stroked her breasts in a gentle, sensuous manner, pinching the nipples between thumb and forefinger tighter and tighter until she yelped in pain. "You'll handle the clamps quite well."

Although he'd told her to keep her hands behind her back, she wanted to roam them over his magnificent chest, down his stomach and take his thick cock in her hand. But she'd submit to him, learn the ways of a submissive because by doing so she might reach that state of ecstasy that Shannon had. More than that, she wanted to please him, wanted to give over the control.

Jack's mouth captured a nipple and tugged on it, and his teeth scraped across the tender skin. He worked the other nipple in the same way until they both were raw and puckered. "Feel good?"

"Yes, very."

He stepped over to the table and picked up the nipple clamps and approached her. "I'm going to clamp your nipples now." Dana bit her lower lip, anticipating the pain. As he tightened the clamp, the pain increased but she tried to work through it. The pain became excruciating but at the same time a jolt of pleasure shot to her pussy. She closed her eyes and moaned, part from the pain and part from the pleasure.

Then the pressure eased up a bit. "Brave girl," he said with a short laugh. "You're not telling me when you're feeling too much pain. But fortunately, you have very expressive eyes. Is that better?" He adjusted both clamps until there was pressure and a slight amount of discomfort but the kind that was pleasurable.

"Better, yes."

She knelt on the slant bench, and Jack strapped her forearms and ankles down. Her upper body rested lower on a padded board so her ass was elevated.

His hand slid over her ass and around to her slit. "I've made you wet." His finger slid inside her cunt, then rubbed over her clit. "Yes, I think you're ready."

Her body quivering, she tugged against the restraints as a climax quickly approached. "You're going to make me come, Master." She hoped. If she didn't come soon or get fucked soon, she'd jump out of her skin.

"No, punish you." He pulled his hand away. "And don't come yet. Not until your punishment is over."

"Yes, Master."

Jack picked up a flogger from the table and caressed her with the leather lashes down her back and ass, making her shiver. "Relax. If you let go the pain can bring pleasure."

Her teeth were clamped shut, anticipating the first hard blow. Jack moved around to the front of the bench and bent to kiss her. He used his tongue to part her lips and deepen the kiss. She moaned and relaxed. Then he stood, moved beside her and swatted her ass with the flogger. It hurt, a lot. She tensed and bit her lip, determined not to cry out. The tails of the flogger struck again and again, equally on each side until her skin burned. Briefly, he stopped and rubbed her ass.

"Hmmm. Turning a little pink now." His fingers followed the curve of her hip, slipping down the cleft of her ass and probed the opening of her anus with the tip of his finger. "How would you like it if I fucked you here?" He pressed a little harder but her sphincter muscle tightened. Her body jerked.

She didn't know what to say to him, she didn't want to call an end to their evening.

"I would love to take your ass like this but I can tell by the way you're tensing, you're not quite ready for that. We won't go there tonight. Another night then."

"Yes, Master." Her words sounded slurred to her.

The smacks of the flogger began again, she closed her eyes, floating with the pain, feeling her heart throb in her temples. As the pain increased, her skin tingled and her clit swelled. Juices from her pussy dripped down her thighs. She couldn't move. She was trapped. The pounding in her head increased, not a headache, more like a head rush. Any moment she was going to scream, "Fuck me, Jack". It took all her willpower to keep from crying out.

He walked over to the table and dropped the flogger, picked up a condom and slipped it on.

Strapped down onto the bench, she felt helpless, completely under his control. A flutter of panic rose to the surface. But then Jack moved in front of her, claiming her lips again, and kissed her until she gasped for breath. Watching him step back, she felt the heat build inside her and desperately craved his touch. She admired the rigid thickness of his cock and had to feel that fullness deep inside her. His hands slid over her back, her breasts, easing the tension from her body. "Let's see how ready you are for me."

His hand moved over her bottom and between her legs, then he plunged a finger deep into her dripping cunt. "God, yes, Master." She arched her back, tugging on the restraints.

"You're ready for me to fuck you then?" He buried his finger deep. Her body bucked.

"Yes, please fuck me, Master. I want you." Every muscle in her body trembled with need. Jack knelt on the bench between her legs and nudged the head of his cock at her entrance. Easing in just enough to open her cunt, he then stopped. Her pussy clenched, aching for all of him. She whimpered. Sweet torture. Restrained as she was, Dana's pleasure was completely under his control. "Please, Master. Fuck me deep."

Grasping her hips, he eased in and out of her in small movements. Reaching around her hip, he pressed his fingertips onto her engorged clit. The pressure was almost too much to bear but it felt so good. Then he thrust hard into her all the way to the hilt of his shaft.

Dana cried out. Her head spun. The restraints inhibited her ability to move, heightening her pleasure. The pressure and slight movements on her clit and the rhythmic thrusts of his cock sent her racing toward an orgasm. "Master, I'm going to come soon." She felt the tension building in her cunt. If he told her not to, she wasn't sure how she could stop.

"Come for me, come for me now." It was an order not a request, and the command in his voice sent her over the edge.

She screamed as the waves of her climax radiated through her, the intensity more powerful than any orgasm she could remember. "God, yes."

When he let out a low groan, he grasped her hips, and she felt his cock pulsing in her cunt. Moments later, he slipped his cock from her body and leaned over her back. Gently, he stroked her body, shoulders, breasts and ass. His hands moved in slow, sensuous touches. Her mind and body drifted as if she was floating on a raft in the ocean.

She glanced at the black robe hanging on the wall and thought of the entertainers in the forest. What were they doing in there? Was Jack a part of it? Could they be drawing her into some bizarre, evil thing? Or had she watched too many horror movies?

"You're so beautiful." She heard Jack say, but he sounded far away now.

Someone was touching her between her legs and it felt good. Jack? Of course, it was Jack. Were there more than two hands? Or was it her imagination? Shadows danced around the room from the flickering flames. She imagined other people touching and stroking her, bringing her closer to another climax. Almost there.

Her gaze fell upon the black robe again, and she wanted to get away from it. Were there other people in the room? Dana tried to lift her arms, her legs, she couldn't.

Trapped. Panic gripped her. She struggled against her restraints. She had to get out, get away from them.

Far away, she heard Jack's voice, but she wasn't sure what he said. Then the air was sucked out of the room. She had to get out, now!

Then she remembered.

"Butter!"

Like a fire alarm, when Jack heard Dana's safe word, he instantly yanked off the Velcro straps two at a time, both wrists, then ankles and lifted her off the bench. Searching around the room, he looked for a blanket, then cursed himself for forgetting that one item when he'd set up this scene.

Instead, he grabbed the black robe off the wall and wrapped her in it. Although she struggled to get away, he scooped her in his arms, brought her over to the cushioned lounger and cradled her onto his lap. He had to find out what went wrong, if he had hurt her.

"Dana, you all right? Did I hurt you?" He held her close against his chest. Feeling her body shake nearly broke his heart.

"No, Jack, you didn't hurt me. In fact, I was enjoying it. I don't know why I freaked all of a sudden. I'm sorry."

Relieved, he chuckled as he stroked her hair. "No need to be sorry. That's why we have a safe word. Hold still, let me take the nipple clamps off. This might hurt a bit."

As he loosened the first clamp, she sucked in air. "Ow!"

"One more."

"Damn, that hurts."

"I think you might've reached sub space, and it scared you." He took off the other one and gently rubbed the circulation back into her sensitive tips. "Better?"

She nodded and leaned her head against his chest. "Subspace?"

"It's like a light trance. Your perception can be altered and it can be disorienting."

"That must explain it then." She frowned.

His guts were twisting in knots. How the hell did he lose control of the scene? "You have to be honest with me. What was I doing, or what were you thinking that made you panic?"

"Nothing." Squirming out of his lap, she stood, picked up her clothes from the chair and got dressed. "I didn't panic. It just got to be too much I guess. Maybe this lifestyle isn't right for me."

Jack didn't say anything for a moment. He pulled on his pants. "I disagree, I can tell by how you were responding but that's something you have to decide for yourself. I think there was something else bothering you."

As he hung up the robe, she turned away and started up the stairs. "I have to go."

"Stop, Dana, hang on." He slipped on his shoes and chased after her, catching her halfway up the stairs. Turning her in his arms, he raised her chin. "Please tell me what happened." He saw fear in her eyes. *What the hell went wrong?*

"What are the black robes about? Why do the others go into the forest? Where are they going? I saw the robe in your closet. Are you in some kind of cult?" Her voice had a dream-like slur to it.

"It's not a cult."

"They looked like a bunch of Druids or something. It's pretty freaky."

He nodded. He was beginning to understand. "The robe spooked you."

"Yeah."

"The people in this town are very conservative, but they respect Celtic rituals. If they were to see people entering the woods in black robes, they wouldn't think twice."

"Is that what Damon, Shannon and the others are doing, Celtic rituals?"

"They're going to a private club called Unfettered. It's like an invitation-only BDSM club. The robes hide their fetish outfits, which might cause some concern with the neighbors. Bad publicity for the dinner show. The robes are for privacy, nothing overly mysterious. Maybe a little."

She let out a breath. "Have you been to this club?"

"Yes, once you've been there, you're welcome to return."

"Were you going to ask me there?"

"If you were receptive to it."

She glanced away, unable to meet his gaze. "Not now though." The sadness and disappointment in her voice were unmistakable.

"Maybe we went too fast. I know we've talked online, but we really don't know each other that well." He gave her a hug. "Come on. Let me pack up and I'll take you back to your cottage."

She stood her ground. "So that's it? What if I want to try this again? What if I want to go to Unfettered?"

"It's more intense than the scene in the dungeon. This lifestyle isn't for everyone and that's okay."

"No, it's not okay," she snapped at him. "I don't know enough about a D/s relationship yet. And I want to learn more."

"I've never had anyone…call a safe word before." He was going to say freak out during a session but held his tongue. "I should've seen your discomfort before it went too far. That's my fault, my failing. You don't know enough yet to know when to quit."

Concern creased her brow, then she smiled, put her arms around his neck and kissed him. "Thank you for being protective of me. Clearly I was aroused during the session. I just need us to try again."

He groaned. "We will then. If you can surrender as my slave, I'll help you find ecstasy beyond your wildest fantasies."

"So you'll take me to Unfettered?" The thought of a forbidden place even more wicked than the dungeon made her horny again.

"No, you're not ready for Unfettered."

She turned and started up the stairs.

"Dana, stop!"

She couldn't ignore the command in his voice. Turning around, she spoke calmly. "Jack, I'll trust you to make that decision but tonight I'd rather go to my cottage alone."

"That's fine, but I'm walking you back. Wait for me to pack up."

Her shoulders slumped and she sat down on the steps. "Okay. I'll wait."

Back in the dungeon, Jack stuffed all the sex toys and devices on the table into a duffle bag. He made sure everything was cleaned up. The fire would burn out soon, so that was safe, but not the fire burning within him. He knew he would be Dana's Master, if only she'd let go of her inhibitions. He pushed aside other thoughts that might be causing her fears and hesitations—like his own failing in past D/s relationships.

Damn it, he knew how to reach her. He could master her.

Chapter Six

ꟻ

Over the next several weeks, Jack introduced Dana to many aspects of a D/s relationship. During their sessions and lovemaking, she discovered a deeper level of sensuality and pleasure she hadn't expected. By the end of August, she was considering the possibility of staying on in Ireland, but the email from her old boss caught her off guard. It dropped a gloomy shadow over her entire summer. She'd been avoiding the actual decision of what she would do after the musician job ended. Safe and secure had always been her way, and now the email only made the decision harder. He was offering her a raise and a new position if she returned as planned to her job in the security company by September first.

A text message from her friend Karen said she couldn't wait to see Dana or hear about her summer. As much as she loved Ireland and was falling for Jack, she was also feeling homesick. Was she like a kid on summer break trying to hang onto a foolish dream by considering relocating to Ireland? That was a huge decision and not very practical.

The idea of leaving Jack was painful but there wasn't much she could do. She had less than two weeks before her return flight. Jack had offered suggestions on where she might find work, but the prospects weren't hopeful. The security company was the logical choice. Her father was right, performing as a harpist wasn't a real job, it was a hobby, something she should be proud of, but still a hobby, not something she could make a career on. She should stop acting like a gypsy and get her act together. What she and Jack had was a hot summer romance, nothing more.

After the dinner show, Dana bade the guests farewell as she usually did and snuck down into the dungeon to wait for her Master. The dungeon was their secret place for pleasure and pain. And tonight she'd planned a little test of her own. She loved the strong, Dominant voice Jack used as he commanded her in sensual, reassuring ways through adventurous sexual games.

In the dungeon, she added on another turf brick to the fire that was already burning. With what she had planned, they might be there a while, if not all night. Undressing out of her costume, she got completely naked and slipped on the come-fuck-me red heels she'd bought in town and had stuffed in her purse. She untied her hair from the twist it was in for the show and let her brown waves drape over her shoulders and back. As usual, he had the table filled with hedonistic supplies.

There was something frightening and exciting about being restrained. Her cunt was soaked and clenching. She hoped tonight's session ended with him fucking her because she wanted to feel his hard cock thrusting inside her. The sound of footsteps on the stone steps made tremors course through her body. Quickly, she took the position on the slant bench, legs spread wide, ass high and her breasts resting on a padded board.

When he entered the dungeon, he said, "Mmmm. My slave is anxious. Naked already and in position. I like the shoes."

"Thank you, Master. I wore them to please you."

He shed his renaissance clothing and stood in front of her naked. His cock, hard and erect, swayed in front of her face, teasing her. Licking her lips, she was tempted to lean forward and take him into her mouth. "Why did you choose the bench? I had ordered you to stand by the wall restraints," he asked as he moved closer and stroked her breasts. His cock was an inch from her face, she could smell his musky scent but she didn't dare take him without permission. What she planned later was bad enough.

Shifting position, his hand slid over her ass, down her cleft, then he sank a finger into her cunt. "You're dripping."

She gasped. "I always love to be flogged, Master, but I'd hoped to suck your cock tonight and then feel you fuck me."

He gave a sexy, low laugh. "I like when my slave expresses her needs as long as she doesn't try to top from the bottom. Or maybe you're hoping I'll punish you more tonight."

"Yes, Master, if that's your wish."

"My slave should trust me more. If she would surrender herself completely, her pleasure would be greater."

"I do trust you, Master."

"Not completely. Get up and stand by the wall like I'd asked." His words were firm but gentle. Stretching her arms straight up over her head and spreading her legs wide apart, he strapped her into the shackles that were anchored into the wall and floor. "Comfortable?"

"Yes, Master." Anticipation made her pussy twitch and her nipples harden, erect and sensitive, aching for his touch or the sting of the nipple clamps. Her eyes drifted over to the hammock suspended from the ceiling, the one Shannon had been writhing in and screaming in pure pleasure. She didn't believe she'd reached that level of ecstasy that Shannon had.

Jack lifted her chin and brought his face close. "Where are your thoughts, my lady?"

"I was remembering Shannon for a moment."

Jack let out a breath then squeezed her nipple until she yelped. "Keep your thoughts here and you'll enjoy this much more." He unshackled her ankles and turned her around to face the wall, then reshackled her ankles. "Extra punishment should keep you focused." Grinning down at her.

"Yes, please, Master."

He began with the flogger, swatting her buttocks and thighs and gently stroking the sides of her breasts. The rough, cool stone rubbed against her nipples and heightened their sensitivity. Rocking her hips, she ached to rub her clit against something to ease the throbbing. If he touched her there, she could come with little effort. The flogging stopped and she caught herself before she groaned out loud.

"We're going to try something different tonight." She heard him pick something up from the table but didn't turn her head to look. His rough hand rubbed her ass then she felt a sharp sting on one side.

She cried out from the sharp pain. "What was that, Master?"

"A cane." *Swat!* He struck her again on the other side and the sting rang through her body. Clenching her teeth, she waited as the pain converted to waves of throbbing in her pussy. Her pulse pounded in her head. She hoped she'd feel another strike because her body was humming. *Swat! Swat!* She groaned. Her hips and knees quivered as her groin craved attention. His mouth, fingers or any stimulation would send her over into a blissful orgasm.

He stopped and rubbed her ass, then slipped toward her pussy. "Edge," she cried out.

He pulled his hand away. "Very good, slave. I hadn't given you permission to come." He put the cane down and picked up something else. When he returned, he worked her nipples between his thumb and forefinger and attached nipple clamps.

Manipulating her already raw and sensitive nipples was pushing her to the brink of another orgasm. What if she ignored his order and allowed herself to come? Would he give her more punishment? Maybe then she'd reach that level of ecstasy like Shannon.

"Is my slave's mind drifting again?"

"No, Master. I liked the cane."

He gave a short laugh. "I could tell. You like the clamps too."

"Yes, they feel good."

Sliding his hand between her legs, he thrust a finger inside her and pressed his hard cock against her tender buttocks. Dana rocked her hips as he fucked her cunt with his finger. She wanted more, she wanted his thick cock filling her.

"Wet, yes. But I don't think you're quite ready." His hand slipped from her body and he moved to the table. A moment later the cane struck her again and again.

Instantly, her pussy was clenching and dripping. Her clit was so hard, it ached. "How about now?" Sliding his hand around, she knew the moment he touched her she would come, but she didn't warn him this time or fight to hold back.

His fingers stroked her swollen and sensitive clit and she plunged over the edge in an intense orgasm. "Master, I can't stop it. I'm coming."

"Fuck." Jack dropped the cane and pressed his body to her, stroking her clit until the tremors of her orgasm eased. Why hadn't she warned him sooner? It happened, especially to a novice, but they'd been together for a couple months now. After the spasms from her body ceased, he left her shackled and didn't say a word. As much as he wanted to fuck her, he had to give her a punishment for defying him.

Walking over to the table, he picked up a black scarf and returned slowly. Dana strained to look over her shoulder to see what he was doing, her eyes wide. He blindfolded her, then left her there. Long moments passed. She kept lifting her head as if trying to hear what he was doing but he was very still. When her body began to tremble he began pacing the room so she'd hear him walking, then he shoved the lounger, the noise made her jump.

"Master? I'm sorry, I didn't let you know. I was testing you."

He squeezed his eyes shut and didn't answer. *Not good.*

Damn, she was so beautiful, and so innocent, it was killing him to do this. When she whimpered, he thought his heart would break but he bit his lip. It wasn't the orgasm, it was the fact that she did it to defy him. Her safety was in his hands. He couldn't have a sub "testing" him. He slipped on a condom and picked up a crop. At the lounger, he swatted the brocade material with the crop. Dana jumped and cried out from the sharp crack.

Without a word he unshackled her ankles, and Dana attempted to turn around. He pressed her against the wall to keep her back to him. She didn't protest. When she tried to squeeze her legs together, he roughly pushed them apart. His commands were by touch, and she followed his orders without hesitation.

Legs spread and arms over her head, Dana remained quiet until he struck her with the crop on her buttocks. She let out a yelp and her body jerked. Her breathing quickened. The crop glided up and down each leg, to her pussy, up her back, over her breasts, then arms, like a gentle caress, a tease, then slowly back down and rested on her buttocks. He gave her another swat. She yelped. Her body quivered. God damn, he wanted to take her now, but his lesson wasn't over yet.

Sliding his hand between her legs, he felt her cream soaking her pussy. She was ready for him.

He struck her again, not as hard because he saw she was slumping in the restraints. She never moved her legs even without the shackles. *Good slave.* His cock was so hard and his balls so tight, he didn't know how much longer he could stand not fucking her. Finally, her groans of pleasure were too much of a temptation. His slave loved pain so much but he didn't want to overdo it. He had to be inside her.

Dropping the crop, he spun her around and lifted her legs to wrap around his hips and plunged deep into her cunt.

"Omigod," she cried out.

Her hands gripped around the chains that held her to the wall as he drove his cock rapidly into her. The sight of the nipple clamps on her distended peaks drove him deeper and harder with his thrusts. Tightening her legs around his hips, she let out a groan that told him she was coming again. He felt the pressure build, then let out a bellow as his orgasm exploded inside her.

When the pulsing eased, he slid out of her, unfastened the shackles, wrapped her in a blanket from the table and took her into his arms. He brought her to the lounger and sat her down. After discarding the condom, he brought her a damp cloth from the table of supplies. Pulling her onto his lap, he gently removed the nipple clamps.

"Ouch. They hurt worse coming off." She gave a chuckle.

"So I've heard."

She held him close and looked up at him, giving him a tentative smile. "I had a reason, Master." There was no defiance in her voice, the gentleness in her eyes twisted in his gut.

"Why, Dana? You're not a novice anymore. You've always told me when you were close before, but this time I think you defied me on purpose."

"Not to anger you, but I do want to be punished, punished harder."

He studied her for a moment. "It's more than that. Tell me."

"I think you hold back. I wanted to disobey an order to receive a more severe punishment to see if…"

"To see if what?" His words were sharper than he'd intended.

"If extreme pain would bring the ecstasy that Shannon experienced that first day I arrived."

He shook his head. "No, slave. It has nothing to do with the level of pain. Something else is holding you back. Lack of trust, fear. I don't know. I bring you right to the point where I think you'll completely surrender and then you backpedal. A lack of communication between a Master and his sub can be dangerous. I'm responsible for your safety."

"I know." She nodded and rested her head on his chest. "Jack, I'm leaving in less than two weeks. I'm running out of time."

"Maybe that's it. You're thinking about leaving." He pulled her back to look into her eyes. "Stay then. You can live with me. I'll help you find some kind of work, maybe where you can play your harp."

She shook her head. "I have a good job at home. There's no guarantee here."

"Who said life has guarantees? Follow your heart."

She looked at him, and he was surprised by the emotion in her eyes. "Why don't you come back to the states with me?"

He shook his head. "I can't. I just signed the loan to buy my uncle's store yesterday. If I were to sell it, he wouldn't have any place to work. Since my aunt died, working is the only thing that gives him joy. I can't take that away from him. What gives you joy?"

She considered that for a moment. "You. My harp."

He kissed her, slow and deep then kissed her forehead. "Dana, stay here with me. We can work out the details together. I want more than a sexual submissive. I want you."

Her heart was breaking. Did she love him? Maybe but she didn't want to give him any promises she couldn't keep. "I'll have to think about it."

"Do that. Like you said, you don't have much time." He got up, got dressed and began packing up his devices and toys in a duffle.

She dressed and started up the stairs.

"Wait, I'll walk you back," he said.

"I can find my way." She continued walking.

"I know, but I'm walking you back. Wait."

She came back down and sat on the lounger.

Returning to the table, Jack stuffed the rest of the items into the bag. *My sub needs to trust me.* He was about to shut off the lights when he noticed a small, white piece of paper left in the center of the table. A cold shiver went up his back. It wasn't there a moment ago. He didn't want to touch it. Finally, he picked it up and turned it over.

It was a business card with the text: 1-800-DOM-help.

He groaned. *What the fuck?* Was Damon around? There were no hidden passages leading into the dungeon, as far as he knew.

"What's wrong?" Dana asked from the lounger. She couldn't see what he had in his hand.

"Nothing. Let's go." He crumpled the card and threw it on the floor. Then he groaned, picked it back up, and stuffed it in his pocket.

Not again. I don't need any fucking help.

* * * * *

When Dana got back to her cottage, she boiled water and added it to the teapot, then pulled out a tank top and jeans to wear. It was late but she couldn't sleep. Jack said he needed to do some work and didn't want to keep her up so he was going to his cottage. Just as well, she needed time to think. Why couldn't she make this decision—go or stay? Probably because she'd never had to make any big decisions in the past.

After the discussion with Jack she should be pouring herself a large goblet of mead. The herbal tea was a better choice. The mead would make her a bit daft and she needed a clear head to sort out her troubles. As she stepped out of her costume a white card fluttered out of the bodice and dropped to the floor. It was the same business card. How could the card have been inside her dress all evening, and then never fallen out in the dungeon when she'd taken it off? This was a new card too. The other ones she'd torn up. This was insane.

She laughed. Was Jack trying to make up with her, cheer her up? She finished dressing and with the card in hand she ran over to his cottage and knocked on his door. No answer.

"Jack? You there?" No answer. There weren't any lights on inside either. Odd. She returned to her cottage and took out a teacup from the cupboard.

She was about to pour hot water into a teacup, when she found another business card sitting inside the cup. She cried out and nearly dropped the kettle.

Slamming it down on the stove, she looked around her room. "Hello? Jack? Are you in here?" She checked under the bed, in the bathroom and closet but there was no sign of him. Next she went outside again and over to Jack's cottage. Still no light inside. What was going on with these business cards?

She was going to find out. Back inside her cottage, she picked up her cell phone and punched in the number.

The phone rang and someone picked it up.

"Thank you for calling 1-800-DOM-help. This is the Operator. How may I be of assistance?" the male voice said.

She hesitated for a moment. It didn't sound like Jack, but the same calm and pleasant voice she heard the first time she called. "Hello, ahmm..." She wasn't sure what to say. She was still trying to figure out how the number could work at all.

"We're pleased that you called."

"Are you selling something? What's going on? Who keeps giving me these cards?"

The Operator chuckled. "No, Dana we're not selling anything. Receiving one of our cards is a special and rare opportunity."

A chill crept up Dana's back. She never told this guy her name. He must have caller ID or something. "Then what's it about?"

"You received this card because you have a need. Something in your D/s relationship is troubling you and we're here to help."

She plopped down on the bed, angry at Jack for talking to strangers about their sex life. "Did Jack call you?"

"No."

"Then how did you—"

"You're a sub?"

"What?" She was pissed now. "Who put you up to this?" Her voice was shaking with anger. *How dare this stranger ask these personal questions?*

"How you came to have the card is not important. Do you have questions about your current relationship? Yes or no? Be honest." His voice was firm, yet compassionate. A lump formed in Dana's throat and tears filled her eyes. She wanted to figure this out.

"Yes, I do."

"Are you a sub or a Domme?"

"A sub."

"Very well. Hold on and I will connect you with someone best able to assist you." She heard a click on the phone and then a woman's voice came on. "Dana?"

"Yes?"

"Hi. I'm here to help. Do you have something sexy to wear? A club outfit, preferably leather?"

"Can you tell me what's this all about? How do you all know my name? Did Jack put you up to this?"

"We keep a very selective list of clients who come to Unfettered. Once invited, you're always welcome for as long as you remain in the lifestyle. We're also here to help Dominants and submissives work out their very unique problems. You can continue to deny your true nature and be miserable, or sense there is something missing, or you can come to Unfettered with me and let the Master help you break down the barriers."

"Barriers?" She hadn't thought about that. "Is this safe?"

"Completely. I can stay with you the whole time if you wish. Now, do you have something sexy to wear?"

"I have a leather skirt. Jack bought it for me and a tank."

"That will do. Get changed into that. I'll be by your cottage shortly to escort you to Unfettered." The woman hung up before she had a chance to ask any more questions. The voice sounded familiar but she couldn't place it.

Racing out of her cottage, she ran over to Jack's cottage and pounded on his door. It was well past midnight and it was dark inside. He still didn't answer. Maybe he'd gone into town to stay at the store? She doubted it, because his car was parked in front of the cottages right next to her rental. *Damn. Where the hell was he?* Was she finally going to Unfettered alone without him?

Back in her place she quickly changed into the black leather skirt, a midnight-blue shimmery tank and strappy black heels. As soon as she finished dressing, a knock at her door made her jump. She had to take a couple breaths before she had the nerve to open the door.

"Shannon!"

"Ready to go?" Shannon was smiling and wearing a black robe. She had another robe draped over her arm.

"That was you on the phone?"

Shannon nodded. "Hurry up, the Master is waiting."

"Who's the Master?"

She continued smiling. "You'll see. You'll love Unfettered. Put this on first." Shannon handed her a black hooded robe. "We'll walk. It's not far."

"Can I walk in these heels?" She suspected they'd be going into the forest.

Shannon nodded. "You'll be fine."

Outside there was no breeze, and the sounds of the crickets and frogs had stopped. Dana's heart pounded, taking her breath away. What was she getting into? If only Jack was with her. "Shouldn't we find Jack and ask him to come?"

"Follow me. It's not far." Shannon led her into the forest.

After a few minutes, Dana saw the golden glow of lights through the trees, that same strange glow she'd seen weeks ago. She and Shannon passed through two stone pillars and an open wrought iron gate. The level of excitement was almost overwhelming. *I can do this.* Her hands grabbed fistfuls of the robe as they walked closer to the building. At the end of the walkway was a stucco house with a thatched roof that looked like an old farmhouse. "This is Unfettered?" There was no parking lot, no cars, just forest. She couldn't see any road that led to the house.

"Yes, it's quite nice inside." Shannon showed her to the entrance, a large man stood at the door. He nodded and opened the weathered wooden door for them. "This is Hayden," Shannon explained. "If there's any trouble, Hayden will handle it. But you won't have any problems. You're safe here." Hayden remained at the door like a human brick wall.

Inside Dana was stunned. Unfettered didn't look like an old farmhouse. It was surreal, as if she'd walked into a luxurious hotel with polished woods, overstuffed leather chairs and couches. An elegant bar and tables were at one side of the large room and hallways led off from the main area. Sensual music with a steady beat played in the background. Soft candlelight flickered from tables and the bar. The air was heavy with spicy scented candles, leather and sex.

Women were dressed in scanty leather and lace, boots or heels and the men wore leather or black trousers and black shirts or no shirts. A few people were naked or close to it. "We have something here for everyone's taste. I'm sure you'll find what you're looking for."

Shannon removed her robe and took Dana's and handed them to a petite woman at the door. "I'll hold these until you're ready to leave," the woman with several facial piercings and black, spiky hair said. She wore a black lace body stocking that left nothing to the imagination and outrageously high platform heels. Another attractive woman with long dark hair approached them, holding her hand out to Dana.

"Hello, Dana. Welcome. So glad to have you here. I'm Dru." The woman shook her hand and Dana was stunned by the sexy, black dress. The V in the front came down to her navel and the hem barely covered her ass. She also wore thigh-high boots.

"Thanks, I'm still a little confused." Dana noticed Kevin and Thea, two of the entertainers from the dinner show, at a table by the bar. Kevin wore only a leather vest and a collar around his neck. He was bent over the table and Thea held his leash while she whipped him with a cane. Each crack of the cane sent chills up Dana's spine. Kevin's cock was hard and swayed with each strike, and a glistening drop of pre-cum dribbled from its tip.

At the far side of the room a woman was hung upside down, her legs spread slightly and her arms bound behind her back while her Dom held a large vibrator at her pussy. The woman moaned and writhed.

Dru smiled, not giving the hedonistic display a second glance. "Unfettered is a special place. There's something for everyone here. By the time you leave, your questions will be answered. You're troubled by your relationship and have a few big decisions to make." Dru's brutal honesty stabbed at Dana's heart.

"Yes, you sound like a fortuneteller."

"Not at all. I'm just well informed. If you want your answers follow me. But first a lesson in trust." Dru walked over to the girl who had taken their robes and was handed something that looked like a masquerade mask. She came up to Dana and handed it to her. "Put this on. It's a blindfold. When you can't see, you have to trust other senses."

Dana glanced at the mask in her hands, hesitating.

"It's all right, Dana," Shannon said. "Hurry, the Master waits."

"But what about Jack?"

"You love him, don't you?" Shannon asked, with a reassuring smile.

"Yes." She realized she'd never told Jack.

"And you want to break down the barriers between you two."

Dana nodded.

"Then Jack would want you here."

Dana put the mask on, then Dru and Shannon led her down a long hallway. The farmhouse didn't seem quite this large from the outside. The cracks of whips and moans and an occasional rattle of a chain were heard as she was guided down the hallway. They stopped then and she heard them open a door and walk her inside. She felt so helpless not being able to see. The familiar smell of a turf fire filled the room, as well as the scent of leather and another herb, eucalyptus. Just the smell of leather immediately made cream flood her pussy and her clit throb with a sexual need.

"Did you want Shannon to stay, Dana?" Dru asked.

"Yes," Dana answered.

"The Master says no, it's not necessary," Dru said. "Safe words here are 'stop' and 'slow'. Understand, Dana?"

"Yes." Panic was setting in. Did this Master expect to have sex with her? "Shannon? Jack would agree to this? I mean, I know I have things to learn about the D/s lifestyle, but this can't be right me being with someone else."

"Jack would approve, Dana," Shannon said. "You want to understand what's holding you back, right?"

"Yes."

"We'll be leaving you now. You'll be fine," Shannon said. Dana heard the door close and rough hands gripped her and drew her across the room and up against the wall.

"Can you tell me what we're going to do, Master? I'm very nervous." Since Dru and Shannon referred to him as Master, she had better too. "I'm fairly new to this and Jack, my

Master, wishes for me to live with him and not return to the states. That's a big decision, I—"

Pressing his fingertips over her lips, he signaled her to be silent. Then he raised her arms and clamped them into shackles. Dana gasped. Her feet were shoved apart and secured into a spreader bar. She was still clothed. Would this experience with this Master help her to break down any remaining resistance she had with Jack so she could completely surrender to him? Would this also help with her decision to stay or return home?

The Master stroked her cheek with his knuckles. If he'd only talk to her maybe this would be easier. Every inch of her body shook partly from fear and partly from anticipation.

She kept reminding herself that this Master was trained and she was doing this for Jack and herself. Right now, her body shook and muscles tensed as she heard the Master moving around a few feet away. The first crack of a flogger made her jump. Her cream flowed but she also tensed since it wasn't Jack. The flogger stuck the wall close to her but never touched her. How could the Master help her?

Moments later, the sound of chains replaced the cracks of the flogger and he released her arms and ankles, but shackled her wrists in cuffs and chains and walked her over to a chair. The heat from the fire warmed her flushed skin and calmed her. He pressed something to her mouth and at first she resisted. The thought of a ball gag made her cringe. "Master, I know I shouldn't speak, but if you gag me we haven't discussed safe signals."

He pressed his fingers to her lips to silence her, and she nodded. Then the object was at her mouth again. It was cool and she opened. He popped it in and she rolled it around in her mouth and bit down. The juice was sweet and squirt over her tongue. A grape. She giggled.

This time another piece with bumps, a raspberry? And several blueberries, then a spoonful of honey. The sweet syrup dripped down her chin and he lapped it up with his tongue.

The first intimate touch made her stiffen but she didn't protest. In the back of her mind, she was still worried about where this would eventually lead. She truly loved Jack, she knew that for sure now and she didn't want to be with another man. Still, she was confused.

Tenderly the Master brushed her hair back and stroked the nape of her neck. It felt nice but she wished it was Jack. Images of their weeks together rushed through her mind, all wonderful times but always with the heavy feeling of knowing each day brought her closer to the time she would have to leave him. Tears flooded her eyes and dripped down her cheeks. And now she knew why she couldn't surrender to Jack.

The Master gently brushed her tears away. Then his fingers roamed down her neck to her shoulder and over to the side of her breast. Dana squirmed. "Stop!"

The Master pulled his hand away. "Why are you crying, my lady?" It was Jack's voice.

"Jack!" Her heart leapt.

He lifted her mask and smiled.

"Because I know why I haven't been able to surrender to you completely." She quickly glanced around the room. It could've been any upscale hotel room with a bed and door to a bathroom except for the eyehooks on the ceiling and floor, various chains and straps hanging from them and also a table of bondage devices and sex toys.

He knelt in front of her looking so hot in leather pants and no shirt, his chest gleaming in the firelight. "Are you going to let out the secret?"

"Because I love you."

He smiled, then frowned. "Then why can't you surrender to me, trust me?"

"If I love you and surrender to you as your slave, it will be unbearably painful to leave you."

"Don't think about tomorrow or next week or leaving. You'll make the right decision when the time comes. Surrender to me tonight. Just tonight."

Her chest tightened. "Okay." She let out a breath.

He undid the shackles around her wrists and ankles. "Undress for me, slave, but leave your shoes on. I like the heels."

Heat traveled to Dana's pussy as she unzipped her short skirt and let it drop to the floor. She hadn't worn panties so she stepped out of the skirt and kicked it aside. Already wet and aroused, she felt a trickle of her juices slip down her thigh. After pulling the tank over her head, she tossed it by her skirt. Completely naked except for her five-inch heels, she felt exposed and aroused under his inspection. When he removed his shoes and leather pants, her heart nearly stopped. Standing naked, he was so gorgeous, every hard muscle outlined, his cock hard, ready to satisfy her beyond her imagination.

"Good slave. Will you submit to me tonight?"

"Yes, Master."

"Show me." His words were a command but she wasn't sure what he wanted her to do. The walls in her vagina fluttered with need. She wanted to please him but how?

"I don't understand, Master."

"Show me that you will surrender and completely submit to me tonight. Show me."

After a panicked moment of hesitation, she walked up to him and knelt down.

She bowed her head in submission. Her face was inches from his cock. The temptation to take him in her mouth was strong but she waited for his permission.

"Yes," he breathed with a ragged breath. Lifting her chin, he gazed into her eyes. "My beautiful slave, I'm going to pleasure you and fuck you until you beg me to stop."

She smiled and glanced longingly at his cock.

He laughed. "You'd like to suck me first."

"Yes, Master."

"Take me into your mouth, but just for a moment."

"Thank you, Master." Running her tongue up and down his rigid shaft, she took him into her mouth and cradled his scrotum with her hand. He held her head, guiding her up and down. She was rewarded by his groans and loved the musky male and soap scent of him. When she released his shaft, she moved to his balls, gently sucking one into her mouth, and rolled her tongue around. Taking his cock into her mouth again, she slid down to the base in quick thrusts. Pleasuring her Master gave her joy. Hearing his groans warmed her inside and made her cream flow. A salty drop of pre-cum slipped from his slit and she lapped at it, wanting more.

His fingers tightened around her head as he thrust his cock, matching her rhythm, faster and faster, then abruptly pulled away from her. "God, that's so good. But I have to stop," he groaned. He drew her up to her feet, embraced her and kissed her deeply, held her close for a long time. "I love you, Dana. More than you'll ever know. Trust me, I will take care of you, my slave."

"Yes, Master."

"Now over to the swing."

She did and waited. Would he flog her first? Probe her ass with a butt plug?

"Hands behind your back," he ordered. She did, and he pinched her nipples, sucked them and grazed them with his teeth. Then clamps were attached to the distended tips. The nipples were still raw and sensitive from earlier but the pressure and sting made her clit throb and swell.

"That feels good, Master. I liked that very much. I like what you do to me, how I feel so intensely loved. It's a deliberate and powerful loving."

"There are many things in a slave/Master relationship we could explore." He sat her in the swing, then attached the straps to her wrists and ankles, adjusting the rigging so her arms and legs were spread and pointing upward. This gave her Master access to her pussy and ass. "But tonight it's going to be about your threshold of pain and pleasure and trust. You seem to be obsessed with pain and to respond well to it. Still I don't want you to hesitate to tell me when something becomes too much."

"I promise, Jack."

"Good." He kissed her then gave a swat on her ass with his hand. She yelped and giggled.

Picking up another device from the table, he unwrapped a condom and slipped it over a dildo and applied some lubricant. When he brought it to her she noticed the straps. Spreading her labia, he gently worked the dildo into her channel and secured the straps around her waist to keep it in place. Then he turned it on. The vibrations sent shudders of sensations through her body and her clit began to swell and throb. Even her nipples throbbed as all her nerve endings came alive.

His fingertips rubbed her clit until she was about to shout out "edge" but then he stopped and picked up the flogger.

"Do not climax until I give you permission, slave."

"Yes, Master," she answered him through clenched teeth. She wasn't going to last long like this.

The flogger struck her ass in repeated strikes and her body quivered as she absorbed the pain and it transferred into pleasure. She moaned. Several more times and between her legs. "Edge!" she cried out.

He stopped the flogger and turned the vibrator down but not off. "Don't come. Hold it."

She was on the brink of an orgasm, but she held back. A moment later he switched the vibrator to high again and swatted her with a paddle. This hurt a lot. She was still tender from her early lashings and each strike shot waves of sensations throughout her body. She cried out with each smack but didn't ask him to stop. Her hands gripped the straps and tightened as she tried to control her climax. So close.

Her clit throbbed and her pulse thumped in her head. Two more smacks and the thickness of the dildo in her cunt would push her to a sweet release. "Edge, Master. Edge." The words were harder to get out.

She tried focusing on something other than the vibrations in her cunt, the sharp pinching of her nipples, then felt a sharp swat on her ass. It was a cane, not the paddle. This hurt the worst. But good too. The pain absorbed into her body and turned to pleasure, an odd sensation that disconnected her from the physical world. She felt as if she was a feather drifting on a warm breeze. When the cane hit her the third time, her whole body hovered in the swing, aching for release. "Master," she breathed. "Edge. No strength left."

He stopped. "I need to be inside you."

"Yes, Master."

He removed the vibrator and then put on a condom. "But I'm going to fuck your beautiful ass tonight."

"Yes, Master." But her words held a tone of doubt. What if she couldn't do this?

"Relax, this is all about pleasure. I won't hurt you."

He lapped at her slit, his tongue worked her clit, bringing her closer to climax. "Soon, you'll have more pleasure than you can stand." His hands grasped her breasts and tugged at the nipple clamps. She moaned and wriggled in the restraints.

"Oh yes, Master. That's so good."

Bending lower, he rimmed her anus with his tongue, then coated his finger with water-soluble lubricant and circled the entrance with his finger. Gently, he pressed slowly through the ring of muscle. She tightened with the initial pain.

"Easy, slave, breathe easy, relax. That's it." He slid in deeper and moved in and out slowly. "How does that feel?"

"Burned and hurt a little before. Feels good now." With his encouraging words and gentle movements, she relaxed a bit. The idea of taking his large cock like this made her nervous but also excited her.

Then he slid two fingers in a little at a time. She sucked in a breath from a twinge of pain. "Easy, breathe slowly. Relax." Once the pain eased and he was moving his fingers freely, he removed them, then picked up a butt plug from the table and coated it with lubricant. "This will help you open some more for me." He eased the plug in and moved it around, in and out. "Good, slave."

"Master, that feels good. Please, fuck me. I need your cock now."

"Not yet. I want to make sure you're ready."

Finally, he took the butt plug out and added a heavy amount of lubricant to his condom. "I'm going to fuck your ass, Dana. Slow, easy now."

"Yes, yes."

He eased in, inch by inch, giving her time to become accustomed to his size. "Damn, your ass is so tight."

"Fuck me. Please, fuck me."

He groaned and sank into her. She gasped, but he wasn't in her all the way. Holding back must be pure torture. He stilled. Was he trying to keep from hurting her or coming?

He glanced at her and the dark look he gave her was so full of love and lust. Her heart soared. The final surrender. "Fuck me, Master. Deep, all the way."

She sucked in a ragged breath as his hand stroked her clit. Shattering into a fierce orgasm, she cried out as the sensations coursed through her body. The climax was so intense, almost unbearable. "Never been so good," she murmured. Afterward, she hung limp in the restraints.

"My pleasure." He closed his eyes and thrust into her ass the rest of the way, then held still as her body accepted all of him. He was so hard and thick, and his slow, easy strokes gradually increased and drew the most exquisite pleasure. Tugging against her restraints, she raised her hips slightly, urging him deeper.

The muscles in his face, his arms and chest were rigid and coated with a thin sheen of sweat. Her muscles strained against the binds, but she found the complete loss of control, and giving her power up to him, elicited the most delicious sensations and joy. "Master, yes," she breathed and wriggled her ass. The movement sent him over the edge. He sucked in a breath and groaned as he reached his climax.

Gripping her buttocks, he held tight until the aftershocks subsided. He slipped from her body, unfastened the straps and helped her down. For a long moment he held her close. She didn't want to let go. She didn't want to think about tomorrow and the decision she had to make.

After they cleaned up, he scooped her up in his arms and sat her down on the bed. "Let's remove these." She cried out in pain as he released the clamps and tossed them on a side table. "How are you doing?" He brushed her hair back from her face and kissed her forehead.

"Drained but wonderful," she said, smiling.

He chuckled. "Hmmm. I figured that." He gave her a long, loving look that made her heart break. "Are you ready to go home?"

"Home?" She groaned. "I don't want to think about that. I haven't decided yet."

Jack smiled and tapped her nose with his finger. "I meant have you had enough of Unfettered for tonight? Would you like to go back to your cottage?"

"Oh yes. I'd like to go back now."

"Dana, I love you, and you know I want you to stay in Ireland. But I'll understand if you have to go."

"I know, Jack."

Chapter Seven

ꕥ

She awoke in her bed to the sound of birds chirping outside. Sunlight streamed into her cottage and she reached over to the other side of the bed and it was empty. "Jack?" There was no movement in the bathroom and she didn't see any of his clothes on the floor. Had he gotten up and left without waking her? She stood and looked around for a note or something but didn't see anything. It was still early. Maybe he went into town to work at the store. After showering and getting dressed she strolled outside to a warm August morning. She looked into the forest where Shannon had taken her to Unfettered last night. The trail was still there. It wouldn't be hard to find now in the daylight. Her curiosity drove her into the forest. The walk was about fifteen minutes if she remembered correctly.

Dana entered the forest and followed the trail. It was overgrown and narrow. She was glad that she'd followed Shannon last night because she didn't think she could've found her way in the dark. After several minutes, she found the stone pillars with the wrought iron gate and walked through.

She screamed. An icy terror gripped her as she stared at the place where Unfettered should be. It hadn't been but twenty or thirty yards from the gate and now there was nothing. The building was gone, and there was no sign that anything had ever been there.

Had she been hallucinating? Dreaming? Running back to the cottages, Dana knocked on Jack's cottage and when he didn't answer she tried Kevin's and Thea's, Damon's and Shannon's. No one was around. Could it be possible that she imagined Jack and the others too? Covering her face with her hands, she ran up to the castle and it was closed. Checking her watch, she noticed it was too early for visitors.

A crushing weight slammed into her chest. *Jack, where are you?* What if he'd been a ghost all along? What if they all were? She looked up at the ancient castle. A five-hundred-year-old fortress must have many ghosts. Had she lost Jack for good?

Her hand went up to her mouth to smother a sob. My God, it couldn't be. She loved Jack. Yes, she was sure of that now. He was her Master. And given the chance she would stay in Ireland with him and not go back to her old job. She could visit her friends and family or they could come to see her. Why had she been struggling with that decision before? It was so clear to her now. But if Jack was a ghost, he was lost to her forever. Tears filled her eyes and spilled onto her cheeks.

She barely registered the sound of footsteps on the gravel walkway. "Morning, my lady, have you had breakfast?"

"Jack!" She ran over and into his arms.

"Hey, what's wrong? You've been crying?" He lifted her chin and studied her through narrow eyes.

"I woke up and you were gone."

"Sorry, I promised Donegal to help move some furniture this morning. I figured I'd be back before you woke up. It took longer than expected."

Taking her by the shoulders, he held her back. "What else is going on? You're shaking."

"I took a walk into the forest."

Jack groaned.

Dana ignored him and continued. "I followed the trail to Unfettered and it's gone. I found the gate where Shannon took me through, but the building is completely gone."

Jack nodded. "Yeah, it does that."

She looked at him strangely, but then it seemed to make sense. "Will it come back?"

Jack shrugged. "Probably. When it's needed or wanted badly enough." He pulled her into his arms. "Want to tell me why you were crying?"

"I thought I lost you."

"Ah, because you woke up and I was gone?"

"No, never mind. I'm staying here with you. I love you, Jack. Although it scares the hell out me having to depend on you for a while until I can find work, I can't imagine leaving you. This is where I belong. The security job may pay well but it doesn't give me joy. You were right. Playing my harp gives me joy. Loving you gives me joy. Being your sex slave gives me joy."

Jack smiled. "I love you, Dana. I need you in my life, and I want you as my submissive for as long as you want me as your Master." He kissed her hard, crushing her to his chest. "And I could take you right now."

"Yes, I'm ready for whatever you have in mind, Master."

He chuckled. "Be careful, remember I own a store full of bondage devices."

"Now you're teasing me." Her pussy clenched thinking about the new things he would try with her.

"Go back to your cottage, strip and wait on the bed. I'll come down and teach you a few things about knots and ropes, then feed you breakfast while you're bound."

"I'll be eagerly waiting, Master."

* * * * *

As the guests from the dinner show began to file out of the castle on the night of her last performance, she noticed Jack talking to a few of the entertainers. She was hoping to see him later tonight to discuss her plans for moving out of her cottage and into his apartment over the store. Although depending on Jack for a job and a home wasn't ideal, he insisted she would soon find employment either with her harp or in the security business. She was following her heart, trusting him and their love, even though she felt like she was jumping out of an airplane without a parachute and expecting the ground to provide a soft landing.

Jack's Uncle Lee had been in the audience that evening and after the show he came up to her. "Glory, Dana, you do play the folk harp beautifully."

"Thank you, Mr. Keagan."

"Call me Lee. And can you forgive an old goat for being harsh with you?"

Dana smiled. "Of course, it's all right." He gave her a kiss on the cheek.

"I'm pleased you'll be staying," he declared. "In truth, I've not seen my nephew this happy in a long time."

Dana pressed her hand to her heart. "Thanks for saying so."

"I'll see you at the store. Good night." After a few words with his nephew, he left the great hall.

While she waited for Jack, she strummed out an old folk song Kevin was teaching her. Mr. Donegal walked over to her. "Lovely performance, Dana, a gift you have there," Mr. Donegal said, admiring her instrument. "Like listening to an angel play."

"Thank you. Your other harpist, Jane, should be back this week."

"Wanted to talk to you about that now." He scratched his chin. "Jane has decided to stay home with her babe. She won't be coming back to Rathmore Castle. She'll fill in as needed but I'd hoped you'd considering staying on with us."

"Really?" Her fingers gripped her harp so hard she thought she'd leave permanent dents. Glancing around the room, she looked for Jack. He was going to be thrilled. Or was he? Jack was with a group of guests and entertainers and had just left the room, taking the stone stairway to the lower level.

She'd have to talk to him later. "Thanks, Mr. Donegal, I'd love to."

He asked her to stop by the office the next day to make arrangements then left the hall. Shannon came over. "You're all smiles, Dana."

"Jane has chosen not to come back to the show, and Mr. Donegal asked me to stay and replace her."

"And you agreed."

Dana nodded.

"Wonderful. I'm sure Jack will be pleased. Does he know yet?"

"No, could you tell him to meet me on top of the castle? I want to surprise him."

"Sure thing. So glad you're staying with us. I was going to miss you terribly," Shannon said, giving her a hug.

* * * * *

Standing on top of the ancient castle, she looked out at the glow of lights from the cottages. A warm breeze swayed the pine trees. And the sounds of night creatures drifted up from the forest and bog. No lights could be seen deep within the trees. Unfettered had vanished for now.

Dana wondered how many lovers over the centuries had stood looking out from that turret, a lord and lady, a crusader and maiden, struggling or arguing over some impediment. Jack was in love with her. And she was in love with him.

This would be her new home. The excitement and anticipation tingled through her. Yes, this was where she belonged. The door to the roof creaked open and Jack stepped out. The sky was clear except for a few clouds but it was a warm August evening.

"Shannon said you had some news." He took her in his arms and kissed her.

"Jane isn't coming back. Mr. Donegal asked me to stay on. So you don't have to put me up in your apartment if you don't want to. I can stay in the cottage."

"I love you, Dana. I want us to be together as lovers and friends, as Master and slave." He hugged her then squeezed her breasts through the thick fabric of the costume. Her body heated up. She wanted him right there, right now on top of the castle. Gripping the material of his medieval tunic, she pulled him closer. Time seemed to stand still for a moment. Looking into his eyes, she saw lust and also love. How could she have considered leaving him?

"Would you rather stay in the cottage or at the store?" His face was emotionless but intense.

"I'll stay with you."

"Great. You can still work in the store if you like. I'll give my uncle a good talking to. I'm sure over time he'll get to love you. He's cautious about people and remembers how a woman broke my heart years ago."

"I think we'll get along fine," she said.

He hugged her again. "I'm so glad you're staying with the troupe. When did Donegal give you the news?"

"Right after the show."

"And you didn't come to tell me straight away? I might have to punish you for that," he teased.

"Please, Master, please." Turning around, she raised her skirt, facing out at the forest where Unfettered had once been. Where she learned about glorious surrender. Bending forward, she stuck out her naked bottom to him. "My lord, I'm ready for my punishment."

"No panties? Hmmm." His hand rubbed the bare skin of her ass. "My lady, I do believe a most severe punishment is in order."

Also by Delilah Devlin

eBooks:

1-800-DOM-help: Begging For It

Altered States: Unleashing the Tiger

Arctic Dragon

Desire: Garden of Desire

Desire: Prisoner of Desire

Desire: Slave of Desire

Ellora's Cavemen: Jewels of the Nile I *(anthology)*

Ellora's Cavemen: Legendary Tails III *(anthology)*

Ellora's Cavemen: Seasons of Seduction I *(anthology)*

Ellora's Cavemen: Tales from the Temple III *(anthology)*

Frannie 'n' the Private Dick

Fun With Dick and Jayne

Handy Men

Jacq's Warlord *(with Myla Jackson)*

Jane's Wild Weekend

Lion in the Shadows

Lockdown

My Immortal Knight: A Long Howl Good Night

My Immortal Knight: First Knight

My Immortal Knight 1: All Hallows Heartbreaker

My Immortal Knight 2: Love Bites

My Immortal Knight 3: All Knight Long

My Immortal Knight 4: Relentless

My Immortal Knight 5: Uncovering Navarro

My Immortal Knight 6: Silver Bullet
My Immortal Knight 7: Knight of My Dreams
Raw Silk
Red Stilettos: Bad, Bad Girlfriend
Ride a Cowboy
Silent Knight
Sin's Gift
The Pleasure Bot
Warlord's Destiny
Witch's Choice

Print Books:

A Hot Man is the Best Revenge *(anthology)*
Altered States *(anthology)*
Desire: Pirate's Desire
Ellora's Cavemen: Jewels of the Nile I *(anthology)*
Ellora's Cavemen: Legendary Tails III *(anthology)*
Ellora's Cavemen: Tales from the Temple III *(anthology)*
Ellora's Cavemen: Seasons of Seduction I *(anthology)*
Fated Mates *(anthology)*
Feral Fixation *(anthology)*
Jacq's Warlord *(with Myla Jackson)*
My Immortal Knight 1 & 2: Twice Bitten
My Immortal Knight 3 & 4: Endless Knight
My Immortal Knight 5 & 6: Silver Shadow
Red Stilettos *(anthology)*
Royal Bondage *(anthology)*
Running Wild *(anthology)*
Un, Deux, Trois, Menage! *(anthology)*
Veiled Alliance *(anthology)*

About the Author

ஐ

Delilah Devlin dated a Samoan, a Venezuelan, a Turk, a Cuban, and was engaged to a Greek before marrying her Irishman. She's lived in Saudi Arabia, Germany, and Ireland, but calls Texas home for now. Ever a risk taker, she lived in the Saudi Peninsula during the Gulf War, thwarted an attempted abduction by white slave traders, and survived her children's juvenile delinquency.

Creating alter egos for herself in the pages of her books enables her to live new adventures. Since discovering the sinful pleasure of erotica, she writes to satisfy her need for variety--it keeps her from running away with the Indian working in the cubicle beside her!

In addition to writing erotica, she enjoys creating romantic comedies and suspense novels.

Also by Francesca Hawley

℘

eBooks:

1-800-DOM-help: Controlling Interest

Protect and Defend

Red Stilettos: Whirlwind Affair

Seeking Truth

Print Books:

Protect and Defend

Red Stilettos *(anthology)*

Seeking Truth

About the Author

ℬ

Hi. I'm Francesca Hawley and I'm a fat chick. A woman with dangerous curves just like my heroines. Many people don't like the word, "fat" but I do because it's the truth and I've learned to own it. I am a fat chick and I always will be.

When I began writing, I wanted to create a fat heroine who loved herself—or at least learned to love herself—and a hot alpha hero who liked her jiggly bits just the way they were. Since I didn't find many big girls to read about, I decided to write about them myself. After all, I loved to write and had been writing almost as long as I'd been reading, so Francesca Hawley - author of "Romance with Dangerous Curves" was born.

In a Francesca Hawley romance, my readers will find authentic, sensual, fat heroines who love and are loved by their intense, passionate, and seductive Alpha heroes. I hope you enjoy their dangerous curves just as much as their hunky heroes do.

Also by Samantha Cayto

ཀ

eBooks:

1-800-DOM-help: Mistress Mine

Cougar Challenge: Locked and Loaded

Illegal Moves (*with Dalton Diaz*)

Print Books:

Cougar Hunt *(anthology)*

Illegal Moves (*with Dalton Diaz*)

About the Author

ᢒ

Samantha Cayto is a Boston-area native who practices as a business lawyer by day while writing erotic romance at night—the steamier the better. She likes to push the envelope when it comes to writing about passion and is delighted other women agree that guy-on-guy sex is the hottest ever.

She lives a typical suburban life with her husband, three kids and four dogs. Her children don't understand why they can't read what she writes, but her husband is always willing to lend her a hand—and anything else—when she needs to choreograph a scene.

She is a member of the Romance Writers of America and the New England Chapter and credits RWA, NEC and the wonderful friends she's made there with helping her become a published author.

Also by Kathy Kulig

ഇ

eBooks:

1-800-DOM-help: Emerald Dungeon

Damned and Desired

Desert of the Damned

Dragon Witch

Secret Soiree

Seducing the Stones

Wild Jade

Print Books:

Damned and Desired

Desert of the Damned

Wild Jade

About the Author

꧁

Kathy Kulig spins stories with passion and adventure. Her characters enter both paranormal and contemporary worlds with steamy or erotic romances woven in. Gutsy heroines and hunky heroes face the unexpected and overcome formidable odds, because with courage, true love can find a way. These are the stories she loves to read and the stories she loves to write.

Besides her career in writing, Kathy is a cytotechnologist and has worked as a research scientist, medical technologist, dive master and stringer for a newspaper. Propelled by her love of travel and adventure, Kathy has visited a few places not usually considered vacation hot spots-and lived to tell about it. When not writing or dreaming up her next story, Kathy enjoys traveling, relaxing by the beach with a book, mountain biking, movies and dinners out. She lives with her husband in a 100-year-old Victorian house in Pennsylvania.

꧁

The authors welcome comments from readers. You can find their websites and email addresses on their author bio pages at www.ellorascave.com.

Tell Us What You Think

We appreciate hearing reader opinions about our books. You can email us at Comments@EllorasCave.com.

Why an electronic book?

We live in the Information Age—an exciting time in the history of human civilization, in which technology rules supreme and continues to progress in leaps and bounds every minute of every day. For a multitude of reasons, more and more avid literary fans are opting to purchase e-books instead of paper books. The question from those not yet initiated into the world of electronic reading is simply: *Why?*

1. ***Price.*** An electronic title at Ellora's Cave Publishing runs anywhere from 40% to 75% less than the cover price of the exact same title in paperback format. Why? Basic mathematics and cost. It is less expensive to publish an e-book (no paper and printing, no warehousing and shipping) than it is to publish a paperback, so the savings are passed along to the consumer.
2. ***Space.*** Running out of room in your house for your books? That is one worry you will never have with electronic books. For a low one-time cost, you can purchase a handheld device specifically designed for e-reading. Many e-readers have large, convenient screens for viewing. Better yet, hundreds of titles can be stored within your new library—on a single microchip. There are a variety of e-readers from different manufacturers. You can also read e-books on your PC or laptop computer. (Please note that Ellora's Cave does not endorse any specific brands.

You can check our website at www.ellorascave.com for information we make available to new consumers.)

3. ***Mobility.*** Because your new e-library consists of only a microchip within a small, easily transportable e-reader, your entire cache of books can be taken with you wherever you go.
4. ***Personal Viewing Preferences.*** Are the words you are currently reading too small? Too large? Too... ANNOYING? Paperback books cannot be modified according to personal preferences, but e-books can.
5. ***Instant Gratification.*** Is it the middle of the night and all the bookstores near you are closed? Are you tired of waiting days, sometimes weeks, for bookstores to ship the novels you bought? Ellora's Cave Publishing sells instantaneous downloads twenty-four hours a day, seven days a week, every day of the year. Our webstore is never closed. Our e-book delivery system is 100% automated, meaning your order is filled as soon as you pay for it.

Those are a few of the top reasons why electronic books are replacing paperbacks for many avid readers.

As always, Ellora's Cave welcomes your questions and comments. We invite you to email us at Comments@ellorascave.com or write to us directly at Ellora's Cave Publishing Inc., 1056 Home Avenue, Akron, OH 44310-3502.

ELLORA'S CAVE
ROMANTICA PUBLISHING

CPSIA information can be obtained at www.ICGtesting.com
Printed in the USA
BVOW050538130911

271047BV00001B/1/P